The Bomb Maker's Daughter

The Bomb Maker's Daughter

This is a work of fiction. Names, characters, organisations, places, events, and incidents are either products of author's imagination or are used fictitiously.

Text copyright 2018 Thomas Ryan
All rights reserved.

No part of this book may be reproduced, or stored in a retrieval system, or transmitted in any form or by any means, electronic, mechanical, photocopying, recording, or otherwise, without express written permission of the publisher.

Cover design by: Good Cover Design

ISBN – 13: 978-0-473-42500-5

Published by Far and Wide Publishing.

ALSO BY THOMAS RYAN

In the same series:

The Field of Blackbirds
The Mark of Halam
The Ottoman Conspiracy

Short Stories

Far and Wide Publishing

For Meg
always steady
always strong
forever courageous

THOMAS RYAN

The Bomb Maker's Daughter

CHAPTER ONE

The rumble of thunder disturbed the sleep of Arina Marcos.

The eleven-year-old tossed and turned until she woke. Entangled in white cotton sheets she lay on her back, eyelids flickering as they adjusted to the darkness. But now, wide awake and staring at the ceiling, she was confused. The noise of the thunder had not stopped. It had not been a dream.

Weeks earlier, a typhoon had smashed its way across the Philippines and devastated Mindanao Island. The howling winds rattling her house had frightened her. Her chickens blew away while still in their cage. Was this another typhoon? Her fingers fumbled in the dark until she found the photo of her Lord Jesus on the bedside table. She held it to her chest and whispered a small prayer.

Light through the slats of the shutter windows danced across the pearl-gray walls of her bedroom. Arina knew enough to realise that lightning flashes do not dance across walls. Relieved it was not a storm, she freed herself from the bedding and sat up. She reached across and shook her sister.

"Leave me alone," Sarah moaned.

Arina crept to the window. She wrapped her fingers around the long dowel strip in the centre of the shuttered window and pulled it down. The shutters widened enough for her to see outside. Her eyes focussed on the scene at the entrance to the camp. She saw the cause of the thunderous sound, the whirling blades of a hovering helicopter. Her bewilderment grew as men in black uniforms emerged from the rain forest encircling the camp. Guards, keys in hand, opened the padlocks and pulled back the gates. Two vehicles, headlights blazing and engines revving, raced into the compound. To Arina, they looked like small tanks but without the big gun. The armed men from the jungle formed a line in front of the armoured vehicles. The guards then re-locked the gates.

Arina's bedroom door opened. Her father stood in the doorway.

"Arina, Sarah. Out of bed."

The urgency in his voice unsettled Arina.

"What is happening Papa?"

"No talking. Quickly. Get dressed."

Arina pulled on her jeans and slipped a T-shirt over her head. She felt around on the floor for her slip-on shoes.

"Hurry girls, we must leave."

"What is it Papa? Why are there soldiers in the camp?" Arina asked.

"Don't talk. Just hurry. Quickly now."

Sarah wrapped a sarong around herself and tied it in a knot above her breast. She reached for her flip-flop sandals.

"Not sandals, Sarah, wear shoes," her father ordered.

Once they were dressed, he pushed the two girls into the small sitting room of the two-bedroom hut which had been their home for the past six months. The light from outside made it possible for Arina to see her mother standing by the front door. The smell of spices from last night's dinner hung in the air. Arina was hungry. She eyed the fridge and made to move toward it.

"Stand by your mother," her father ordered. "Sofia, keep them with you. I need to think."

"Papa, tell us what is happening," Arina pleaded.

"No talking."

"But Papa."

Her father turned on her, his face flushed. In recent days, his illness had made him irritable. In Arina's view he was now irritable almost all the time. Her father opened his mouth to admonish the two girls. But instead, he bent forward, a hand covering his mouth. His free hand was on his knee, and a fit of coughing shook his body. He stayed bent over until the coughing became simply gasping and wheezing. Slowly, he lifted his head.

"Do you see what you have done? This happens when disobedient daughters irritate their father."

His shoulders heaved as he struggled for breath. He coughed into his handkerchief then turned away as he folded the bloodied cloth and pushed it into his pocket. Arina watched the shadow of her father as he stepped to the window. She pulled her hand free from her mother's grip and joined him. She could pick out figures dashing between the dwellings nearer the entrance gates. She could see well enough to identify the runners as her neighbours. Some, caught by the men in black, were gathered into small groups and forced to sit on the ground. Arina strained to listen to a garbled message that was being broadcast over the camp loudspeaker. A sound like cracking whips made it difficult to hear clearly.

Her mother said, "Carlo, the man on the loudspeaker is telling us we need to go outside."

Carlo ignored his wife.

The helicopter continued to hover above the main gate. A searchlight, fixed underneath, swung back and forth.

For an instant it lit up a man dressed in a black uniform. Then Arina saw the cause of the sound of the cracking whips. He lifted a rifle to his shoulder, and the barrel flashed. Her best friend fell to the ground. Arina held a hand to her mouth, her widening eyes staring at the still form. She waited for her friend to rise to her feet.

"Papa! It is Rosa! Something has happened to her."

Her father put his arm gently around her shoulder and guided her back to her sister and mother. "No matter what happens tonight, girls, you must do what I tell you." Her father led them to the back door. He pulled it open just wide enough to poke his head through. "To get out of the compound we need to go through the hole in the fence that Sarah uses when she meets Tulus."

"Papa!" Sarah said, mortified he had found her out.

Arina's mouth fell open at learning of her sister's deception. She thought her father should reprimand her sister, but instead he didn't appear the least bit annoyed. It wasn't fair. Yesterday she had been yelled at for not making her bed.

"Sarah, can you find the hole in the dark?"

"Yes, Papa."

"Good girl."

"But the man on the loudspeaker said we have to go outside," Arina said.

"Hush, Arina. You will do as I say. Sarah, take this." He passed her a small box the size of a cigarette packet. "This is your birthday present. I made it for you in the workshop. I am giving it to you now." Sarah stared at the box. "Inside is money. Use it to get to Uncle Felipe."

"Why give it to me now, Papa? Are you and mother not coming?"

"Of course we are. But you have younger legs. You can run faster and we will be slow." He touched her shoulder. "When you get outside the fence you must run as if your life depends on it. And it does. Whatever happens, you are to look after your sister. Your mother and I may need to hide out in the jungle for a few nights. You must not wait for us."

"But…" Her eyes welled.

"No arguments."

Sarah wiped her eyes. "Yes, Papa." She put the box into the red leather purse which hung from a strap around her neck.

"We must go," her father said.

He reached out and placed his arm against the door jamb. His head dropped as another fit of coughing spasms began. Arina couldn't remember when he first got sick. But now he was always coughing and usually didn't stop for a long time. When it was her turn to wash their clothes Arina had noticed blood on his handkerchief. She showed her mother, but was told to get on with the washing.

Carlo took deep breaths; steadied himself.

"I'm ready," he gasped.

Sarah pushed the door open.

"We must run to the left of the light," Sarah said. "Do you see the small bush against the fence?"

"I see it."

"It is behind that bush."

"Arina," her father said, "you must do what your sister tells you and be brave."

"Yes, Papa."

"Lead the way, Sarah."

Sarah raced across the open space towards the bush. Frightened friends and neighbours ran directionless across their path, pushing each other. Arina risked a glance over her shoulder. The line of soldiers was advancing. Sarah reached the communal clothesline. Sheets and assorted clothing items hung limp in the windless night. They pushed through the washing, which now shielded them from the men with guns. Dust from the downdraft of the helicopter also helped hide their movements. Arina closed her ears to the screams and the gunfire, her eyes fixed on her sister. Sarah reached the bush and fell to her hands and knees. Arina, who was now beside her, helped pull away branches as they searched for the hole.

"I've found it," Sarah cried out.

Arina looked at the black shape of the jungle beyond the fence; a leafy sanctuary offering their only hope of survival.

"Mama and Papa," Sarah called out. "Hurry."

Arina, still on her hands and knees, turned in her parents' direction. To her horror they were still a long way away. Her father was staggering, his arm across their mother's shoulder.

"He is too heavy for Mama," Sarah said. "Arina, as soon as the lights of the helicopter turn away, I am going back to help. You stay here. Crawl under the bush, find the hole and go through it. Then hold it open for us."

"But I should help."

"Arina, don't argue," Sarah said. "Please, just do as I ask, just this once." She slipped the strap of her handbag over her head. "Hold this until I get back."

"What if you don't come back?"

"Arina, get through the fence!"

"All right," Arina grumbled, but did not move.

"Now!" Sarah screamed at her, and gave Arina a shove.

"All right, all right." Arina dropped again to her hands and knees and crawled through the hole. Once outside the fence she lifted her head high enough to see over the bush. Sarah had reached her father's side. She swooped under his right arm and helped prop him up.

"Almost there," Arina heard her sister yell.

The helicopter swung its light back towards the trio and lit them up like actors on a theatre stage. A voice yelled for them to stop. Arina's eyes widened as men with rifles ran toward her family.

"Hurry, hurry," she screamed at them.

"Arina, run away. We are right behind you," Sarah called.

Arina stayed where she was. Her hands pushed against the fence, her fingers poking through the wire mesh. "Hurry, hurry!"

Sarah and her mother were struggling with her father. The soldiers were getting closer. To her right Arina saw a military jeep racing along the fence line. Arina screamed a warning, but her voice was lost in the din. A soldier standing in the passenger side swung a swivel gun toward them and fired. Erupting dirt followed the flashes of light. Her Papa held his hands in the air and shouted at the soldiers not to shoot. Her Mama held onto her Papa's arm and Sarah's hand. Soldiers yelled more orders and her mother, father and sister dropped to their knees. The helicopter turned away as the soldiers surrounded them.

Arina's fingers slipped from the wire. She knew what she must do. Find Uncle Felipe. She slung the strap of Sarah's bag around her neck and ran into the jungle. Spikey plant tendrils tugged at her clothes and scratched her arms. She did not slow until the sounds of violence had faded.

CHAPTER TWO

The Philippines Airlines A320 taxied to the Auckland Airport arrivals terminal. On board the almost-full jet were one hundred and twenty Filipino businessmen and women. The chartered flight, organised by the Davao City Chamber of Commerce, had brought the delegation to Auckland to discuss trade opportunities. The chamber CEO had spent a year arranging the trip, organising discussion round tables, visas and accommodation. The response from chamber members had been positive. The addition of latecomers had brought the passenger list to one hundred and twenty, a good-sized tour party. The CEO was more than happy.

The aircraft would return to the Philippines via Sydney, Australia. It would fly passengers on behalf of Air New Zealand to Sydney and passengers from Sydney to the Philippines as a normal scheduled route. In seven days it would return to New Zealand for the Chamber of Commerce travellers.

As passengers and crew cleared customs, the Sky Chefs' catering truck manoeuvred into position under the aircraft's loading doors. The Asian driver climbed out of the vehicle, secured the wheels, and then entered its box van body through a side door. The van body, with a platform protruding out over the cab, lifted until it was level with the aircraft door. The driver, wearing an iridescent yellow jacket, stepped out onto the platform and made his way across the walkway and into the plane. For the next ten minutes he off-loaded empty food trolleys and replaced them with new.

The fifth empty trolley that was wheeled onto the van had a strip of red tape along the top edge. The driver pushed it into a space near the side door. Once he had completed the trolley swap, the aircraft door was shut. The driver pulled a lever and the hoist and the box van lowered onto the truck frame. Next, the driver dropped two black sports bags beside the trolley with the red markings. He opened the trolley door and emptied out Kalashnikovs, pistols and grenades. Into the second bag he loaded extra rounds, full ammo clips and two American-made grenade launchers. He zipped the two bags shut and dragged them across to the open side door.

An airport employee driving a forklift stopped within arm's reach and waited. The bags were hidden amongst other unloaded commercial freight already on the pallet. The catering driver waited until the forklift disappeared from sight then slammed the door shut.

His job was done.

CHAPTER THREE

Jeff Bradley strode up the wheelchair ramp and entered the Auckland Central Police Station. The cop manning reception was focussed on whatever subject matter filled his computer screen, and ignored Jeff's presence. It was probably the end of a long day. With his shift almost over he didn't need a civilian messing up his going-home time.

Jeff rubbed the top of his thigh. Earlier, he had run five kilometres followed by a strenuous workout at his gym. Manny, his fitness trainer, had coached him through a new exercise regimen, had him pound a punchbag and then finish off the session with a few rounds of sparring. He ached and was stiff. The discomfort made him irritable. He was in no mood to be ignored. Jeff slapped his hand on the counter. It worked. The cop looked up and fixed his eyes on Jeff. Thin lips curled into a practised smile, polite but lacking sincerity.

"Yes, sir, how can I help?" The cop remained seated, one eye cocked on Jeff, the other on the screen.

"I have a meeting with Sergeant Te Kanawa."

The cop picked up the phone.

Jeff moved away from the counter and studied the posters on the noticeboard. Senior Sergeant Moana Te

Kanawa had been cagey when she made contact with him. The last time Jeff had seen her, Moana was beating up a terrorist who had resisted arrest. She was trained in martial arts, and had fought in UFC bouts. The terrorist had chosen the wrong woman. Even then, at age forty, Moana had been too tough an adversary.

Jeff tried to recall any activity over the last few weeks that might have led to Moana's request for him to come to the station. Nothing obvious came to mind and he hadn't broken any laws that he was aware of.

A side door opened and the cop manning reception appeared.

"Come with me."

It surprised him when he was shown through to the staff cafeteria and not her office or an interview room. Moana was waiting in the doorway, and greeted him with a genuine beaming smile. They embraced as old friends.

"Where would you like to sit?" she asked.

The cafeteria was empty. Jeff opted for a table by the window.

"Can I get you a coffee, bottle of water, tea?"

Jeff shook his head. "I'm okay."

They sat.

The policewoman clasped her hands together and leaned forward, elbows on the table. Her mannerism reminded Jeff of a time when his mother scolded him for shooting his cousin's doll to bits with an air rifle.

"Two weeks ago we raided a sauna parlour, The Playhouse on Customs Street. Do you know it?"

"Yes, I know it. And no, I haven't been there."

Her question puzzled Jeff, for no other reason than the sex industry was legal in New Zealand. They even paid taxes. Even if he had used The Playhouse's services, and he hadn't, what did it matter?

"Why a raid?" he asked.

"It was a routine check on the Asian girls. We carry one out every few months. Some of the girls are in New Zealand illegally, others overstay their visas. Sex slavery has not been much of a problem, but now and then it pops up. Girls brought in on a promise of work. Their fares and accommodation are paid for, and then they are forced to work off the debt as prostitutes. You know how it works..."

Jeff indicated with a motion of his head that he did. He wriggled in his chair, feeling uncomfortable. His eyes narrowed. "You're not accusing me of human trafficking?"

Moana laughed. "If I thought that, we'd be in an interview room and not the cafeteria. Relax."

Jeff scratched the back of his head.

"I found two girls who had overstayed their visas. I rummaged through their handbags, and in one I found a small sachet of cocaine. Both women were from the Philippines. In their country they shoot users and dealers. They were as scared as hell. I didn't reassure them we don't shoot druggies in New Zealand. I made them an offer. Tell me your supplier and they can fly back to Manila. It worked. They told me what I needed to know."

"Moana, I know you're a good cop. No need to brag."

"Let me finish. My story has a point."

Jeff folded his arms and leaned back in his seat.

"At the address the women gave us we found a large quantity of drugs–no hard stuff, just marijuana–but enough bags to classify the holders as dealers. We arrested three Filipino males and one female. There was a young Filipino girl in the house. Not yet a teen was my first assessment. One of the men said she was his sister. She was too young to be left alone, so I brought her back to the station."

Jeff eyed the coffee machine a few metres away. He decided he needed one after all. "Keep talking." He stood up and walked to the machine and filled a foam cup with black liquid. Back at the table, he sipped coffee and made a face. It was lukewarm.

Moana continued. "We contacted the Philippine Embassy in Wellington and sent them a copy of the young girl's fingerprints. They sent them on to the police in the Philippines, who came back with a name. Her father worked for the government. They had her fingerprints on file. Apparently, because of the secrecy surrounding his work, they fingerprinted the whole family."

"Okay," said Jeff, still not seeing what any of this had to do with him. "I'm assuming the news from the Philippines on the kid was interesting."

"Her first name is Arina, and she is eleven years old. The embassy told us her family believed criminals had kidnapped the girl and sold her into prostitution. They thanked the New Zealand police for Arina's rescue and said they would arrange for her to fly back to the Philippines. I told them this is not the way it works in New Zealand. If they wanted the girl, her parents needed to make contact with us.

"The idiot I was dealing with at the embassy said it was a Philippines matter and the girl was now under the protection of the Philippines government. They sent embassy staff to Auckland and when they arrived, they demanded I hand her over. Their attitude pissed me off so I didn't oblige. Anyway, it's what they didn't say that worried me most."

"Like what?"

"They never mentioned the likelihood of the parents coming to get their child and they refused to make them available to speak with me over the phone. I smelt a rat. Besides, no one from a foreign country is going to tell me what to do. Not even a bloody upstart Ambassador."

"Moana, will you get to the point?" Jeff said, half laughing, half serious.

"When I told Arina that the Philippines were sending police, her eyes flittered about like a frightened bird that had just seen a cat. I know fear when I see it, Jeff. I've seen it enough times. The poor kid was so upset she scratched at her arm until it bled. I brought her here to the canteen, fed her, and after half an hour in my charming company I calmed her."

Jeff gulped more of his undrinkable coffee and made another face.

Moana said, "Arina asked for her purse. I tipped out the contents and saw nothing of consequence except for a small red box. Inside the box was a locket and a note. Her eyes were set on the note. I gave it a quick check, but the writing was in Filipino. She reached for it and I gave it to her. She unfolded the piece of paper, which was wrapped around a business card. Then she gave me the card and the paper. Like the envelope, the writing on the card was Filipino, or Tagalog to be correct. I asked Arina to translate it for me."

Jeff sighed. He opened his mouth to speak. Moana held up her hand. Jeff held his tongue.

"Almost there," Moana said. "The girl then pointed to an underlined word on the page and said, "This word, the one written in capital letters and underlined, is the word *trust*." Moana then looked at Jeff, held his eyes, and recited the full message from memory. "Trust no one. If you are in trouble, go to the police and tell them you will only speak with Jeff Bradley."

CHAPTER FOUR

Jeff reached for the business card and read the name on it: Felipe Mendoza, Inspector, Davao City Police Department.

Jeff knew Davao City was on Mindanao Island in the southern sector of the Philippines archipelago. There were thousands of islands. The exact number he had no idea, but Mindanao was one of the largest. Felipe had to be Feelie, a man he had met at university. Jeff only knew two Filipino men, Felipe and his brother-in-law, Carlo. Why had Feelie given this girl his contact details? And if he wanted her to make contact, why had she not already done so?

"What is it you want from me, Moana? I knew Felipe a long time ago and I have never met this girl."

Moana said, "I need to get her talking. Her uncle told her to trust you."

He glanced at the business card again and flicked it with his forefinger.

"I guess you better take me to her."

Moana led Jeff through to her office. It was not much bigger than a closet but size didn't matter. The space came with her promotion to senior sergeant and she wasn't about to complain. She'd made it work. A three-drawer grey filing cabinet stood in the corner beside her desk. Atop the filing cabinet was a silver frame holding a photo of Moana's two sons. Jeff knew both boys were at university, and Moana never missed an opportunity to brag.

Arina wore blue denim jeans, a yellow T-shirt and light blue tennis shoes. She sat on the two-seater couch. Her legs were folded to her chest, her two thin, light brown arms wrapped around them. Her chin rested on a knee. Jet black hair which was tied in a ponytail was held in place with a bright yellow hair band. The tips of the ponytail were between her lips. Her brown eyes fixed on him.

"Arina, meet Jeff Bradley," Moana said.

She offered Jeff a shy smile. He held out his hand. Arina slotted her fingers across his boxer's palm and gave them a gentle squeeze. He pulled up a chair from the front of the desk and placed it as close to her as space allowed, and then sat. Moana sat opposite.

Moana said, "Jeff, Arina is eleven years old, and she speaks excellent English."

"Did you learn English at school?" Jeff asked.

Arina, her head slightly inclined, said, "Yes, and also my mother taught my sister and me at home." Her voice, barely a whisper, was not easy to hear. Jeff leaned forward. He tapped the business card.

"Felipe is your uncle?"

"Yes, he is my uncle."

"Your Uncle Felipe is a friend of mine which makes us family. When your uncle says that you are to trust me, you know you can do that, don't you?"

Arina nodded.

"Sergeant Te Kanawa, told me that you don't want to go back to the Philippines. Why don't you want to go home? Be with your family. Your mum and dad must be worried."

Arina's bottom lip trembled.

"Mama and Papa and my sister are dead. The soldiers killed them."

She lowered her head and wiped a hand across her eyes. Jeff glanced sideways at Moana. Moana responded with raised eyebrows; the unspoken communication that Arina had just contradicted the statement from the Philippines police. Moana placed a hand on Arina's arm. Jeff waited. Finally, the young girl looked up. Lips tightened, fighting to control her emotions. But he sensed she wanted to continue.

"How do you know your parents are dead, Arina? Did you see it happen?"

Arina shook her head.

"No, I didn't see it actually happen, but they were taken away and they never came to Uncle Felipe. I saw my best friend fall down when a soldier shot at her." Her eyes welled. "Mama and Papa must be dead."

Jeff decided to steer Arina away from the fate of her parents. "And where did this happen?"

"In the camp."

"Was this a holiday camp?" Jeff asked.

Arina shook her head. "It was a work camp. Papa had a job there."

"What type of job?"

Arina shrugged. "I don't know."

"Can you tell me how you came to be in the camp?"

Arina dropped her legs over the edge of her seat. She flicked her head. Her ponytail swished back over her shoulder. She dropped her arms across her thighs and entwined her fingers. Jeff waited for her to settle.

"We live on the outskirts of General Santos City on the Island of Mindanao. Papa came home from work one day and told us he had been offered a job. He would earn enough money for us to buy a house. But the job was a big secret, and the whole family needed to go into a camp with him.

"We travelled by bus. It was a long drive, many hours. When we arrived it was exciting, like going on a holiday. Inside the compound everything looked new and shiny. The small houses, the sheds, and the hall we held meetings in, everything. Papa said it had been built especially for us and the other fifteen families. It was so new the ground was still dirt. There had not been enough time to grow grass. Even the fence built around the compound for our protection was new and shiny. We were told that we could not leave the compound until Papa's job was finished. This was okay. Whatever we needed, food, magazines, toys, anything we asked for, came in a truck at the end of each week. And for four months it continued to be like this. Then it stopped."

"Delivering the goods stopped?" Jeff asked.

Arina nodded.

"One night, Papa told us the work was almost over and soon we would go home. My sister and I hugged each other. In the beginning it was fun but then the fun part wore off. We missed our friends and wanted to see them again. Sarah and I pestered Papa the rest of the night for an exact date. He growled and said we would be told soon enough.

"It was from this time on the soldiers stopped filling our weekly orders. They brought the food, but nothing else. This upset Sarah. She had a boyfriend, Tulus; a boy she had met in the camp. And she had run out of some of her makeup. My mother gave her what she had, but it was not the same. Not the right colour."

Jeff gave a sympathetic nod although it wasn't a problem he could relate to.

"Did you ever go to where your father worked?"

"Only once. He had some ipads and he let me play with them."

"Did anything else change?"

"The guards were not nice anymore. I used to talk with them every day. One of them used to bring me candy. Now when I went near them they ignored me. When I asked Papa why they were so rude, he told me it was best that I not talk to the guards anymore. So I didn't. But from then on, everyone in the camp was unhappy. Mama and Papa whispered to each other at night. Sarah and I never knew what they said. I didn't like the camp anymore. I wanted to go home."

Jeff was glad Moana had used her office and not an interview room. The cosiness of the three of them in the limited space had put Arina at ease. Her voice grew stronger and she sat more upright as she went on and related the events of the night when the soldiers came. Jeff did not interrupt her until she finished.

"But you didn't see what happened to your family?" he asked.

Arina shook her head. "My sister screamed for me to run, so I ran."

Tears appeared in the corners of her eyes. "I ran away. I was so scared." She looked at Jeff. "Was it okay for me to run away?"

Moana took hold of her hand. "You could not have helped even if you had stayed. Your family wanted you to be safe."

Arina wiped her eyes.

The shootouts Jeff had experienced with the Special Forces were noisy, deafening and scary. His first time in battle was frightening. For an eleven-year-old girl it must have been terrifying.

"What happened after you ran into the jungle?" Jeff asked.

"I ran through the trees for a long time, tripping over tree roots and fallen branches. The dark scared me. And I hate snakes. I came to a river. Papa told me if I am ever lost in the jungle to find a river and follow the flow. The sides of the river bank were pebbles and not covered by jungle. I walked until the sun came up. I saw a man standing outside a café. There was money in my sister's purse and I paid him to let me use his mobile phone. The only number I could remember was for my aunt in General Santos City. I phoned her and she told me to hide, my Uncle Felipe would come for me. And he did."

Arina turned to Moana. "Am I going to jail?"

Moana gave her a reassuring smile. "No, you are not going to jail, but for the moment I need to find you somewhere to stay."

Moana caught Jeff's eye.

"Jeff and I are stepping out of the office. We won't be long. Just stay where you are until we get back."

Arina lifted her legs and wrapped her arms around them, and again rested her chin on a knee. Her eyes dropped to a spot on the floor. Jeff followed Moana out of the room. Moana instructed the policewoman waiting outside to sit with Arina and then continued to lead Jeff along the corridor. When they had enough distance so the girl would not overhear their conversation, she stopped.

Jeff frowned, and said, "The Filipinos were lying to you if Arina is telling the truth, and I believe she is. No eleven-year-old kid could make that shit up."

"She needs somewhere to stay. How about it, Jeff?"

Jeff's head pulled back.

"You can't be serious. I'm a thirty-something divorced male who never had children. I have no idea how to look after an eleven-year-old girl. Isn't there a police procedure you need to follow?"

"Usually, we would give Arina over to social services if we can't find a responsible family member. You did tell Arina you and her are family."

"Not funny. Besides I think she should be in a safe house?"

"A safe house? Why would she need a safe house?"

"If what Arina said is true, and we both agree it is, then she may be in a lot of danger. You've told the Philippines authorities where she is. She has witnessed a massacre. Whoever is responsible might decide to eliminate the only survivor."

"That's a little over the top, isn't it?" Moana said.

"You've been warned."

"Then you'll take her home and keep her safe?"

Moana folded her arms and waited for his response.

"I have a dinner date, Moana."

Moana stayed silent.

Finally, Jeff's shoulders sagged, defeated.

"All right, I'll do it, but I need time on my own to speak with Felipe and organise the house, and ring my date."

Moana grinned. "Good boy. You go home and speak with Arina's uncle and I'll deliver her to you in a couple of hours."

CHAPTER FIVE

A police car delivered Jeff to the Fuller's terminal and he caught the twin-hulled ferry across the harbour to the one-hundred-and-fifty-year-old settlement of Devonport. When Jeff's grandmother died she bequeathed him several properties, his Devonport home one of them. He enjoyed life in the village, but it did have drawbacks. Its site at the end of a peninsula meant at rush hour the roads became gridlocked. Lucky for him he didn't need to travel at peak hours, otherwise he would have moved out to his West Auckland vineyard long ago.

He hung the door key on its hook and scanned the freezer for his evening meal. Pizza looked easiest. The instructions on the packaging said twenty minutes cooking time in a pre-heated oven. He set the temperature control and pushed in the knob. With dinner underway, he went to his office and phoned Felipe's number.

A male voice answered in Filipino. At least Jeff assumed it to be the Philippines language.

"Felipe Mendoza?" Jeff asked.

"Felipe speaking."

"This is Jeff Bradley. An old friend from your university days."

A pause from Felipe. Jeff waited. When Felipe spoke again his voice was guarded. Tense. Understandable, under the circumstances.

"My guess is you're not phoning to rekindle an old friendship?" Felipe asked.

"I've been speaking with your niece."

"Is Arina safe?"

"Yes. She said you are her uncle."

"Arina is Sofia and Carlo's daughter. You remember my sister and you must remember Carlo?"

Jeff's memory switched back to the night he attended a farewell reception for one of his professors. As he walked from the staff faculty rooms to his car on Waterloo Quadrant, he saw four men beating up an Asian student.

Jeff rushed across the street.

He landed a few good punches, but four against one were four too many. The thugs ran off when they heard police sirens. A bloodied face, a black-and-blue body and two broken ribs were reward for his instinctive reactions. The man he had saved was a Filipino engineering student, Carlo Marcos. After the rescue, Carlo and Jeff became friends. Carlo introduced Jeff to another Filipino student, his brother-in-law, Felipe Mendoza. Felipe was a law student. Carlo was married to Felipe's older sister, Sofia. When Sofia came to visit, the four of them shared many a dinner together. Every time they met, Sofia told Jeff how indebted she and her family were to him for saving her husband. Her continuing display of gratitude embarrassed him. But she would not be stopped.

As he remembered it, Sofia and Carlo had children and he had now met one of them.

On graduation, Carlo returned to the Philippines. Felipe stayed on for another six months. Jeff and Felipe spent time together, but the friendship was not the same as with Carlo. Carlo had been affable and sincere, Felipe was guarded and non-committal, not someone to rely on, and Jeff never quite trusted him. At the time Jeff thought he might have misjudged the Filipino. But when he reflected on it, he didn't think he had. Felipe had done nothing to justify Jeff's mistrust. For Jeff, it was gut instinct. They would never be best buddies. The other students in the law school had nicknamed Felipe, Feelie. The nickname stuck. When Feelie returned to the Philippines to become a lawyer, Jeff joined the military. He had not heard from Carlo or Feelie again.

Not until today.

And now it seemed that Sofia and Carlo were dead. His fingers splayed out across the yearly planner pad on his desk and he stared at a spot on the back of his hand. He conjured up an image of them both, and felt a sudden sadness.

Jeff said, "Yes, I remember Sofia and Carlo. What's going on, Felipe?"

"I don't know, Jeff. Sofia told me she and her family were moving to Manila for her husband's work. I had not heard from her, but thought nothing of it. We quite often went months without contact. To find out Arina was in Davao City was a surprise."

This confirmed Arina's story that secrecy had been a requirement of Carlo accepting the new job. Arina had said the men were soldiers, and Jeff was beginning to believe they must have been. To maintain security over such a large group of people for so long was impressive.

It needed men who were used to discipline. The nagging doubt was, were they Philippines military? He had had dealings with Filipino soldiers in other parts of Asia. They had a good reputation. He had heard stories of corruption in the Philippines Police Force, but not the military. Corruption and well-disciplined troops didn't often go hand in hand.

"When Arina told you her story, did you investigate?"

"Yes, of course. But she had no idea where the camp was and it was difficult getting past military checkpoints without a valid reason."

"But you're a cop."

"Especially cops. Much of the land in that region is controlled by the military. But it wouldn't have made a lot of difference. Arina walked all night. She could have covered many kilometres. And when she made it to the road, she walked many more kilometres to get help. She doesn't remember where she emerged from the jungle. There are streams and rivers all over the place. She could have come out anywhere."

"Why send her to New Zealand?"

"When she first told me her story I didn't know what to believe. Then a directive was sent to all the local police stations giving her description and a Manila number to call."

"And did you call the number?"

"Yes. It was the military. When I asked which unit, I was told for reasons of national security this could not be disclosed."

"You didn't push?" Jeff asked, incredulous.

"In the Philippines, if you want to stay alive you don't ask questions: not until you know who you are dealing with. The military are the power behind the government. They can replace the government if they wish to. If they tell you not to get nosey, you shut up. My first thought was to get Arina off Mindanao Island. I hid her in a friend's house until I could arrange documents and an escape plan.

"A man I arrested a year ago arranged a false passport and a visa for Arina. Then I sent her with a woman friend to New Zealand. They travelled as sisters. The man who organised the passport has a cousin in Auckland. He said he would look after Arina. Pretend he was her brother. I had little choice but to accept their help. I had to promise to never arrest the forger again, no matter what he does."

"Why didn't you send her to me?" Jeff asked.

"I didn't know how to contact you, which is why I gave her your name, just in case. I assumed the police would know how to find you if the need ever arose."

Jeff was first to acknowledge he had been difficult to locate over the past few years. His address and even mobile phone numbers changed many times. His military service and his hunting for the terrorist, Avni Leka, saw him out of the country for long periods of time.

Jeff said, "The New Zealand police made contact with their counterparts in Manila. The Philippines Embassy in New Zealand wants her handed over to their staff."

A pause from Felipe. Jeff waited.

"This changes everything, Jeff. You can't let them take her. If she is brought back to the Philippines I cannot protect her, not now. You need to keep her out of their hands until I can think of what to do."

Jeff took a deep breath, and then let it out slowly. It made a whistling sound. He glanced at Felipe's business card. If these men could intimidate a police inspector, where did it leave Arina?

"And what do you believe, Felipe, are Sofia and Carlo dead?"

"If anyone survived I would have heard from them by now, don't you think?"

"Yes, that makes sense. And you seriously think Arina is in danger here in New Zealand? Whoever is after her will know she is under police protection. They will assume she has told the police her story. It's too late to shut her up, isn't it?"

Felipe said, "She is a witness. When I questioned Arina, she said she spoke with the guards at the camp, but not to anyone in charge; NCOs, not officers. But, the commanders might still believe she can identify them. Now they know where she is, I believe they will not stop until she is dead."

Jeff nodded. If the military were involved, they had the power and capability to send a squad to New Zealand to find a young girl. And if she were sent home, Felipe had no chance fighting them on his own.

"What do you want from me?"

"I will continue to make discreet enquiries. In the meantime I would be grateful if you looked out for my niece," Felipe said.

"You can count on it."

"Thank you, Jeff."

Felipe rang off.

Jeff pulled the pizza tray out of the oven. It looked edible; so much for the need to pre-heat the oven. He cut off two wedges. Before he sat at the breakfast bar to eat his only-too-familiar bachelor dinner, he took a beer from the fridge. Holding onto the opened door he stared at the empty shelves and grimaced. What did young Filipino girls eat? Fruit, for starters. He would need to go shopping.

Sitting down, he bit off a piece of pizza and gulped a mouthful of beer.

He pondered his conversation with Felipe. Days had passed since the New Zealand police had contacted Manila. If Felipe was right, was a hit squad already on its way?

The front doorbell chimed.

CHAPTER SIX

Diego, with one hand on the dashboard and the other on the armrest, kept his eyes fixed on the vehicle two cars ahead.

"Do not lose sight of the police car," he said to his driver. "And don't tailgate. I want no accidents. You're driving a stolen vehicle. If the cops come, it's over. And you know the consequences if we do not complete our mission."

"Yes, Diego, you have made it clear. But I live in this country. Driving on the roads in Auckland is not the same as the Philippines. The drivers are polite. I will not have an accident and I will not lose them."

Diego said nothing to lessen his driver's discomfort. Better the driver feared him and obeyed orders. He had reluctantly agreed to use him, and only because the Colonel had insisted. Firstly, he was from Manila not Mindanao and secondly, he was a serial rapist. Diego disliked men who abused women, especially men who raped young girls. This man's family had paid a lot of money to get him false documents and to the safety of New Zealand. He must have thought he had left his past behind, but the Colonel had needed a man with local knowledge for the mission. The driver was given an ultimatum, help out or the Philippine police would be informed of his whereabouts.

Diego wasn't worried they would lose sight of the police car. The heavy traffic meant slow progress. He monitored the GPS on the black Nissan X-Trail four-wheel-drive. The locator blimp on the screen showed they were driving along a peninsula. Lake Road was the only main thoroughfare to the village of Devonport. But once they got closer, there were many side streets the police car could disappear down. But their informant had given them the police car's final destination. Today, he and his men must take care of the girl. There could be no delay. The plane to fly them back to the Philippines would leave tonight, with or without them.

The only occupants of the police vehicle were the female cop and the girl, Arina, a sure sign they weren't expecting trouble. But that was anticipated. How could the police know he and his men were coming? The final phase of the operation would proceed trouble-free.

"How did an eleven-year-old girl get to New Zealand?" Diego's second-in-command asked from the backseat. "Whoever helped her had the connections to keep her hidden, arrange false travel documents, and smuggle her out of the Philippines."

"I cannot answer this question. The Colonel has men everywhere. He will uncover the truth," Diego replied.

"And at the house the police woman is driving her to," his second-in-command continued, "will they have weapons?"

"Do not fear for this," the driver said, answering for Diego. "Cops in New Zealand do not carry weapons. And no one in the city has weapons in their home."

Diego smiled. "This is good news, but it is not a reason for us to get sloppy. We proceed with caution, as planned."

A kilometre beyond a set of traffic lights, the highway descended, then flattened out. To the left was a golf course. If he had been in Auckland on holiday Diego might have taken the time to play a round. He watched live golf telecasts whenever he could but had never played. One day he would. The road climbed again, a small mountain ahead of them. Mount Victoria was the name on the GPS map.

"It looks like that mountain is the end of the line," Diego said.

"It is not a mountain, Diego," the driver said. "It is an extinct volcano. There are many all over Auckland."

"Mountain, volcano, what does it matter, it is the end of the peninsula."

"Not quite. The road goes either side. To the right into the village, to the left small streets that lead down to the waterfront drive."

At the top of Lake Road, the police car turned to the left of the volcano, then right into, the narrow, tree-lined, Church Street; barely enough room for two cars to pass. After fifty metres the police car pulled over.

"Stop!" Diego ordered.

They waited. After a few seconds the policewoman climbed out and walked to the rear of her car. The girl stayed seated inside.

Diego turned to the men in the back seat.

"It seems an opportunity has presented itself earlier than we had planned for. When the girl gets out of the car, we will drive up and grab her and the cop. If we leave the cop behind, she will raise the alarm so we must bring her with us. If the cop causes trouble, shoot her, and throw her body in the back. There are no pedestrians and if we are quick we will not be seen. Pass out the pistols."

Diego watched as the policewoman opened the trunk of the police car. She bent forward and her upper body disappeared into the trunk's interior. He tapped the driver on the arm.

"Move up behind the car." He turned to the men in the back. "Ready?"

"Ready," three voices responded.

Diego's fingers tightened on his pistol's grip.

The female cop stepped back from the trunk and half turned. Diego gasped.

She held a pump-action shotgun.

CHAPTER SEVEN

The female police officer pumped the handgrip and loaded a cartridge. With the shotgun cocked she scanned her immediate surroundings. Satisfied there was no threat, and holding the weapon in her right hand, a finger across the trigger guard, she slammed the trunk cover shut with her left hand and walked to the passenger door.

An angry Diego turned on his driver. "Cops in New Zealand don't carry guns you said, and what the fuck do you call that fat-barrelled monstrosity."

"Sorry, Diego, in the time I have lived in this country I have never seen a cop with a gun. They don't wear them out in the open. "

"Well, now they do. Okay, we abort. A handgun is no match for a shotgun. And she looks like she knows how to use it. Okay, we now know where the girl is. Let's get out of here and follow through with the original plan."

As they passed, the policewoman was helping the girl out of the car. She glanced their way, dismissed the SUV as no threat, and turned her attention back to the girl. Diego conceded she had won this round. She would not be so lucky next time.

On the GPS, Church Street ran down to the water's edge. But from the bottom end it was one-way, forcing them to make a left turn, then a right, before the road sloped down onto King Edward Parade. The waterfront drive ran along the shoreline from North Head to the ferry terminus and the Devonport business centre. They turned onto the drive and parked but kept the motor running.

Opposite the foot of Church Street was a small sandy bay. Yachts and launches bobbed on their moorings, further out a cargo ship sailed up the inner harbour. The only pedestrians in sight were a family out for an early evening stroll.

"Look, the clock tower," the driver said.

A semi-circular concrete seawall protruded into the water. The clock tower was in the centre, surrounded by a strip of mown lawn. A young boy chased his sister across the grass, around the clock tower and down the bank onto the sand. The parents walked on. Diego waited until the children raced after them.

He said, "With pedestrians out walking, someone might think five men in a vehicle is strange and call the police."

The driver said, "New Zealand is a civilised country. A group of men in a black SUV will arouse no one's suspicions. It is why I suggested we dress the way we did."

All five were dressed in navy blue tracksuits and training shoes; football shirts under their jackets. Diego had even put two footballs in the SUV's equivalent of a trunk.

"We are members of a football team out for a training run. No one will pay us any attention."

Diego pointed to a spot between an old boat shed and a building signposted as The Devonport Yacht Club. Three giant pohutukawa trees hung over the car park and the shoreline. He ordered his driver to park under them. It was a good spot. When they made their way onto the beach, the trees would shield them from prying eyes.

They stayed in the SUV until the twilight faded into full darkness.

Diego climbed down the bank onto the beach and pointed a torch out to sea. He switched it on and off twice. He waited five minutes then repeated the double flash. No reply. The driver and the three men in the back seat climbed out of the vehicle to stretch their legs, then joined Diego on the beach. One of them brought a football and they kicked it back and forth. Two joggers ran past, glanced their way, and ran on without slowing. It brought a smile from Diego. The ruse had worked. After another ten minutes, he flashed the torch again. This time he received a return flash.

"Good, he is in position."

The running lights of a boat came into view.

Earlier, Diego and his team had stolen a seven-metre fibreglass power boat from Westhaven marina. The security gate that blocked access to the jetty had been easily opened. The speedboat had a 150 HP outboard motor, which was enough power for a fast getaway.

Diego punched in the mobile number of his man on the boat.

"You are too close. Go out as far as the other boats and wait for my signal. And remember, when you come in to shore, make certain you've lined up with the clock tower. If you go too far either side of that line you will strike rocks."

Diego waited until the boat disappeared into the darkness. He closed his phone and led his men back up the bank to the vehicle. No matter what happened, he now had a secure escape route. He looked back across the harbour to the Auckland Ports and CBD. Lights sparkled. To the west, the inner harbour stretched for kilometres to tidal rivers and mudflats, to the east were the marinas and beaches. And in the centre were the container ports and terminals for cruise ships and ferries. On the water, pleasure craft, ferries and freighters ensured Auckland harbour was busy, even at night. Once aboard the speedboat, they would easily disappear and never be found. In the Philippines he spent much of his time as a pirate dodging the authorities. He didn't expect the New Zealand Police or Navy would be difficult to evade.

He turned to his driver, "Let's go."

The police car remained parked in the same spot. Diego ordered his driver to go past it and pull to the opposite side of the narrow street a dozen car lengths ahead. The driver parked with two wheels on the footpath.

Diego looked back through the rear window. "I don't see anyone."

"They will be eating dinner and watching television," his driver responded.

Many of the homes on the narrow street had trees in their front yards. Diego doubted anyone in these homes would see him and his men from a window.

They climbed out and gathered at the rear of the SUV.

Diego lifted the door and unzipped the sports bags. His men had already selected their weapons of choice. Once they had armed themselves, Diego gently brought the door down and pushed on it until it clicked shut. Five figures stepped across to the opposite pavement. The street lights made it impossible to not feel exposed. There was shadow, but this would not hide them from anyone out for an evening walk. And it was impossible to hide an American made M16 automatic rifle inside a tracksuit. This was danger time. If seen, five men huddled together clutching weapons would have residents dialling the police emergency number. They had debated whether the use of an automatic rifle was overkill, but Diego decided that overkill was wise. The woman cop was armed. Those in the house might be as well, despite his driver's assurance New Zealanders did not have guns in their homes.

Diego poked his head round the end of the neighbour's hedge.

"I see lights on in the rear of the house."

He pointed to the man standing next to his second-in-command. "You have the M16. Go down the side. Shoot the glass out and toss in the smoke grenade. Whoever is inside with the police woman will fall to their knees coughing. Stay by the window and shoot anyone that moves."

He sent his second-in-command to the rear. Then he turned to the driver and his last man.

"You two, cover the front."

Diego poked his finger at the driver. "You, blast the lock off the front door and smash it open. It may have a chain on the inside. If it does, shoot the bolt out. Then charge in. Don't waste time."

The driver gave a nervous nod.

"Be careful of the policewoman. With her shotgun, she cannot miss. But once the smoke bombs detonate, her lungs will fill and she will be blinded. Move quickly and she will not be a problem."

He checked his watch. "Ten seconds from now. Get in position."

Diego returned to the SUV and climbed into the driver's seat. When the shooting started, neighbours would look out the window but they would see nothing. No one would venture outside, not at first. When they did appear, he and his team would be gone. It would be bad luck for any nosy neighbour who attempted to interfere with their escape. He turned the key in the ignition, revved the engine, and left it to idle.

CHAPTER EIGHT

Jeff switched on his drip coffee maker and spooned coffee powder into the wire cone filter. He filled it with water and checked that the coffee jug was in place.

"It will take a few minutes."

Moana said, "At the station I was beginning to think you were paranoid. But, after you phoned me following your conversation with Felipe, I decided maybe not. I'm not about to be caught with my panties down. So I brought along my trusty friend." She patted the butt of the shotgun that lay across the breakfast bar.

Moana was a tough woman. Jeff had never seen her shoot but had little doubt she was proficient. She had worked hard at self-improvement, and her rise in rank was a testament to her single-minded determination to be the best. Her mobile phone vibrated, and she cast an eye down at the flashing screen. Jeff noted the slow shake of her head as she read the message. She looked up and smiled away the obvious disappointment.

"I had a date and had to cancel at the last minute. Duty called and here I am in Devonport and not at dinner. He said he'd text me. I hoped it might be him. Look at me. I'm over forty years old and I'm acting like a school kid."

"He'll be in touch."

"I hope so. I like this guy, he makes me laugh and he's good in bed." Then she remembered Arina was in the room, and put a hand over her mouth. "Did I just say that out loud?" She cast an eye toward the young girl but Arina was fast asleep and would not have heard the comment. Moana relaxed. "The poor kid. It's not fair this crap is happening to an eleven-year-old, is it?"

"No, it's not. Moana, there's no need for you to stay. I can take care of her. I doubt anyone is going to come smashing my door down tonight."

"I know you're capable Jeff, but she is under police protection. A cop needs to be with her. Those are the rules."

"Okay. No problem. The spare room is across the hall. The housekeeper was in today so everything is clean and tidy." He eyed the shotgun. "Is that our only defence? Do you have a backup plan?"

She pulled her jacket pocket open. A Glock 17 sat snug in its shoulder holster. She let go of the jacket flap and the pistol disappeared.

Jeff grinned approval.

A gurgling sound from the bench drew his attention.

"How do you have your coffee?"

"Black."

Moana said, "Arina has told us everything she knows. And when you think about it, it doesn't amount to much. She doesn't know if everyone is dead, she doesn't know the ringleaders, and she doesn't know where the camp is. In fact, the camp will have disappeared by now, don't you think?"

Jeff nodded. "How can you be certain she has told you everything?"

"I've sat in on hundreds of interviews. Most of the time I can tell when someone is lying, or deliberately holding back information; Arina wasn't holding back."

As Moana mentioned her name, Arina shifted her sleep position. She resettled without waking. Moana dropped her voice.

"She could be killed for no other reason than the killers think she might know something. Maybe if I sent a copy of the interview transcript to Manila. Then they'd know for certain she wasn't a threat."

"Forget it," Jeff said. "I've dealt with some of the world's biggest arseholes. This massacre puts these guys right up there with the worst. They won't stop until she is dead if they've decided that's what needs to be done."

Jeff stood and walked to the coffee machine. He refilled his cup. Moana shook her head no to a second cup. As he walked back to his seat, a shadow flitting across the window caught his eye. Moana was talking, but he wasn't listening. Then he saw a head and a gun barrel. The cup dropped from his hand. He caught a surprised Moana by the arm and flung her toward the lounge. She stumbled backward before crashing onto the carpet. The kitchen window exploded and a projectile came through the hole. Jeff instantly recognised the cylinder shaped object bouncing across the floor.

"Grenade!"

CHAPTER NINE

Jeff swooped.

His shoulder smashed against the breakfast bench-top. The collision bounced him sideways. As he fought to keep his balance, the grenade clattered across the floor and between his feet, smoke pouring out each end. Instinct kicked in. He reached back. His fingers found the small cylindrical bomb and he took hold of it. He swung his arm and tossed it at the window. It went through the hole. A fluke.

Moana was rising to her feet.

Jeff yelled, "Keep down!"

A lungful of smoke brought a coughing spasm. Fumes irritated his eyes and caused them to water, blinding him. He used the bottom of his T-shirt to wipe away tears. One cleared eye caught movement. Moana must not have heard his warning. She continued climbing to her feet. Jeff dived forward and tackled her. Yellow smoke billowed through the shattered glass. Outside he heard sounds of a hacking cough and gasps for air. Whoever had tossed the smoke bomb was having as bad a time of it as he was.

Rat-tat-tat-tat-tat!

A burst from an automatic rifle sent slugs slamming into the walls and ceiling. Clumps of plaster and dust rained down and added to the smothering effect of the smoke. The height of the shots told Jeff that the shooter had backed away. If he had been close, the rounds would have thudded into the carpet. He pushed his face to the floor and found clear air. He inhaled, then coughed deep from within his lungs to clear his bronchial passages.

"Arina," Jeff yelled, now in control of his breathing.

"She's with me," Moana screamed back.

Jeff rolled toward the sofa. He tipped it on its side, plunged his hand through a slit in its underside covering, and pulled out a plastic bag. He emptied the contents; a Sig Sauer pistol and a spare mag. The spare mag he shoved into his pocket. Moana's eyes narrowed into a disapproving frown when she saw the concealed weapon.

"A previous tenant left it," Jeff said.

"Sure they did."

He saw Arina. Her head appeared over the top of Moana's rump; her face ashen, eyes enormous with terror, pupils darting back and forth.

Jeff said to Moana, "Whatever happens, stay with Arina."

She gave him a thumbs-up.

He rolled onto his back and shot out the lounge light. Then the two lights in the kitchen. The room plunged into darkness.

"Have you got your gun out?" he asked.

"In my hand. I'd prefer the shotgun. But I might get shot retrieving it."

A thud reverberated down the hall.

"Someone's trying to break down the front door."

Another battering thud; the door held. A shoulder or boot, Jeff couldn't tell.

"You'll need to use more than a boot against that door," he muttered to himself.

More automatic fire, aimed at the front door. Wood splintered as shots battered the panels.

"They'll be in the house in the next few seconds," Jeff said. "I have double bolts and it's heavy timber, but it won't hold. Moana, aim your gun at the window. If a head rises above the sill, pull the trigger. You're not looking to make an arrest."

"You don't need to worry on that score. Any movement, I'm shooting."

"And don't stand up."

"I'm not an idiot."

Jeff crawled across the floor. The front door crashed open. He put his arm around the doorjamb and fired shots up the hallway. A cry of pain and the sound of a body hitting the floor rewarded his blind shooting. For the moment, anyone else would think twice before running into the house.

He snaked his way further into the corridor and fired off three more shots at a shadow on the front deck. The shadow crumpled. Jeff scrambled to his feet and charged down the narrow hallway. He leapt over the two bodies, and when he hit the deck, dived onto the small lawn, rolled onto his chest, gun hand stretched out in front of him. His pistol swept the area.

He heard shots fired from down the side of the house; not aimed at him. The gunman who threw the grenade must be shooting at Moana and Arina. Jeff rose quickly and in three strides crossed the paving stones. The gunman's M16 swung side to side, as he fired off short bursts. The man sensed a presence and his head jerked round. Then his eyes widened in horror when he saw the handgun pointed at his chest. His lips tightened as he fought to bring the M16 to bear on Jeff.

It was too late.

Jeff pulled the trigger and kept firing. Leaden projectiles sent the gunman's body reeling backward. The M16 dropped from his hand as he slumped to the ground. Jeff moved forward and knelt beside the body. His eyes scanned the darkness of his backyard. Without looking down, he reached out and felt for a pulse. None. The man was dead.

Jeff sidled along the side of the house then dropped to the ground. If anyone else was out there, their silhouette would be easier to see looking up into the light. He counted off thirty seconds; there was no movement. He made his way across his back lawn. There was a fence between his and the neighbour's house, and behind the neighbour's house, the slopes of Mount Victoria.

The sound of running footsteps on the pavement drew his attention.

He raced back down the side of the house and out onto the street. He looked both ways and saw no one. Then to his right, near the entrance to the park, taillights flashed. An SUV, two wheels on the pavement, revved then sped forward. A desperate Jeff chased after the vehicle, but before he got close the taillights disappeared down a side street. Frustrated, he spun on his heel and trudged back toward his house.

Neighbours had emptied out of their homes and bunched into small groups on the pavement; others had gathered at the end of driveways. Their eyes fixed on Jeff as he walked past. Very few New Zealanders had ever heard gunshots and the murmuring crowd would be speculating why their neighbour was setting off fireworks. Jeff ignored them. He needed to stay vigilant. The gunmen might return.

He checked the magazine of his Sig Sauer.

An audible gasp came from someone in the crowd at the sight of the handgun. Those closest stepped back. The chatter was astonishment that Jeff had a gun. It wasn't firecrackers they heard, it was gunshots. Some neighbours, bolder than the others, moved along the pavement opposite until they could see the entrance to his house. Someone pointed at the bodies on the porch. An anxious mother rushed her two children away.

Graeme Whiting, Jeff's neighbour from across the street, waved to him.

"Need any help?"

"Not yet, Graeme. Stay back. Can you crowd control? I need to clear the house."

"Leave it to me."

Jeff climbed the veranda steps. The two men lay unmoving. There was little doubt they were dead, but he checked for pulses anyway. Nothing. They were as dead as the man under the kitchen window. He turned to move back into the house. His door hung from a single hinge. He kicked at it and it fell to the floor.

He called out, "Moana, are you okay?"

"I'm okay."

"Arina?"

"Holding my arm."

"I'm moving forward. Don't shoot."

"Okay, come ahead."

As he stepped through the doorway, he could hear sirens in the distance. Someone had called the police. But, it wasn't the police he needed right now. He hoped the anti-terrorist squad was also on its way.

###

Diego returned to the Devonport Yacht Club carpark, by now almost full. Music came from the clubhouse. Through its windows he could see dancing figures. It was a lucky break. The parking area was close to full. Many of the vehicles were SUVs, like his, and mostly black, like his. He could hear sirens getting closer and expected police cars would be patrolling the streets in the next few minutes. It was a risk staying so close to the crime scene, but he couldn't leave just yet. At any rate, hiding in plain sight often worked. The police would expect him to make a run for it back down the highway. They would establish roadblocks and the checking of vehicles would cause chaos. With the police preoccupied with closing their net in the wrong places, his escape by boat across the harbour would go undetected. Later that night, while the police were still running around in circles, he would be on his way back to the Philippines.

Diego and his second-in-command scrambled down the bank and walked across the sand in the direction of the clock tower

He paced.

He had lost three men. His driver and city guide were among the dead. No matter. Diego knew the escape route. It was not getting to the girl that was his main concern.

The Colonel would not be pleased and he dreaded the conversation he was about to have with his boss.

He pulled out his mobile phone and tapped in the number.

The Colonel answered on the second ring.

Diego related what had taken place then held the phone away from his ear until the tirade of abuse ceased. If Diego had been back in the Philippines, the Colonel might have had him shot.

"Colonel, I need a safe house and I need more men," Diego said. "The intel you supplied us said there were no weapons. The cop had a gun and so did the occupant of the house. We would have been more cautious if we had known."

The colonel went silent. Diego waited.

"You should always expect the worst, Diego," the Colonel said, calmer. "This is how you live your life. Now you want me to clean up your mess?"

Diego decided there was no point arguing. "Three of my men are dead, Colonel. I need more."

The Colonel said, "No more men. You will finish the job with the resources you have."

"But, this is not possible."

"Diego, I paid you money and you accepted the contract. You will complete your obligation. If not I will kill your mother, your wife and your two sons."

The Colonel rang off before Diego could respond. The message was clear. If he did not get to the girl tonight, then he'd better die trying.

CHAPTER TEN

Senior Sergeant Moana Te Kanawa leaned through the rear passenger window of the police car. A policewoman was in the back seat with Arina nestled up against her. Arina watched Moana, face impassive, as if she were in a trance. Her eyes were red from crying, but now the tears had dried and she was putting on a brave face. The poor kid had seen her family and friends slaughtered, escaped to good old New Zealand and now she was being shot at in one of the safest suburbs in the country.

Satisfied that Arina was comforted and didn't need her for the moment, Moana turned her attention to the crowd. Police floodlights lit the surrounds and she could easily see their faces. The excitement and curiosity turned to grim expressions when they saw the unmoving shapes on Jeff's veranda. None had pushed through the police tape around the crime scene and she had ordered two constables to make sure they didn't. Two ambulances, not needed, had parked in a side street. They would ferry the bodies when forensics had finished.

One spectator, a woman, flashed a smile Moana's way. She sipped on a mug of coffee. Moana envied her; she could do with another coffee herself, with a nip of brandy added. A man behind the woman leaned forward and whispered something in her ear. She nodded a reply and carried on a conversation but all the while her eyes never left the gruesome scene. It occurred to Moana one of the assailants might be hiding in the crowd. The attack had failed. Would they try again? She searched for anyone acting in a suspicious manner but no one stood out.

She made her way across the short driveway and joined Jeff who was standing on the bottom step. In the distance she heard more police sirens.

"That will be Brian Cunningham," Jeff said. "As always he is too bloody late." He checked his watch. "Why have they taken so long? They're meant to be a rapid deployment squad."

"You two aren't still feuding are you?" Moana asked.

Jeff smiled. "No. It's a habit. I've gotten so used to criticising him."

Moana knew there was history between Jeff and Cunningham, but she had never discovered the cause of their animosity toward each other. Whatever happened, it was while they were serving in Afghanistan. Both men had left the SAS Special Forces unit under a cloud. On the occasions that she had asked what went wrong, both had tossed *"It's classified"* back at her. Cunningham had been Jeff's commanding officer. Now he commanded the Special Tactics Group known to the public and the media as the police Anti-Terrorist Squad.

Two black four-wheel drives stopped in front of Jeff's house. Men in dark uniforms, ballistic vests and helmets climbed out. They carried Bushmaster M4 rifles, and had semi-automatic Glock pistols strapped to their thighs. Moana relaxed a tad. Cunningham's men, armed and dangerous, were more than capable of securing the immediate vicinity. If nothing else, Jeff's ex-commander knew how to train men. If one of the assailants was in the crowd the presence of the anti-terror squad would be enough to deter any thoughts of a second attack.

Brian Cunningham, dressed in the same battle gear as his men, ignored Moana and Jeff and set about deploying his squad. He snapped orders through the mic on his headset. Then Cunningham disappeared down the side of the house. After a few minutes he reappeared.

Cunningham said, "Why is it, Jeff, wherever the hell you are, people get killed?"

"And a big hello to you too, Brian," Jeff responded.

Cunningham was somewhere either side of forty years. Moana did not know his exact age. His hair held more grey than she remembered; the strain of leadership was taking its toll. She had gained a few grey hairs herself since her promotion. Dye had taken care of the unwanted fibres as they appeared. She didn't see Cunningham as a man who would colour his hair.

Moana waited for the two to finish trading verbal punches. As a woman, she had learned a long time ago that when alpha males strutted and butted heads it was better to let them get on with it. But when the terrorist Avni Leka sent men to New Zealand to blow up an American submarine, she had seen Cunningham and Jeff set their differences aside and work well together. When crunch time came they were professionals.

"And that girl in the car is what all this hoo-ha is about?" Cunningham asked.

"Her name is Arina," Moana said. "She's a tough kid, shaken, but not falling to pieces."

Cunningham, with a tilt of his head, motioned toward the doorway. "I counted three bodies. Are there any more?"

Jeff said, "No, just the two here, and the one down the side of the house, all three Asian males. I think it's safe to assume they are from the Philippines."

"You know this how?"

"The girl they were after is Filipino and the men who want her dead are Filipino."

"Okay, I'll go with that assessment. Anything else?"

"I saw a vehicle drive off. I think another two men in it. But it was near dark so I couldn't be certain. There could be more of them somewhere; it's probably safer to assume there is. I didn't get the vehicle number or model. It looked black and it was an SUV. That's it."

"An SUV, so are half the vehicles in Auckland. Not much help, Jeff." Cunningham turned to Moana. "Have you set up roadblocks?"

"Patrol cars are doing their best, and the station is calling back off-duty staff. It will take time. No reports of a sighting as yet," she said. "Of course, we may have already missed them. We have no identity pictures and the only description we have is they are Asian males and Asians make up more than twenty percent of Auckland's population."

"Okay, so realistically, it's an impossible task?"

Moana nodded. "That's how it looks to me."

Jeff said, "I was warned that men might be sent to New Zealand to kill Arina, but I didn't think it was a serious threat. Luckily Moana did, and came armed."

"Okay, we can talk about that later. Right now I need to get the girl to safety."

"You have somewhere to take her?" Moana asked.

Cunningham scratched the back of his head.

"I have a few places in mind. My men and I will keep her secure but the fewer people that know her location the better. My concern is that they found their way to Jeff's house. You might have a leak in the department Moana."

Moana did not respond. She hated that Cunningham might be right. And worse, she now had to deal with the fact that a cop or cops close to her had betrayed her. She had wanted to take charge of protecting Arina, but she had no defence against Cunningham's accusation. If she was honest, maybe on her part it was ego, not immediately acknowledging that Arina would be better off with Cunningham and his team. After all, they trained for this type of duty. Cunningham should take charge.

"How do we transport Arina away from here?" Moana asked.

Cunningham said, "Moana, I want one of your female constables to act as a decoy. Can you ask for a volunteer?"

He outlined a plan; two cars would leave the scene. One car would transport Arina, the other, a body double wearing Arina's pink jacket.

"I won't need to ask for volunteers. I'll do it myself."

Jeff said, "Moana, you're too big."

She glared at Jeff. He squirmed. "I meant athletic."

"That's better."

"Jeff's right, Moana. For the ruse to work we need someone of smaller stature. That officer controlling the crowd looks the right height and build."

Moana looked to where Cunningham was pointing. "Constable Judy Collins. I'll talk to her."

Jeff said, "Not a great plan, Brian."

"You got a better idea?"

"We stay here with Arina in the house until daylight. In the morning we bring in an armoured vehicle and transport the girl to the golf course. A chopper can take her to safety."

"Works for me," Moana contributed. "Much better idea than getting one of my people shot."

"It will avoid putting the team and Arina in unnecessary danger," Jeff added. His eyes narrowed. "But then that never bothered you in the past, did it."

"Let it go Jeff," Cunningham snapped.

The anti-terror squad leader turned and signalled to one of his men. "Bring me the weapon." Cunningham watched as his man disappeared down the side of Jeff's house. He returned after a few seconds with an M16 automatic rifle and passed it to his commanding officer. Cunningham held up the rifle so Jeff could see.

A shocked Jeff shook his head. "Bloody hell."

Moana stared at the rifle and then at Jeff. The ex-soldier looked worried. "So, they have an automatic rifle," she said. "We already know that."

"It's not the rifle making us anxious, Moana," Jeff said. "The long fat round piece under the barrel is a grenade launcher." He turned to Cunningham. "Where the hell would they get an M203?" Then Jeff held up his hands in a pose of mock surrender. "Okay, don't answer that. It was a silly question."

Cunningham answered anyway. "Any international arms dealer in the phone book."

"It might have been already attached to the rifle," Jeff said. "That doesn't mean they have ammo."

Cunningham reached into his jacket pocket and pulled out a canister the shape of a bottle of underarm deodorant; only a little bigger. "I found this on the body down the side of your house."

A look of alarm crossed Jeff's face. "Okay, you win." He turned to Moana, "The name of this oversized round is M433. It has an explosive kill zone of up to five metres, maybe more. If someone shot this little sucker into my house, anyone in the room would be killed. Fire enough of them and the house might come tumbling down. Brian's men can't cover every backyard and vantage point. Behind us is a mountain. And if they have these they might have something a little more dangerous."

Moana raised her eyebrows.

"Like a rocket launcher," Jeff said. "I hate to admit it, but Brian is right. This house is not safe." Jeff looked at Moana. "And," Jeff held up the M433 round, "fire this bomb through a car window and no one survives."

Moana's jaw firmed.

"I have two unmarked cars and eight men," Cunningham said. He pointed. "We will use those two police cars for our sleight-of-hand manoeuvre. Then we drive to the navy base."

Moana agreed with the navy base. It was a short drive, less than a kilometre. Once inside the base, Arina would be out of danger. They could chopper her to the safe house from there.

Cunningham said, "I will send one of my vehicles on ahead looking for any signs of an ambush. They can spin round at the first sign of trouble. The second SUV will follow behind the two police cars. My men will drive all four vehicles."

Moana's face remained passive. That still meant asking a colleague to put their life in danger. It did not come easy to her. "I'll go talk to Judy."

She gave a thought to home. Her sons would have eaten and she hoped they had washed the dishes. If they hadn't by the time she got back she should scold them. But she knew she wouldn't. All she wanted to do right now was hug them.

Jeff watched on as the charade was played out. Would it fool the Filipinos? It didn't matter, he supposed. With all the cops and patrol cars, he was certain the men who had attacked his house were long gone. With the fire power that Cunningham's men had, any attempt on Arina would be suicidal. Cunningham had planned for the worst-case scenario. The protection detail might be overkill, but it meant that Arina would have police surrounding her every inch of her journey to the base. Moana stood beside Jeff. The vehicle, with Judy Collins masquerading as Arina, followed the car carrying the true target.

A nervous silence had settled over the crowd of onlookers.

The vehicles neared the turnoff where the one-way began.

Then the loud crack of gunfire and explosions. Frightened heads spun toward flashing barrels, and bullets whistling overhead sent Jeff's neighbours diving to the ground.

Jeff, Sig in his right hand, raced down the street.

Metres from the corner the police car carrying Judith Collins exploded.

CHAPTER ELEVEN

The blast wave sent Jeff stumbling backwards into a street-side garage roller door. It prevented him from crashing to the ground. Somehow he managed to maintain his grip on the Sig Sauer. He dropped onto his right knee and brought the pistol arcing across his body. With his left elbow on his left knee, he balanced the Sig across the palm of his hand. Eyes narrowed as he searched for a target. He saw nothing.

He switched attention to the burning police car. He scrambled to his feet and ran towards it. Flames had engulfed the interior and a billowing plume of black smoke poured out through the smashed windows. The explosion had blown open the rear passenger door. Judith Collins lay on the road, her legs still inside the car, her body unmoving. Blood seeped across her forehead from a gash hidden in her hairline. The left side of her face was charred black from the searing heat. Her mouth opened and closed, but she made no sound.

The sight of her spurred Jeff into action. Using his arm to shield his face he took hold of Judith's collar and dragged her clear. She groaned. Then Moana appeared and pushed him aside as she dropped to her knees.

Judith's eyes flickered open. She gave Moana a pained smile.

Arina!

Through the smoke Jeff could make out the first police car. It was halfway around the corner, but stopped. Ahead of Arina's car he saw flames. The anti-terror squad's lead vehicle must have had a rocket fired into it.

Then the inside of Arina's car erupted.

Shattered glass sprayed through the air, as if it were raining diamonds. A second explosion bounced the car into the air, and flipped it onto its roof. If anyone had been alive, they weren't now. The first explosion must have been a grenade, the second the petrol tank blowing or another grenade.

His heart sank. They had killed Arina.

Then, through the flames and smoke of the burning wrecks, Jeff saw running men.

He said to Moana, "I see the killers."

"Get after them," she growled.

Gun in hand, Jeff ran through the smoke and chased after the shadowy figures, now a hundred metres ahead. One of the killer's movements appeared unsteady. Then Jeff saw why. A wriggling, writhing Arina was over his shoulder, her struggling throwing the man off his stride. What the hell were they doing with her? They hadn't killed the girl, and they had no chance of leaving the country with her. It made no sense.

At this distance, Jeff could have stopped, taken aim and fired. He would hit his target, but not accurately. He might hit Arina or one of the bystanders drawn onto the pavement by the sound of explosions and sirens.

The running figures had killed good cops tonight.

Once Arina was safe, he would avenge their deaths.

He ran past the Church Street café, and now it was downhill to the waterfront drive. Jeff was gaining on them; he jogged three to four times per week as part of his exercise regimen. How fit were the assassins? It didn't matter; survival mode would kick in and produce enough adrenaline to keep their legs pumping. But there was no escape. The police had now established roadblocks along the peninsula. They were trapped.

Jeff saw an SUV parked in front of the clock tower. Was it their getaway vehicle? He couldn't see anyone in the driver's seat. The killers would not have time to climb in and start the motor before he reached them. Locked windows would be no protection. He would smash out the glass with his bare fists if he had to.

The two men were now beside the SUV. One turned in Jeff's direction. Muzzle flashes sent Jeff weaving to the right. A slug shattered a car's wing mirror as he ran past it. More flashes. The street lamps gave the shooter good visibility. He was now on the beach side of the SUV, and his arm stretched out across the bonnet. His next shots would be more accurate. Jeff stooped but did not slow. He continued to weave. Even at close range it was difficult to shoot a swerving figure with a hand gun, but at this distance it was almost impossible. The second gunman had dragged Arina down onto the sand.

Why wasn't he getting into the vehicle?

Another muzzle flash from the gun of the man sprawled across the bonnet. Jeff instinctively ducked, but knew it was pointless – you can't dodge a bullet. The shot missed, but he was now closer, and the shooter's accuracy would improve. He ran into the driveway of a waterfront apartment block. A brick wall separated the residents' car park area from a grassy bank circling the building. Jeff made his way along the bank. When he reached the end he was on the waterfront drive. He poked his head around the corner of the building just as a police car sped past; the police oblivious to the action unfolding. Behind the SUV, the gunman remained focussed, looking back up Church Street, anticipating that at any moment Jeff would reappear from the driveway.

Jeff estimated that from where he stood, there was less than thirty metres to the shooter. On the beach he could see the second man had a firm grip on Arina's thin upper arm. She had stopped struggling. The killer had his back to his companion and was looking out to sea.

"That's right, boys. You're trapped, with no way out," Jeff muttered to himself as he weighed his options.

He could hear more sirens. Ambulance, police, fire brigade, there was no way of telling whose siren was whose, but he knew they'd all be coming. The destroyed cars would have blocked off Church Street so all around the narrow streets would become gridlocked. He expected support at any moment but the injured and dying would take priority. Cunningham had lost men, and the survivors would be tending to the wounded. And when reinforcements did arrive, he feared the kidnappers might panic and shoot Arina and themselves. He had little choice but to rescue Arina quickly.

How many rounds left in the Sig Sauer magazine was a guess. A push on the release button and the empty mag dropped out of the handle into his hand. He shoved it into his pocket and loaded the spare. Fifteen 9mm rounds were enough to lay down a protective field of fire when he charged. He dismissed the man on the beach as a threat. The man behind the SUV had all his attention.

Jeff steadied himself, waiting until his breathing was under control.

He counted down in a whisper.

"Three, two, one……" He kicked forward off his right foot and dashed out from cover.

CHAPTER TWELVE

Jeff ran at the Nissan, his pistol at arm's length. The shooter was still leaning on the bonnet and aiming up Church Street. He heard Jeff's running feet. His head spun towards the sound. The hand holding the gun followed. Too late. Jeff pulled the trigger and the Sig Sauer bucked. He kept firing. Sparks flew off the bonnet as the Sig's bullets pinged into it. The shooter's head ducked from sight. Jeff stopped in the middle of the street. He held his fire, and stood silent, waiting, barrel focussed.

The gunman raised his head.

Jeff's pistol cracked twice. Two holes appeared in the gunman's forehead. The impact raised him to full height, his eyes glazed over as he fell forward onto the bonnet, then slid off it into the gutter. Jeff didn't need to check. The shooter was dead.

Behind him, residents from the apartment building had begun appearing. Jeff waved his gun at them.

"Stay back," he yelled.

Jeff recognised one of the men. He'd played golf with him.

"You remember me?"

"Sure, Jeff Bradley."

"Go back up Church Street. Tell a cop I have one of the killers trapped on the beach and I need help. Got it?"

"Got it, Jeff."

"Good. And tell everyone to go back inside. There will be more shooting."

Jeff didn't wait for a response. Arina was his priority now.

He ran across the top of the sea wall and leapt down onto the sand. The man on the beach had run into the water dragging Arina with him. The move by the killer took Jeff by surprise. What did he intend to do? Swim across the harbour?

The water was now up to the killer's thighs and its depth was slowing his progress. He looked over his shoulder and saw Jeff run across the sand to the water's edge. Street lights illuminated the immediate vicinity and Jeff could clearly see the killer's face. He was smiling. When Arina saw Jeff she tried to pull away. The gunman tightened his grip. Her struggling ceased. Jeff dug his shoes into the soft surface of sand to set a solid base, as a golfer does when preparing to play a bunker shot. He raised the Sig and aimed at the centre of the killer's back.

This was a kill shot. No mercy. No asking him to surrender.

Jeff gently applied pressure to the trigger, knowing that soon the hammer would slam onto the 9mm firing cap and launch the projectile. The killer hoisted Arina out of the water and over his shoulder. Her head fell across Jeff's gun sights. He held his fire.

There were two gun flashes to the right of his target.

Jeff dived onto the sand.

A motor boat emerged from the darkness. He squeezed off three shots in its direction. The boat kept coming. The cop killer with Arina over his shoulder waded toward his rescue vessel.

"Damn it," Jeff cursed. The boat was now alongside the killer. He took careful aim and waited. The boatman reached out and pulled Arina aboard. She fought him. The boatman punched her on the side of the jaw. She disappeared from sight. The boatman reached down and grabbed at the back of the killer's shirt to help him aboard. Jeff held his breath, steadied his arm and fired.

The bullet struck the boatman in the shoulder. He released his hold on the killer's shirt and staggered sideways gripping his wound. He lost his balance and fell over the side. The boatman splashed with one arm to keep himself afloat. He was still alive, but wounded and now both men were in the water. Jeff assessed they would struggle to get back in the boat but eventually they would make it. Shooting at two men in the water from this distance would be hit and miss. The second gunman gripped on to the clamp that held the outboard motor in place and managed to pull the wounded boatman towards him. With the outgoing tide, the boat was drifting away from the shore. Jeff had no clear shot and in the next couple of minutes the killer would be aboard. Once he'd helped his companion up they'd be gone. And so would Arina.

Jeff had no option. He needed to get into the water.

He ripped off his shoes and socks and shoved the Sig between his back and belt. He was a competent swimmer. When he was thigh deep he dived forward. His shoulders rolled and his palms reached deep, the smooth strokes gliding his body through the water. Not much more than a dozen strokes and he would be upon them. The boatman was no longer armed; his gun had fallen into the water when Jeff shot him. The killer might be armed but Jeff hadn't seen him with a weapon. He reasoned the killer would have shot at him if he had a gun. When he reached them it would be a frenzied fight. He intended to kill them both.

The killer had loosened his hold on the boatman to concentrate on climbing aboard. The boat had a stern ladder and the wounded boatman clung to the bottom rung with one hand. His wounded arm hung limp in the water. Alongside him the killer needed to pull himself up so as to get a foot on the ladder. He was struggling. He had wasted too much energy escaping and keeping Arina under control. Jeff was close; it was time to end it. He reached behind him for the Sig, and felt nothing. The gun had slipped out.

"Dammit."

Jeff swam at the boatman and swung his fist, hitting the man on his shoulder. He screamed in pain and released his grip on the ladder. Jeff pushed him away from the boat. The boatman, his head back, was gasping for air, his good arm flailing helplessly as he struggled to keep himself afloat. For the time being he was out of the fight. Jeff switched focus back to the cop killer. Two strokes and he reached for the man's legs. The killer kicked out at Jeff's face. The water cushioned the blow, but it was still hard enough to make him wince. It took a moment to catch his breath.

An arm wrapped around Jeff's neck. It was the boatman.

His head was pulled under the water. He bobbed and managed to get his head high enough for a quick intake of air before being dragged under again. Jeff shook his body, trying to wriggle free. The arm around his neck held firm but had slid over his chin and across his mouth. Jeff sunk his teeth into the arm. The hold weakened. He bit harder and was released. When he broke through to the surface he gasped in air and coughed out seawater. A sideways glance brought satisfaction when he saw his attacker thrashing away in the opposite direction. He turned back to the boat.

The killer was on the ladder, almost on board.

Jeff swam, reaching for a dangling leg. It pulled away.

Above him, over the boat's coaming, Arina's head appeared. He felt a huge sense of relief. Jeff gestured for her to join him in the water. The killer lunged for her as she jumped, but too late. The look of desperation told Jeff the killer knew he had lost. He vanished from sight. Seconds later the motor revved, the boat turned away, and disappeared into the darkness.

A frustrated Jeff slapped at the sea surface. Then Arina was beside him, treading water.

"Are you okay?" he asked.

She spat a mouthful of water in his direction.

"Can you swim?"

"I can swim." She turned away and swam for the shore. Jeff swam alongside her.

Once they had reached shallow water and were able to stand, Jeff turned his attention back to the boatman. He was further along the beach and wading knee deep. Jeff strode toward him. He caught hold of the man's arm and a handful of hair and pushed him under the water. The boatman was now too weak to resist and made no attempt to fight back. When Jeff pulled the head above the water, he waited until the gasping, spluttering boatman's breathing grew steady.

Jeff was about to shove the man's head under again when he saw torch lights flashing on the beach.

"Lucky for you the cops have arrived," he growled into pleading eyes.

Jeff dragged his half-conscious prisoner onto the sand.

Brian Cunningham waved to two police officers, who took hold of the boatman.

"You kept him alive," Cunningham said.

"A difficult decision," Jeff gasped. "I should have broken his neck."

"Good call, Jeff. Now we can find out who sent them."

Exhausted, Arina dropped to her knees on the beach. A female officer walked towards them. Arina, sensing the woman had come for her, moved closer to Jeff, touching his arm, an awkward moment. He gave her his friendliest smile, but, knowing what was about to happen, knew straight off it wouldn't console her.

"You need to go with the nice police lady. She will take you somewhere safe."

Arina shook her head. "I want to stay with you."

"I'm sorry, Arina. It isn't possible, but I will come to see you as soon as I can."

Arina, her jaw set firm, rose to her feet. She didn't look at Jeff as she took hold of the policewoman's offered hand and allowed herself to be led away.

"The kid's life just keeps going from bad to worse," Jeff said.

"She's safe now," said Cunningham.

Jeff pulled on his shoes and socks and trudged back up Church Street, now ablaze with the flashing lights of emergency vehicles. Uniformed figures stood beside smouldering wrecks. The crowd of locals had grown but stood back watching on with morbid curiosity. He could see Moana kneeling beside the body of Judy Collins, stroking her blackened hand. She had never been a military officer, but he had known many. They forever bore the scars when the men they had sent into battle were killed. He knew that Moana would never forgive herself.

Someone would pay for what happened here tonight. He would make sure of it.

CHAPTER THIRTEEN

"Felipe, it's Jeff. Men attacked my house tonight, with guns."

"Are you all right? How is Arina? Is she hurt?"

"She's alive. And this concerns me."

"It concerns you she is alive, why would you say such words?"

"Tonight these men did not kill her, they tried to kidnap her. And they killed New Zealand police officers, friends of mine, which pisses me off. Now why do you suppose this was a kidnapping and not a killing? What aren't you telling me?"

"I don't know any more than you do, Jeff, and what I know came from Arina. And she told you the same story. That's it."

Jeff sat back in his office chair. The caustic smell from the smoke grenade pervaded his home. It had been shot up but his phone still worked. His splintered front door, busted off its hinges, lay on the veranda. He would hammer a few nails into it later. Forensics, police and firemen were everywhere. They'd asked him to leave and he'd told them to go to hell. This was his house and he would sort the mess himself. And why did forensics need to be here anyway? It was obvious what had taken place.

Brian Cunningham had stepped in and overrode everyone else's authority and instructed them to leave Jeff alone. He could use his office as long as he wanted, were his orders. Jeff had slammed his office door shut; partly out of frustration that he'd let the cop killer get away, but mostly to drown out the noise.

Armed police had barricades at both ends of the street and they had also staked out surrounding gardens. His neighbours wouldn't be happy. The police had been caught out once tonight, they weren't going to let that happen again. The neighbours had little choice but to put up with the inconvenience. Jeff had been proven wrong earlier, when he believed the attackers would not try again, but now he was confident they were not coming back, not tonight at any rate.

He wanted answers and Felipe had them.

"You need to find out who is behind this," Jeff said.

"As I told you earlier, Jeff, progress is slow. I've listened to gossip in the bars and spent time in the villages on the outskirts of Davao City. But I've heard nothing."

"But are you asking the right questions?"

"Maybe not. I'm treading softly."

"A great policeman you turned out to be, Felipe. How can you protect your niece if you won't do your job?"

"I must be careful."

Jeff pursed his lips. Judy Collins died tonight because the Filipino cop was dragging his feet. If Felipe were standing in front of him right now he would smash a fist into his face.

"What the hell happened to you, Felipe? There was many a night when you bored Carlo and me to death with your speeches on how you would change the Philippines legal system. You wanted to mount a one-man crusade against corrupt authorities. And because you won't act like a cop, Sofia and Carlo might be dead, and it might not be long before Arina is lying on a slab next to them."

"They are still alive, Jeff," Felipe said.

Jeff stopped tapping his fingers on the desktop. His brow wrinkled.

"Who are still alive?"

"Sofia, my brother-law Carlo, and Sarah."

"How do you know this?"

"The men wanting Arina made contact with me, just now. They found out it was me who helped Arina get to New Zealand."

Jeff scratched at his chin then looked over his shoulder, searching for an imaginary eavesdropper. He lowered his voice.

"How did they find out?"

"I don't know and it doesn't matter. They know. I hate to think they tortured it out of either Sofia or Carlo."

Jeff paused. "They told you your sister was still alive. And you believed them."

"I'm not an idiot, Jeff. I asked to speak with all three, and did. They are still alive, but I am assured if I do not do what I am told they will die."

"But why are they contacting you now?" Jeff asked.

"I'd say that one of the men who just attacked you has contacted his boss and informed him they failed. Now they've come to me."

"And what do they want from you?"

"They want me to bring Arina home. I have seven days. If she is not back on Mindanao in a week they will kill Carlo and then Sarah, and then Sofia. This is what they said."

Jeff was thoughtful. "What is it they want from Arina?"

"I don't know. I am as confused as you are. I sent her to New Zealand because I thought they wanted to kill her. Now we know they do not. But it does explain why Sofia is still alive. As long as they have her, they have leverage over me. "

"What else did they say to you?" Jeff asked.

"Once they have Arina and she gives them what they want, they will release everyone, including Arina, unharmed. This is what they have told me."

"Felipe, even you cannot be that naïve. They might not have killed Sofia and Carlo yet, but they killed the other people in the camp. Once they have what they want they will leave no one alive who can bear witness."

"Yes, I know this is a possibility. But what can I do?"

"The best way to save your family, Felipe, is to find the men responsible and stop them. We captured one of the assailants. One of them escaped. The man we captured called out the other man's name. Diego."

"Did you get a good look at this man? Can you describe him?"

"Yes I did get a good look. The boat light lit him up. He looked like an Asian, Felipe," he said, exasperated. "Like you, but better looking."

"How old?"

"Thirties, at a guess. He looked the worse for wear, like he'd been in the sun too long."

"Anything else?"

"Yes. A piece of the top of his ear is missing and another piece off his lobe."

Felipe went silent. Jeff waited.

"I know him. He was a regular visitor to the jailhouse but we never kept him long. Money changed hands and he walked. He is a member of a faction of the NPA, the military arm of the Philippines Communist Party. They hide out in the jungles of Southern Mindanao. Kidnapping, extortion, robbing banks, you name it, they do it. But I'd heard recently the NPA leaders got rid of him. They thought he was a nutcase, too extreme. Can you believe that? How bad do you have to be, for these guys to chuck you out? At any rate, whether the rumour is true or not, I cannot confirm, but he has dropped out of sight. Or at least he hasn't come to our attention recently. He may have moved to another region."

"Could this NPA be the ones who set up the camp?"

"No, Jeff. I do not believe this. They are long-time rebels. A permanent camp is not their style, and besides, the camp was on military land. They'd never go near it. I think it's more likely Diego and his soldiers were hired for this one job. Visas and passports were supplied and they were sent on what appears to have been a suicide mission."

Jeff said, "I'm guessing Diego will find somewhere to hide out in New Zealand. The police will find him."

"He could also be leaving tonight before borders close. From what you have told me, the weapons used are not available in New Zealand. That means they were smuggled in. Not easy to do. Maybe they had help at government level. They might even have diplomatic papers, who knows?"

Jeff said, "I'll have our police notify Interpol and any other security agency that needs to be notified. There are no direct flights from New Zealand to the Philippines, so he'll have to go via another country. Even diplomats get vetted when they go through immigration. He'll be found."

"He will have false papers. And certain countries will be easier for him than others. "

"Well, okay. Then which route will he take?" Jeff asked.

"If I was a gambling man, and I am, I would put my money on the Malaysian capital, Kuala Lumpur. And from there he will catch a domestic flight to the city of Sandakan in Sabah, in Northern Borneo. Diego and his men are pirates, Jeff. They roam the Sulu Sea. From Sandakan to Mindanao across the Sulu is only a few hours in a speed boat."

"It seems a logical route to take. I'll inform the New Zealand police to check all flights to Malaysia."

"What do I tell the men holding Sofia, when they phone again?"

"Tell them you have been in touch with me and I will bring Arina. But I need time. I will be there as close to the seven days as possible."

"Are you going to bring Arina?"

A knock on the door and Cunningham pushed his head through the opening.

"Hold on a minute, Felipe."

Cunningham pointed to the phone, "Any information we can use?"

"Getting there, Brian. A few more minutes."

"We need to talk."

Jeff glared. Cunningham backed away and pulled the door closed. Jeff kept glaring at the door. It had been a long night and everyone was pissing him off.

"What did you say, Felipe?"

"I asked, are you going to bring Arina to the Philippines?"

"Of course not."

"Jeff, if she doesn't show they will kill her family."

"It's why I need the seven days. I'll need time to find them."

Felipe said, "I don't like it."

"It's all we've got Felipe. I am not delivering a young girl into the hands of men who will kill her once they get whatever it is they are looking for."

"If you come on your own, they will know when you leave. They will have the airports manned. They will arrest you when you land."

"I'll make a plan, Felipe. Just be ready to help when I need it."

"It seems I have no choice. Get here as quickly as possible."

CHAPTER FOURTEEN

"There," Jeff said, pointing to the screen. For two hours he had watched video footage of passengers passing through the departure gates. "That's him."

"No wonder we couldn't find him. We were searching for a passenger, and he was cabin crew."

Cunningham phoned the airport. He shook his head as he hung up.

"The plane has gone. It was a charter flight. Not on a scheduled route. But its destination is Davao City, in the Philippines." Cunningham turned to one of his officers. "Contact the Philippines police. Tell them what has happened and tell them our man is on a chartered flight to Davao City. We want him detained. He'll be in the air for another six hours yet. When the plane lands I want a welcoming party."

Diego made himself a drink and sat in one of the empty first-class seats. He peered out the window into the darkness. In another hour the plane would circle Davao City, and his gut churned at the thought of what awaited him when it landed. He had botched his assignment. Four of his men were dead and one had been captured, and the girl was still in New Zealand. It was not his fault; he had been working with misinformation. But he knew his excuses would be ignored. The Colonel did not tolerate failure.

He swigged a mouthful of whiskey then asked the flight attendant for a pen and paper. He would write down all he knew about his dealings with the Colonel and give it to someone he could trust; a lawyer or a priest, he'd think of someone. The threat of exposure should be enough to stop the Colonel killing him. After thirty minutes he had finished. He sat back in his seat and read through his text. It would do. The Colonel couldn't touch him now. He folded it in three, and slipped it into his jacket pocket.

Blinking wing lights on a distant plane caught his eye. His wish right now, was to be aboard that plane, no matter the final destination; as long as it wasn't the Philippines. He finished his drink and waved to an attendant for another. She brought a miniature whiskey bottle, with the top removed. She gave a suggestive smile as she reached across. Diego waited as she emptied the contents into the glass; again the smile. Was it his imagination? They had worked together on his trip to New Zealand, but she had given no signs she found him interesting. Under different circumstances he would have arranged to meet after they landed.

He gulped down half the whiskey.

When he was free of the airport, he was not going home. He would take the stash of money he had hidden in a safety deposit box and disappear. Leave his wife and family behind. Start a new life. Thailand was a possibility. He'd warn the Colonel by phone; if he sent men after him the authorities would receive a copy of the letter he had just written.

He looked out into the darkness again. The other plane was further away but the lights somehow appeared to be flashing more brightly. How could that be? His breathing had become laboured and his head began to spin. He wiped the back of his hand across his forehead. He was sweating. It wasn't the cabin temperature; the interior had cooled with the air conditioner. He gagged as it became harder to breathe. His chest tightened; such pain, like a giant hand was squeezing his lungs. His arms weakened and dropped to his sides. The glass in his hand fell to the floor. Foam dribbled from his mouth and slid down the side of his cheek. What was happening? Why couldn't he move? Frightened, his mouth opened to scream for help, but no sound escaped. Pleading eyes followed the flight attendant as she removed the letter from his pocket. She him gave a reassuring smile as she spread a blanket over his unmoving shape.

Then blackness.

CHAPTER FIFTEEN

Kennedy Patton decided to use her hotel room phone. Her mobile was on a charge and she didn't want it to cut out through the call. She stood looking through the window at the Auckland harbour as she listened to the ring tone.

"Jaggers."

The voice was American and it had a recognisable Texan drawl. It was tinged with sleep. Kennedy Patton looked at her watch. Oops, the Philippines were four to five hours behind New Zealand time. Four in the morning in Manila.

"Dean, it's Kennedy."

"Quick or long?"

"I have a number of discussion points."

"Give me a minute. I need to use the bathroom."

Kennedy tucked the phone between her ear and shoulder and poured herself a coffee. She added a teaspoon of sugar then sat at the small table and stirred. From her hotel window she had a view of the street. It was a new day. The city was coming to life after an eventful night. The street battles in Devonport were breaking news on all the television news channels, local and international. The public were asked to be suspicious of men wearing tracksuits. That news item brought a smile. Half of the citizens of Auckland out for a morning run fitted the description.

Dean Jaggers was the Philippines Chief of Station, a reward for his many years of experience as an operative. He had been her supervisor the day she became operational. They worked well together and she was pleased to be working with him again. Waking him would not irritate him. He knew she never made frivolous phone calls.

"Okay, Kennedy, I'm back. Unload."

Kennedy related details of the attack in Devonport and the attempted kidnapping of the Filipino girl.

"Interesting. Have you gleaned any information from the Filipino girl that might be of use?"

"No, she doesn't know what work her father did and she didn't know why the men were after her. But whatever they want, they need her alive to get it."

"What is your assessment?"

"I've hit a brick wall. But new information from the man looking after Arina, Jeff Bradley, is that her family is alive. The men holding her parents have threatened to kill them if the girl does not return to Mindanao. The others in the compound are presumed dead. To find out what they were up to I'd need to locate the camp. The girl is our only lead and she can't remember how to find it. Understandable; she's a frightened eleven-year-old, and it was night when she escaped. It's not certain the camp has any connection to my investigation. I could be wasting my time. But my recommendation is it needs following up, if only to rule it out."

Jaggers went quiet.

Kennedy waited.

"Then we have little choice, Kennedy. We have to send the girl home."

Kennedy's lips pressed together in a slight grimace. Her head shook slowly. "It doesn't sit well with me. She is very young, Dean. If they get their hands on her, once they get from her whatever it is they want, she dies."

"We need to draw them out. If they are up to what we think they are up to, then many people will die, maybe thousands, and many of them Americans."

She sipped her coffee. "We might be wrong. And she dies for nothing."

"Come off it, Kennedy. I read your report: The trace elements you found on her possessions; her father's illness and the secrecy surrounding his work. Throw in a disappeared workforce and the evidence is building—it's a no-brainer. We work on the assumption it's what we're looking for. If we're wrong, no matter, it's back to the drawing board. But to find out for sure, she has to return to Mindanao."

"What if the New Zealanders won't go for it?" Kennedy asked.

"We will persuade them."

"There is a meeting later today with New Zealand officials at our Auckland consulate office. The Ambassador insisted on it because of the international terrorism link. I suspect the New Zealanders don't like our interference. But they need us if they want to continue receiving up-to-date intel from around the world, so have little choice. You want me to talk to them about the girl at the meeting?"

"No, the Consul can do that. I'll let the Ambassador know what we want and he can speak with the New Zealand Government. As for you, I want you on your way to the Philippines, today."

"I want to attend the meeting, but I will fly out tonight. It will give me three to four days to get organised before the girl returns. I don't see her getting there any earlier. One more thing," Kennedy said.

"Yes."

"The New Zealander, Jeff Bradley."

"What about him?"

"He is protective of the girl. He might cause trouble. Try to block her from leaving."

"You want me to get rid of him for you?"

"No, on the contrary. I think we make sure he goes with the girl. The girl's father and he went to the same university. They're old friends, and the girl's uncle, who Bradley also knows, happens to be a cop. It will work in our favour having the two of them working together. Bradley is ex Special Forces. He can handle himself."

"Okay. He stays in the game, for now."

"And what about the girl when she arrives?"

"That's up to you, Kennedy. Keep her alive."

CHAPTER SIXTEEN

Auckland City's one and a half million citizens, spread across fifty kilometres, left their homes and places of work twice a day and brought the central city business district and motorways to a standstill. It meant nowhere to park, unless you were a cop. The driver eased the yellow, blue and white police car across into the bus zone. Commuters waiting for their transport were forced to wait as buses banked up behind the police. Annoyed faces tightened lips and flung undisguised glares at the car, but no one dared rebuke the police outright.

The constable in the front passenger seat climbed out and opened Jeff's door. He waited until Jeff was beside him on the pavement then pointed at the multi-story, grey granite, Citibank Building opposite. The entrance was wedged between the Kiwibank, a travel agency and an Esquires Coffee Shop. Jeff scratched at his chin. Why had he been brought here and not the Central Police Station?

"Take the lift to the sixth floor, and ask for the US Consulate office," the constable said.

The police officer climbed back into the car. Jeff, nonplussed, watched the police vehicle squeeze back into the traffic. He had been to the US Consulate office on more than one occasion and it was on the third floor, not the sixth. Once he'd safely dodged his way through the lines of slow-moving cars, his first stop was the Esquires Café. The spray of bullets fired through his kitchen window had smashed his coffee machine. With an Americano in hand he rode the elevator to the third floor. When the doors opened he was struck by the smell of fresh paint. He poked his head out. Ladders and trestles were standing on ground sheets. The whole floor was undergoing a revamp. Next stop was the sixth floor.

A makeshift sign on the wall read US Consulate.

Why was he in the US Consulate office?

A Marine in familiar dress uniform; a dark blue jacket over light blue trousers, and a white buckle belt and cap stood next to a security arch. The Marine waved him forward. Careful not to spill his coffee, Jeff walked through the arch. No alarm sounded. The Marine pointed towards what looked like a temporary reception desk. The second hand on his watch had not completed a full circle when a woman appeared through a side door. Early thirties, was Jeff's initial assessment. She wore her charcoal trouser suit and scarlet crew-neck top under the jacket like a uniform. Stiff backed, she approached him with a polite smile and an outstretched hand.

"Mr Bradley."

Jeff shook the offered hand.

"My name is Kennedy Patton. I'm the Consul's assistant. I'll take you through to the meeting."

Jeff followed Kennedy Patton into the meeting room. The US Consul, an African-American, rose to greet him. Jeff was over six foot and this man dwarfed him. He had the muscled upper body of an athlete, but the uprightness and assuredness of a high-ranking military officer; a retired American colonel or even a general, perhaps.

"Mr Bradley, I'm Redfern Washington. Thank you for agreeing to this meeting."

Redfern Washington's welcome had genuine warmth. Whatever it was they wanted from him, it was not about to get him shot.

The woman who announced herself as the Consul's assistant took up a position at the back of the room. In Jeff's hurried assessment of her, she was an observer and probably not the assistant she claimed to be; CIA, at a guess. Compared with Redfern she looked small, but then anyone standing beside Redfern would look small. Jeff guessed she was five foot five, maybe taller. She looked athletic and fit. He'd expect a CIA agent to keep herself in shape. Her thick hair, the colour of wheat and cut short, enhanced her facial features, green eyes and full lips. Her smooth, milky complexion had a light tan. Jeff wasn't convinced it was from lying on a towel in the sun; possibly the result of a recent tour of duty. Her eyes followed his movements and stayed fixed on him when he sat. The friendliness displayed in reception had gone. Her demeanour had changed to passive spy mode.

The light-coloured veneer-topped meeting table was long enough for five executive leather chairs along each side and a chair at either end. Washington introduced the attendees to Jeff. Jeff had already met most of them. He was seated next to the Commander of the Police Anti-Terrorist Unit, Brian Cunningham. Opposite Cunningham sat two men he didn't know, introduced to him as Percy Croydon, the head of the SIS, New Zealand's Security Service, and George Mahon, the Minister of Defence.

Mahon and Croydon had flown up from the capital city, Wellington. Sergeant Moana Te Kanawa sat on the other side of Cunningham.

Jeff, dressed in a dark blue polo shirt, jeans and running shoes, appeared casual compared with the others who were wearing suits. His house needed airing and all his clothes needed washing. Everything smelled smoky. He'd bought new clothes on the way to the meeting. He'd left a message for his housekeeper to put his entire wardrobe through the washing machine but, with his house still secured by the police that might not happen for a few days.

Minister Mahon held up a document and looked at Jeff. Jeff noticed the others had copies of the briefing paper. He didn't and none was passed to him. He assumed the content was for their eyes only and he was not to be trusted. That annoyed him, but he sipped his coffee and kept his mouth shut.

"I've read through the main points of this brief prepared by Mr Croydon," the Minister said to Jeff. "I have to say the government is not happy. Mr Croydon is all for your going to the Philippines and hunting the men responsible for last night's shootout and I understand why. If it was only you to consider, Mr Bradley, I'd say, go for it. After all, New Zealand citizens and police officers have been killed."

Jeff opened his mouth to explain his plans for travelling to the Philippines. The Minister held up his hand.

"Let me finish, Mr Bradley, please."

Jeff nodded.

Mahon continued, "If the citizens of our nation ever found out its government allowed a civilian to venture off on a trail of vengeance they would crucify us. And if the Philippines Government found out that we gave approval for someone to enter their country, knowing this person intended to shoot the place up, we could get dragged into all sorts of international legal crap. Officials from my Ministry and from Foreign Affairs are meeting with the Philippines Ambassador in Wellington today. We will make the strongest of protests, but you know politics; it's all gobbledegook and nothing will be resolved. They will promise to look into who these men are, but if these killers have had help from government employees, which we suspect they have, then the ass covering is already under way. Small nations like ours have to take it on the chin."

The Minister paused and took a sip of water.

"Officially, the Filipinos deny any involvement and they are feeding us all kinds of bullshit; playing us for idiots. And now, this morning, we hear this man, Diego, was found dead on board his flight when it landed last night; he had conveniently died from a heart attack. Natural causes; do you believe that shit? I don't, not for a minute."

Jeff raised an eyebrow. He had not heard about Diego. He turned to Cunningham and received a nod of confirmation.

Jeff gave a half-smile, "Some good news after a shitty night."

He was about to add, one less to kill, but Cunningham, anticipating, nudged Jeff in the side. The Minister wanted his say, and although Jeff understood the government's position, the tone of the conversation worried him. He could not get into the Philippines without help. If the government dug its heels in, they could block him from leaving New Zealand.

"I'm sorry, Mr Bradley, but the government can do nothing to help you."

Jeff shrugged, "You must do what you must do, Minister. But I want to emphasise I am not on a vengeance trail. A friend is in trouble and my first concern is to help him save his family."

"A regular one-man army, God help us."

The Minister of Defence gathered the papers in front of him into a manila folder. He raised himself from his chair and dropped the folder into his briefcase. He pushed down the lid and shut the latches, all the while with one eye fixed on Jeff.

"I cannot stay for the rest of this meeting, Mr Bradley. Officially, whatever you are about to do, the government washes their hands of it. If you go to the Philippines, you are on your own. I might add that before I flew out from Wellington, confiscating your passport was on the table."

The remark caught Jeff by surprise. Before he could respond, the Minister leaned forward, his two hands, now fists, pressed into the table. His manner was belligerent, almost threatening.

"I do not want to hear your name ever again."

Then the Minister smiled and winked.

The gesture left Jeff dumbstruck.

"From here on you will converse with Mr Croydon, and this meeting and any discussions you are about to have never took place." The Minister held out his hand.

Jeff shook it. "Good luck. My personal message to you is, go get the bastards."

Jeff exchanged an uncertain glance with Brian Cunningham, who had a half-grin on his face, but said nothing. No one spoke until the Minister had left the room. Jeff, bewildered by the Minster's frank comments and departure, turned his attention to the head of the SIS.

"And there you have it, Mr Bradley, a fine example of political double-speak," Percy Croydon said. He looked down at his briefing paper. "What we do now is discuss how we sneak you into Mindanao,"

To Cunningham he said, "Anything from the prisoner?"

Cunningham shook his head. "Nothing more than we already know. He says their leader Diego hired him and he was following orders. Whether or not that's true, it's too soon to tell. So, nothing new, but we'll get the truth, eventually."

Jeff turned his attention back to Croydon.

Croydon said, "Our American allies have a keen interest in the Philippines, which is why Mr Washington invited us to meet in the consulate."

Jeff glanced toward Kennedy Patton. What had any of this to do with the CIA, apart from their brief to spy on everyone?

"Might I ask what the American interest is? A bunch of Filipinos shooting up the streets of Auckland is not an everyday occurrence, but why would it interest the US?"

"We monitor terrorist activity anywhere in the world," Washington responded.

"So it's your opinion we are dealing with terrorism," Jeff said. "And not a bungled kidnapping."

"We are also keen to learn whether what the young girl has said is true. If a massacre has taken place then those responsible need to be held accountable."

Jeff paused. "No other reason?"

"Why would there be, Mr Bradley?"

Jeff shrugged.

"My government supports your trip to the Philippines, and anything we can do to help, just ask. We want to know what's going on, nothing more."

"If you say so."

Percy Croydon smiled. "Take careful steps, Mr Bradley. After all, the Americans are our friends."

"Then if we are all agreed, I'll get out of here. I have much to do before I leave."

"Not so fast, Mr Bradley," Washington said. "As I said, my government supports your lonesome cowboy heroics, but our concern is, without the young Filipino girl, your chances of finding those involved are slim. With you, the girl could draw them out."

Jeff frowned. "I'm not taking Arina with me, if that is where this conversation is leading."

"The purpose of your trip is to find the men who want the girl. If she were to go, it would be dangerous for her, I agree. No one at this table will dispute that, and we will not force her. After all, she is only eleven. We might be in the intelligence services, but we do have scruples."

This brought a wry smile and a shake of the head from Jeff. He didn't believe a word of it. None of them would hesitate offering Arina up as a sacrificial lamb if it suited their purposes.

"I have spoken with Arina and explained that her family is still alive. She is keen to help save them and will do whatever it takes," Percy Croydon said. "Let's ask her if she wants to return to the Philippines. We owe it to her to ask."

Jeff, incredulous, sat back in his seat. "You're not seriously considering sending her?" he asked.

Croydon turned to Moana. "Can you please escort the girl in, Sergeant?"

Moana walked across to the door. A shy Arina entered. Jeff had not seen her since the attack. She looked smaller. His heart went out to her. She offered a hint of a smile when she saw him. Jeff gave a wave and pulled up a chair so she could sit beside him. He was not about to let anyone intimidate her. Moana led her to the table. She clung to Moana's arm as if it were a life raft. When she stood beside him he hesitated, feeling awkward; should he hug her? She sat down. How could Arina ever comprehend the gravity of the conversation they were about to have?

Croydon waited for everyone to settle, and then cleared his throat to gain attention.

He said, "Arina, I have told you your mother, father and sister are still alive and they are being held captive." Arina nodded. "The men holding them have said if you return to the Philippines they will free your parents and no harm will come to you. Arina, these are terrible men. They might not keep their promises. Do you understand this?"

Arina nodded.

Percy Croydon asked, "Are you prepared to return to the Philippines? You won't be going alone. Jeff will go with you."

Arina looked at Jeff.

"You don't have to do this, Arina. They can't make you go," Jeff said.

"But I want to help my family." Her eyes welled. She paused. "I don't want Mama and Papa and Sarah to die. Not because of me." Her voice had a determined tone. "I want to save my family, if I can."

Anger flickered in Jeff's eyes, his lips tightened, uncomfortable with Percy Croydon's blatant manipulation.

"Arina," Croydon began, "I need to ask you, do you know what these men want from you?"

Arina shook her head, "No, I don't."

"Do you know what they were making in the compound?"

Another shake of the head.

Washington said, "The United States Government wants to know if this girl witnessed a genuine massacre. And we want to know if what was taking place in the compound is a threat to our nation. We could send our own people but we have no leads. We don't know where to start searching." He then looked at Percy Croydon. "If Mr Bradley and young Arina can speed the process my government will be grateful."

Jeff caught the exchange of glances between Croydon and Redfern Washington. The meeting was a farce. They had prearranged Arina's fate. And he had been horse traded, along with the girl.

Croydon said, "Jeff, why don't you tell me your plan to get into the Philippines?"

"My plan is for me and me alone, not Arina."

"Tell us, Jeff."

Jeff took a deep breath. "I will fly to Malaysia and catch a domestic flight to Sandakan City, Sabah. I'll be meeting up with Arina's uncle Felipe. He has organised a boat to take me across the Sulu Sea to Mindanao."

There were nods of approval from Croydon and Brian Cunningham.

Cunningham said, "It works for me, Jeff. And if Arina is with you, her uncle will use whatever resources he has available to keep her safe. He hid her from them once, he can do it again."

"I am not taking Arina with me," Jeff said.

Percy Croydon said, "The decision has been made, Jeff."

Jeff noted Croydon now addressed him by his first name.

"I'm afraid it's a matter of either Arina goes with you or you don't go at all."

Now it was on the table. The Minister of Defence's threat to confiscate his passport was not idle chat after all. He scratched at his cheek. They had him. He could argue but   would   lose.

"I'll need travel documents for Arina," Jeff said.

"That might be a problem. You heard the Minister. They want to be kept out of it. Issuing a New Zealand passport to Arina is direct involvement," Croydon said.

"My government will give the girl a passport," Washington said. "I am advised to provide anything within reason to make sure this succeeds."

Jeff said, "It might look a little dodgy to the Malaysian border control; a New Zealand male travelling with a young Asian girl on different passports. They might decide to ask awkward questions."

Washington said, "I'm sure my government would be happy to issue you an American passport as well, Mr Bradley."

"I don't have a lot of time."

"The passports will be ready in three days."

Brian Cunningham said, "I know Sandakan. I had a few days there when we were training in Brunei. It's known for orangutans, believe it or not. A good cover story. A nature trip for Arina. You could be cousins. Your uncle married a Filipino woman."

"Well then," Croydon said, "it's settled. Travel safe."

Jeff stood and placed his hand on Arina's shoulder. He glared at Croydon but it changed to a smile when he looked down at his young charge. "I guess I better go book us two air tickets, cousin. We leave when we have the passports. In three days."

Arina brightened, and her face broke into a smile. Jeff eyed Kennedy Patton. The CIA agent, if that was what she was, tilted her head towards him. Jeff read the gesture as, *I have what I need.* What the hell did that mean?

CHAPTER SEVENTEEN

Jeff and his new cousin, eleven-year-old Arina Marcos, breezed through border control in Kuala Lumpur, their new American passports accepted without question. It crossed his mind that Redfern Washington might have asked the US Embassy in Malaysia to intercede on their behalf. After a few hours in transit they boarded the 10.30am Malaysia Airlines flight to Sandakan City.

Jeff's memory of equatorial climates had faded. He had not spent time in Asia for well over a year. He had passed through, but it had always been in transit and he never left the air-conditioned lounges. The moment he exited the modern Sandakan City airport terminal, it all came flooding back as a wave of heat slapped his face. Asia reminded him of what life would be like living in a hot oven. Born in New Zealand, he was used to temperate to cold climates.

Arina didn't flinch, but he was already sweating.

A line of plain white cars and further out, red-and-white taxis, awaited new arrivals. He steered Arina across to the red-and-whites, walked past the first two and took the third. A meaningless precaution perhaps, but he was in an unfamiliar environment, and had moved into double-alert mode. He expected trouble from the men chasing after Arina, but also had to consider the international terrorist Avni Leka. Leka had sent men to kill him previously and he had to assume more were on their way. Paranoia had become a trusted friend and this mission to the Philippines might prove to be a fatal distraction if he wasn't watchful. But, because of Leka, he was forever watchful and always erred on the side of caution.

Before he left New Zealand, Jeff attended a briefing session with an SAS intelligence officer, who had given him a general overview of Sabah.

"Malaysian citizens form the majority of Sandakan City's population and Filipinos are the majority of the non-Malays," the officer said. "Pirates from Mindanao Island in the Philippines have rampaged across the Sulu Sea for many years and are still active. Some of those pirate groups are NPA members – the Philippines Communist Party - the group Diego belonged to."

"And I'm guessing they'll be all over the city."

"You've got it. Take care to keep a low profile. They get a lot of tourists because of the orangutans, so you won't stand out just because you're a strange face."

"And crossing the Sulu Sea?"

The intelligence officer smiled. "You'll find a seaman to ferry you to Mindanao easy enough. But finding someone you can trust is another matter."

Jeff frowned. The officer had shrugged.

"It's the way it is," the officer had said. He passed Jeff a small piece of notepaper. "This is a man the squadron has used in the past. He is reliable enough as long as you pay him well."

Now, as he climbed into the taxi, Jeff subconsciously tapped at the plastic pouch in his shirt pocket that held the notepaper and US dollars.

The taxi driver could have been any age from thirty to sixty. He wore a loose, white, short-sleeved shirt over a pair of black trousers, and he looked like he needed a decent meal. But he had a ready smile and Arina seemed taken by him. Felipe had given Jeff the name of a hotel, the Sandakan Star. It was near the port. Jeff gave the hotel name to the driver and settled back for the eleven-kilometre drive to the city centre. Arina had her face to the window, watching the passing cars, the shop fronts, and jungle. She had been quiet for most of the trip, but now that they were closer to the Philippines, she grew more fidgety and sucked the end of her ponytail. Biting her bottom lip had started in Kuala Lumpur.

He wanted to comfort her, but didn't know how. He had bought her a duty-free iPod and iPad, but she ignored them both. For the moment she was quiet, so he decided that leaving her to it was best. It concerned him that, if a dangerous situation unfolded, he would need to consider his young charge. His instinctive reactions were a major asset in his defensive arsenal but now, with Arina in tow, it worried him that putting her first might slow his responses.

Bringing her along was a mistake.

The road into Sandakan was much better than he expected and as the taxi sped along the four-lane highway, his initial impression was that the city looked clean, tidy and prosperous. But then again, he recalled that Malaysia was one of the Asia's leading economic powers, and Sandakan City was part of Malaysia. But by contrast he observed that amongst the factories and warehouses lay many rundown four to six-floor apartment buildings that needed rendering and paint. Unstable balconies were cluttered with lines of drying washing and unused furniture. Close to the city, they drove through a rain forest before entering the city proper. The cabbie slowed at a roundabout and glanced over his shoulder.

"We are now in Sandakan City. The hotel is another five minutes."

Arina straightened.

The streets were busy with pedestrians. The sight of women wearing hijabs reminded Jeff that Sabah, along with the rest of Malaysia, was an Islamic state. But, of the four hundred thousand municipal population, only one hundred and fifty thousand were Islamic Malays. The rest were Indians, Chinese and Filipinos. The SAS intelligence officer had told Jeff that Sandakan was not a security risk. "It's peaceful. The pirates are there, but they make trouble at sea, not on land."

Jeff dismissed the peaceful comment. In his mind he had already reclassified Sandakan City as a red-alert territory.

Felipe had also given Jeff a mobile phone number. He would come to the hotel and meet with Jeff and Arina as soon as they arrived. But Jeff was not about to contact Felipe until he had sighted the hotel. They drove past a KFC takeaway on the right, and took the next turn on the left. The cabbie drove to the end of the street and pulled over.

"The hotel is thirty metres down that street. It is one way. I cannot drive to it. You have backpacks. You can walk from here. Yes?"

The street was narrow, the buildings dilapidated. Jeff did not like the look of it one bit.

"Arina, I need you to stay in the taxi. I won't be long."

Arina, tired from the trip and mystified by all that was happening to her, gave Jeff an undisguised look of horror at the thought of being left alone.

Jeff leaned toward her. "I need to check out the hotel."

"I should come with you. If you need to ask questions I can speak the language," Arina said, a hopeful look in her eye.

"I promise I won't be long."

Arina inserted the iPod earplugs and turned away.

Jeff shook his head in despair. "Just stay here."

He gave the cabbie money and received a cheerful and grateful smile. Jeff was a foreigner and he had money. The cabbie would wait as long as Jeff wanted.

So far, travelling with Arina had been easy enough. There had been no awkward moments. But this was about to change. Tonight they would stay in a hotel. He would have been much happier if Moana had come with them. He hated leaving Arina, and he didn't exactly trust the cabbie. But in this part of the world money bought loyalty. His worry was that if the men responsible for the attack in New Zealand had found out he was meeting Felipe they might have laid a trap. In the next few minutes he could be fighting for his life, and he needed Arina safely out of the way.

Would Felipe betray him? He hoped not, but this didn't mean Felipe had not been followed and was unaware of it.

Arina had now turned her back to him. Her small hands clasped together.

After six paces he stopped and slapped the side of his head, "Idiot." What was he doing leaving her on her own? Someone could be watching him right now and he'd left the girl as a gift. He turned back and pulled open the taxi door.

"Grab your pack."

She beamed. Put her iPod away and climbed out. Jeff took his pack.

He said to the cabbie, "We might be back. Can you wait five minutes before you leave?"

"I will wait."

As they rounded the corner an old man sitting on a chair held out his hand. Jeff ignored the gesture. Arina took out a coin Jeff had given her and gave it to him.

Jeff smiled.

The hotel was fifty metres from the corner, not thirty as the driver had said. Not a lot of extra distance, but from the corner the street had looked shiny and inviting. Twenty metres further along began a line of dingy, run-down buildings and the hotel was slap bang in the middle. It looked out of place. A quick look into the foyer suggested it was clean, acceptable accommodation, but more of a bed-and-breakfast than a hotel. He made his way past the entrance and down the alley at the side of the hotel. The surrounding streets were narrow, and full of dead ends. If Jeff was going to set an ambush for anyone, this was the spot he would select.

Felipe was desperate, and desperate men made irrational decisions. After all, his life was under threat, and his sister's life was under threat. The men holding Sofia and her family were desperate to get Arina back. Many had already died. These guys, whoever they were, would have no compunction killing anyone who stood between them and their goal. And right now, Felipe stood between them and the girl.

If Felipe was setting him up, Jeff was not about to make it easy for him.

He made his way back to the taxi and asked the cabbie to take them to the Sabah Hotel instead. Brian Cunningham had recommended it. Jeff had Googled the hotel before he left New Zealand. The aerial photos showed the hotel was close to the city, but surrounded by areas of jungle, which hid a network of roads and tracks. But now that he could see it first-hand as the taxi made its way along the hotel driveway, at ground level much of the undergrowth was sparse. However, it would do. If necessary, he and Arina could run into it for cover.

The hotel was four stars, but compared to the hotel Felipe had booked him into it was five stars. It was air-conditioned, had a swimming pool, restaurants, wi-fi and room service – a better option for Arina.

He asked for two rooms. Arina overheard and tugged on Jeff's arm and pulled him aside.

"Jeff, I don't want to be on my own," she said.

He shook his head, then looked to the ceiling, closed his eyes for a second and blew out air. This was one of the expected awkward moments he had been dreading.

He went back to the booking clerk and asked for one room with two beds.

The room was bigger than he expected, with two double beds. A wooden bench ran along one wall, and on it sat a television and a bowl of flowers. He gave Arina the choice of beds. She chose the one furthest from the door, and placed her backpack on it. Moana had taken her shopping and bought her new clothes. She now unpacked her meagre collection of possessions and placed them in the dresser drawers. She sat on the bed with her iPod plugged in her ears and played a game on her iPad. Jeff dropped his backpack on the second bed. Travelling light had been the order of the day. Within the next twenty-four hours he expected they would be on a fishing boat crossing the Sulu Sea.

"Arina, are you hungry?" Jeff asked. She nodded, and he passed her the room menu. "Choose whatever you want and I will order it. Then I need to go out for a short time."

She put down her iPad and bounced onto her knees. "I'm coming with you."

"I won't be long, I promise."

Arina shook her head. Jeff rubbed at the back of his neck. Then he squeezed the bridge of his nose.

"A short time. Not even an hour."

She crossed her arms. "I'll run away."

CHAPTER EIGHTEEN

Jeff relented, then had to wait for Arina to take a shower. She reappeared wearing a new red T-shirt tucked into her new green slacks, and new blue canvas shoes. Jeff showered and changed into a white polo shirt and navy slacks. He changed from his running shoes into Timberland boots. He had no idea how the meeting with Felipe would turn out. If there was trouble, a hard-heeled boot and toecap would leave a more lasting impression on a man's face.

It was mid-afternoon when they set out.

Arina agreed to walk into the city. After hours in an aircraft Jeff needed some exercise to loosen his limbs. Arina had a spring to her step, not so him. The heat sucked his energy, as it always did. When Jeff had trained in Asia it had always taken a week to acclimatise. He remembered the first time. Fit as hell, but he and the rest of his unit struggled to finish a mile run. As the blazing sun and almost one hundred percent humidity sapped their strength, they soon discovered there was no escaping the sauna-like conditions, even under a shady tree. Asian humidity hid under every blade of grass.

They walked a number of streets as Jeff searched for a secure meeting spot. An outdoor café was his first choice, but he found none. At night, tables would cover the pavement, but in the mid-afternoon heat patrons preferred air-conditioning or ceiling fans. The many shop windows attracted Arina's attention, and her progress slowed. He didn't force her to move faster. She was not complaining or asking to stop. The new sneakers weren't hurting her feet. After another ten minutes, Jeff found the ideal spot. The road had a tree-lined walkway down the centre and was a single lane on either side. It might have been two lanes, but the city fathers had opted for diagonal parking, and today, cars filled all the spaces. Plenty of obstacles to give him cover if he needed to make a quick getaway. On the corner of an intersection was a familiar red-and-white building.

He pointed across the road. "How about fried chicken or ice-cream and a milkshake?"

Arina's eyes sparkled and her face spread into a smile.

Jeff ordered two chicken burgers with fries, and two strawberry shakes. The restaurant had an upstairs section with a table next to the window. He pulled out a chair for Arina then sat in the chair opposite. His seat gave him a view of the street, the intersection and the opposite corner. He did not know the street names, but on the next corner was an electrical goods store, which butted up against the Hotel Western. Across the street from the Hotel Western was a small café/restaurant with a wide, open entrance, and no doorway. At the end of the day, a roller door would rattle down and a padlock would secure it. He could see a white plastic table and four white plastic chairs at the entrance. Behind them, more tables and chairs.

He pulled out his phone and dialled Felipe's number.

###

Jeff had little trouble picking out Felipe. His friend from university days had plumped out. The extra weight threatened the buttons of his shirt and grey streaks tinged his black hair. Years had passed. At university, Felipe was eight years older, which meant he must now be fortyish. For the next ten minutes he watched Felipe and the surrounding area, side streets, doorways, shadows, and parked cars. Arina had finished her fries and caught Jeff's preoccupation with the window. She leaned forward and followed his line of sight. Jeff sensed she was ready to move on. If he wanted her co-operation, he needed to be honest.

"See the sign, Restoran Fathimah? Underneath the sign is a green canvas awning with the word 'Milo' on it."

"I see it." Her eyes drifted below the sign. She stiffened. Her head jerked back. "Uncle Felipe!"

She rose from her seat, but Jeff reached across and touched her arm. "Not yet. Soon."

"Why do we have to wait?" Her bottom lip trembled. "Why can't I see my uncle?"

Jeff gave her a half-smile.

"I am just making sure no one is following your uncle. The men who attacked you in New Zealand know your uncle helped you. They may have followed him here to Sandakan. Do you understand?"

Arina gave a grudging nod. She was not happy. Jeff attempted to soothe her with more apple pie and ice cream. It worked to a degree but as she ate she kept her eyes on her uncle.

Felipe bought a bottle of iced water. He checked his watch several times. He was growing impatient. But Jeff waited. Another five minutes passed. He saw no suspicious movements. If Felipe was under surveillance, the men or women were professionals.

The five minutes were up; time to meet Felipe.

But just as Jeff bent forward to rise from his chair, he saw the figure of a man lurking in the shadow of an awning which covered the entrance to the electrical store. The man wore sunglasses under the peak of an American baseball cap. It was obvious he was watching Felipe. Jeff looked for a second tail. He saw no one else. The pavement on both sides of the street was busy. For a moment Jeff debated taking Arina, blending in with the crowd and disappearing. If he met with Felipe, would he be walking into a trap? The man hiding on the corner might not be an enemy. He might be a colleague Felipe brought along for protection. Jeff had little choice; he had to speak with Felipe. The pedestrian-busy pavement and cars would provide cover for an escape, should he need it.

"Arina," Jeff said, as he leaned forward. "How much of an adult are you?"

"I'm an eleven-year-old. I'm not an adult. Not for a long time yet."

"Okay, my mistake. What I meant to say was, can you act like an adult if I ask?"

"Yes, I can."

"Good. I want you look at the next corner."

She leaned forward.

"In the doorway, see the man wearing the baseball cap and sunglasses, in a light blue shirt and grey trousers?"

"I see him."

"That man is watching your Uncle Felipe. I don't know why, but it's possible he might know we are meeting him. It could be dangerous for us. There might be more men."

Arina leaned forward for another look.

"I need you to wait here while I go meet with your uncle. If they attack me and your uncle, I need you to be in a safe place so I can just concentrate on protecting your uncle and myself."

"Okay, go ahead."

Jeff smiled and stood. "Come and sit in my seat. You will be able to watch me and your uncle. " He put money in her hand. "If anything goes wrong and I have to make a run for it, that is enough money to take a taxi back to the hotel. You wait for me there. Got it?"

"I've got it."

He pulled out a small notebook and scribbled a number onto a blank piece of paper and ripped it out."

"Keep this safe," he said as he passed it to her. "If I don't get back to the hotel, phone this number from there. It is Mr Croydon, the man you met in Auckland. He will take care of you."

"Why won't you come back to the hotel?"

"Well, you know, sometimes not everything goes according to plan."

An anxious look clouded her face.

"I don't want you to get hurt. Promise me."

"I promise you," Jeff said, already knowing it was a promise he might not be able to keep.

CHAPTER NINETEEN

Felipe looked up as Jeff approached. He smiled and stood.

"Jeff, is it really you?"

Jeff held out his hand. Felipe pushed it aside and gave Jeff a hug. Jeff returned the gesture then pulled back.

"Good to see you again, Felipe."

"I wish I could offer those words of greeting with sincerity, my friend. As glad as I am to see you, I wish you weren't here." Felipe looked over Jeff's shoulder, eyes scanning the immediate vicinity. "Where is Arina?"

"In a safe place."

Felipe gave a half-smile. His lips tightened with displeasure, and a quick flash of anger crossed his face, almost hidden. Jeff caught it and could tell the Filipino was fighting to restrain himself. He remembered during their university days, Felipe had a temper and when upset would often unload a tirade of abuse. Not bringing Arina along had thrown him. Too bad.

Felipe gestured toward a chair, "Take a seat. Can I get you a drink?"

"Water will do."

Felipe waved to a waiter hovering out of earshot and ordered two bottles of water.

"You had me worried. I went to the hotel to collect you and they said you hadn't checked in. You have a problem with the hotel? It is one of the best in the city."

Amused by the comment, Jeff raised an eyebrow.

"I booked a hotel when I bought my air ticket."

"Did you bring Arina with you?"

"Yes, but I'm being super cautious. After what happened in Auckland, I am making sure I'm not the one who gets her killed."

"I see. I am her uncle, Jeff. And, I'm the one who helped her escape; remember?"

"You also told me the men who are after Arina threatened you. I wanted to make certain you weren't followed."

Felipe fiddled with his drink bottle. "You wouldn't be messing me about, would you, Jeff? A lot is at stake here. I have Sofia and my family to consider."

"We have had this conversation. The best way to help your family is to find out where they are, and rescue them."

"And this rescue team is me and you?"

Jeff nodded.

Felipe raised his hands in mock surrender. "Do you know what I think; I think you have decided to play games with me. Maybe because of the policemen killed in New Zealand. For them you want revenge. Okay, this I understand, but what you are asking me to do is not reasonable. We have no chance against these people. We don't even know who they are. Now bring Arina. With her I can save Sofia. They said they will not harm my niece. This is all that is important."

"I am not bringing Arina into the open until I am certain no one will harm her, and right now I'm not convinced."

"I am sorry you have chosen this course."

Felipe looked across Jeff's shoulder. A slight nod.

Jeff did not have to turn around to know Felipe was signalling to the man in the shadows. Was he alone or were there more? He pushed the table into Felipe and sent the policeman crashing to the ground. Jeff sprinted out of the café and across the street. His eyes widened when he saw Arina was standing on the pavement. He rushed to her.

"Follow me."

Arina stood her ground. "You hurt my uncle."

Jeff stooped and eyeballed her. "Arina, those men with your uncle are the men who have your mother. If they get you, they will kill your parents. Do you understand?"

"Yes, I understand, but Uncle Felipe......."

"We can discuss your uncle later; right now we need to run."

The man Felipe had signalled dashed towards them. Jeff ran at him. The move caught the man by surprise. Jeff swung a right cross and his fist crushed the assailant's nose. He screeched with pain, his hand grabbing his face. Jeff swung again, this time a right hook into the side of the head. The fight was over.

Jeff took hold of Arina's hand and pulled her along as he ran. She dragged her feet, fighting him. He picked her up and threw her over his shoulder and ran through the pedestrians. Arina kicked her legs and screamed. Pedestrians were pointing. Jeff shook his head. The local police would soon be all over him if this continued. He ran into an alley and placed her on the ground. He held her shoulders so she couldn't run off, then bent over until their faces almost touched.

"Now listen, Arina, I am doing what I need to do to protect you. Do you believe me?"

A slow, but confused nod. "But my uncle?"

Jeff decided he needed to be honest with her.

"Your uncle believes if he gives you to the men who have your family they will release your mother and father and not harm you. This is not true, Arina. They will kill you all. The only way to save your family is for me to find them, and to do that I need time."

Arina was calmer and at least listening, Jeff let his hold on her arms relax. She didn't run away.

"You need to trust me, okay?" She nodded. "Good." He heard sirens. "The police are coming. We need to get away from here." He took her hand. "Let's go."

From his earlier reconnaissance he knew there were markets at the end of the next side street. As they ran between the stalls he looked over his shoulder. He saw no one following. On the other side of the market they made their way through a maze of alleys. After walking almost six blocks, Jeff flagged down a taxi. He needed to get a terrified Arina back to the hotel and keep her out of sight. And he needed to get out of the damned heat.

CHAPTER TWENTY

Jeff phoned the contact number given to him by the SAS intelligence officer. Omar, the skipper of the fishing boat, named his price for taking Jeff and Arina to Mindanao Island, and told Jeff to come to the fish markets.

"Find the Sheraton 4 Points Hotel, walk to the water's edge, turn left and you will see a circular building on a small area of reclaimed land jutting out into the sea. The wharf surrounds it. You can't miss it," Omar had said over the phone. "This is where I will be. And don't forget to bring the money."

Jeff checked out of the Sabah Hotel and decided again they should walk into the city; he liked to keep up some form of exercise routine. He had offered to carry Arina's backpack, but she was adamant it was hers to carry and she didn't need help. It had been a difficult night. When they had made it back to the room she was still upset that she had not spoken with her uncle. Arina had stuffed the iPod plugs into her ears and turned her back to him. At breakfast she was more animated and had at least said good morning.

The street leading to the entrance of The Sheraton 4 Points Hotel and the waterfront road was lined with palm trees. Arina ran around each of them. It slowed progress and Jeff resisted admonishing her and pointing out they did not have time for games. He just kept walking. When they reached the water's edge and a single chain railing, she was beside him. He turned left as Omar had instructed. A few hundred metres away, stood a round, two-storey cream-coloured building; the fish market hall.

Jeff led Arina down the centre of the road between lines of parked cars. A road circled the fish market building, and from where Jeff stood he could see it had steps down onto the wharf. Men leapt on and off boats unloading goods. He could hear raised voices from within the market building. He guessed they belonged to sellers and buyers haggling over the price of the day's catch.

Fishy smells assaulted his nose.

The city was one hundred and fifty years old, and Jeff pondered on how many decades fishermen had bashed their catch to death on the concrete and rock surrounds. Nine fishing trawlers were lined up beside each other. They were all old, all wooden, and all appeared unstable. Their fragile appearance left Jeff thinking; if any of them were caught in a decent storm, they would end up at the bottom of the ocean. If Omar's boat was in a similar condition then crossing the Sulu Sea was going to be risky. If he was on his own he wouldn't give it a second thought, but he had Arina with him and had to consider her safety.

Three smaller craft loaded with watermelons were moored between the rock sea wall and the fishing boats. A human chain passed the melons up to road level where they were loaded onto small flat-deck trucks. A second chain loaded melons into large wicker baskets for sale in the markets. Jeff led the way past the trucks and down the steps to the lower level, sidestepping baskets and empty plastic bins.

Arina, uncertain in the strange environment, stayed close.

The hull of the last in the line of fishing boats was painted bright blue with a yellow stripe along the waterline. The cabin covered two thirds of the deck and was painted yellow, white and the same colour blue as on the hull. Six car tyres hung over the side just above the waterline for protection against boats moored alongside. Omar had said his boat was the most colourful, and most beautiful. It was certainly colourful, but Jeff doubted it belonged in the beautiful category.

On the foredeck, five Malaysian or Filipino men were sitting on crates smoking cigarettes and talking. Grizzled faces, as leathery in look as tanned hide, turned his way as he approached. Their thin bodies might look in need of food but Jeff was not fooled. These men were sinewy and tough and right now they appeared menacing.

Arina pushed in closer to him and Jeff placed a hand on her shoulder.

One man stood. He wore a red-and-gold headscarf tied around the top of his head. It had been knotted at the back, and the tails dangled down to his shoulders. A thick gold earring hung from his right ear lobe, and a sparse growth of black bristles sat under his nose; a failed attempt at growing a moustache. He wore a sleeveless khaki singlet tucked into green military trousers tucked into boots. He had the look of the quintessential pirate and would have not looked out of place in the pages of a comic book.

A welcoming smile broke across his face, displaying a row of yellowing teeth. He leapt off the bow onto the wharf.

"Mr Bradley, I am Omar. It is a big pleasure to meet you." Jeff shook the offered hand. "Welcome to my boat. She is beautiful, is she not?"

"Yes, it's very pretty Omar, and old," Jeff said. "Is it safe on the open sea?"

"Is it safe?" Omar's wrinkled brow showed he was genuinely offended.

Jeff continued, "As I said on the phone, I need to get to Mindanao. Will your boat get me there?"

"Of course, I make the crossing all the time. I am going to the port of Zamboanga, on the western side of the island. I can take you there, for the price I told you."

"How long will it take?"

"Maybe thirty hours, depending on patrol vessels. The Indonesian and Australian navies patrol this area now. Don't worry, it is a big sea. They will not catch us."

"Why would navy patrol boats concern you? Are you a pirate, Omar?"

Omar placed a hand on his chest close enough to where his heart might be found. "Mr Bradley, you offend me by making such a remark."

Jeff said, "I have a young girl to look after."

Omar moved his eyes to Arina, now hiding behind Jeff.

"I must be certain she is not in danger."

Omar smiled at Arina. "Do not fear, little one. My friends and I," -- he gestured toward his men who had stopped talking and were now watching their Captain and

Jeff -- "We are businessmen. We ferry goods between Sandakan and Mindanao."

Jeff scrutinised the four-man crew, all dressed in similar garb to Omar. His first thought was that somewhere beneath deck would be weapons of all varieties. Out at sea, how long would it be before they attacked him? It was the worst plan he had ever concocted and he hoped, for Arina's sake, it wouldn't be disastrous. But he had little choice; he had to get to Mindanao, and this was the only way to slip into the Philippines undercover. Despite Omar's protests, Jeff had little doubt the captain and his crew were pirates. But the SAS officer had vouched for Omar and that was good enough for him.

Earlier, he had toyed with the idea of buying a weapon. At least then, if Omar and his men turned on him, he could defend himself. But he hadn't, and now it was too late. Four sets of eyes turned to the petite figure of Arina as she stepped out from behind him. She stood as tall as it was possible for a person of her stature. She locked eyes with the men until they looked away. Jeff smiled and gave a nod. Arina had spunk.

"When can we leave?" Jeff asked Omar.

"Have you got the money we agreed?"

Jeff pulled an envelope from his backpack. Greedy eyes zeroed in on the bulging packet. Omar held out his hand and Jeff placed the envelope into it. Omar turned to his men and yelled an order.

"We go now. Jump aboard."

Jeff helped Arina over the railing. One of the crew released the mooring ropes, and the boat drifted away from the dock. Two of the men disappeared below deck.

A few minutes later Jeff heard the low growl of an inboard engine as it chugged into life. A plume of black smoke coughed out through the exhaust. Captain Omar, the trader, stood at the helm and turned the wheel until the boat was on the correct bearing; and then the speed slowly increased.

After twenty minutes on the Sulu Sea, the gentle roll and diesel fumes had begun to work on Jeff's stomach. Queasiness forced him to grip a handrail. He shook his head. He needed to take his mind off the urge to vomit. Arina seemed happy enough. She had settled herself at the galley table, which was also a section of the bridge, and was rocking her head to the music on her iPod and playing games on her iPad.

Jeff stepped into the cabin. His nostrils were greeted with a mix of unsavoury smells, body stink, cooking odours and stale beer. Unwashed dishes were stacked in the small stainless sink. The contents of his stomach began to churn.

"How well do you know Zamboanga City?" Jeff asked Omar.

"My business takes me to the port many times. After one or two days I will ferry cargo to General Santos City on the eastern side of the island. I call General Santos my home. Do you know it?"

Jeff shook his head.

"It can be dangerous in Zamboanga if you are a foreigner. It is dangerous in most parts of the southern Philippines, but Zamboanga is bad. Many rebel groups operate in the region; communists, Islamists, locals fighting for their land rights, corrupt police, military and government officials. The rebel groups are always on the lookout for a wealthy foreigner to kidnap. You will need to be careful."

"And what about you, Omar, do you kidnap for ransom?

Omar laughed. "Not me, Mr Jeff. I am a businessman, a trader. Do not worry. For the right price I will protect you, even from me."

Jeff didn't smile. He was debating whether Omar's last comment was humour or a veiled threat.

"What are you going to do in Zamboanga? Why do you go there?" Omar asked.

"I am going to Zamboanga because you are going to Zamboanga. But I need to get myself and Arina to Davao City. I have business there."

"Illegal business, I think. To sneak into the Philippines like this is not normal. Are you a wanted man? I need to know if I am putting myself in hot water as you say in the West."

Jeff smiled. "You're a pirate. How bad would I have to be to be worse than what you do?"

Omar laughed. "I've already told you, Mr Jeff, I am not a pirate, I am a trader. Pirates steal from the sea, I steal from the land, and I do not kidnap tourists on sailing boats." He flashed another yellow-toothed grin at Jeff. "For the right price I will arrange for you to get to Davao City. I have a cousin who has a hotel in Zamboanga. If you need to stay the night, I can get you a cheap rate."

Jeff shook his head. "Okay, I believe you. You're a business man."

One of Omar's crewmen poked his head through the door and spoke quickly in what Jeff took to be Tagalog.

"We are being followed," said Omar.

The crewman took the wheel and Omar took binoculars from a shelf and hurried to the stern. Jeff followed. Omar scanned the approaching vessel then passed the binoculars to Jeff. The following craft had the look of a navy patrol boat. Maybe it had been that, at one time. Everything was for sale nowadays. It was sleekly shaped and the gunmetal-grey hull might have been steel. Sixty feet long at a guess, and it looked much stronger and faster than Omar's wooden craft. At the pace it was moving through the water, it would catch up within the next ten minutes.

"Are they the authorities?" Jeff asked.

"This is not a boat the navy would use. I think pirates. They will think we are locals taking tourists out for a cruise. When they get close, they will see we have nothing of value."

"Don't you pirates know each other?"

Omar grinned. "Many pirates roam the Sulu Sea. But we do not work together. And I told you, I'm a businessman."

"Is this as fast as your boat can go?"

"Yes, it is all the speed we need."

The pirate boat had closed to a few hundred metres. Jeff took up the binoculars again. This time he could clearly see five men. They held automatic weapons. Two were Kalashnikovs for sure. He could not make out what type the other weapons were but it didn't really matter. They were armed and he wasn't. He would leave it to Omar to send them on their way. He scanned the rest of the boat, and then he froze. He refocussed the lens to ensure his eyes had not deceived him. There was no doubt.

At the stern, with one hand holding onto the railing to steady himself, stood Felipe.

CHAPTER TWENTY ONE

"Omar," Jeff said. "Those pirates are after me. They will shoot you and your men to get to me. Do you understand?"

Jeff wasn't about to tell Omar they were after Arina. They'd toss her into the water in an instant. Omar's brown eyes darkened to black as he glared at Jeff. His attention then swung to the approaching boat.

"Why are these men chasing you? What have you done?" Omar was incredulous, his face clouded in anger.

Jeff thought quickly.

"The man at the stern of their boat is a wealthy drug dealer. I took his money. He wants it back."

Omar eyed Jeff. "For endangering me and my men it will cost you more money. Now, follow me."

Jeff followed Omar along the deck into the cabin. Arina was listening to her music and playing a game on her iPad, oblivious to the unfolding drama. The pirate captain pulled back a faded bamboo mat. He knelt and poked his finger through a hole in one of the floor boards. It came loose and when he pulled it back it revealed a cache of weapons. Jeff looked over Omar's shoulder and smiled when he saw the array of firearms. He was familiar with the Kalashnikovs, Glocks, a Beretta, two

Israeli Uzis, an M16, and two Carbine rifles. There were several older weapons he did not recognise.

"You could start a war with this lot, Omar."

Jeff received a broad grin. "You know these weapons?" Omar asked.

"I have fired some of them."

Omar threw Jeff a quizzical glance.

Jeff saw no point in hiding his experience. If he was to take control, he needed Omar on his side. "In another life I was in the military."

Jeff went back to ferreting through the remainder of the stockpile but saw nothing that would give him an edge or packed a decisive punch.

"I don't see any rocket launchers."

"No, Mr Jeff. This we do not have."

"Arm your crew," Jeff said.

Jeff helped himself to the Uzi. It had a magazine attached. He checked the auto-select slide and moved it to automatic. More foraging and he found two more magazines, both loaded with 9mm rounds. He removed the magazine on the weapon and pushed down on the top bullet. It depressed then bounced back. The magazine was full, with plenty of oomph in the spring. He cocked it and pulled the trigger. The firing mechanism worked. It had a fold-out stock, but he left it in place. It was as good as any pistol submachine gun he had fired. The Uzi was useful in tight spaces. He reloaded the magazine. He pushed a Glock into his belt and the two extra Uzi magazines into his trouser pockets.

"What about smoke grenades?" Jeff asked.

"This we have. How many do you want?"

"How many have you got?"

Omar knelt on the floor, reached further back and pulled out five grenades. "This is all."

"That will do. Let's get back on deck."

When he looked up he saw Arina was no longer sitting at the table. Worried, Jeff rushed onto the deck, and then relaxed when he saw her standing at the stern. She was watching the approaching pirate boat.

"What is happening, Jeff?"

"Pirates."

Her eyes widened in alarm, and her fingers pressed the locket she was wearing against her lips. Her cocoa-brown Asian complexion turned pale. Jeff took one of the life jackets stacked against the wall.

"Arina, come here," Jeff ordered. It was not a time to be gentle, and he hoped she wouldn't be stubborn. She obeyed. He slipped the life jacket over her head and tightened the straps. He placed his hands on her shoulders.

"What are you going to do with me," Arina asked.

"I need to make you safe, okay?" Arina nodded.

He guided her along the deck until he was certain they were hidden from the pirate boat. Then, taking a deep breath and praying she might one day forgive him, he grasped her shoulders, picked her up and tossed her overboard. She surfaced after a few moments then splashed about as she caught her breath and steadied herself. It did not take her long to get through the shock of finding herself in the water. Then a pair of hostile eleven- year-old eyes fixed on him.

"It's for your own good," he yelled at her. "Don't wave your arms. The pirates might see you."

She was now a good three boat lengths away bobbing up and down with arms splashing about as she drifted away. She either hadn't heard him or didn't care. Now for Arina's sake he had to make sure he came out on top of the looming fight. If he didn't it was a long swim back to shore or she'd be on her way to Mindanao on the pirate boat. It occurred to him that she might be hard to see in the choppy sea once it was over. It was too late now. He'd find her.

The pirates had closed the distance and their boat was not slowing, their intention clear - to ram Omar. Omar and his men exchanged high-pitched babble as they pointed toward the danger. Omar looked in all directions in search of a miracle. The closer the pirates got, the shriller the voices became.

Omar screamed an order; Kalashnikovs appeared in hands and all barrels turned toward the pirate craft. One of his men climbed onto the cabin roof. He aimed his Kalashnikov and pulled the trigger. The rocking boat ruined his aim and most of his spray of bullets bounced off the pirate's metal hull. Flashes of light came from the pirate boat as they returned fire. Omar's crewman's body jerked about like a dancing marionette. His dance of death sent him staggering backward before falling from the roof into the water. Jeff looked over the side. The body lay still, head down, unmoving, the water turning crimson.

"Give me a few of those smoke grenades," Jeff ordered.

Omar gave him three.

Jeff pulled the pins and dropped them onto the stern deck. Omar followed Jeff's lead and pulled the pins on his two. Red, yellow and white Smoke spewed forth from the canisters.

"Everyone to the foredeck," Jeff ordered.

He stopped by the wheelhouse door and turned to Omar standing behind him. "Tell your man to turn the boat. Get the stern facing the pirates."

The boat turned.

The smoke was building, creating the cover he hoped it would.

Jeff climbed onto the cabin roof, and cocked the Uzi. The pirates had closed to under fifty metres. The steel bow of their boat, in the shape of a wedge, protruded further than normal. They had modified their vessel into an assault weapon. In a few minutes it would scythe through Omar's wooden hull, and he had little doubt, the pirates would shoot any survivors floating in the water. They would have Arina. And if he survived the crash, would Felipe let him live, maybe, maybe not? He wasn't about to put Felipe's integrity to the test.

"Make sure your man on the helm keeps the smoke between us and the pirates," Jeff yelled down to Omar.

He received a thumbs-up.

"You two," Jeff called to two of Omar's men on the deck directly below him. "Get up here."

Puzzled faces stared up at him. Jeff pointed at the boat, through the smoke, now only a few metres away. "Follow me," he yelled, waving his arm.

They scrambled onto the roof and crouched down as Jeff had done. Then the smoke did its job, and the pirates disappeared from sight. Jeff ran across the roof until he was near the stern. Then the pirate's vessel emerged from the smoke. Omar's boat rocked sideways as Felipe's attack boat struck. Jeff almost lost his footing. He grasped a handrail and steadied himself. The sounds of splintering timber told him he needed to act. Through the smoke screen he was able to see the pathway he needed. He ran and leapt through the haze onto the foredeck of the pirate vessel. Holding his finger on the trigger, he sprayed bullets until his magazine was empty. Two of the pirates died as bullets slammed into their chests. Another reeled sideways and disappeared over the side. He heard two thuds behind him. Omar's two men had jumped aboard. He reloaded a new magazine and moved forward.

He was now clear of the smoke.

A pirate on the bridge was taking aim through a glassless window. Jeff brought the Uzi up, knowing he was too late. His ears rang as an automatic weapon fired behind him. The face in the window vanished. Omar's men raced past him through the first door and into the cabin. The cabin walls muffled the sound of automatic fire. Two pirates ran out and onto the deck. Jeff sprayed them with 9mm rounds. They fell where they stood. He jumped onto the cabin roof and raced the length of it and leapt onto the stern deck as Omar's men emerged.

Felipe, had remained seated. His nervous eyes followed Jeff's movements. Omar's men aimed their Kalashnikovs at Felipe's chest. They looked to Jeff for the order to fire. Jeff waggled his forefinger at them.

"No," he shouted.

Disappointed, they lowered their weapons.

Omar, standing on the bow of his sinking boat, gave a wave. One of his men rushed to the wheelhouse of the pirate boat and steered it back towards his captain. Omar and his remaining man stepped aboard. In despair he watched as his boat sank, then relief followed. He was still alive.

Jeff ordered the boat to circle back and search for Arina. He climbed back onto the cabin top. After five minutes he spotted her and waved. She waved back. Gutsy kid. When the boat was close enough, he scrambled down from the roof and yanked her aboard. She sat on the deck, her back against the wall, exhausted. He checked on Felipe. The policeman from Davao City wasn't going anywhere. One of Omar's crew had his weapon trained on Felipe's chest.

Felipe gave Arina a wave. She climbed to her feet and walked toward her uncle. He opened his arms. Arina stopped. Picked up a half-empty plastic bottle of water and threw it at him. It hit him on the shin. She turned away and went inside the cabin. Jeff laughed.

Gunshots.

Jeff swung the Uzi toward the sound. He relaxed when he saw it was Omar. He shot a surviving pirate attempting to swim away.

Jeff entered the cabin to check on Arina.

She looked up at him. "What about our bags?"

"I'm sorry, Arina. They went down with the boat."

Her eyes welled. "My new clothes. My iPod and my iPad."

"I'll buy you more, don't worry."

Arina turned away, wiping her eyes with the bottom of her T-shirt. Jeff's heart almost broke. The poor kid had been through so much and now she had lost the few possessions she owned. He reached out to comfort her then pulled his hand away. He didn't know what he should do. She sat in drenched clothes, but in thirty degree heat they would soon dry out. He searched the cabin and found a bottle of water and brought it to her. As an afterthought he tapped at his thigh. His waterproof holdall was still strapped tight. He had cash, passports and credit cards. He and Arina would get by when they made it to Mindanao.

Time to speak with Felipe.

###

Jeff strode at Felipe, grabbed a fistful of his shirt, pulled him off the seat and forced him onto his knees. Felipe did not resist. Jeff pulled the Glock from his belt and pushed the pistol barrel against the side of the Filipino policeman's head.

"If you want to kill me, Jeff, do it. I deserve it. But do it quick."

"Don't think I won't. Why, Felipe? Why?"

"I can explain."

"Go ahead," Jeff growled.

Felipe reached inside his jacket pocket. Jeff's finger increased pressure on the trigger. Felipe held up a hand. "I am not reaching for a weapon." Jeff did not relax. Felipe pulled out a photograph and held it up. Jeff let go of his hold on Felipe's shirt, took the photograph and stepped back far enough to be beyond Felipe's reach. He glanced down at the photo. It was of a family. He recognised Felipe. His arm was around an attractive woman. Not Sofia. Felipe only had the one sister, so he guessed the woman must be his wife. There was an older man seated. Standing beside the older man was a young boy and girl. Beside Felipe and his wife were two men; of a similar age to Felipe.

Jeff looked up from the photo.

"This is my family, Jeff. The men after Arina have threatened to kill them. I was followed to Sandakan. They guessed I was here to meet with you and Arina. They hired the pirates and ordered me to go along. The plan was to get me close enough to speak with you and talk you into giving up Arina. But they are pirates, and pirates cannot be trusted."

Jeff shook his head.

"And did your plan include killing me?"

Felipe shrugged. "They want Arina. They will stop at nothing to get her."

"Felipe, you're her uncle. Fight back."

Felipe glared, he was angry. "It's all very well playing the hero in a country where the bad guys get arrested. But here in the Philippines, justice does not work that way. If you are wealthy and connected, you can do whatever you want. You're hell bent on creating mayhem to find these men. It is not the way. We need to appease these people before it gets worse."

Jeff leaned forward, "Get it into your thick skull once and for all, Felipe. You cannot appease these guys. They are killers and they will kill everyone. Do you understand?"

Felipe's shoulders slumped, defeated.

Jeff lowered his weapon.

"What can I do? I cannot fight them. I am fighting ghosts. I have run out of choices. Taking Arina from you seemed the only way for me." He shook his head, shame clouding his features. "I was prepared to let my sister's family die, to save my own family. I am an evil man. Satan controls my heart."

"Listen to me, Felipe. We will find Sofia. The man who threatened you and your family, how did he contact you?"

"Apart from the man following me in Sandakan, all contact has been by mobile phone; untraceable."

Jeff gave him a puzzled look.

Felipe shrugged. "I put a trace on my phone after the first call. It served no purpose. Each call was on a throwaway phone or a payphone."

Jeff was thoughtful.

"What now, Jeff, are you going to kill me?"

Jeff pushed the Glock back into his belt. "Perhaps later, but for now, my pirate friend Omar is taking you, me and Arina to Zamboanga City, and then you are taking Arina and me to Davao City."

"This is not wise, Jeff. In Davao, whoever is behind this will have men all over the city. They might not recognise you but they know me. If they see me, they will make contact. What will I tell them?"

"You tell them you tried to get Arina, but the men they hired were no match for me. Their man in Sandakan, who was watching us, can verify that you went on the boat with the men he hired. Tell them I let you live only because of Arina, but because of your betrayal, I no longer trust you. But I have not returned to the safety of Malaysia. I am somewhere on Mindanao. You believe this because I am an honourable man and would not let your family die. You tell them you are confident I will make contact within the week. Why? Because I do not know anyone and will need your help."

"And what if they don't believe me?"

"They lose nothing by waiting. And they gave you seven days. Hold them to it." Felipe's eyes brightened slightly. "And from here on in, Felipe, investigate as much as you can. Act like a cop. And let's find these assholes."

Jeff turned to Omar. "How do you like your new boat?"

"I like it very much. But as much as it has made me happy, I am also sad. I lost a good man today. But I am a businessman. You will get my bill."

"And will your new boat get us to Zamboanga? Is there enough diesel?"

"Do not worry, my friend. For you, if we run out of fuel I will row. All part of the service."

Jeff grinned. Omar was costing him a fortune.

He turned to Felipe. "Your niece needs her uncle. Go comfort her."

CHAPTER TWENTY TWO

Felipe turned off the main highway onto a dirt road. The bungalow at the end of the road was not what Jeff had expected. With a manicured lawn and neatly tended gardens, the house, surrounded by rainforest, had the look of an idyllic oasis. A blast of cold air struck Jeff when he entered the home. The house had air-conditioning, quality furniture and furnishings, a huge kitchen, two bathrooms and five bedrooms.

Jeff had little choice but to trust Felipe. He was a Davao City police inspector. If nothing else, he could make sure investigations did not come near the bungalow. And Jeff knew no one else in the Philippines. He couldn't keep moving about, not with Arina.

"What does this friend of yours do for a living?" Jeff asked.

"He is a policeman, like me," Felipe said.

Jeff raised an eyebrow, but made no comment.

"From the state of the grounds I take it your friend has gardeners. Make sure they stay away."

"I'll take care of it when I leave here. There is a housekeeper. I phoned ahead and had her turn the air-conditioning on."

"Probably best she stays away as well," Jeff said.

"The refrigerator has food and drinks. Help yourself to anything you need," Felipe said, and he turned to Arina. "My friend's daughter is a similar size to you. Have a look through her wardrobe. She will not mind if you wear her clothes. Her room is at the end of the corridor."

Arina hesitated and glanced at Jeff. After receiving a nod of approval, she slid off her seat and went in search of the room.

Felipe gave Jeff his contact details and left.

Arina reappeared wearing a change of clothes and sat at the table. Jeff gave her a warm smile. He received a blank look in return. She bit at her bottom lip and then the end of her ponytail was back in her mouth. He took a cola and a bottle of water from the fridge. He pushed the can across; she stared at it, but made no attempt to touch it.

Jeff opened up the map Felipe had given him.

The Americans wanted to find the compound as much as he did and had lots of military toys to play with. But they had not managed to find it. If they had, he and Arina would not have been sent. He was certain US satellites would have scanned the search area, but satellite scanners could not penetrate foliage, and if the camp no longer existed, no thermal infrared images would be detected. And even if they did pick up movement, it could be any one of the twenty million or so inhabitants living on Mindanao.

Jeff said to Arina, "Are you up to helping me find the compound?"

"You threw me in the water," she said.

"I'm sorry."

"You didn't need to. I can look out for myself."

"I know you can. Next time I promise not to throw you in the water."

Arina didn't look convinced.

Jeff reached across and took the cola can. He ripped off the tab and pushed it back to her.

"Thank you." Her voice was soft.

Jeff said, "Now, let me see. If I remember, you set out from General Santos City, here."

Jeff stabbed the spot on the map with his finger and highlighted it with his yellow felt-tip marker.

"Yes. At 6pm."

"Okay, take me through your trip."

"We drove there at night. They had covered the windows. Where I sat, there was a small hole. I saw out. But everything went by so fast."

"Could you find it again?" Jeff asked.

"No, I could not find it. But I could see Mount Apo from the compound."

"Mount Apo?"

"Mount Apo is the biggest mountain on Mindanao."

"How long did it take you to travel to the compound?" Jeff asked.

"It was four hours from General Santos City?"

Jeff gave a quizzical look. "How come you can remember the exact time?"

Arina gave a ghost of a grin.

"I kept asking Papa, 'When are we leaving?' He told me to hush. But I looked at my watch when the bus started and it was six o'clock. Then later I was hungry, we'd had no dinner, and kept asking my father, 'How long to go?' He kept saying, 'Ten more minutes.' I kept checking my watch. We stopped at ten o'clock."

"That's something," Jeff said.

It occurred to him that if he could find out what the roads were like, he might at least be able to mark out a search area on a map. For the next twenty minutes Jeff talked Arina through the details of her trip. Ten-minute toilet stops every hour. But always, there were soldiers. Military posts, not townships. There were no food stops.

"Good. And you said from the compound you could see Mount Apo?"

"Yes, it was a long way away, but I could see it."

"And were you looking north or south."

Arina looked confused. She shrugged.

Mount Apo appeared to be halfway between General Santos City in the south and Davao to the north, but well to the west. She must have been looking south if they drove past Davao City. Jeff marked Mount Apo with his highlighter. He ran a straight line from the mountain to the north of Davao City.

"Now you said it was about a three to four-hour drive.

"Four hours."

"Okay. Good. It's about a three-hour-plus drive from General Santos City to Davao City? Another half-hour inland puts the general area about here. But when you went inland did you travel north, south or west."

Again Arina shrugged.

Jeff drew a circle on the map.

"At least we now have a search area."

"Are you going to save Mama and Papa and Sarah?"

Jeff gave a reluctant half-grin.

She continued, "I heard you and Uncle Felipe talking. What happens if you don't find them in seven days? Are you going to give me to the bad men?

Jeff rubbed the top of his forehead.

"I promise you, Arina, I will find your family, and no, I won't give you to the bad men."

Arina studied Jeff, searching his eyes for the truth. Jeff waited for her to finish. She looked down at the map. "What do we have to do, to find my family?"

"We take one step at a time, Arina. First, I need to find the compound. I might find clues. If there are any men in the camp I will make them tell me where they are holding your family."

If he had learnt anything from his SAS training and field experience, it was that it was hard to cover up and wipe clean an area occupied for a long period. Whenever they patrolled, they were careful never to leave any rubbish. Now and then they missed small items. Something as innocuous as a cigarette butt or ration wrapper in enemy territory might start a manhunt. A compound occupied by many people for months would leave a trace. He frowned when he looked down at the map. He had circled a huge search area. Impossible maybe, but it was all he had. The best way to search such a big area was by helicopter or small plane.

His other lead had been Diego. And he was dead. Diego's crony, who he had captured in New Zealand, had so far given up nothing. Not because the interrogation methods were not working, but in Brian Cunningham's opinion the prisoner had no knowledge of Diego's activities. Jeff would have to rely on Felipe to discover the whereabouts of Diego's rebel group.

Arina yawned.

"Tired? Jeff asked. Arina nodded.

"Why don't you go to bed? Get some sleep."

"I'm not that sleepy." She yawned again.

Then Jeff remembered she hated to be on her own. Jeff pinched the bridge of his nose. What the hell was he supposed to do with her? He looked toward the settee. "I have more work to do. How about I get blankets and a pillow and you can sleep on the couch? And I'll be right here at the table."

He received a half-smiled nod of acceptance.

Jeff stripped a blanket and pillows off the bed in the first bedroom. Arina sat at the table watching him make up a bed for her. He stood beside it until she was under the sheets and comfortable. He was grateful for the air-conditioning. With the room as cool as it was, Arina soon drifted off to sleep.

He made fresh coffee, went back to the table and phoned Percy Croydon, the head of the Secret Service in New Zealand.

Croydon said, "Today the Americans told me they'd sent someone to the Philippines. Kennedy Patton, the woman from the Auckland consulate office."

Jeff had suspected she was CIA, and now Croydon confirmed it.

"Her cover is that she is working with an aid group, bringing medical supplies and equipment to outlying villages."

"What's happening in the villages?"

"A typhoon ripped through Mindanao. Many villages destroyed, many people killed. Huge tracts of jungle flattened. It might make your search easier."

"I'm sure it will," Jeff said, not bothering to hide the sarcasm. "How much budget do I have? I need to hire a plane."

"You don't have a budget; you're spending your own money. What else?"

Jeff related the details of the events in Sandakan City and the pirate attack. His first thought after hanging up was that he'd better find the locations of Davao City ATM machines. He was going to need access to a steady supply of cash.

The CIA sending an agent confirmed his earlier suspicions that the Americans were interested in finding out what happened to Arina, but not to help save her family. They had ulterior motives and they weren't about to share. He sipped his coffee and scanned the map again. A knock on the door had Jeff swing his head toward the entrance hall.

He felt for the pistol at his back, but there was nothing. Felipe had insisted no weapons. Felipe's reasoning had been that if he was stopped by the military or the police, and Felipe was not with him, he might be arrested for terrorism. Jeff didn't like it but he had made the stupid decision to place his and Arina's security in Felipe's hands. He might live to regret it but it meant he had little choice but to accept the policeman's judgement calls.

Jeff surmised the late-night caller had to be either Felipe or a nosy neighbour seeking to find out why a light was on. No one else knew he was here and if it was the men chasing Arina, they wouldn't be knocking on the door, they'd be smashing it down. He softly stepped across to the window by the front door and looked through the wooden slats. It was Felipe.

Jeff opened the door.

Standing beside Felipe was a tiny older woman, perhaps in her fifties or sixties. Village women had harsh lives, their ages hard to tell. She wore a tomato-red T-shirt that hung over the top of white shorts – on her feet, flip-flops. A head of thick black hair surrounded a smiling round face and dancing brown eyes. Felipe was not a tall man, but the top of this woman's head was inches below his shoulder.

"This is Mama Soo," Felipe said by way of introduction. Jeff received a beaming grin that bared a row of white teeth, which took Jeff by surprise. Whatever Mama Soo's upbringing might have been, she had been to a dentist. "Mama Soo speaks perfect English."

Felipe carried a small brown leather suitcase. He held it out to Jeff. "Her belongings."

Jeff looked at the case, but did not take hold of it. Felipe placed it on the floor.

"Mama Soo is here to look after Arina. She will stay as long as is needed. She won't leave Arina's side. Now, I need to go. I am on duty and I'm expected back at the station."

Jeff touched Mama Soo on the shoulder. "Give me a minute, I need to talk with Felipe."

Jeff followed Felipe halfway to his car.

"This woman is trustworthy?" Jeff asked.

"She was a nanny to my children."

Jeff nodded. "Okay, good enough. I need to hire a plane."

Felipe looked puzzled.

"I have a search area. A flyover might find the camp."

"It would be best to use a foreign pilot. The NGO aid organisations have planes. The pilots meet at Rosie's Bar. It is not a typical Davao club. It's more like the clubs they have in Angeles City. You have heard of Angeles City?"

Jeff said he had. Angeles City, north of Manila, was the Philippines equivalent of the red-light districts of Bangkok.

"Rosie's was opened to cater for foreigners," Felipe said. "The police leave it alone. Major cities need to cater to everyone's needs, don't you think? Ask for the pilots' table. Now I need to get back to the station. I will organise for two colleagues I can trust to guard the house from tomorrow. I don't think anything will happen tonight."

"Nor do I," Jeff said. "But the fewer people who know about this house and where I am, the more secure we will be."

"These men are like my brothers. They will not betray me."

Jeff was sceptical but said nothing.

"How do I get to the city from here?"

"Walk out onto the main road and take a taxi. It's only fifteen minutes to the city centre. I'd take you myself but I need to get to the station and I also don't want to be seen with you."

Felipe spun on his heel and walked off to his car. Jeff walked back to Mama Soo, waiting on the veranda. He picked up her suitcase.

"Come on in, Mama Soo."

She followed Jeff down to the farthest bedroom and Jeff placed her bag on the bed.

"This room is for you."

"Thank you. This is a nice room."

Mama Soo's English was faultless. Not a hint of an accent.

"Your English…." Jeff started.

"A long time ago I was a school teacher. I taught at an English school. Where is the girl Arina?"

"Asleep in the lounge."

"I think she should be in her bed. She'll sleep more comfortably. Will you carry her for me? She will not wake. Young girls, they tend to sleep deeply." Jeff lifted Arina and carried her through to her room. She stirred as Jeff gently placed her on the bed, but did not wake. Mama Soo covered her with a blanket. Arina rolled onto her side and settled. Jeff led Mama Soo back to the lounge.

"I need to go out."

"I will watch over her."

"If she wakes and a stranger is sitting beside her, it will frighten her."

"Do not worry. She is in good hands."

Jeff hesitated. "Okay. Make yourself at home. Help yourself to anything."

The woman bowed and placed a hand on her heart. "You are a kind man. Thank you."

"Now I must go, I need to find a pilot."

CHAPTER TWENTY THREE

Rosie's Bar was much bigger on the inside than it looked from the street. It had a good-sized crowd but was not packed. It had a sex-bar look to it but not of the kind found in Bangkok as Felipe had implied. To Jeff the flashing lights gave it a disco look and most of the girls, dressed in denim shorts, white T-shirts and black vests, looked more like cheerleaders than sex workers. The girls in denim shorts walked between tables delivering drinks and taking orders. The music was loud and the dance floor crowded. Other girls clung to men from all nations, the couples rocking back and forth to a music beat he didn't recognise. By night's end the men would have built sizeable tabs buying the girls non-alcoholic drinks at three times the usual price.

Jeff made his way to the circular bar in the centre of the room. He climbed onto a bar stool. There were two barmen and both were busy filling orders.

"You look like a man looking for someone or something."

The accent was German. Jeff gave the man next to him a sideways glance. A handle of cold beer rested on a mat in front of his neighbour. His head drooped, eyes reddish. The beer on the mat was not his first.

"I'm looking for the pilots' table," Jeff said.

The German aimed his forefinger at eight people seated around two tables that had been pulled together.

"They sit there every other night," the German said. He wavered on his barstool. "They drink too much alcohol. Whatever you do, don't go up in a plane with any of them. Me, I would rather risk driving through rebel territory than fly over it with any of that lot."

Jeff slid off his stool.

"They dislike being disturbed," the German went on. "If you don't plonk a bottle of bourbon on the table, they'll tell you to piss off."

Jeff waved to the barman and dropped a handful of pesos on the bar top. The barman stood a bottle of bourbon next to the money and counted the notes. Whether it was enough, the barman didn't say. He didn't ask for more and he didn't offer Jeff any change.

Jeff nudged his way through the patrons on the dance floor. When he reached the pilots' table, one man eyed him. Jeff held up the bottle of bourbon and received a nod of approval. As he placed it on the table the German from the bar appeared, took a chair from the next table and squeezed his way into the circle.

The German said, "Drink up guys, the rest of the night is on my new friend."

Jeff smiled and gave a mock salute to the German who had conned him.

"I'm looking for a pilot who has a helicopter for hire," he said, his voice loud enough to be heard over the music.

The pilot closest to him looked up. A woman's face. It was Kennedy Patton. She smiled. Not of recognition, but the kind of smile a business person gives a potential client. Percy Croydon had said she was undercover but not that she was a pilot. Croydon should have forewarned him. He would play the game and follow her lead.

Kennedy stood. The top of her head came to just above his chin.

"No point talking to her," the man who had eyed him called out, his accent South African. "You want a reliable chopper pilot for this region. You need someone with experience. She's only been here a few days. Still wearing the same underwear, I'd bet. Don't waste your money."

"Don't pay him any attention," Kennedy said, and took Jeff by the arm. "I'm the best pilot here by far. Come to my office."

Jeff allowed himself to be led away.

"You've been warned," the South African yelled after him and then waved a hand in dismissal.

Kennedy walked ahead. Her baggy white blouse and loose cotton navy trousers showed no body definition, but from the spring in her step, Jeff guessed her to be fit and supple. She picked an empty table at the opposite end of the bar, and away from the music.

"Much quieter," she said, by way of explanation.

The American waved to a bar girl, held up two fingers and yelled for two beers.

"Take a seat," Kennedy said.

Jeff sat. Her pleasant manner was genuine. If it surprised her to see him she did not show it. He couldn't decide if she was attractive or handsome. The fine features were strong, the eyes had mischief, and she looked like she enjoyed herself. A free spirit.

Her hand reached across the table. "I'm Kennedy Patton."

Once again he was taken by surprise, they had already met. Jeff shook the offered hand. "Jeff Bradley. But that you already know."

"Let's get down to business. You need a chopper. I charge three hundred and fifty US dollars per hour, but we can talk about reducing the fee if you want my services for longer than four hours. Now where do you want to go?"

Jeff gave her a questioning look. Had she forgotten they had met? She must realise he knew she wasn't a contract pilot. In fact, in Kennedy's own words, she was an assistant to the US Consulate in Auckland, New Zealand.

Kennedy leaned across the table and dropped her voice, "Every wall and corner has ears in Davao City," she whispered.

He nodded. In the Special Forces Jeff had operated in cities filled with spies.

"I'm a photojournalist. A magazine has commissioned me to write a travel article on the Philippines, with pictures. For the photos I'm looking for something spectacular. I have nothing in mind, but I'll know when I see it." He unfolded the map from his back pocket. "Here is my area of interest." He ran his finger along a line highlighted in pink. "A researcher for the magazine told me if I looked in a line from here to Mount Apo I would find breathtaking landscapes. I have a particular interest in rivers and waterfalls. Have you flown this region?"

Kennedy swivelled the map toward her.

"That's one hell of a search area." She placed her finger on a spot. "This could be a problem. It's just been designated a no-fly zone by the military. It's not policed, but all the same I'd be breaking the rules flying over it."

"Pretty up-to-date information for a pilot who's been here less than a week," Jeff said.

"I work for an organisation that prides itself on maintaining an up-to-date database." She smiled.

Jeff glanced up from the map. "Does that mean you won't take me near here?" He placed a finger where Kennedy had indicated.

"No, just laying down the rules. The Philippines Air Force can get finicky. Any fines incurred will be at your cost. I expect payment up front or I don't leave the ground. But I think a small plane to start, not a chopper. We have a lot of ground to cover, we need to get high."

"Whatever you say. You're the pilot."

The bargirl returned with two bottles of beer, the caps removed. Kennedy picked up her bottle.

"Are we doing business, Mr Bradley?"

Jeff smiled, then picked up his bottle and tapped it against Kennedy's. "I guess we are."

Kennedy took a notebook from her pocket, wrote on a page, then tore it out and pushed it across to Jeff.

"Come to this address. The taxi driver will know where to bring you. Three o'clock tomorrow afternoon. Don't be late."

CHAPTER TWENTY FOUR

After one hour of flying in the Cessna 172, Jeff had not seen any tell-tale signs of cleared jungle and regrowth. He checked his map. Each time they had flown over an area, he circled it. Circles now covered most of his marked-out search area. Kennedy banked to fly over the last section. The wing dipped and Jeff was looking almost straight down. He saw a dust cloud trailing a military jeep speeding along a dirt road. As he focussed his binoculars on the vehicle, Kennedy banked away. He tapped her on the shoulder and pointed.

"Over there."

Kennedy turned the plane so she could see from her window. They watched the jeep disappear deep into the jungle. Two miles ahead the road reappeared. They waited, but the jeep did not re-appear. They circled high above, but kept a distance; Kennedy was careful not to enter the no-fly zone. Then the jeep reappeared from where it had entered, followed by two trucks. Jeff marked the spot on his map.

"I want to take a closer look."

"Not today," Kennedy said. "It's back to the airport. Tomorrow we can use a chopper."

"Okay," Jeff said, disappointed, but he had little choice. Kennedy was the pilot, and she was going back to base.

It had been a long day. Jeff was hungry. Kennedy said she was too. She took him to a different bar; one off Roxas Street. The night markets were opening. The bar served food and there were no bargirls. Jeff ordered two beers and a menu. He laid his map on the table and focussed on the spot where he had seen the military vehicles.

"I can't remember the last time I went to dinner with a man and lost out to a map," Kennedy said.

"I hadn't realised we were on a date."

"Don't kid yourself. But polite conversation during dinner isn't a big ask."

Jeff folded his map and swigged a mouthful of beer. He hadn't taken the CIA agent for the type to engage in small talk. Agents didn't gab away unless they were fishing for information. If she was looking for secrets from him she was wasting her time. He had none.

"Where did you learn to fly?" Jeff asked.

"My father gave me my first lessons and then I joined the Marines."

Jeff raised an eyebrow. "Interesting life."

"I grew up in a small town in a place I like to call Nowheresville, Kentucky. Near to where General George Patton lived. Yes, as you can guess by my name, Patton, we're related. Although, the connection was never clear. I had lots of Patton cousins, but none of us could show a direct family link to the great General. But to my brother and father, the name was enough. We were Pattons, and from the time I could walk, my future would always be military."

"And the first name, Kennedy?"

"After President Kennedy."

Jeff looked surprised. "He was a Democrat, wasn't he?"

"Yes, but he stared down the Russians. Good enough for my family. They declared him an honorary Republican. As a name, it was okay. My parents had many name choices. Kennedy is better than most; it might have been George."

Jeff smiled. "And your dad, he was in the Air Force?"

"He was a crop duster, and he taught me to fly. Working for my dad is how I paid my way through college. He always thought that once I had a degree I'd come home and help grow the family business. My brothers weren't interested."

"And why didn't you?"

"I love my dad. He's a good man. But crop dusting is not for me. And I might add, it's not called crop dusting anymore. Nowadays we call it aerial application. Anyway, it wasn't the future I saw for myself, and the Marines pay more."

Jeff said, "And why the Marines? Why not the Air Force?"

"Kentucky is a long way from the ocean. I was eighteen before I walked on a sandy beach. I liked the feel of it. From that day on, a life near the sea was it for me. I ended up on a carrier, flying planes."

"And what about marriage and a family?"

Kennedy said, "No man would ever give me the same thrills I got from landing a fighter jet, at night, on an aircraft carrier that was rocking and rolling on the high seas."

"I guess that would be a hard act to follow. Bad luck for men."

Kennedy added, "And any man I ever gave the time of day, wanted to put me in a dress and take me home to meet his mother. What about you, Jeff? What's your story?"

"I joined the Army after university. Made it into the New Zealand SAS. Got married and then divorced. My wife didn't like me being away from home all the time, or living in military camps. She wanted to go back to her hometown and be near her family and I didn't want to leave the Army. That's my story so far. Dull, don't you think?"

"Is that it?" Kennedy complained. "I give you my life story and you throw me a few crumbs."

Jeff leaned on the table. "You gave me a story that's easy to check. Nothing confidential. I'd say if I googled you, I'd find you have your own Wikipedia page. The pretence of sharing your life story to get me talking didn't work. I was in Intelligence, remember? I know how the game is played."

Kennedy smiled. She turned and waved to a waiter to bring more drinks.

The face of a man sitting with two others a few tables away caught Jeff's attention. The face looked familiar, but he couldn't place it. As he continued his conversation with Kennedy, he continued to search his memory. The steak arrived. As he cut his meat, his eyes flicked back and forth, between the man and Kennedy. She was making small talk as they ate. Finally, she picked up on his lack of attention.

"Am I boring you?"

Jeff shook his head. "Not at all. There's a man at the table to your left; I thought I recognised him. Unlikely, I know. I've never been to the Philippines."

Jeff turned his attention back to his meal. The dice of meat on the end of his fork was midway to his mouth when he remembered. The man at the table was the man he'd seen tailing Felipe in Sandakan City. Felipe had said it was him who had hired the pirates. This man worked for the men holding Felipe's family. Jeff laid his knife and fork side by side on the plate; a sign he had finished eating. He sensed Kennedy's eyes narrow. She turned her head toward the table occupying Jeff's attention. The three men rose from their seats. One dropped paper currency on the table. They walked towards the door.

Jeff half turned to Kennedy. "I'm sorry, but I can't stay to finish dinner. It's time for me to go home."

"What?"

"I'll see you at the airfield tomorrow."

He caught the flabbergasted look on Kennedy's face and the scowl. He would make it up to her. He followed the men out of the bar.

CHAPTER TWENTY FIVE

Jeff didn't need to keep a great distance behind the men he tailed. They had not looked back. They weren't expecting anyone to follow them. It was night, and Roxas Street buzzed with activity; tourists and locals enjoying the night markets. Despite the throngs of meandering pedestrians, Jeff kept his targets in sight. The three men chatted as they walked. Slaps on the back followed bursts of laughter; the camaraderie of friends. He needed to isolate the man from Sandakan. Then he would wring his neck until he coughed up the information he needed. He must be patient. Eventually the group would split.

As the three made their way between the many market stalls dotting the pavement, Jeff considered his options. If they didn't split, he'd have a problem. Fighting three men at once didn't swing the odds in his favour. He could phone Felipe and ask for help, but if the man from Sandakan saw them together, the kidnappers would know Felipe had lied to them. They might kill Sofia as punishment.

The street vendors offered a wide array of merchandise, from clothes to DVDs, but the friends showed no interest. Clothing gave way to food stalls. The smells coming from the barbecue eateries, spicy titbits on skewers slowly basting on hot grills reminded Jeff he hadn't finished eating his meal and he was still hungry. The trio stopped next to an ice cream cart before crossing the street. A few more side streets and they entered a nightclub. A bouncer gave Jeff the once over, decided he wasn't a threat and turned away to give his practised sour glare to the next patron.

Inside there were girls. Not bar girls, Filipina girlfriends out for a night of dancing. It was a live band and the music was loud. The female performer sang in a language he took to be Filipino. Strobe lights flashed across the dance floor, creating the illusion the dancers were moving in slow motion.

The men sat at a table and waved to a waitress.

Jeff kept walking until he was in the corridor that led to the toilets. At the far end was an emergency door, the kind that only opens from the inside. A quick look over his shoulder; no patrons were headed his way. The door opened onto a small yard and beyond it an alley. From the direction of the alley Jeff assessed it led back onto the main street. The yard would do for interrogation purposes. If the man from Sabah continued to drink as much as he had been, he'd need to take a leak, and Jeff would have him.

He made his way back to the bar. Two Filipina girls in their twenties approached him. Both offered themselves up as dance partners. Jeff shook his head and pointed to his ring finger, which was minus a ring, but indicating he was married.

"We like married men," the one nearest him said.

"Sorry, girls, I'm not interested."

Disappointed, the two women moved towards an expat further along the bar. Lucky man. Jeff cradled his beer but had not drunk any. Another ten minutes passed before the man from Sandakan City stood and made his way to the corridor. This was it. Jeff moved away from the bar and followed. He waited outside the toilet door and counted to twenty before stepping inside. The man from Sandakan was standing at the urinal. Jeff walked past him and entered the first cubicle. He waited until he heard water rushing. Then he stepped out. The man from Sandakan was head down rinsing his hands. Jeff moved. He struck him below the kidney. His man groaned and dropped to his knees. Jeff grabbed a handful of hair and pulled the man's head back. He looked up at Jeff. Eyes blinked.

"What do you want?"

"You and I are going outside, I have a few questions."

Jeff pulled the man to his feet and punched him in his windpipe; just enough to leave him gagging. Unable to catch his breath, he offered no resistance as Jeff dragged him into the corridor. He slammed his prisoner against the exit door, crashing onto the handle. It flung open.

Jeff was about to step out onto the three-step stair and into the yard. A loud voice caught his attention. From the tone and pitch of the words, Jeff had little doubt it was directed at him. He half turned. It was one of the friends. He ran at Jeff. Jeff smashed his fist into the side of his prisoner's head. It sent him reeling backwards down the stairs. Then Jeff spun to face the new threat.

Too late.

The friend dived onto his back and they both tumbled down the stairs onto the dirt. Jeff managed to get to his feet but the friend stayed behind him with an arm around his neck. Jeff twisted and turned but could not free himself. He reached around with his right hand and took hold of his attacker's thumb and wrenched it backwards. The attacker screamed and the hold loosened but not enough for Jeff to break free.

The man from Sandakan was sitting up. He shook his head to clear the grogginess. Jeff was still struggling to get the friend off his back. If these two got the better of him and forced him to the ground, they'd kick him to death. He concentrated on balance and getting the man off his back. He yanked on the thumb again and heard a distinct crack. A cry of pain followed. The friend released his hold and fell away.

Freed, Jeff stood tall, moving forward onto his toes as his boxing training kicked in.

The friend gave Jeff a murderous glare. "Now you will die, you piece of shit." The threat lacked venom. The friend's thumb was broken and he was in pain.

Jeff flicked out his right fist and caught the friend on the nose. Another to the nose and an uppercut to the jaw followed. The friend was dropping. Jeff finished him off with a right cross onto his falling head.

He spun around ready to confront the man from Sandakan. He had gone.

Jeff ran into the alley and followed the lanes all the way back to Roxas Street. The street was still busy. He scanned the crowd but knew that finding the man from Sandakan amongst the thousands of people in the markets would be hopeless. He gave up and made his way back down the alley. The friend was now his only lead. When he made it to the yard the friend had gone.

"What is so urgent that you had to interrupt my dinner?" General Hono demanded.

His intelligence officer, Colonel Wang replied, "Believe me, General, I wouldn't phone if it wasn't important. It's about the man I told you about from New Zealand; the man who has the girl, Arina Marcos."

"What about him?"

"He is here."

"What do you mean, he is here? In the Philippines?"

"In Davao City. He saw the man I sent to Sabah last night out walking with a friend. Another of my soldiers. He chased them. There was a fight. My men were lucky to get away."

"Interesting. Does this mean the policeman was not telling the truth when he said he does not know where this man is? How can he be in Davao City without help?"

"This I will find out. If the policeman lied to us he knows the consequences," Wang said.

"What I would like to know is, how did this man defeat two of your men?" Hono asked

"I made enquiries after our attempt to kidnap the girl failed. His name is Jeff Bradley. What her uncle did not tell me, when I discussed Bradley bringing the girl back, is he was a soldier. No more. He is now retired. But he was with the New Zealand SAS, a Special Forces unit. This would account for the way he handles himself."

"And you don't think the policeman is helping him?"

"No. I do not think so. He was with the pirates when they attacked the boat with Bradley and the girl aboard. My man in Sabah verified this. I do not think the policeman is lying. He has too much to lose. And remember he does not know who we are. To him we are voices on the phone. He will think we are watching his every move and he will not risk losing his family. "

"Then why is Bradley here?"

"The policeman told me this man Bradley is a man of honour. He will want to stop us from killing the girl's family. But now he does not trust the policeman. If I was in his shoes I'd try to find the men responsible. He probably thinks if he does, he can stop us. Foolish man. It means he has to come out in the open and ask questions. When he does we will find him."

"You will sit and wait?"

"No. I have men checking all the hotels. My contacts in the police stations are looking and I have men all over the city. We will find him."

"And what about the policeman?"

"The cop said he believes Bradley will make contact. He has the girl, and he is on his own, and he will need help."

"How can you be certain the policeman is not playing games? How do you know he is not helping the man from New Zealand? Maybe he helped him get onto Mindanao, and now he is hiding him."

"If he is betraying us, I will find out."

"Good," the General said. "And the two men who fought with this Bradley, if he sees them again, they might not be so lucky next time. Make sure that doesn't happen."

CHAPTER TWENTY SIX

Jeff had breakfast with Arina and then set off to meet with Felipe. The girl had stared at his eye knowing something was not quite right. Jeff cheerfully carried on talking about life on the farm when he was young. It had distracted her from the scars he bore as a result of last night's fight. He left before she started asking awkward questions.

Jeff walked a half-mile and then stayed hidden in the undergrowth, beneath the palm trees, until Felipe's car pulled over. He slowed enough for Jeff to run out, open the front passenger door, and climb in. Before the door had shut Felipe depressed the accelerator and his car sped away.

Jeff said, "You're fifteen minutes later than you said you would be. You had me worried."

"I was being cautious. A car behind me stayed there far too long. It made all the same turns I did. I did not know if it was following me or not. It took time to shake them."

"Or maybe they were just driving down the same stretch of road."

"Yes, that's possible. Our station received instructions to search for you. You now have your own wanted poster.

And they will distribute them around the streets. Something has triggered this. I will try to find out what, later."

"What are they accusing me of?"

"They do not specify, only that you are a person of interest."

"Who issued the order?"

"It is from someone in the military. A number to phone, that's it."

"And where the hell did they get photos of me?" Jeff asked.

"On the internet probably. You have not lived a quiet life, Jeff. If I can Google you, so can the men who are after Arina."

Jeff sighed. "I guess so."

Felipe said, "What I don't understand is how they found out you are on Mindanao and here in Davao City?"

"I chased a guy last night; the man you met in Sabah. I spoke with him," Jeff said. He turned in his seat to gauge Felipe's reaction.

"Good God, Jeff, look at your face. You've got a bruised eye. Did you kill him?"

Jeff shook his head. "No. He escaped."

Felipe slapped the top of the steering wheel.

"He will tell his bosses he has seen you. What if they decide I am helping you? This could be bad for me." He gripped the steering wheel tighter. His knuckles whitened.

"Relax, Felipe."

"How can I relax?"

"Pull over."

Felipe did as instructed. It worried Jeff that Felipe was slipping back into panic mode. In Sandakan a desperate Felipe tried to have him killed. Jeff could not afford to have him losing the plot again.

As the car came to a stop, Jeff turned to face him.

"Felipe, you need to stay calm. Nothing has changed. If they ask, you still do not know where I am, and you still believe I will make contact. The plan stays the same."

"What if they decide I'm lying, or test my honesty by harming my family?"

Jeff shook his head. "They won't target your family. Not yet. But they will keep putting the pressure on. They'll stress the hell out of you. You need to refocus your energy into finding these men. It is still our only option. I'm going in the air again today to search for the compound. I think I know where it might be."

Felipe's eyebrows lifted. His demeanour brightened. "This is good news. When will you know for sure?"

"I'm hoping to identify the spot later today. Then I need to take a walk in the jungle and confirm it. But while I do that, try to find the man I chased from the bar last night. He is another lead. Get me in front of him, and I will get the information we need."

"You have changed since the days we spent together at university. Then, you were against beating people up."

"I'm older now. I've learned there are very bad people living in our world. I have a simple philosophy these days. If somebody wants to kill my friends then I'm going to kill them back. Now, are you going to help me find the man from Sandakan City?"

"I only met him for the first time in Sabah. He is not from Diego's group. I know he is from the Davao region, but that's all. He will have gone back to his village, I would think. Or maybe, because you found him, the men he works for have got rid of him; cleaning up loose ends like they did with Diego on the plane."

Jeff said, "At least with the military issuing orders to look for me, we have a definite military connection."

"And if they are distributing posters of you, it is a sure sign they're running scared."

Jeff shook his head. "It might be too big a jump to say they are running scared. I think it's more likely they are flexing their muscles, and it seems they have a lot of muscle, Felipe."

"With so many hunting you, maybe you might think it best to leave Davao City?" Felipe said. "Maybe even leave the Philippines?"

"I'm not going anywhere. Now drop me near a taxi. I have a plane to catch, and I don't want to be late."

CHAPTER TWENTY SEVEN

Aircraft used by aid organisations were located at the eastern end of the Davao City airfield. Moveable modular homes had been trucked in to use as administration offices. Jeff now sat in a converted bedroom. The furnishings comprised of a filing cabinet, two desks, office chairs and a small meeting table. A whiteboard hung on the wall behind the desk. Lines of writing in blue marker ink on the whiteboard provided a list of names. Alongside the names were dates and times: a duty roster.

From where he sat, looking through the open window, Jeff could see a helicopter. He leaned forward in his chair, hands on knees, ready to move. He checked his watch, then glanced out the window again; a not-too-subtle attempt to indicate to Kennedy that he was anxious to leave. Kennedy didn't move. She sat back in her chair, hands clasped behind her head, and remained impassive, showing no interest in his impatience to take to the air. He had expected a hostile reception after running out on her, and here it was. He had no defence.

With help from Mama Soo, he had patched himself up as best he could. The cut on his lip was noticeable, as was the bruising around his eye. Arina had stood in the doorway, watching. She wiped her eyes at one stage, and

Jeff could not tell if it was tears or tiredness. When Mama Soo had finished, Arina had returned to her bedroom.

Kennedy said, "Last night you ran off and left me to pay for the bar tab and both meals. Not the best way to impress a girl. Didn't your mother teach you any manners?"

Jeff spread his hands in an apologetic gesture and shrugged.

"The man I pointed out to you last night, I remembered where I had seen him. He was the one who sent the pirates after me off the coast of Sabah."

"And you thought you might exact a little revenge."

Jeff answered with a tilt of the head and a lopsided grin. Kennedy waited.

"It was a thought. But no, I did not have revenge on my mind. Maybe later, but right now I have Arina's family to rescue. He was a lead, that's all."

"So you played the lone wolf and came off second best. He escaped and no doubt has already told his boss, which means they know you're here on Mindanao. They'll have men on every street corner hunting you. Your job just got harder and that means my job just got harder. Why didn't you invite me along as backup? Or didn't that option occur to you?"

"I'm used to working alone."

"Bullshit. In the SAS you were trained to work as a team. So what was it? Because I'm a woman?"

Jeff squirmed, and decided not to comment. Instead he said, "You haven't said what this mission of yours is. We might be better off joining forces. "

"If that time ever comes, I'll let you know."

"At any rate, I'm not certain my job did get harder," Jeff said.

Kennedy leaned forward, placing her arms on the desk. "Explain."

"You just said it yourself. If men are searching for me, they will be asking questions. I'll ask Felipe to send out trusted colleagues to nab one of them. Then we use some of the persuasive techniques I've been taught and extract the information we need."

"That might be wishful thinking." Her green eyes darkened. "These people have come across as slick. No mistakes as yet. They might not be that easy to find."

"Arina was a mistake. So, are you going to take me flying or not?"

"The chopper is outside, fuelled and ready to fly."

"The Robinson."

Kennedy looked surprised. "You know helicopters?"

"They've had safety issues in New Zealand. It looks old and small."

"It's twenty years young and it's got two seats. Don't worry, soldier boy. I won't crash it."

###

After ten minutes in the air and now closer to the ground, Jeff could see the level of devastation caused by the typhoon. Whole villages had been flattened. Sheets of corrugated iron were strewn across open areas and lying atop trees. Sunlight flashed off metal and blinded Kennedy for an instant as the chopper banked. Jeff saw two aid trucks, laden with supplies, travelling along the road that Kennedy now followed. He pointed them out.

"Food and medical supplies," Kennedy said. "And volunteers from around the world, armed with a hammer and a pocket full of nails. They will build makeshift huts, install water pumps, generators, and distribute food, the usual disaster relief projects."

Jeff had seen disaster recovery in third world countries before. Volunteers struggled against corruption and red tape, and governments preferred cash rather than foreign interference. He hoped that wasn't being repeated in the Philippines.

"Must have been really strong winds to cause this much damage," Jeff said.

"Typhoons are a powerful force. These villages are close to the major cities. No difficulties getting supplies to them. It's worse in the more isolated areas and islands. One pilot told me he saw corpses hanging from trees. No one was prepared. They rarely get such storms on Mindanao."

Kennedy swung away to the north. Jeff pointed to the west. She shook her head. "I told you, it's a no-fly zone."

Jeff frowned.

"Okay, I'll be straight with you. I also used Arina's directions and I've flown in and out of this area several times. I found nothing. The only reason I agreed to fly you is because going back over the same trail sometimes works."

"We need to take a look, Kennedy. Those military vehicles yesterday came out from under that jungle canopy. The only explanation I can come up with is a camp."

Kennedy nodded and then turned the chopper towards where, the day before, they had seen the vehicles. After another few minutes Jeff pointed. "Look, a river, and it's flowing from the direction of Mount Apo and through that section of jungle. Arina said she followed a river when she escaped."

Kennedy nodded an acknowledgement.

Jeff made a note on his map. A back road ran parallel with the road on which he had seen the jeep. He decided the back road would be his way in. Once he was back on the ground he would make a list of the required kit. He would be likely to find what he needed from the markets. Jeff tapped Kennedy on the shoulder. He pointed down.

"We need to go lower."

Again she shook her head and banked away from the no-fly zone. In the distance Jeff saw a glint of light, then a fighter jet swooped overhead. It waggled its wings and then sped skywards before levelling off.

"That plane is a Bronco, ex-USA. In reality it's an observation aircraft," Kennedy said. "I've flown one. They were retired out of the navy, but they do have armaments and they aren't so old they couldn't shoot this chopper out of the sky. They want us to get the hell out of here."

"That's how I read it too," Jeff laughed. "It confirms they're hiding something. I guess you'd better do what he says or we'll be hanging upside down in one of those trees."

CHAPTER TWENTY EIGHT

A knock on the door stopped Jeff mid-stride. It couldn't be Felipe; he had just spoken with him on his mobile. Jeff gingerly stepped across to the window and looked through the slats. The angle only allowed him to see the cuff of a pair of trousers and the khaki-coloured canvas shoes beneath them. They belonged to a woman. He pulled open the door.

"How did you find me?"

"I told you once before," Kennedy smiled, "I work for an efficient information-gathering organisation."

"I don't remember the Yanks I worked with from your agency being that slick in the past. How did you really find me?"

"I followed your cab, careless Jeff."

Jeff thinned his lips and scratched the back of his head. "Yes, it was careless."

"Are you going to invite me in?"

His quick glance over his shoulder would, he knew, to Kennedy's trained eye, look as if he was hiding something. But he hadn't had time to clean up, and wasn't about to let her in. Instead, he stepped onto the veranda and pulled the door closed. She stood legs astride. Arms crossed.

"What are you up to, Jeff?"

"I was about to take a siesta. I'm tired. Jet lag is catching up with me."

"If you'd been on a plane I might believe you. Cut the crap and don't treat me like one of the bimbos you date."

She attempted to walk past him. Jeff stepped in front of her.

"Anyone ever told you, a man's house is his castle?"

She held out her arm and Jeff allowed her to push him aside. Kennedy threw open the door and entered. She stopped just inside the room and looked around. An array of equipment covered the floor; a knapsack and a sheet of plastic, a torch and general camping items. She raised her eyes. A young girl and an older woman sat together on a settee watching her.

"Your family?"

"You've met Arina." Arina lifted her hand and gave a small wave. "And next to her, Mama Soo, my Nanny-cum-housekeeper and anything else I need her to be."

Mama Soo smiled.

Kennedy returned the smile, then turned back to Jeff. "Is this old lady all the protection Arina has when you go out?"

"Two cops are sleeping outside somewhere. I wake them when I leave."

"Holy crap, Jeff. I just walked in without so much as a howdy-do from anyone."

"I must remember to boot their backsides. You should have been shot before you got close to the house."

Kennedy turned her attention to the floor. "And what's this? Going on holiday?"

"Well, you know, I miss my times in the jungle. I thought I'd spend a night or two on the side of Mount Apo. I like camping." He smiled. "I need to spend some time alone."

"Yeah, right. Funnily enough, I feel the same way. A night under the stars would do me a world of good. Lots of fresh air…"

"You have no equipment and you need boots. You can't go traipsing through jungle in those shoes."

"I have boots in the trunk of the car. Even a small backpack."

Jeff rubbed his hands together, searching for a reason he could use to deter Kennedy. He struggled to find one.

"I was scared as hell the first few nights I spent in a jungle. Have you ever heard of snakes, leeches, spiders the size of a human fist, and other creepy-crawlies?"

"I'm a woman, Jeff. Every bar I go into I get covered with creepy-crawlies. I have a job to do and hanging out with you has just become part of it," Kennedy said.

"And you still won't tell me what your mission is?"

"I told you, I can't do that." Kennedy glanced toward Arina and Mama Soo. "Should they be here, listening to this conversation?"

"It's their home."

"I'm coming with you."

"As a marine pilot, you've completed basic training and you've had a refresher in the CIA. This will not have given you the skills to go after these people on your own, in a jungle and at night. And it takes careful walking techniques otherwise they'll hear you coming a mile away. Stay here. When I get back I'll share whatever I find."

"I have my orders."

Jeff shook his head. "Then tell me your mission. If we're about to go into combat together we need to trust each other."

"It's classified. All I'll give you is that something might have been going on in the compound that has attracted the interest of the US Government. I need to take a look. If I don't find what I'm looking for, it's all yours and I'll be on my way. But the bottom line is, I need to see first-hand."

"If soldiers are protecting the area there might be shooting. Can I rely on you to have my back?"

Kennedy stepped up to Jeff. Her face inches from his. "Classified documents will tell you, as a CIA agent I've walked the streets of some of the shittiest third world countries. Cities filled with hostiles nursing a hatred for Americans and trying to add my scalp to their belt. No one ever succeeded. If the going gets tough, I can defend myself, and I can even rub two sticks together and make a fire."

"Well then," Jeff said. "You're definitely on the team, because I sure as hell can't. But we leave now and we go with the equipment I've got here. I don't have time for you to go to the hotel and pick up personal items. Time's against us and we need to get to a campsite before dark."

"Fine," Kennedy glared, "but I have a stipulation of my own."

Jeff smirked. "You want to know if you'll need pyjamas. Not in the bush."

"Very funny. I want to clear up a point. We might be spending a little quality time together, but don't get any ideas. Lay one hand on me and I'll shoot your balls off."

Jeff shook his head and burst out laughing. Mama Soo slapped her thigh and cackled; Arina looked confused.

CHAPTER TWENTY NINE

Jeff drove as close to the search area as he could without entering the military no-go zone. He spotted an opening in the trees, slowed, then drove into the jungle as far as the damp ground and dense undergrowth would allow. Tall trees snaking overhead provided enough cover to ensure the vehicle would not be seen from above. He switched off the engine, but left the key in the ignition. Felipe had said to dump it. It was an unclaimed stolen vehicle and could not be traced back to anyone.

He turned to Kennedy. "Let's do this."

His pack made a heavy thud when he dumped it on the bonnet. He had brought extra bottles of water to cover for Kennedy's presence. She had a smaller pack and insisted she had enough water, but walking through jungle in hot climates was thirsty work. Drinking from the river was not an option.

Jeff opened the map. Kennedy stood beside him.

"My best guess is we are here." He stabbed at a spot with his finger. "By my reckoning, it will take two to three hours to reach the river. Then we follow it to this point. Another two hours and it will be dusk. This looks like high ground so we'll spend the night at this spot." He moved his finger across. "Tomorrow, an hour or so after dawn, we move forward, no earlier. The world's military train their troops to 'stand to' an hour before dawn, which is the most likely time of an enemy attack. I see no reason to believe these guys will be any different. They'll be alert for another hour and then they'll have coffee and relax. That's when we walk about and see what we can find."

"If it's a military base, do we go in?"

"I'll decide after we reconnoitre."

Kennedy's lips tightened, but she said nothing. Jeff suppressed a grin. Kennedy did not like being under his command. Fair enough, he wouldn't like taking orders from her either.

"It's not much of a strategy, is it? I thought you guys plotted everything, right down to the length that your toenails need to be trimmed."

Jeff grinned. "Our Special Forces move in small teams. We are not normally assault units. Most times we just observe. The only forward planning we do is the kit we carry, the landing zone and pick up point. The intel we initially work on when we start an op might have changed. In fact, it usually has; so decisions are made as circumstances allow. We react to the environment or enemy movement, as we are going to do now. There may or may not be a military base hidden amongst those trees. If we do find one, we need to assess how many men and how penetrable is the camp. Once we know this, we can make a decision about what to do next. Got it?"

"Got it. And then what?"

"If the decision is go, we return to our camp, wait until dark and then we go in. Have a look round. Then we get out and follow the river to the main road. It will only take one or two hours."

"Why did we not come in this way?"

"Because all around here at the bottom are houses and people," he said dabbing his forefinger again at a spot on the map. "If we were seen driving in, or if the car is found, someone might call the authorities. The army might decide someone is trespassing and send a search party." He ran his finger across a mark on the map. "This was the best way to get to the destination without a hassle."

"Okay."

Jeff looked at Kennedy. "Ready?"

"Lead the way. I'm right behind you."

Jeff took the first step. In the past, when on military ops, he worked with professionals he could rely on. Kennedy was a mixed bag. How would she react if shooting started? Would he have to look out for her? Be responsible for her? However, he did admit that he was starting to enjoy her company.

The light was fading. A full moon was expected. Jeff knew that for the first couple of hours before the moon rose, all around them was about to turn black.

"We camp here."

Kennedy dropped her pack and sat on it. She pulled out a water bottle and chugged two mouthfuls.

"Be careful with your water. All you've got is what you've carried, and you can't have any of mine."

A flicker of amusement crossed her face.

"Where do you intend pitching the tent?" she asked.

"No tent. I left it behind. It didn't look like rain, so there wasn't any point lugging it along."

"Ground sheets it is then. I have slept in the open before."

"I'm sure you have, being a country girl. But as I have already said, it's not the same as sleeping in the jungle."

"I'll survive."

Jeff indicated the jungle with a tilt of his head. "All around us, creatures you couldn't envisage in your worst nightmares are waking from a day's rest. And, they are attracted to body heat." Jeff smiled as he remembered the same comments given to him by the old hands when he spent his first night in the jungle. He slept with a machete in his hand. It was all garbage but he wasn't going to tell Kennedy that. The tall stories were part of the baptism of jungle training. He threw her a small plastic bottle. "That's mosquito repellent. Cover any exposed skin."

"I need to pee."

Jeff pointed back the way they had come in. "Go back there. And while you're at it rub some repellent on your butt. You might want to go again later. I'll put on dinner. He held up two cans. Beans or beans?"

Kennedy didn't answer. She walked back down the trail. Jeff smiled at her careful steps. "Look out for snakes."

She slowed, then walked on.

They ate the beans from the cans in silence. Jeff wiped off the utensils and buried the rubbish. In his military days they would have taken the rubbish with them, but he had no intention of returning and he doubted there would be any soldiers patrolling the jungle. It wasn't a war zone. So it wouldn't matter if a wild animal dug it up.

Jeff sat on his groundsheet and drank from his water bottle.

"Do you mind if I ask you something, Jeff?"

"Go ahead."

"Why are you doing this? I know Felipe and his sister are friends of yours, but that was a long time ago. Surely that can't be the only reason."

"No, that's all it is. I'm helping a friend. Nothing more."

"I don't believe that. What else?"

Jeff took another swallow from his water bottle, then screwed the cap on. He scratched at his chin.

"Tell me," Kennedy persisted. "It's dark, we're in the jungle, no witnesses. You can let your man thing slide for a time and reveal the real Jeff Bradley. I won't tell. Promise."

"My man thing?"

"I want to know."

"Well okay. It's nothing complex. No great insights. I have this overwhelming sense of responsibility for other people. Even when I was a big lug of a kid I was always looking out for the younger kids. So when Arina came my way with men wanting to hurt her, I was compelled to protect her. That's it, as I told you, simple, nothing complex."

"You chose the wrong profession. Maybe you should have been a doctor?"

"If I was a doctor I couldn't help Arina, could I?" Jeff said.

"Arina is fond of you, Jeff. I could see it in the way she looks at you."

Jeff said, "I've noticed and I'm growing fond of her, and it worries me. She has high expectations. I'm dreading I'll let her down. If I do, she loses her family."

"That's an unfair burden to load yourself with, but you know what, I don't believe you will let her down."

"Okay, time to sleep," Jeff said.

Earlier, Jeff had put Kennedy's ground sheet next to his. She had pulled it back a metre.

It had been a long time since Jeff had listened to the sounds of the jungle at night. Leaves rustled, as animals stalked and their prey scampered for safety. Atop trees, monkeys hooted and shrieked. Toads croaked and any insect that could make a sound joined in the cacophony. He was half asleep when he heard Kennedy move her plastic sheeting closer.

"I hate snakes," she whispered.

He dozed off, a half-smile across his face.

Jeff woke Kennedy at dawn. He tossed her two muesli bars.

"There's enough nourishment in those to keep you going for a few hours. We can eat something more substantial once we know the lie of the land and we know where the camp is. It might prove to be only metres away and any cooking smells might bring unwelcome guests."

Kennedy ripped open the packaging. She sipped water as she chewed. Jeff noted she was using her water sparingly. After they had packed their gear away, he produced a tube of two-tone camouflage cream. He applied the brown and green colours to his bare skin before passing it to Kennedy. He watched as she applied it. She had used it before.

They moved in single file in the general direction that he'd assessed the base might be. With each step, he placed the side of his foot to the ground first and let it roll to the centre. The soft walking style lessened the sound and the risk of breaking branches. He'd shown Kennedy how to do it and she was walking the same way. This wasn't war. There would be no listening posts, but his training had kicked in. At any rate, there was still a need for care. As they neared the camp, a soldier taking a morning stroll might hear them. Kennedy allowed a ten-pace gap to develop. She had been on patrol before.

Jeff called a halt when he heard voices and music. He listened for a few seconds and assessed the camp was still some distance; they walked on. The sounds told Jeff that security must be lax. The camp might be hidden, but the guardians weren't concerned about intruders. Why would they be? It was military land and everyone in the region knew not to enter. And the local rebel groups had no interest in getting into a gun fight with the military.

Jeff was only metres away when sunlight glinted on metal and he saw the wire. He dropped to one knee and held up his right hand; a stop signal. After pulling away a rotting mossy log, he dropped onto his stomach in the cleared space and crawled forward. When he reached the wire, the dense green undergrowth blocked his view. He moved along the fence line, over a blanket of dead leaves and fern fronds. He glanced over his shoulder. Kennedy's head was almost touching his boot. Another ten metres and he was looking into the camp.

Kennedy crawled up beside him; they were now shoulder to shoulder. He breathed in the subtle hint of the perfume she had applied the day before. He gave her a sideways glance before refocussing on the compound. Jeff estimated the camp was close to one hundred and fifty metres in length and one hundred metres wide. There were three buildings. The nearest was less than fifty metres from where they lay; a building Jeff took to be a storage warehouse. In front of it was a barracks and further down, a gatehouse. A sealed road ran from the gate to the warehouse, and the area in front of the barracks was also sealed. The trees had been cleared, but the surrounding area was covered by undergrowth, only inches high, but enough to give it the look of a natural forest clearing. Dotted across the tops of the buildings and over the sealed surface were poles, and across the tops of the poles, camouflage netting. Jeff pointed to the netting.

"Now we know why we couldn't see it from the air," Jeff said, his voice low.

"They've gone to a lot of trouble to hide something," Kennedy whispered back. "And this doesn't seem to be the camp Arina described. But I have a feeling her camp was once close by."

A truck drove in through the gate and stopped next to the warehouse entrance. A roller door was pushed high enough to allow men to walk through. Soldiers entered and returned carrying crates. Each was as long as a man and heavy, needing four men, one on each corner, to carry it. A soldier climbed onto the step-board at the rear of the truck, and pulled back the canvas covering the opening to the truck's box body. He rolled up the canvas and used dangling strips to tie it in place. Another soldier climbed onto the step-board beside him and they pulled the first crate inside. After loading another five crates, the ties were undone and the canvas dropped.

The warehouse roller door fell back to the ground. The truck started up and drove away. A guard locked the gate behind it, then all the soldiers disappeared into the barracks.

"Interesting," Jeff whispered to Kennedy. "They look like soldiers, and they act like soldiers, but they have no unit insignias anywhere on their uniforms."

"A rogue outfit?" Kennedy asked.

Jeff shrugged. "I don't know. In combat operations no one wears insignias and never a badge of rank, but this is a camp. I'd like to get a look inside the warehouse."

"Or, we could listen in on a conversation. Where is your listening equipment?"

"My what?"

"Spy gear. How do you expect to carry out effective surveillance if you don't have the right gear?"

"I'm a civilian," Jeff said. "You're the spy. Why didn't you bring something?"

"I'm undercover. I can't get caught with anything incriminating. The aid group I work for gained approval from the Philippines government to allow me to fly the chopper on special request from the US Government. I can't compromise them."

"And yet here you are, with me. But what does it matter? They'd be speaking Filipino."

Kennedy nodded.

"How do you propose we get in to take a look at the warehouse? We can't climb a three-metre-high fence. Not without being seen. We can't drive in. I don't suppose you thought to bring wire cutters did you?"

Jeff shook his head. "But I have an idea."

CHAPTER THIRTY

Jeff left Kennedy at the fence and retreated a few metres. He found an identifiable spot and stashed the packs at the base of a tree, then found old palm fronds to cover them. He hung three lighter-coloured bushes on the tree's branches. They looked like giant dots. If they had to run, it would be best without the packs. He would find them again easily enough.

He returned and lay back down beside Kennedy. She held a finger to her lips, a hush signal. She pointed. Two soldiers were walking the fence line and were about to come within metres of their hiding place. Jeff heard Kennedy's sharp intake of breath. He reached out and held her arm, his forefinger stroking the cotton sleeve of her shirt. She didn't pull away, but he felt her muscles tighten. He suddenly realised what he had done and relaxed his hold. He dreaded the time when they'd be alone; a tongue lashing was on its way for his patronising manner. No matter how long he lived he would never get it right. His instinct was to protect women. How the hell was he ever going to get over that?

The two soldiers ambled past, too engrossed in their conversation to take notice of the surroundings. In Jeff's view, the two men were out for exercise, not surveillance.

It was now time to make a decision. Without weapons, they were at a disadvantage. Twice he had demanded a firearm from Felipe and twice the policeman had said no. This time Felipe reasoned they could claim they were lost hikers if they were discovered. The soldiers would grumble, but they would accept a couple of foreign tourists losing their way as long as they had no weapons. Jeff now admonished himself for not insisting. If they were injured tonight because they couldn't defend themselves, he'd be pissed off.

The soldiers had continued to follow the fence line and disappeared behind the warehouse. Jeff pulled the foliage back. He took out his machete and dug it into the ground. It was soft. He stabbed at it then scooped it back with his hand.

"Is this your grand scheme?" Kennedy whispered. "Dig a tunnel?"

"Why not? The soil is soft; this is agricultural country. I grew up on a farm. I know how to dig holes. Keep an eye out and let me know if the soldiers come back. I'm exposed digging this close to the fence."

After fifteen minutes he was a foot deep and, as he suspected, the wire did not continue below ground level. He kept digging until he was half a metre down, a metre wide and back two metres.

"Okay that will do it."

Kennedy studied Jeff's handiwork.

"Not bad," she said.

He covered the hole with fern fronds.

"Now we wait until dark. Come on. Let's go make a coffee and rest up. We'll come back just before sundown."

###

At dusk they were back in position. Jeff dug out the rest of the hole.

"Ready?" he whispered.

"Ready."

"I don't see soldiers wandering about, and from the loud music and voices coming from the barracks, I'd say they've called it quits for the night. The gates are closed and there's no light on in the guardhouse. These guys are tuned out. Let's not do anything to switch them on."

"What's the plan?" Kennedy asked.

"I didn't see infrared motion sensors next to any of the floodlights, so I don't think we need to worry we might trigger an alarm. As long as we aren't seen, we'll be fine. If not, worst-case scenario, the lights come on, and we'll be dead before we get back to this hole. But for now the residual light from the barracks is enough. We could wait for the moon to be high, but I like it a little dark." Jeff paused. "What do you think?"

"You're asking for my opinion?"

"I'm being polite."

"Just get on with it."

"We run across the open to the far end of the warehouse wall, furthest from the barracks. From there anyone looking out a window won't see us. We go in through the window at the end."

"Won't it be heard if we smash a window?"

"Not if we use this."

Jeff held up a glass cutter.

"You thought to bring a glass cutter, but not wire cutters."

"I couldn't find any at the markets. Okay, let's get going. Ladies first."

Kennedy crawled through the hole and crouched on the other side until Jeff joined her. Keeping low, the two sprinted across the ankle-high undergrowth to the warehouse wall. When they reached it, Kennedy bent over, hands on knees to catch her breath.

"Give me a moment. I'm a little unfit," she panted.

"Okay, while you catch your breath I'm going to take a quick look through the barracks window to see what we're up against."

"That's risky. What if you're seen?"

"I won't be."

Jeff ran around the rear of the warehouse and sprinted down the side until he was close to the barracks. The first window was in shadow. He ran to it and raised his head above the sill. Six men sat at a table, playing cards. Another sat on a lounge chair reading a newspaper. He moved across to the next window. He stiffened.

"Bloody hell," Jeff muttered.

A woman sat in a chair next to a bed. She was holding the hand of a man spread out across a bare mattress on the floor. Jeff could see enough of her face to recognise her; it was Sofia, Felipe's sister. A woman was asleep on a mattress on the floor. Jeff figured it was Sarah. Sofia blocked the man on the bed from his view, but he assumed it was Carlo. Jeff's eyes turned cold. Muscles tightened. His hands closed to fists. If he was armed he would crash through the door. He held his breath and backed away. He'd seen enough. There was nothing more he could do tonight, but at least he now knew where they were. He ran back to Kennedy.

"What did you find?" she asked.

"Felipe's family. They are here!"

"Anything we can do to rescue them?"

"Not a chance. Not against armed men. I counted seven and there could be more. Let's have a look inside this warehouse, then we go get reinforcements."

Jeff licked the rubber sucker on his glass cutter and pushed it onto the window. When it held there he worked the cutter in a circular arc until the circle was complete. A gentle tap and the segment came away. He placed the glass on the ground, careful not to drop it. He pushed his arm through the hole, found the lock and released the catch. The window swung open.

"You're handier than I gave you credit for," Kennedy whispered.

Jeff climbed in and then he turned to help Kennedy.

"It's black in here," he said. "Wait for our eyes to adjust." He pulled two slimline torches from his pocket. "These are set to low beam. The light won't travel far and they aren't bright, but still try to aim them down and not at the windows."

"Gee, thanks for the tip, Jeff. A dumb broad like me would never have thought of that."

Jeff ignored the jibe—fair though it was—and led the way down an aisle of crates. "These crates are the same as those we saw being loaded this morning. I'm guessing they must contain some type of armament. By the size, I'd say rockets or launchers."

As he moved forward, he tripped. Kennedy grabbed his arm, just stopping him from falling to the wooden floor.

"Steady," she said, holding him until he found his feet.

"There's something on the floor."

Two torches shone down.

Kennedy exclaimed, "A trapdoor."

Jeff knelt down and pulled at the handle. It didn't budge. A padlock held the latch in place.

"I don't have bolt cutters. We won't be getting in there tonight. Come on, let's have a look inside one of those crates."

Jeff made his way down the aisle until he found a crate stacked on top of another, its top at waist level. He tried to pull the lid off with his fingers. It didn't budge.

"You go to the rear and I'll go down here. See if we can find anything we could use as a tool to lever this lid."

Jeff walked to the front of the warehouse. On the way, he side-tracked to the window and peered into the dimly-lit compound. There was no sign of roaming guards.

"Jeff!"

He returned to Kennedy's side.

She held up a claw hammer. He couldn't see her face but he sensed she was smiling. He reached out to take it, but she held on to it and walked past him. "I can probably do this. You might not believe it, but I know women back in the States who have driver's licenses, and their own cars. Clever of them, don't you think?"

Jeff held his tongue. He stepped back as Kennedy put the claw through a gap in the wooden lid and pushed down. As the board rose, nails screeched and the sound echoed throughout the building. She stopped.

"Don't worry, no one would have heard it," Jeff said.

Kennedy pushed the two-pronged hammer claw back under the wooden cover and worked her way along the front until the nailed timber came free. Grabbing the raised timber in both hands, she pushed it up then twisted it to the left until the remaining nails gave way and it pulled free. Jeff helped to put it on the floor. Kennedy retrieved the torch from her pocket. Jeff watched as she shone it into the crate.

"What do you think these are?" Kennedy asked.

"Exactly what you think they are. What the bloody hell is going on here?"

CHAPTER THIRTY ONE

"Coffins?" Kennedy said.

"That's what they look like," Jeff said. He tapped his glass cutter on a coffin lid – it was metal. He ran his torch around the side of the coffin. "Look at that; welded shut. Sealed tight. Why the hell would they do that?"

Kennedy ran a finger along the welded seam. "To make them airtight is my guess. Ever smelt a dead body left in the heat for a few days?"

"Too many." He stared into the crate.

"Could these be Arina's camp mates?" Kennedy asked.

"No doubt in my mind."

They had already ruled out this camp as being the one where the soldiers had held Arina and her family. But finding the coffins meant Jeff was leaning towards Kennedy's assessment that the other camp had been nearby. The dead had been moved and the camp erased. It would be logical for the soldiers to stay in the vicinity until the jungle had completely concealed it.

He replaced the crate lid and pushed the nails back into their original holes. He covered the nail heads with the bottom of his t-shirt to muffle the sound and tapped them down with the hammer.

"I'd like to look under the trap door," Kennedy said. "Maybe we could pry the hinges open with the hammer?"

"Worth a try."

Jeff followed Kennedy down the aisle to where they had seen the trapdoor. She knelt beside the hinges and pushed the hammer's claws into the space where the padlock held the hinge in place. She pushed down on the handle. A deep groan echoed throughout the warehouse, as screws ripped from the timber floor.

Kennedy stopped.

"You'd better go stand by the window, Jeff." She paused. "One moment."

Kennedy stood and disappeared into the darkness. When she reappeared she held her hand in the air, between her thumb and forefinger, a key.

"I saw this beside the hammer. Can we be this lucky?" She knelt and inserted the key in the lock. She turned it and the U-shaped shackle sprang open.

Jeff smiled. "Brilliant. With the lock back in place when we leave they'll never know we were here."

"There is still the hole in the window."

"With luck, they might not see it. The men we saw loading the truck came in through the roller door and the guards walking the fence line came nowhere near the window. In less than forty-eight hours it won't matter. I intend to be back tomorrow to rescue Sofia."

The hinges squeaked as Kennedy raised the trapdoor and pulled it back until it lay flat on the floor. They both looked down into the black hole. The stairwell was wide enough for three men to walk down shoulder to shoulder. The slope of the stairs was not steep. Jeff took a moment to think through their next move.

"Going underground would be walking into the perfect prison cell. If someone slams this trapdoor shut, we'll never get out. One of us needs to stand guard."

"Good idea. I'll let you know what I find."

"You know what, Kennedy, I'm not confident you would." He scrubbed a hand through his hair. "Okay, go ahead. I'll play sentry."

Halfway down the stairs Kennedy switched her torch onto full beam. The light rays bounced off the walls until they disappeared. He checked his watch every few minutes. Ten minutes passed before she reappeared. Even in the dim light he could see her grim demeanour.

"Go have a look," Kennedy said.

Jeff made his way down the stairs. Like Kennedy, he switched on his torch to full beam on the third to last stair. At the bottom he stood for a moment flashing the torch about, as he studied the underground complex. White contamination suits hung on hooks along the wall. A corridor ran between glass-panelled rooms. He walked along the corridor, shining his torch into each room. There were four rooms, all similar in size, and to his untrained eye they looked like laboratories.

He opened the first door past the labs. It was a storeroom the size of two school classrooms. It was a quarter filled with drums. Stickers on the sides of the barrels showed skull and crossbones inside the shape of a red diamond; other stickers had "Dangerous Goods" in stencilled white lettering across black strips, but it was the last sticker that caught Jeff's attention. All white, and at the top of the diamond shape was a skull and crossbones; underneath the crossbones was the word, *Toxic*.

Jeff ripped a label off each drum. Forensics might discover the origin of the drums from residue still on the labels. He bundled them together and pushed them into his pocket. Next, he pulled out his phone and took photos. As an afterthought, he went back and took photos of the four labs. When he'd finished, he went further along the corridor. At the end were thick aluminium doors; the type used in industrial freezers or chillers in food factories. He pulled on the handle and slid the door sideways. He stepped in.

It was a chiller.

He flashed his torch across the interior. He pursed his lips and blew into the chill air, as his eyes focused on the contents. His breath fogged like hot air does on a frosty morning. Then his jaw slackened and a series of blinks followed. He rubbed his eyes. Improved vision did not suspend the disbelief that what he was looking at was real. Floor-to-ceiling racking covered the walls. Each section of racking had three shelves. Each shelf held a body. Two of the bodies he recognised. The man from Sandakan City and his friend; a clear message the kidnappers did not tolerate mistakes.

Sadly, he and Kennedy may also have found some of Arina's missing neighbours.

Why store them here? He could only surmise the intention was to move them somewhere else for cremation or burial. It made sense, in a macabre way. A mass grave might be found and lead back to the camp. The ruthlessness of the slaughter and placement of bodies in the chiller made Jeff fearful for Sofia and her family. He had to get them out.

Jeff dropped the trapdoor, slotted the padlock back in place and locked it. He and Kennedy did not discuss what they had seen. There would be time enough once they made it to safety.

"Let's get out of here," Jeff said.

Lights flashed through the window. They froze.

CHAPTER THIRTY TWO

Jeff ran to the window.

"There's a truck at the gate."

Kennedy joined him. "It could be here for more crates. We need to get out of here."

Jeff looked toward the fence line to reassess the position of the escape hole. Crossing the open ground was the only way out. The moon was on the rise.

"The damn moon is not going to help and now, with the camp lights, it's almost as bright as day out there. Out in the open, if they look our way they'll see us for sure. We could creep down the side of this building and hide at the rear and hope to hell no one comes walking our way. If they do, then we have no hope, not against armed men."

Kennedy said, "I agree, we don't have a lot of options. If we stay here, they'll have us corralled. Out in the open it will be like a turkey shoot, and turkeys don't survive turkey shoots."

"Let's get outside first." Jeff said, and clambered through the window. He helped Kennedy down and they lay flat on the ground. "Okay, Kennedy, make a decision. Do we run for the hole and dive under the fence, or crawl to the rear of the building and stay still and hope to hell there's no patrol?"

"You're the boss, hero. You decide."

Jeff assessed the distance from where they were to the gate. He guessed it would be over a hundred metres – far enough for the guards to have difficulty hitting a running figure in bad light. But if they had machine guns they could get lucky.

"Your decision-making is too slow," Kennedy said, and climbed onto her knees. She set herself like a sprinter about to race. "We go for the hole."

She ran. Jeff, taken by surprise, chased after her and stayed on her shoulder. He shone his torch ahead, scanning for the hole. He saw it. In the distance he heard shouting. Puffs of dirt erupted around them. He glanced toward the gate. The men at the guard house were shooting. Soldiers would soon emerge from the barracks, and the barracks building was closer than the guardhouse. But those soldiers would be too late. Jeff made it to the fence first, dived forward and crawled under the wire. When he was through, he turned to help Kennedy.

She lay on the ground. Unmoving.

"Kennedy," he yelled. Still no movement. "Dammit."

Jeff crawled back through the space and grabbed hold of her shirt collar and pulled. Shadows were rushing towards them. Her shirt caught on the wire. He yanked harder and heard a ripping sound, but kept pulling until she was clear. He did not bother to feel for her pulse. She grunted; a sign she was alive. He was on his feet crouched and running; dragging her behind him until the ground sloped away. Now, bullets fired at them went harmlessly over their heads. He found the packs. He pulled Kennedy over his shoulder in a fireman's carry, and with the two packs in his free hand, he moved forward, walking as fast as he could. He had enough light to see. There was no point in wandering all over the place to lay a false trail. Right now, distance was his best friend. There weren't enough guards to mount a patrol to come after them. They would need to secure the compound and guard their prisoners.

After twenty minutes it was time to rest. He dropped the packs and lowered Kennedy to the ground.

Another grunt.

"Sorry," he muttered.

He listened. There were no sounds. No chasers he could detect. Soldiers did not like moving about in a jungle in the dark. It was clumsy and there was no way to detect the enemy. And movement could be heard hundreds of metres away. Night attacks only succeeded when well planned. Running blind through the jungle wasn't a reliable plan.

He needed to check Kennedy's wound. Should he risk using his penlight torch? He decided he had little choice. If she was shot, her wound needed tending. He flicked on the light. Blood trickled across her face from a gash along her hairline. A head wound. He pulled out a bottle of water and a T-shirt from his pack. He poured the water over the T-shirt and used it to wipe away the blood. Then he targeted where he believed the wound was and emptied the bottle. He ran his finger over the developing lump. There was no hole. No tell-tale sign of scalp penetration. He opened a second bottle and poured more water on her face.

A murmur. Jeff leaned forward to hear Kennedy's words. Her eyes blinked open. He was above her, looking into her eyes.

"What is it you're doing?" she whispered.

"Saving your life."

"By lying on top of me?"

"I am not lying on top of you." Jeff leaned back. "I thought you caught a bullet. I was checking for wounds. You haven't got any. There is blood all over your face, and a bruise on your head, which will be the size of a basketball in a few hours. But your hair will cover it and you will live."

Kennedy ran a finger over the side of her head. She winced when she touched the wound. "I tripped. I must have hit my head on a rock."

Jeff kept his thoughts to himself and let Kennedy believe it was a rock. He hadn't seen any when he dug his way under the fence. It was more likely a bullet grazed her skull. She was lucky.

"Are we safe?" Kennedy asked.

"We have distance between us and the base but we need to get to the road and meet up with Felipe. They might send out patrols. But my thinking is, they won't do that until dawn. However, roadblocks could be up within the next few hours."

"Part of my CIA training was evasive manoeuvres."

"Good. Then between the two of us we should be able to outsmart this lot."

"Help me to my feet."

Jeff reached down and pulled her up. She wobbled and Jeff held her shoulders until she was steady. He shone the torch on the wound. "At least the bleeding has stopped."

As part of his SAS training he had spent time in an ER hospital unit. But he had never liked it; too much blood and too many examples of how smashed up a body could become. But he had learnt a lot. Enough to ensure a comrade did not die in the field.

He picked up the packs. "Ready?"

"You came back for me; dragged me through the hole and carried me to safety." Kennedy touched his arm. "Thank you, Jeff." She brushed past him but then turned and paused. "I mean it."

"All in a day's work," Jeff said and gave her a mock salute, then immediately admonished himself for feeling awkward and acting childishly. "We need to get out of here. Keep close and take care. The moonlight will let us see ahead, but not deep holes."

CHAPTER THIRTY THREE

Colonel Wang stood at the window looking down into Hono's yard. The General poured two glasses of whiskey and passed one to his Intelligence Officer.

"And your soldiers have no idea who these people were?"

"No. My men are still searching for them, but they've probably got away by now. In which case, I fear we might have a problem."

"Why a problem? What do you mean?"

"If these people are able to stay hidden from my men, then we are dealing with professionals. I'm confident one of them was the man from New Zealand. It is too much of a coincidence for it not to be him. I don't know the woman."

"Then the girl, Arina Marco, has remembered enough details to guide him here."

"It would appear so. Enough details for him to identify a search area and be lucky enough to find the camp."

Hono raised his eyebrows, his face not hiding his disbelief. "How could this be possible? He went wandering through the bush and came across it? I don't believe this."

"There was an incident a day ago. The Air Force scrambled a jet fighter. A helicopter from an NGO aid group had entered the no-fly-zone. The helicopter left at once and the fighter pilot put it down to the chopper making a mistake and veering off course."

Hono said, "From the air he might have seen something."

"Yes, I agree."

"And do we know who the pilot was?"

"Not yet. But it will not take long. Only ten pilots to check. I have men investigating. They will find out who it was."

Hono finished his whiskey and poured another. "I thought this man's only reason for coming to the Philippines was to bring the girl home to her uncle. We paid the uncle a lot of money to make sure the girl returned. He said the New Zealander would do what he asked."

"I do not know for sure if the policeman paid him off as we ordered him to do. If he had, we would have the girl. I am beginning to think his coming to Mindanao is not about money."

"Why wouldn't he take money?"

"A misguided sense of duty is my guess. Protecting a child. Playing the hero."

"But she is nothing to him," Hono said. "And, he cannot know of our objectives, can he?"

Wang shook his head. "No, it is not possible. The girl was the only one to escape, and she had no knowledge of the operation. We know this from our informant in the New Zealand police department."

"Then what is his objective?"

"It is my assessment he does not trust we will release the girl and her family. I'd say he is thinking, to rescue the family and keep the girl safe, he needs to find us or find the camp and discover a clue that will lead to us. And now he has come close to finding where the camp had been."

"But he hasn't found us and the compound has gone. What's his next move?"

"He will keep looking. To do that, he needs to come out into the open. And when he does, we will find him and the girl."

"For both our sakes I hope you're right. We need the girl, Wang. Time is running out for us. We have a deadline. You know this. The men we are dealing with will not accept delays."

"The girl is close, I'm sure of it."

"And you implied there was another reason driving this man from New Zealand," Hono said.

"Diego killed people in New Zealand. Maybe close friends."

Hono gave Wang a quizzical look. "Revenge?"

"I think it's reasonable to think there might be an element of vengeance involved. At any rate, it doesn't matter what his motive is. He is here in Davao City and my men will find him."

"And are you confident he found nothing at the base?"

"He found a military base. It has soldiers in it. The warehouse is full of crates. Nothing to see."

"Could he have opened one?"

"My men say, no."

Hono eyed Wang. "It is safer to assume he did."

"If you say so, General."

"I do say so, Colonel. Clean up this mess."

CHAPTER THIRTY FOUR

Just before midnight they climbed into Felipe's car. He gave Jeff a slow, disbelieving shake of the head when Jeff informed him he had found Sofia. A beaming grin followed and then a wrinkled brow. Felipe was ecstatic his sister was safe, but now worried about her rescue.

Jeff said, "Drive by Kennedy's hotel. She can get changed and then come back to the house with us. We have plans to make."

"I'll need a half-hour. I want to shower," Kennedy said. "Then a decent meal. No offence to your canned beans and muesli bar menu, Jeff."

"I could eat a juicy hamburger myself right now."

Felipe turned, and slowed as Kennedy's hotel came into view. In the distance, soldiers milled about in front of the hotel's entrance.

"It seems you've been found out, Kennedy," Felipe said. "I don't see any cops. Looks like you two have upset someone in the military; this is not good for either of you."

"How could they know about me?" Kennedy asked.

"Somehow they have connected you to Jeff, but just how, it doesn't really matter now, does it?"

"Take us back to the house, Felipe," Jeff said.

"What about my stuff? My clothes?" Kennedy asked.

Felipe said, "Do not worry. After I drop you off I'll pay a visit to the hotel. The soldiers want you, not your belongings. I will insist I take these and hold them at the station. They will not care. What about Sofia?"

Jeff said, "For the moment she is in no danger. We need to plan her rescue. We go in tomorrow night."

###

Kennedy showered first. Arina and Mama Soo were in bed. Jeff was thankful he didn't have to lie to Arina about finding her parents. Not tonight at any rate. He had considered telling her the truth, but what would have been the point? He would have had to tell her he had left them behind and had not tried to rescue them. But she was sleeping, so it didn't matter.

When Jeff finished washing the grime from his body, he joined Kennedy in the kitchen. She wore a bathrobe. Her wet hair had been roughly dried with a towel and gave her a tomboyish look.

"I hope Felipe gets my clothes, this bathrobe is all I could find to wear."

Jeff was thinking she probably didn't have underwear on underneath it. An image of a naked Kennedy Patton came into his head. A soft aroma from a scent she must have found in the bathroom added to his imaginings.

"How is the bump on your head?"

She ran a finger over the lump. "I'll live."

They'd been in a tight spot tonight, and Kennedy seemed unflustered by the experience. She was a CIA agent and a jet pilot. Flying dangerous missions and living in the shadows had to count for something.

"How do we go about getting into the camp without starting a war with the Philippine Army?" Kennedy asked.

"We'll need men; a small army of our own. Those guards will be doubly alert and they'll bring in reinforcements for sure. But I do not believe they are regular army, unlike the soldiers at the hotel. I'm not certain the real Philippine Army would be kidnapping a cop's wife, murdering innocent civilians and sitting on a chiller filled with bodies. Not the Philippine Army I know, at any rate."

"A private army?"

Jeff shrugged. "I don't know, but it makes more sense if it is. In the Philippines private armies have been about for decades and especially on Mindanao. Most of them are run by ex-military officers; hence the military connection. A few bucks here and there, and heads look the other way, and a few more bucks and a garrison of troops can be sent to an American CIA agent's hotel room. Soldiers follow orders. Only the commander needs to be paid off."

Kennedy said, "And Felipe did say the men at the hotel were army, not private, and he should know."

"Correct."

Kennedy was thoughtful.

"I need to secure the crates and the labs under the trapdoor," Kennedy said. "Now that they've had intruders, it's likely they will think about clearing the house."

"I agree," Jeff said, and drummed his fingers on the table. "In Zamboanga there is a US Special Forces base. Can you not get them to help?"

Kennedy shook her head.

"I wish it were that simple, Jeff. They're here to train the Philippines' forces to combat local rebel groups, and now that ISIS has appeared in this part of the world, they have their hands full. Even if they had a few men to spare, they won't become involved in covert operations against the Philippines' military just on my say so. Besides, what do we have? We found a warehouse and an army base in the jungle and it has a basement with white suits and dead bodies. That pretty much describes the local morgue. The first question will be, so what? We can't go to war because you found dead bodies. Shit, if that were the case, we'd be invading every third world country on the planet."

Jeff said, "I have labels from the drums, and I took photos with my phone camera."

She smiled. "I did the same and I've already sent them to my boss. But it won't be enough evidence to support US military action. The photos could have been taken anywhere, and this type of label can be found on barrels in any chemical factory. Plenty of those in the Philippines."

"What type of evidence do we need to convince your government to pay attention."

"I have instruments in my bags back in the hotel. If you'd given me time, I could have run tests in the underground labs, and right now we'd be having a different discussion. If the boys in Zamboanga were too busy, my boss would call in the Marines that are on the aircraft carrier cruising somewhere in the Pacific or Philippines Sea."

Jeff continued to drum his fingers.

A knock on the door had them instantly alert. Jeff held a finger to his lips and slowly raised himself from his chair. A second knock.

"It's me," Felipe yelled through the door. Jeff let him in. Felipe placed Kennedy's bag on the floor and two pizza cartons on the table.

"You said you were hungry."

Kennedy said, "Felipe, you are a star. Thank you." She pulled open the lid on the top box and removed a slice.

"Did you find out why the soldiers were at the hotel?" Jeff asked.

"Yes. They received a tip-off that the woman staying in the room was a Russian spy."

"What did you say?"

"I said it was ridiculous, and that Kennedy was an American aid worker with a police clearance. You only had to speak with her to know she was American. She is here helping our country. She does not deserve the harassment. Then I asked who gave the orders. No answer. But they insisted they had their orders and would continue their search. Two soldiers were left behind to guard the entrance. The others left."

"And they let you take my bags?"

Felipe shrugged. "The two soldiers were outside guarding the entrance. I packed it all up for you, and two of my men carried the bags to the car. No one tried to stop us."

"That confirms it," Jeff said. "The military unit at the base is a private army. If the regular army were truly after you, your room would be locked down tight and squads of troops would be roaming the streets. And that isn't happening. The local commander was paid off to send out some token soldiers because a private army would not have the authority to enter your hotel room. Do you agree, Felipe?"

Felipe nodded. "You are correct, Jeff." He asked, "What is the plan to rescue Sofia?"

"We need to go tomorrow night," Jeff said. "We need men, Felipe."

"How many?"

"Thirty should do it, but fifty would be best."

Felipe shook his head. "I cannot get fifty men. I would need to call in colleagues from the station. Only a few have fired a gun in the line of duty. But I have other concerns. Even amongst my friends, I don't know who I can trust. It would be impossible to keep it a secret."

Jeff scratched his chin.

"I have an idea. Felipe, go and sign off duty or whatever you have to do and be back here early morning. We need to take a drive."

Jeff watched Kennedy unzip her bag and reach under the top layer of clothing.

"Aha, here it is."

She held up a bright-yellow electronic gadget the size of a handheld telephone. She placed it on the table and helped herself to another slice of pizza.

Jeff's eyes widened as he stared at the instrument. Kennedy munched into her slice of salami and cheese, and watched closely to gauge Jeff's reaction. He knew what the instrument was, and he could see she knew he did. And that Kennedy needed a radiation detection meter scared the hell out of him.

CHAPTER THIRTY FIVE

Omar, the pirate, met them halfway between Davao City and General Santos City. The café wasn't yet open. Omar talked with the owner to keep it closed until they had finished their meeting. Then he asked Jeff for money to cover the café owner's loss of early morning trade. Omar gave half to the owner. The four sat around the table and Jeff explained why he had called the meeting.

"You ask me to put my life and the lives of my men in danger to help a policeman?" Omar laughed. "Mr Jeff, why are you helping this man, anyway? He tried to kill you in Sabah. He tried to kill me and he destroyed my boat."

"Forget about the boat, Omar, you ended up with a better one."

Omar shrugged. "Okay. On this you are correct."

Felipe turned to Jeff. "I told you this was a hopeless idea."

"Omar is a pirate, Felipe, and pirates always want something. That's why they're pirates, right Omar? So why don't you stop fucking us around and tell us what you want."

Omar smiled. "You are a clever man, Mr Jeff. And I have told you many times, I am not a pirate, I am a businessman."

Jeff used the back of his hand to wipe sweat from his forehead, and looked around for a cloth. The ceiling fan was not rotating; the owner had not turned it on. With the windows and doors closed, the interior had become a sauna. The others didn't seem to notice. He reached across to the table beside him and pulled off the cotton table cloth.

"What do you want, Omar?" Jeff asked, as he wiped his face.

"My brother and three of my men are in General Santos city jail." He turned to Felipe. "I want them out."

Felipe threw his hands in the air. "And how am I meant to do that? I am not even from General Santos."

Omar flicked the back of his hand at Felipe. "You want something, I want something. What you want is dangerous for me and what I want is dangerous for you. This makes us even."

"Why are they under arrest?" Felipe asked.

"It is all a big misunderstanding. They were accused of kidnapping a tourist. But this is not true. My brother is a generous man. He was driving the tourist to his hotel, nothing more."

Felipe said, "I know this case. They were arrested collecting the ransom." Omar shrugged. Felipe said to Jeff, "This is a very serious crime. What is their current status?" he asked Omar.

"They are being held on remand, and have not yet been to court."

"This is an advantage, but getting them out will still be difficult. They did not harm the tourist, which is also in their favour. But they face a long term in prison.'

Omar stood. "I am going now. Let me know when you have decided."

Jeff wiped his forehead. The attack on the compound could not take place without Omar and his men.

Felipe and his two officers led the four handcuffed men out to the waiting police van. General Santos policemen held the arm of each man as they stepped up into the back of the wagon. Once the prisoners were inside, the two rear security doors were locked. Felipe's men climbed into the passenger and driver's seat; Felipe in the back seat. He allowed a brief sigh of relief as they drove off. So far, the plan was working.

Felipe had called in a favour. Last year the police had arrested a banker's daughter for shop lifting. The banker had come to him and Felipe had arranged for her release and the charges dropped. And now the time had come for the banker to return the favour. He signed an affidavit swearing Omar's brother and his three friends robbed his bank. Felipe had then had a court order issued to have the men transferred to Davao City to face the charges. As expected, the General Santos City police grumbled, but in the end had little choice but to comply with the court order.

After thirty minutes on the open road, an SUV passed. It caught Felipe's attention and he straightened. He ordered the men in front to be ready. Another four bends and as they rounded the fifth, the black SUV was stopped side-on blocking the road. The police vehicle stopped. Two figures, one on each side of the road, and wearing balaclavas, aimed Kalashnikovs at the occupants. The windscreen was not bulletproof. One gunman stepped forward and waved for the police officers to leave the vehicle. Felipe and his two men climbed out. The gunman grabbed the SUV's keys.

The second gunman waved his Kalashnikov and the three policemen moved to the side of the road. Four surprised men stepped through the now open double-security rear doors. The gunman gestured with the barrel of his weapon for the four handcuffed men to get into the SUV. They hesitated; uncertain. This time the gesture with the Kalashnikov was more forceful, and the men, still handcuffed, ran to the SUV, squeezing awkwardly into the rear seat. The two gunmen climbed into the front seats and the vehicle drove off.

A camera mounted on the front of the police vehicle had recorded the attack. Jeff and Kennedy had made convincing kidnappers. Felipe was in the clear with his superiors. And Omar had his brother.

Even better, Jeff had his army.

They waited until just before dusk.

Felipe led the convoy of trucks back to the river. But this time they stopped on the main road. They were taking the shortcut. Felipe was a cop, and he was prepared to use his authority if anyone got in his way. Omar's men looked capable enough. He had seen them in action; they would do. At least now they outnumbered whatever troops were in the camp. Felipe had a determined demeanour. He assured Jeff he was taking his family home, no matter what the cost.

This pleased Jeff and he believed the words of his often-unreliable partner. And Jeff was happy to let Felipe take the lead until he felt the need to step in. Omar had armed his men with handguns, submachine guns and two shotguns. Felipe had supplied Kennedy and Jeff with Glocks. Kennedy's bosses had refused her the right to carry arms while she worked under the UN banner. Jeff had argued that her bosses weren't on the ground, tonight they were going into battle, and you don't go into a gun fight without a gun.

Earlier, Felipe had driven the same roads Jeff and Kennedy had used on their previous incursion. There were roadblocks, but lightly manned; only two men on each barricade - another reason for Jeff concluding that the hunt for him and Kennedy and the job of protecting the camp was not an official military operation. If it had been, there would have been a squad of at least ten men sharing sentry duties.

Jeff expected to find beefed-up security at the base. How many more men, he couldn't even guess at. Jeff would proceed with an assault until he'd assessed the situation as best he could from the fence line. He would not lead his makeshift army on an impossible invasion. Felipe had said he was not bringing the force of the law to these guys. They had his family and if he had to kill everyone to get them back, then he would.

In the fading light the ad hoc militia troops made good time moving along the river bank. When they reached the point Jeff had marked on his map, they turned away from the rushing waters and deeper into the rain forest. After thirty minutes Jeff saw shimmering light through the foliage. Brighter than last time. As they neared the wire he could see the lights atop the poles. They looked like small moons. He held up his hand for all to stop.

"Felipe, you stay here with Omar and his men. Kennedy and I are moving forward for a look. Don't let anyone follow. If we are seen it's game over. Do you understand?"

"Yes, I understand."

"And Omar, one more thing," Jeff said. "Make sure no one shoots at us when we return."

"Ah my friend, this I cannot guarantee," the pirate grinned. "But do not fear, I will give the order to hold fire."

Jeff crawled the last few metres to the wire. Through a gap in the ferns he could see into the compound. The area from the fence to the buildings was lit up like day. The mission had just become mission impossible. He kept his thoughts to himself. He would make an assessment before he made a final decision but if he saw a heavy machine gun, he would end the raid. His militia did not have a rocket launcher or even grenades. Charging across open ground against a barrel spitting out more than 300 rounds per minute would be suicide.

Jeff tracked his way along the fence line to the farthest point of the camp. Kennedy was right on his heels. He had a good view of the warehouse, the gatehouse and the barracks. He pulled out a small pair of binoculars and scanned the buildings.

Jeff whispered, "Where the hell are the guards?"

He passed the binoculars to Kennedy. After a few moments she passed them back.

"I see no one."

"Hmmm…,"Jeff said. "It could be the changing of the guard. Let's give it a few more minutes."

He turned his wrist and with one hand covered the dial on his Patriot Special Ops watch. He waited until the luminous seconds hand completed two circuits. There was still no movement inside the camp. He scratched his chin, pondering. Then he pulled the wire cutters from his pocket and crawled forward.

"What are you going to do?" Kennedy asked.

Jeff leaned into Kennedy. "I'm going to run to the rear window," he said pointing at the warehouse. I'll go down the side of the building to the barracks. It shouldn't take longer than a minute. You wait here. If I come running, flash your torch in my direction so I know where the hole in the fence is. You have a gun. If you need to, use it."

Jeff cut through the wire. This time he made a gap wide enough for a man to walk through.

"Okay, I'm ready. Cover me."

"Be careful," Kennedy said.

"You don't have to worry about that."

Crouching low, Jeff dashed across the open ground to the rear of the warehouse. Leaning against the wall, he took a moment to bring his breathing under control. He crept along the wall to the window he and Kennedy had climbed through on their last visit. The outside lights aided his sight but not enough to easily scan the entire floor area. He pulled the pen torch from his pocket and poked it through the hole before switching it on. The beam of light lit up the darkness. He flashed it around the interior then switched it off.

The crates had gone.

Jeff ran around the back of the warehouse and then along the side closest to the fence. Kennedy would no longer be able to see him. He made it to the barracks. From where he stood it appeared someone had switched on every light in the building. He made his way to the window where he had seen Sofia and her family. The room was empty. He looked through the other windows. The rooms were all empty. He climbed the three steps and entered the barracks. After a few minutes he had cleared the building.

The soldiers had gone.

He climbed back through the fence.

"What did you find?" Kennedy asked.

"No soldiers and no crates."

"No surprise there," Kennedy said. "We spooked them. They must have found the box with the loose lid and guessed we'd had a peep."

"And, no Sofia and family. We'd better tell Felipe."

"He won't be happy."

"Felipe," Jeff yelled. "You can come forward."

Felipe and Omar appeared. Felipe said, "Why are you yelling?"

Felipe's face froze as Jeff broke the news. His colour drained and he began to sway. Jeff reached out and held the policeman's arm, fearful he was about to collapse. He had expected disappointment but what he saw in Felipe as his shoulders sagged was utter defeat. The mask was gone and Felipe was showing a human side Jeff had not expected to see. But he needed him to snap out of it or he'd be of no use.

"It's a drawback, but not a complete loss. Sofia is still alive. If they had killed her, they'd have left her body."

Then Jeff remembered the trapdoor and the bodies in the refrigeration room. He caught Kennedy's eye. He could see she was thinking the same. "We're going back into the camp to search for clues."

"Felipe, we need to search all the buildings. Kennedy and I will go into the warehouse. You and Omar's men search the barracks."

Felipe slowly nodded. He made no attempt to hide his dejection.

Jeff went back through the fence, Kennedy right behind him. Felipe, Omar and his men followed.

Jeff climbed in through the window of the warehouse and then opened the door for Kennedy. He ran his hand down the door jamb until he found a switch. Fluorescent lights flickered momentarily, and then stayed on. As Jeff's eyes adjusted to the brightness they settled on yellow and black cables that crossed the floor and ran along the walls. It took his befuddled brain precious seconds to comprehend where he had seen them before and why they were significant. The he remembered. His squad had used detonator cables of this type to blow a Taliban arms cache in Afghanistan.

He grasped Kennedy's upper arm as she walked past and dragged her back through the door.

"Run!" he yelled into her face.

He increased pace while still pulling Kennedy, until she ran beside him. He waved to Felipe and Omar.

"Felipe," Jeff yelled. "Explosives. Get everyone out of the buildings!"

Felipe screamed the warnings in Filipino. More shouting came from Omar as he ordered his men from the buildings. Jeff heard a rumbling sound and then the ground rolled under their feet. The interior of the barracks and the warehouse buildings erupted. The force of the explosions lifted the structures into the sky. A tsunami of hot air and debris and dust raced across the open ground towards them. There was nowhere to hide. Jeff flung Kennedy to the ground and covered her with his body.

CHAPTER THIRTY SIX

Jeff's lungs filled with smoke and dust. With his hand at his throat, he gagged, coughed and gasped, fighting for air. Kennedy wriggled beneath him. He rolled off her and then raised himself onto his hands and knees. Another cough. Spittle drooled down his chin. He wiped it away with the back of his hand. After the next cough, he managed to take a deeper breath, and then followed this up with slow intakes until his breathing became more regular.

A pair of boots planted themselves before him, inches from his face. He raised his head, still spluttering. Kennedy held out her hand and pulled him to his feet.

"Turn around," she ordered.

Jeff turned. Kennedy ran her fingers through his hair then down the back of his shirt.

"No blood that I can see. How do you feel? Any aches? Pains?"

"My body feels like it's been inside a washing machine, but I'll survive."

"Good. I was about to thank you for saving my life, but there are no injuries that I can see, so it appears you didn't."

She turned her back on him. Jeff smiled as he brushed away the dust. He was gaining a hell of a lot of respect for this female ex-Marine pilot. She needed to work on her people skills, but overall he felt she had earned his admiration.

He scanned the area.

Bundles of rags scattered across the field moved as Omar's men climbed to their feet. Two of the bundles did not move. Jeff hoped they were unconscious and not dead. Any of Omar's men, who were still inside the buildings when they exploded, would not have survived.

Felipe, his face blackened, made his way across to Jeff and Kennedy. Jeff noted he was standing taller. A defeated amble would have been understandable. He had been so close to rescuing Sofia and now she, her husband and his niece, had vanished again. But Jeff caught his eye and saw a hint of steel in the policeman's demeanour.

Jeff glanced toward the warehouse. The dust was settling but flames and smoke plumed into the air. There would be no trace of anything once the fire had died. Another explosion rumbled underground, and Jeff reckoned it came from the basement, probably filled with accelerants. It would make the perfect crematorium furnace. If Sofia, Carlo and Sarah were dead and their bodies had been below in the chiller with the others they would never be identified. When the flames finally died there'd be nothing but ash.

Omar was dusting off his shirt front.

"Any casualties among your men, Omar?"

"Four missing."

"I'm sorry."

Felipe stood hands on hips. "Do you think Sofia is still alive?"

Jeff shook his head. "I can't say for sure, but they still want Arina, and Sofia is all they have to trade. You need to protect your own wife and children, Felipe. After tonight they might come after them."

"I flew them off Mindanao today. They're in a safe place."

"Good move. Now we can concentrate on rescuing Sofia. Are you ready to start hunting these people, Felipe?"

He kicked at the ground, then eyed Jeff. "You can count on me from here on."

"Then we better get out of here before the authorities arrive."

"I am the authorities," Felipe spat out.

Felipe dropped Jeff and Kennedy back at the house and left. Arina and Mama Soo were watching television. When Arina saw Jeff she came running to him, but stopped a step away, hesitating. A shadow of alarm crossed her face. Jeff glanced at Kennedy who was covered in dust, ash and soot. She looked a fright and so must he. He bent forward and flashed Arina a warm smile.

"No need to worry," he said. "Kennedy and I are a mess, but we aren't hurt or anything like that."

Arina shifted her eyes toward Kennedy.

"We're okay. Honest," Kennedy said.

Arina turned her attention back to Jeff.

"Did you find Mama and Papa and Sarah?"

Jeff shook his head. "I'm sorry, Arina. Not yet. But I will find them, I promise."

Jeff hated telling stories to his young charge, but a ray of hope at that moment seemed appropriate. If it didn't turn out, he would deal with it then. But she didn't light up as he had expected. Arina was learning to live with disappointment. He hated that she had to.

She turned away and walked back to the open arms of Mama Soo.

Jeff poured Kennedy a whiskey and took a cold beer for himself. They sat at the table, not speaking. They had been in the equivalent of battle tonight and had come close to dying. It was normal to want to sit in silence and dwell on the shitty life they were both leading.

They had not discussed in detail the warehouse basement and Kennedy had not explained why she carried a yellow radiation detector. No intelligence reports he had ever read on the Philippines showed anything like a radiological weapons program. The drums of chemicals in the labs were labelled toxic but that was a long way from needing a radiation meter. But she had one, and she'd had it on her tonight. Had the USA lost something, and was Kennedy here to recover it? And were the lost goods radioactive waste?

"Why don't you tell me what's going on?" Jeff said.

"You know the business I'm in. You were in it yourself. We keep our secrets."

"Twice now I've saved your ass. That must count for something."

Kennedy said nothing.

"Well, I have a theory. Your government has been careless. Somehow or other you have lost drums of toxic waste or a load of chemicals, including radioactive waste. They've found their way to the Philippines and into those underground labs. Whatever these guys have been doing with it concerns you, and now, after tonight, the level of concern must have increased because the crates and drums are gone."

Jeff paused. Kennedy stared into her whiskey.

"So far, the resources available to your agency have counted for nothing. I'm the one who found the camp. I'm the one who can help pick up the trail. What have you got to lose? And remember, your government sent me here. So come on, Kennedy. Tell me why you're here, and let me help."

Kennedy tapped the side of her whiskey glass. She raised her eyes.

"Have you ever heard of Salvation Island?"

Jeff scratched at his two-day-old stubble. He needed a shave.

"No, I've never heard the name before. Should I have?"

"Not really. It's an island in the Pacific, somewhere near Tonga."

Kennedy related the events as she knew them.

"Before the invasion of Iraq in 2003, Saddam Hussein shipped chemical weapons to an island in the Pacific, Salvation Island. He made a deal with the local chief, and then sent men to build a concrete bunker for secure storage. Saddam's commanders, those who hid the chemicals, ended up dead. As you know, our military tracked down Saddam and he went to the gallows. When the chief of the island learned that Saddam was dead, he decided to keep the secret to himself and not inform the international criminal agencies. He was fearful they would arrest him, and he'd lose the money Saddam had paid him. Over the years, the jungle concealed the bunker and the chief forgot about it.

"Then one day, soldiers came. They killed many of the locals, and the concrete bunker was emptied. A team of cops from Australia were sent to investigate. The chief told his story, and a report was sent to my colleagues at the CIA headquarters in Langley. One of our agents made a trip to Salvation Island. He showed the chief photographs of Saddam's cohorts. The chief identified one of the men as the one who had contacted him. We now knew what had happened to some of Saddam's weapons of mass destruction, his chemical weapons at any rate. We suspected that along with the drums had been storage containers of radioactive waste. Unfortunately it all went missing before this was verified. And more worrying, it seemed they had fallen into the hands of an unidentified terrorist group. We had no leads, and the trail went dead."

"I thought Saddam's nuclear power stations had been destroyed?" Jeff said.

"They have now but he had built three. The Israelis destroyed the Al Tuwaitha complex in 1981 and the other two were destroyed during Desert Storm in 1991. But Iraq had been generating radioactive waste for decades. They had no disposal facility so it was stored in secure lockup. No one knows how much he had and no one knows how much went missing. This factor went on the top-top-secret list. But we always knew he had hidden an amount somewhere and as you can imagine we needed to find it."

"Was that the real reason for the attack on Saddam?"

"I can't confirm that."

Jeff nodded. Kennedy was giving him a broad outline but was not about to give away state secrets. Fair enough.

"Then Arina came to our attention with her tale of the massacre in the compound and her ailing father. We know from the symptoms she described, it was toxic poisoning. Amongst Arina's clothes, was a small red box, and it contained a locket. When we ran tests, we found traces of mustard gas. It turns out her father's family were jewellers, and he learned the family trade when he was young. He made a locket for Sarah, Arina's sister, while he was working in the underground lab.

"Among the stocks taken from Salvation Island were Sarin gas and mustard gas. The Sarin gas would have long ago passed its use-by date, but mustard gas stays dangerous for a long time. If you fool around with it, your skin will blister, and it will cause severe respiratory and general health problems. Arina's description of her father's illness was close enough to the effects of mustard gas to make us want to find out more.

"We dismissed the Philippines as the source of the mustard gas, as they'd never had a chemical weapons program. We concluded the contaminant had to have been brought into the country. It is my belief the men chasing Arina were the same men who invaded Salvation Island. I just have to prove it."

"And you'd been getting nowhere until I came along," Jeff said. "The US Consul was helpful in arranging for Arina and me to get here; even gave us American passports. Were you, the CIA, behind it?"

"We did what we had to do," Kennedy said.

"So, I was the bloodhound, and Arina the bait."

"When the men attacked you in New Zealand, it was obvious they weren't there to kill Arina. We needed to know why? The decision by the US to use Arina was desperation. And it has proven to be the right decision. We have drawn them out."

"That's a wishful statement, I think. The men and the chemicals have disappeared. We still don't know who these guys are and we don't know where they are."

"We're getting closer."

Jeff sat back in his chair. "The bio suits hanging on the wall might have given it the appearance of a facility for handling toxic waste, but they also use bio safety suits in the manufacture of methamphetamine, which, if you aren't aware, is prevalent in this country."

"Yes, you are right, and it crossed my mind, but if that's all it was then why kill everyone in the camp and chase after Arina. They could have moved the lab and sent everyone home, and paid off any government officials sent to investigate.

"Fair comment. Should we have worn the suits?" Jeff asked.

"I'd given thought to that, but the soldiers were there, walking in and out. I took the view that the contamination levels weren't high enough to be a health threat. And any radioactive material would have been secured in sealed containers anyway. Only Arina's father and one or two others were sick and that appears to be from handling the mustard gas."

"So, I guess your concern is, were they making dirty bombs in the compound?"

"It scares us to death," Kennedy said. "We have any number of enemies wanting to kill Americans, and we are worried that if bombs have been made they will end up in the States."

"But why did they only send you? Why isn't the place crawling with CIA agents?"

"We have agents all over Asia searching. And we are following up on many leads. As you can imagine, there have been many dead ends. Even now I still can't say for certain that Saddam's weapons are here in the Philippines. I need to find them."

Jeff said, "When I was in the underground lab, I went into a small office. There was a piece of paper pinned to the wall and scribbled on it was *Claire Dances. Port of General Santos City*. I took a photo." He scrolled through his phone until he found the photo and turned it to Kennedy. "My guess is the *Claire Dances* is a ship. The crates might have been taken to the port. We need to go take a look."

Kennedy nodded. "Okay, good move. And I think we can now jump to the conclusion that the sealed coffins are holding the radioactive material," she said. "Or, they've already made the bombs and each coffin is a weapon of mass destruction."

"Remind me how dirty bombs work?"

"Easy, pack the radioactive material with explosives and explode it in an open area. It contaminates the immediate vicinity. A big enough bomb could make a city's business centre uninhabitable, for example."

"Okay, got it. If we're quick enough and we find them, you could at least get the Special Forces team to secure the port."

"I need to call my boss."

\#\#\#

Kennedy stepped outside. The night was sticky. She needed a shower, and she needed sleep. But that would have to wait. She needed to find the crates.

"Jaggers."

"Dean, it's Kennedy. There have been some developments."

She related details of the raid on the compound.

"You have been busy. And you say the crates and drums are on their way to the port of General Santos City."

"That's my best guess."

"But you can't say for sure?"

Kennedy took a deep breath. "No, Dean, I can't say for sure. I need a Special Forces unit from Zamboanga to secure the port."

"Right now, those troops are working with the Filipino military fighting off ISIS and any number of the other shit-bag groups hiding out there."

"We need to do this, Dean."

"But you don't know for certain these goods are at the port. It ain't gonna fly, Kennedy. Go find the crates and ring me back."

Jaggers rang off.

CHAPTER THIRTY SEVEN

General Santos City was a three-hour drive from Davao City, and Jeff used the time to catch a few minutes of shut-eye. Felipe had posted two more cops to Arina's protection detail. She would be safe, he was sure of it. He couldn't have brought her with him. Kennedy sat in the passenger seat and chatted with Felipe, who was driving. Jeff drifted off to the soft sound of her voice, enjoying its easy lightness during this brief interlude of peace.

Felipe drove into a pot hole and bounced Jeff awake. A quick look out the window told him they had entered the outskirts of the city. Traffic was building. Motorbikes, three-wheeled taxis and Jeepneys fought for road space with cars and trucks. A giant billboard above a pharmacy was advertising Jollisavers. Jeff had never heard the name, but a huge photo of a hamburger set his mouth salivating.

Felipe said, "The big building on the left is Robinson's shopping mall; very modern, like those you have in America. It is air-conditioned and has a food hall. If you are hungry I can stop."

Jeff said, "We can eat later. Keep going."

Kennedy snapped a quick look over her shoulder, but said nothing. Jeff shrugged. "I promise we will eat."

"I need my food," she responded.

Felipe had used his connections in the General Santos Police department to enquire at which wharf the ship, *'Claire Dances'* would dock. He had the name of a shipping clerk who worked in the Makar Wharf shipping office. Felipe drove through the security gates, his police credentials enough to allow them through without questioning. He drove past the container yards and then pulled over and parked.

"Port Services is in the white building set amongst the trees," Felipe said.

From the rear seat Jeff looked over Kennedy's shoulder to where Felipe was pointing.

"I can come in with you," Felipe said. "My family is safe. I don't care if I am seen with you. I'm a cop and I've had enough of these people. My authority might help inside the port if they give you the run-around. Neither of you speaks Filipino."

Jeff said, "No, Felipe. You stay here. If anything goes wrong and the soldiers arrest you or kill you, we're screwed. In Davao we need the protection your Inspector's rank gives you. Besides, I'm certain the clerk will speak some English. It's the language of trade. And you're all taught it in school here, aren't you?"

"Some schools. Okay, I will stay out of it, but be careful."

"No need to worry on that score. You ready, Kennedy?"

"I'm ready."

###

Jeff found the office he was looking for easily enough. It had a 'Reception' sign in English and Filipino above the door. He and Kennedy entered. A woman in her late twenties stopped typing and smiled a greeting. Her jet-black hair flowed down over the collar of a white blouse onto her shoulders. She sat back in her high-backed office chair and studied her visitors.

"My name is Jeff Bradley."

"I have been expecting you. How can I help?"

"A freighter is about to arrive to collect freight that I am shipping. I want to check that my goods are packed in the correct manner. Don't want any broken chairs. Can you tell where I can find my boxes?"

Jeff smiled. Kennedy rolled her eyes.

"What is the name of the ship?"

"*Claire Dances*."

A shadow crossed the clerk's face. It was only for an instant, but Jeff caught it. She searched through a pile of files covering her desk, then gave up looking and wheeled her chair behind the computer screen, almost half the size of the desk. As she typed, twice she glanced sideways in Jeff's direction.

She looked up from the screen. "The *Claire Dances* is scheduled to arrive within the next forty-eight hours. The cargo is in Shed 2."

"Does it say which port was its last call?"

"It is coming from Tampa Bay, Florida."

As Jeff and Kennedy left the office, Jeff glanced back over his shoulder. The clerk had her eyes fixed on their backs and the telephone to her ear.

###

A hundred metres back from the dock were the entrances to three transit sheds. Above the second entrance and just below the roofline of the faded-yellow building was a sign, *Transit Shed No. 2*.

"This is the one," Jeff said.

"Really," Kennedy said. "What gave it away?"

Jeff smiled but refused to be baited by Kennedy's sarcasm. He'd even it up at a later date. He liked she had a smart ass attitude in a dangerous situation. They'd been through a great deal over the last few days and she was toughing it out. He now felt confident she would have his back.

The entry into *Transit Shed 2* was through a giant, battleship-grey sliding door. It was half open. Jeff stepped inside, Kennedy was right behind him.

"There, in the corner, the crates," Jeff said. "Now that we've found them you can call in the cavalry, right?"

"Why are there no guards?"

Jeff shrugged. "I think the answer is they believe they have covered their tracks and no one knows about the ship and the crates. Remember, by now they will know Arina doesn't know anything. They think I'm only here to help save Felipe's family. And they probably have men on the docks watching if anyone comes to this warehouse."

"If that's the case, we'd better be quick. Can we open a coffin and look inside?" Looking at Jeff, she raised her eyebrows slightly and tilted her head. "I'd hate to bring in the troops and find the coffins only had bodies in them. Or worse, nothing."

Jeff shook his head. "You have to be bloody kidding me."

Kennedy said, "Think about it, Jeff. They cleaned the base out and booby-trapped it. These guys are not dummies. The crates could be a false trail. If they do have dirty bombs, they've already shown they'll do anything to protect them. So, we need to open one up before I can call in the troops."

There was a toolkit on a desk just inside the door. Jeff rummaged through it and produced a long screwdriver. He prised open the lid of the closest crate and tossed it onto the floor. There was no longer any need to cover their tracks.

"Okay, great. We have a metal coffin."

He ran a finger along the seam.

"It's not fused all the way around, just spot welds. But to break in we need welding gear. Secondly, we don't know what's inside. It might not be safe. I don't want my hair falling out, do you?"

"Bald suits me. But I think, if there was fear of contamination everyone would steer clear. The men in the camp were put at risk and none of them looked ill. I'd say the bombs are encased or at least any radioactive material will be. My thinking is, the metal coffins are for transport only; maybe to fool the authorities. Remember they are being sent out of the Philippines. "

"Okay, you could be right. We could steal one and take it with us," Jeff said.

"What! Tote it out of here on our shoulders?"

"I was thinking of finding a small truck. Like the one parked outside." Jeff grinned, and walked to the door.

"A pickup truck; the perfect transport. I have no idea what the Filipino writing says, but the light on top of the cab tells me it's a port vehicle." He ran to it and peered through the window. "Just as I thought, the keys are in the ignition."

Jeff pulled back the warehouse's sliding door until the gap was wide enough to drive the vehicle through. He reversed inside and backed up until the crate was only inches away. After dropping the rear flap, he lifted one end of the crate and dragged it until it was over the edge of the load deck. Then he and Kennedy lifted the bottom end until it was waist-high, and pushed it in. The crate was too long and overhung the bed of the truck. But it was far enough in for it to be stable.

"Let's get out of here and get this sucker opened up," Jeff said. "We passed a number of small vehicle workshops on the way in. Any workshop worth a damn will have a welder, and for a few bucks…" Jeff stopped mid-sentence. "Sirens."

Kennedy rushed to the doorway, Jeff, a stride behind her. "We have company; two trucks of troops and two jeeps. At least that answers my question about why no guards. They have the whole goddamn army protecting the crates."

Jeff ran back to the pickup truck. He revved the engine as Kennedy climbed into the passenger seat.

"Are you ready?" he asked Kennedy.

"Ready for what?"

Jeff pushed the accelerator to the floor. The vehicle surged forward and raced through the opening. One truck swung across to block the corner, but was seconds too late. Jeff sped past it and raced into the open. "I can see a bunch of soldiers blocking the exit road."

"Run them over," Kennedy spat out.

Jeff frowned and gave her a sideways glance.

"Don't give me the look of horror. I'm not spending the rest of my life in a Filipino jail."

"These guys are regular army. The uniforms and insignias are not the same as the men at the compound."

"I'm not in the diplomatic corps. If they get between our vehicle and the exit, that's their choice. Don't you dare stop."

Jeff laughed. "At least they can't block off the whole port. I have another option. We go back past the admin office and down the road along the water's edge. My guess is it circles back onto the main road."

"How can you be so sure?"

"I checked it out on the way in. It looked clear all the way."

Jeff, as a habit, never went into unfamiliar territory without checking the lie of the land, where possible. This time he had been half asleep and had taken no notice. But Jeff didn't want Kennedy second guessing him. He had no idea where the road led, but his gut said, go right. They couldn't go back through the main gate. As they sped past the admin block, he saw Felipe standing beside his car. He did not pay the pickup truck much attention. Jeff gave a honk on the horn. Felipe looked up and then his mouth fell open as they sped past.

"Felipe looks confused," Jeff said.

"I'm sure he is. The two jeeps are following. The trucks won't be far back."

Jeff weaved his way through lines of shipping containers and past a crane, before swinging round the last corner.

Kennedy said, "More guards ahead and a barrier arm blocking the way out. We're trapped."

"Not yet, we aren't. We're in a pickup with bull bars. It's like driving a tank. We can smash through anything."

"I don't like the look of those machine guns, Jeff."

"They aren't raising them. They don't know we're the bad guys. It must be that this is a port vehicle. Our advantage. And they are security, not soldiers." He slowed. "I'll cruise until we're close, then speed up."

Fifty metres from the gate, Jeff pushed the accelerator to the floor.

"Hang on!"

CHAPTER THIRTY EIGHT

The two security guards realised the danger too late. More concerned with self-preservation than stopping the vehicle hurtling toward them, they dived sideways. Jeff smashed the port vehicle through the wooden barrier arm. A loud thud and a splintering sound as the wood bent back and broke away from its mounting. Jeff glanced into his wing mirror. The broken barrier arm had been flung high and now crashed back onto the roadway, narrowly missing a guard getting to his feet. Jeff kept the accelerator to the floor until he reached the main road.

"Which way?" Jeff asked.

"Left."

"How do you know?"

"I've flown over this area twice. To the right is a river and the road to Davao City. They will expect that. Left down any of these roads will get us to the airport."

"And you remember all of this in detail, from one flight?"

She held up her phone. "And my phone GPS agrees."

Jeff smiled. "Smart ass. And then what?"

"Beyond the airport is the road to Zamboanga or we can loop back to Davao City." Kennedy pulled Jeff's map out of her trouser leg pocket. "I'll check for other options.

The map phone does not cover a large enough area." She opened it on her lap and ran her finger across her planned route. She looked up. "Turn right here and drive until you hit the main road, then turn left."

Jeff did as ordered.

Kennedy buried her head in the map. Again, her finger followed a line.

"Yes, if we take the road to Zamboanga, we can go through Koronadal, then right at Tacurong, up to Matalam and down into Davao. A long way around but we'll get there."

"You're the navigator."

"The aid organisations have a section of the General Santos airfield set aside like they have in Davao. If we have no choice, we might get lucky and find an aircraft at the airport we can borrow."

"What type of plane?"

"A light plane or a chopper. Take your pick."

Jeff shook his head. "Neither of them excites me. Both are slow and once we were in the air, if we got in the air, even the slowest air force jet would catch us up. I'd much rather go hide in the jungle."

Kennedy said, "The army is behind us and the rest of the Mindanao military is probably out front somewhere setting up roadblocks. The choice of roads is limited. Look around, there's nowhere to hide. No jungle, only city streets. Outside the city it's open range, as my daddy used to call it. The airport is close, and it's an option if we have no other choice."

"And if we don't find a plane?"

"Be positive. There will be a plane and when we get in the air we will have at least ten minutes before they respond. We can fly fifty kilometres and find somewhere to hide. But, it might not come to that."

Jeff sped along the road as fast as he dared, swerving around vehicles and taking care not to hit pedestrians. He wondered if the soldiers chasing were as cautious.

Kennedy kept looking behind. "Still don't see anyone. Turn right after the Shell gas station."

Jeff pulled into the right lane and turned the corner.

"This road takes us to the airport."

He pushed down on the accelerator. After ten minutes, Kennedy pointed left.

"There's the airport but if we turn right at the intersection, we'll be on the road to Zamboanga." Jeff turned then slowed. Ahead the traffic had stopped.

"A roadblock up ahead it looks like. No wonder we hadn't seen anyone following. They are the army, they have radios and there's shitloads of them. All these roads will have roadblocks and they're coming up behind us. We've just run out of choices."

Jeff turned into the airfield, and Kennedy directed him to the section set aside for NGOs. He smiled when he saw three light planes and two helicopters but they were over five hundred metres away.

"I see two jeeps behind us," said Kennedy. "Still a good distance away. It will be tight, but we should have enough time to get in the air."

"Helicopter or light plane?" Jeff asked. "Which one?"

"I can fly both."

"Decide."

"The helicopter," she said. "Easier to land and hide."

"Looks like we have another problem," Jeff spat out.

At the far end of the runway he could see military vehicles crossing the tarmac and making for the choppers. The noose was tightening.

Kennedy said, "At least we now know where the other half of the army is. The trucks up ahead will get to the choppers and planes before we do."

"That's the NGO squadron ruled out. What now? We can't go back, and the way ahead is shut off. A straight drive across the tarmac into the open space beyond isn't an alternative. We'd be easy to track, and I'd say military choppers are on their way."

"What's the decision, Jeff? You're in charge, remember," Kennedy said.

"Further along is another gate. I saw it on the way in. I can see it now. No soldiers, only cops. Felipe said there's no love lost between the military and the police. He also said the cops won't play hero. Not enough money in it for them. What do you say?"

Kennedy said, "I say go for it."

Jeff spun the wheel and accelerated. The pickup bucked as it sped forward. Kennedy gripped his arm.

"Over there."

Jeff looked to where she was pointing.

"The two fighter jets?"

"They're Broncos. It was a Bronco that chased us away from the no-fly zone. It's a two-seater. Or it used to be. If it only has one seat, you'll be sitting on my lap."

"Apart from the cramped space, the thought appeals," Jeff said.

Kennedy smiled.

"What if there isn't a key?"

"They aren't cars, Jeff."

CHAPTER THIRTY NINE

"I hate to leave the crate," Kennedy said. "It's the only evidence we have."

"Right now, saving our asses comes first. We can't take it with us, so forget about it."

Like Kennedy, Jeff hated to leave the crate. His list of failures was filling a page. He had failed to rescue Sofia, and Arina was now alone and vulnerable. Felipe could not hide her forever, and without Jeff's support, Felipe's new-found resolve would crumble and everyone would die. They hadn't stopped the ship, and it would soon load its cargo. Now they were about to steal a Philippine Air Force fighter jet. If they were caught, the UN would be pissed to hell to learn they'd been lumbered with a CIA agent. It could affect their operations in other third world countries. Some governments might be reluctant to allow aid groups in if they thought they were providing a cover for international spies.

"They've left the ladder in place. I'll climb up and open the cockpit."

"Need help?"

"No. This isn't like a normal fighter jet. The cockpit opens like a bird's wings, not front-up like a car bonnet."

Jeff looked behind. The trucks were still a distance away. They had slowed. All avenues of escapes were now cut off. They must have decided that monitoring from a distance was sensible. No point getting shot up when you have the enemy surrounded. Kennedy had opened the cockpit and climbed into the pilot seat.

Her head appeared.

"Quick. Climb up and get in the backseat."

Jeff obeyed and manoeuvred himself into position.

She passed him a helmet. "Put this on."

Jeff set about pulling the helmet onto his head. Kennedy plugged his radio set in.

"Can you hear me?" she mouthed. Jeff shook his head. She leaned back and fiddled. "What about now?" He gave her a thumbs-up.

Kennedy closed the cockpit canopy, and checked the instruments. Jeff waited. "How do we get to the runway with those trucks blocking the way?"

"No need. They designed the Bronco for short take offs, and it can land in small spaces or on any decent surface. That's why they were on carriers. They can take off without a catapult, and land without using the arresting wires. And that just gave me the answer to the question busting my head; where the hell do we go once we're in the air? There's a US aircraft carrier somewhere in the Philippines Sea, on manoeuvres. The Chinese sent an aircraft carrier, frigates and destroyers into the region, and we sent a carrier, cruisers and destroyers. There's probably a submarine or two from both sides. And support vessels. The carrier is where we go. The Philippine fighters won't follow us there."

"You're the pilot."

Two noisy jet engines roared the twin turbo props into life. The plane moved forward. Jeff had seen only one Bronco before, the one which had warned them off. From the inside it appeared to be an observation aircraft, not a true jet fighter. The cockpit seats were high and the glass canopy allowed good viewing in the front, above and on both sides. Jeff noticed that the military trucks had stopped. Soldiers were leaping to the ground, rifle butts hitting shoulders as their weapons targeted the aircraft.

The Bronco was gathering speed.

An officer waved his arms at the squad, and they climbed back onto one of the trucks. The truck sped toward the runway.

Jeff tapped Kennedy on the shoulder. "I think they're intending to block our take off."

"Too bad for them. Wrong choice," Kennedy said into her mic. "We aren't going anywhere near the tarmac.

The Bronco's engines revved, and the plane gathered momentum as it raced across the open grassed area. The soldiers in the trucks had not expected them not to use the runway and were now too far away. They could only watch as the fighter raced past them and lifted into the air.

Wang put the phone down and turned to his lieutenant.

"Contact the Air Force. Get planes in the air. Tell them spies have stolen one of their jets."

"It will be too late by the time they get in the air. How will they know where to go?"

"That's easy. The pilot is an American. They will fly to the American aircraft carrier. Do not let it land. They have information vital to the security of our country. Shoot them down. The Bronco is slow. The fighters should be able to catch it."

"*Carrier Independence II*, do you read me?" Kennedy said.

"This is a classified frequency, pilot. Please identify yourself."

"I am Lieutenant Kennedy Patton, retired Marine pilot. I am flying a stolen Philippine Airforce, OV-10 Bronco aircraft in your direction. I request a bearing and permission to land. I am a CIA agent. Contact them; they will verify who I am. I have vital information that must get back to Langley."

"Please hold, Lieutenant." After a short pause. "You are cleared to land, Lieutenant."

The air traffic controller gave Kennedy a course heading.

"We have you on radar."

"Three minutes to landing, Jeff. Hang on."

"Hang on to what?"

"And be prepared. When we land, a lot of shit will go down. We stole a fighter and we're implicating the US Government by landing it on the carrier. Hell, they might even decide it's too much hassle and shoot us out of the air."

"Would they do that?"

Kennedy shrugged. She banked the Bronco to the left then straightened. The jet began its descent. From Jeff's perspective, the carrier was racing toward them. He could see men running across the four-hundred-metre-long landing strip.

"You're off course, Major, please execute a go around."

"Roger that."

Kennedy turned the Bronco away from the carrier. Jeff was looking straight up as they continued to fly a wide arc.

"What happened?" Jeff asked.

"I was off course. I'm going around again."

"We have a problem. Company at two o'clock," Jeff said.

Kennedy looked to her right.

"It can only be the Philippines Air Force. So much for them not following us," Jeff said.

Kennedy said, "Independence, we have a problem. A Philippines fighter is closing. Are you able to give assistance?"

"Negative, Lieutenant. We can only fire on a Philippines aircraft in self-defence. The plane you are in is Philippine Air Force. You're on your own, Major. Once you have made it onto the ship, we can help."

A beeping sound.

"Is that a warning signal?" Jeff asked. "Are we running out of fuel?"

"Lucky for us, the Philippine Air Force fitted the Bronco with a missile warning system. And that beep is telling us the jet just locked on."

"What does that mean?"

"We're about to be shot down."

CHAPTER FORTY

"The carrier is just there. I can see it," Jeff yelled. "Don't they have missiles?"

"Yes, but even if the carrier changed its mind and sent a plane to help, they'd never make it. They will not fire missiles at an ally's aircraft."

"What are our options?" Jeff asked, already dreading the answer.

"We need to eject."

"I've heard ejecting from a plane can kill you."

"I won't lie to you. It could fracture your spine, pop your shoulder, or even break your arms. But if that happens, you'll drown anyway, so it won't matter."

"Thanks, and here I was beginning to worry."

"Did I mention the chute might tangle, and you'll hit the water with the same impact as falling off a ten-story building?"

"Have you ever been in command? The pep talks must have been worth attending."

"If we survive and make it to the water, the carrier will send a rescue chopper."

"Great, when we're dead the Navy will come to the rescue. What if these guys shoot at us in the water?" Jeff asked.

"At least it will be quick."

Kennedy steadied the plane.

"This is it, Jeff. Take a deep breath. Tap me on the shoulder when you're ready. Grab the loop between your legs and pull."

"And kiss my ass goodbye?"

Jeff reached forward and patted Kennedy on the shoulder; he then took hold of the ejection loop. A loud bang. The glass canopy disappeared and the rushing wind exploded in his face, turning his cheeks into flapping jowls. Like a giant boulder slung from an ancient catapult, he pitched into the sky. Tumbling through the air disoriented him. He had completed many parachute jumps in the Special Forces but they had been straightforward compared to this. Now, he was upside down and plummeting. The chute deployed, and as air filled the canopy it jerked him as if he'd hit a brick wall. His head snapped back and he grunted. A feeling of nausea swept over him. And then he righted and saw Kennedy's chute a hundred metres away. He looked for the Bronco, but only saw smoke.

Luckily, Kennedy had not waited. The missile had fired and she had reacted. Good girl. He found the guide ropes and steered himself towards her. In a few seconds they would both be in the water. He looked around for hostile jets. He didn't see any, but that didn't mean they weren't there, circling but wary of the Americans and keeping their distance.

A Seahawk helicopter was in the air and racing towards them.

Now, they were about to have real problems. He and Kennedy had sparked an international incident and the evidence to justify their actions was in the back of a pickup truck at General Santos airfield. And now, in a few seconds, he would be floating in the ocean. He felt his shirt pocket. His throwaway phone was gone. Kennedy had already emailed the photos, so the loss of his photos was not a problem. At least they had the name of the ship, *Claire Dances,* and its last port of call. This was a lead.

The chute fell over him as he plunged into the water. He floundered about under the silk until he found the release buckle. Once he had freed himself he dived deep and stayed under until he had swum clear. When he emerged, he spat out a mouthful of salty water. The chopper was above him, its rotor swirling the sea and causing droplets of spray to pound his face. He looked up. A harness was on its way down. When it was within arm's reach Jeff slipped his arms through the loops. As the hoist pulled him from the sea, he saw Kennedy swimming towards the harness dropped from a second Seahawk. He waved. She gave him a thumbs-up.

In the distance he saw the carrier, Independence II. A cold beer would go down well about now. Did they have beer on board American naval ships?

When Jeff saw Kennedy enter the officers' mess, he was sitting at a small table in the far corner. He had been stirring his coffee for a minute or more, thinking of Arina. He needed to get to her as soon as was possible, but that depended on how much trouble he and Kennedy were in. The military didn't like its personnel making their own rules. And they disliked it even more when the out-of-control personnel dragged them into an international incident.

The only others in the mess were two officers deep in conversation. They were too far away for Jeff to hear what they were saying. Kennedy poured herself a coffee then walked across to join him. They had both been given dark blue T-shirts and navy denims to wear until their clothes dried. Jeff said nothing when she sat. She spooned a half-teaspoon of sugar into the brown liquid. As she stirred, she stared into the cup.

"Are you certain we couldn't have landed? I didn't need the swim," Jeff said.

She shook her head. "No, Jeff, we couldn't have outrun the missile. I had little choice. I made the right decision and because of it, you're alive."

He rubbed his right shoulder.

"Get a medic to check it."

"I'll survive. Next time, if there is a next time, we go down with the plane."

Kennedy smiled. "Sure we will. What now?"

"We have the name of the ship, *Claire Dances*. It made a delivery to the States and is due to dock at General Santos Port. We need to know what they delivered to the US. It could have been crates similar to those we found."

Kennedy frowned.Dirty bombs headed for American soil. Let's hope we're wrong."

CHAPTER FORTY ONE

Special Agent in Charge, Nathan Ross, like the rest of his team, wore a blue top over his bulletproof vest. Oversized yellow letters, FBI, were displayed, front and back. Out front and leading the raid were the agency's swat team dressed in dark clothing, dark bulletproof vests, and helmets, with holstered SIG Sauer pistols and MP5 submachine guns at the ready. Like deadly shadows, they moved forward. Ross listened to the communications between the squad on his headset and waited for the team leader to radio that they were in position.

The Tampa Bay Port was the largest in Florida. It had taken hours to find someone to open the files and find out where the *Claire Dances* had moored. The ship had gone four weeks earlier, but its cargo had been off-loaded before being trans-shipped to a bonded warehouse off West Hillsborough Avenue, near the Airport Industrial Park.

Special teams for handling chemical weapons were standing by. Ambulances were queued further along the street, out of sight. Ross had been watching the warehouse for two hours and had seen men come and go. As yet, he had seen no suspicious activities. He had counted twenty men, all engaged in unloading trucks and moving the goods into the storage unit. There could be more men inside and if there were, he hoped not more than ten. He had no idea if they were terrorists or warehouse workers. If they carried weapons, he and his anti-terror squad would be outnumbered.

If the men he was observing were storemen working a shift and not terrorists, they would be processed and then released. If they resisted, his men had orders to shoot. He saw more squad members moving to the rear of the building. Weapons were at the ready and in a few moments they would be seeking out targets. Ross knew the stomachs of the men and women under his command would be churning right now. Two members of his team had fired weapons while on the job. The others hadn't, and his wish was for it to stay that way.

He heard the words, "In place," over his earpiece.

Time to move.

Weapon in hand, Ross moved forward, Rodriguez, his partner, a pace behind. They made it to the first of a line of shrink-wrapped pallets, without being seen. From the new vantage point they could see into the warehouse.

"What do you think?" Ross asked.

They watched as a man walked outside and bent to pick up a carton. As he bent, his waist-length jacket lifted at the back, revealing the butt of a handgun pushed into his belt.

"Did you see that?" Ross asked.

"I saw it; I'll pass it on to the others."

Rodriguez whispered into his mouthpiece.

"This changes everything," Rodriguez said. "Twenty, maybe thirty armed men are too many. We need help. I'm not happy risking my life over a few pallets of freight, no matter what those packages contain."

"Too late, the forklift is about to load that truck. In a few minutes they will finish and leave," Ross said. "My orders were explicit. Nothing leaves the warehouse."

Rodriguez was irritated. "Yes, and the man who gave that order is sitting behind a desk right now. We are looking at a small army, Ross. And they have the advantage. They have cover. We're out in the open."

Ross turned to his partner. "Reinforcements are on their way but we can't afford to wait. Now give the order to move in. But make it clear, I don't want any heroes."

Rodriguez glared, but gave the order. Ross saw movement to his right. He knew that, as much as Rodriguez was pissed off with him right now, he would still have his back. The man on the forklift was thirty metres away. Ross stepped out of cover and held up his badge.

Ten heads turned his way. "FBI. You are under arrest. And, you are surrounded. On the ground."

The men froze. Then, from within the warehouse, machine gun fire smashed into the cartons beside him. Ross dived behind a pallet.

###

Ross stepped over a body and entered the warehouse.

The SWAT team leader came up to him. "No wonder these guys put up a fight. All these cartons are full of crystal meth. Is this what we were looking for?"

Ross shrugged. He watched his agents stacking plastic bags of white crystals into neat stacks on the concrete floor. "I don't know for certain, but I have a feeling, as good as this bust is, we just bombed out."

He turned to Rodriguez.

"You take over here. I'd better phone it in."

CHAPTER FORTY TWO

Jeff nodded to Kennedy when he saw the skipper of the carrier approach. Both he and Kennedy stood. Respect for a superior officer had been drummed into them from the day they'd signed up. Captain James Maxwell, waved them back into their seats and sat opposite Jeff. An orderly approached, and the Captain held up his hand and gave a shake of his head.

"I'm afraid I have bad news. The FBI raided a bonded warehouse in Florida. They found the *Claire Dances'* cargo. There was a shoot-out, which the FBI called all-out war. These guys were fighting to the death to protect the goods. The FBI killed several of them and an agent lost his life."

Jeff's mouth set in a grim line. "I'm so sorry to hear that. Too many people have died already."

Maxwell said, "Unfortunately, I have more bad news."

"They found the cargo?" Jeff asked.

"They sure did. But not crates holding coffins filled with toxic waste. They found drugs, kilo bags of methamphetamine crystals. Loads of the stuff, I'm told."

Jeff looked at Kennedy, then back at Maxwell, and scratched his chin. "The crates were for real, Captain. We both saw them."

"I'm assured by the FBI that all goods offloaded from the ship were in the warehouse. Is it possible that what you thought was a facility for making dirty bombs was in fact for drugs?"

"It's possible they might have manufactured drugs there," Kennedy said. "They destroyed the labs before I could take a reading to test for radioactivity. But drums of toxic waste were there, as were the biohazard suits. You don't need those types of suits to manufacture drugs. Arina's description of her father's illness and other men in the camp is in keeping with the symptoms from contact with certain types of toxic residues, in particular mustard gas. And again, these types of illnesses do not appear when handling methamphetamine crystals."

"There was also the attempted kidnapping of the girl, Arina," added Jeff. "They want her. We don't know why, but it sure as hell isn't about drugs. I'll concede it is not beyond reason these guys are manufacturing and dealing drugs. Why not? They seem to have the power to do whatever they want. When you rule a territory the way these guys appear to be doing, then all types of illegal money-making ventures are possible. But we know what we saw in the basement. We didn't imagine those sealed coffins. If the FBI did not find them, it could mean the ship dumped them elsewhere before or after docking in Florida."

Maxwell replied, "The FBI assessed the value of the drug seizure was many millions of dollars. For that kind of money, they might go to any lengths, including building a camp, bringing in workers, and then silencing everyone involved. Bearing in mind, they shoot drug dealers on sight in the Philippines."

Kennedy said, "I hear you, Captain, but what happened on Salvation Island was real. My gut tells me the chemical weapons and the radioactive waste from the island were in the basement, and something terrible is going down."

Maxwell, hands clasped together, leaned on the table. He looked from Jeff to Kennedy. Jeff could see he wasn't convinced.

"Look, all I'm saying is, when I look at the information you have given me, there are two perspectives. Kennedy, you had no leads to chemical weapons until this girl turned up in New Zealand. Then a series of circumstances led you to believe you had found Hussein's lost weapons of mass destruction. But the cargo from the ship *Claire Dances* was drugs. Did either of you see inside the coffins?"

They both shook their heads.

Jeff said, "I have to go back to Davao City. I have a young girl who needs my protection."

Maxwell looked uncertain. "It will be dangerous. They will be on the lookout. If they find you, you will just disappear."

"Can you drop me close to the shore?"

Maxwell said, "Yes, I can arrange that."

"I need to go tonight."

Maxwell nodded. He walked across to where two of his officers were talking and returned with what looked to be an iPad. He brought up a map of southern Mindanao. He placed it on the table to allow Jeff and Kennedy to see.

"I am sending a Seahawk with needed equipment to our troops in Zamboanga. General Santos is on the flight path. The Philippine Air Force is watching us. They blame us for you two stealing their Bronco. The chopper will be on their radar the entire journey so we can't touch down. We will go inland here and then we can fly low enough to drop you into Sarangani Bay. As you can see it is an inlet from the Celebes Sea. Here is the Pacific. Can you swim to shore, from maybe a mile or two out?"

"I can do that. I will have Felipe meet me."

"Meet us," Kennedy said.

Jeff was about to object, then changed his mind. She had proven herself, and two would have a better chance of surviving. Besides, he might need her to fly them both to safety again. At any rate, he was getting used to having her around.

"And remember," Maxwel said. "You and Kennedy destroyed a million-dollar airplane. You don't only need to worry about some rogue unit anymore. The entire Philippines military is now hunting you."

CHAPTER FORTY THREE

Jeff and Kennedy wore wetsuits. The water was warm and the air hot. They didn't need protection from the elements, but if trouble found them, the wetsuits would keep them afloat. They had packed sets of dry clothes into watertight bags that they would use like boogie boards. When Jeff phoned Felipe from the carrier, the policeman's wary reaction told Jeff that Felipe had assumed he had left the Philippines for good, and had been fretting.

"Felipe, have you found Diego's village yet?"

"Not yet."

"And Arina?"

"She is safe, but we are running out of time. I cannot hold off these killers much longer. If they capture me…" He paused, no doubt wondering how long he'd be able to hold out against their methods of interrogation. "You need to get back here. Are you coming back?"

Jeff detailed the plan for his return. Felipe brightened and agreed to follow Jeff's instructions.

Looking out through the Seahawk pilot's window, Jeff could see the lights of General Santos City. The co-pilot turned in his seat and gave a thumbs-up. The crewman pulled back the door. Jeff pulled on his flippers and, in a sitting position, moved across the floor to the open space until his legs were over the edge. He looked down through the darkness. The light under the chopper lit up the immediate area. The downdraft from the rotors churned the water to froth. Fifty metres further out, there was hardly a ripple. Jeff was thankful they were on the west coast of Mindanao, and not the west coast of New Zealand. New Zealand's western coastline was a mix of violent surf waves, crashing seas and dangerous undercurrents. But, when he thought about it, as dangerous as the New Zealand shoreline might be, it might pale when compared to the danger that awaited him and Kennedy as they made their way back on to the Mindanao mainland.

Kennedy nudged Jeff as she moved next to him. Her legs dangled, and the palms of her hands were flat to the floor as she readied herself to push off. There was no point talking, the din from the helicopter made communication impossible. The crewman tapped Jeff on the arm and gave him a thumbs-up. Jeff touched the top of Kennedy's thigh. She nodded she was ready.

They leapt together.

Jeff could see the signal light ahead. He had arranged to meet on the shoreline southeast of the city, a little way past Bula. It was a long way out of the city but most of the inner coastline was built upon. Lots of shanty towns. It would be difficult for him and Kennedy to come ashore in a wetsuit and not be seen.

Jeff paddled to the right, pushing the buoyant waterproof pack containing dry clothes in front of him. After a few hundred metres he turned towards the shore. Then he slowed.

"What's up, Jeff," Kennedy asked, floating beside him.

"I asked Felipe to use a green light. As you can see, it's blue."

"Blue, may have been the only colour at the markets."

"Not the point. The green colour was the signal that it's safe to come ashore."

Jeff kicked out with his flippers, continuing to swim towards the shore. After fifty metres, his feet touched the sand. Another few paces and the water was only chest-deep. He caught Kennedy by the arm and pulled her past him.

"Thanks, I can touch the bottom now."

Jeff released his hold, reached down, removed his flippers, and held Kennedy as she did the same. They waded forward and as the water became shallower, they stooped until on their knees and crawled through the increasingly shallow water until they reached the sand. Lying flat, Jeff looked up the sloping beach. The moon was high. He scanned the horizon looking for movement.

"See anything?" he whispered to Kennedy.

"Nothing."

"Right, I suggest we crawl up the beach, change into our dry clothes, and keep moving to the right."

"Do you think Felipe has betrayed us?" Kennedy asked.

"I don't think betray is the right word. The wrong-coloured light is a warning. He may have had little choice."

"What do we do now?"

"Get off this beach and find somewhere to hide out. Then find a lift to Davao City."

"The military may have roadblocks and soldiers everywhere."

"No, I don't think so. As far as the military is concerned we have fled and they shot our plane down. No one will expect us to return. If Felipe has men with him, I'm betting it's from the private army. However, I'm sure they'll have more than enough men to look for us."

Kennedy said, "If we can't use Felipe, what do you plan on doing? Steal a car?"

"I have an idea, but we need to get off this beach first."

Jeff heard the clanking sound of the brightly coloured Jeepney's engine long before he saw the vehicle. Jeff knew the history of the Philippines Jeepney began at the end of the Second World War. Locals reconfigured abandoned US Army Jeeps. They extended the backs, added roofs, fitted seats to carry passengers and painted them with vibrant colours. The Jeepneys became the cheapest form of public transport. In recent times they had been modernised. In Jeff's assessment, from the fragile appearance of the transport approaching, it may easily have been one of the first to be modified. It amazed Jeff it hadn't rattled to bits on the bumpy roads.

Omar the pirate beamed when he stepped down from his vehicle.

"Mr Jeff, so soon, you need me again. You have become my best customer. You have troubles?"

"Lots of troubles, Omar."

"The soldiers I have passed along the road. You are hiding from them?"

"Yes. We need to get to Davao City. Can you take us?"

"I know a few alternate routes."

"Good man."

Omar coughed. He held Jeff's eye. "You know, Mr Jeff, a trip like this will take time out of my busy day, and I have a number of families to feed."

He gave Jeff a toothy grin.

Jeff laughed. "You have busy days? Good for you." Jeff reached into his pocket and pulled out a wad of Pesos, the equivalent of two hundred US dollars. "Is this enough?"

Omar plucked the cash from Jeff's hands and counted it.

"Climb aboard," he said, as he stuffed the notes into his pocket. "This is a good vehicle. Very comfortable. You and your lady can relax."

"I am not his lady," Kennedy corrected.

Kennedy climbed in, Jeff following. When he saw the wooden seats, he groaned. The three or four-hour trip to Davao City would be uncomfortable.

CHAPTER FORTY FOUR

Felipe paced.

Arina ate her breakfast and kept her eyes on her uncle. Mama Soo sat beside her and chatted away to gain her attention. But Arina would not be drawn into the conversation. The day after the old woman first came to the house, he noticed Arina become more animated. The village woman had been a good choice. Arina had become friendlier toward him, and he sensed his niece now trusted him - and she could. After all, it was his responsibility to look out for her. Many of his decisions might have been unorthodox, but they were always made with her best interests at heart. But, after Jeff and Kennedy went missing, she had become withdrawn.

And she was not alone in suffering a bout of depression. He had also panicked and feared all was lost. He was at the point of giving Arina over to the men chasing her when Jeff made contact. The longer he spent with his old university comrade, the more convinced he became that Jeff could perform miracles. With him about, there was hope.

But the men who wanted Arina were now applying more pressure. They had paid him a sizable amount of money to bring Arina to Mindanao and their patience was wearing thin. They were angry too that Bradley was causing them so many problems. They made it clear they held Felipe responsible. If he had taken the girl from Bradley in Sabah, they would be finished with her, and Felipe and his family could get on with their lives. Now time had run out. If he did not produce the girl, his sister would die in the next few days. But they stated again that if he handed over Arina, she and her family would not be harmed.

However, Felipe now accepted that once Arina had done for them whatever it was they wanted her to do, she and Sofia and Carlo and Sarah would be killed. Then they would come after him.

Jeff had been right all along.

And Jeff had also been right that the key to rescuing Sofia was finding the men responsible. To date, this had been an impossible task. The men last night in General Santos City had been regular soldiers. They had been given information he was in the city to meet the man and woman who stole the fighter jet. That he was meeting them on the seashore. When Felipe had tried to convince them this was nonsense, he received a phone call from the kidnappers. They had tapped his phone and knew the truth. He was to co-operate with the soldiers and take them to the rendezvous point. It had never occurred to Felipe they had tapped his new phone. How had they even found out about it?

Luckily, Jeff had insisted on the coloured lights, and Felipe was able to warn him. On the phone, Jeff had been careful not to mention which colour Felipe should use, only to match it to the jacket he wore at university. Smart Jeff.

###

Felipe, Arina and Mama Soo were standing on the terrace when Omar the pirate drove his Jeepney up the driveway. The look of relief on Felipe's face was clear to see, almost a smile. Before they had turned off the main road, Jeff had made Omar pull over. He had then checked around the house out to three hundred metres. No one was lying in ambush. The two policemen providing Arina's security were sitting, backs against a tree, in conversation and unaware they were being watched.

"Thank God you are both safe. I was worried," Felipe said.

Jeff watched Omar's Jeepney until it had disappeared then turned to shake Felipe's hand. The grip was firm, almost a grasp.

Arina rushed to Jeff, then slowed. She smiled. "Hi, Jeff."

Jeff bent down and placed a hand on her shoulder. "I have something for you."

He undid the flap on his backpack and pulled out the iPod Omar had sold him. He passed it to her. She clutched it to her chest, and her face spread into an even bigger smile. She gave him a quick hug before rushing back to Mama Soo. Arina's nanny gave Jeff a nod of approval and then ushered Arina inside.

In the kitchen, Jeff pushed the button on the kettle. "I need a coffee. Anyone else want one?"

Kennedy and Felipe shook their heads.

Kennedy went to use the bathroom while Mama Soo and Arina settled on the sofa. Arina had the iPod plugs in her ears and Mama Soo was engrossed in a programme on the television. Jeff needed to talk, and he did not want

Arina to hear the discussion. The iPod had taken care of that. He filled his cup and sat at the table. Felipe turned his butt against the bench-top and folded his arms.

"What happened on the beach, Felipe."

"They'd bugged my new phone and heard our conversation. Sorry, Jeff. I've no idea how they got the number."

"Well, no harm done. I got the warning and we got away. But we need to be cautious from here on in. We're getting closer and they will probably get nastier. You may need to change your manoeuvres when you head out in this direction. You've been lucky getting rid of tails so far, but now they know I am back they will concentrate their efforts."

Felipe nodded.

"How bad is the fallout over Kennedy and I stealing the plane?" Jeff asked.

"The military now believe Kennedy really is a spy. She is now number one on their most-wanted list."

Jeff sipped his coffee. "How bad is it?"

"It isn't as bad as it could be. In a few days the roadblocks will come down. They have ISIS and other rebel groups to deal with. You're an unwelcome distraction."

"Good. Now we can focus on finding Diego's village. The base has gone, the compound has gone, the bombs have gone, the village is our last link. Without it, we have nothing."

Felipe said, "I think it might be easier to concentrate on finding a member of the NPA, the communists. Diego was a long-time member. Other NPA members in the region must know him. They might know his village. If they won't talk, I will accuse them of being drug dealers, and threaten to shoot them. But like all the rebel groups, finding them will be difficult. I need to make a few enquiries. Find someone who can tell me where they meet."

###

Jeff had a shower. He spent longer than usual under the stream of warm water until he felt fully cleansed. He threw on a T-shirt and jeans, and joined Kennedy in the sitting room. She had made herself a gin in a long glass, with ice, a slice of lemon and tonic water, and was sitting in a chair. She held up the glass when she saw him enter.

"Want one?"

Jeff shook his head. "No, thanks. I drink beer."

"Aren't you a vintner?"

"Yes, but I inherited the vineyard from my grandparents and made a promise I would turn it into a successful business."

"And have you?"

"It does okay. The wine business is difficult. I have people managing it."

"It doesn't sound like a money spinner to me."

Jeff shrugged. "My grandparents left me more than enough. It doesn't need to give me an income."

"Lucky you."

"How is your body? Any bruises, bumps or other injuries."

"You're not thinking I'll let you give me a check over, do you? Forget it."

"I have spent time in a hospital ER clinic, remember. I'm a trained medic."

271

"Not trained enough for me."

Jeff grinned. "We've just been on a rollercoaster of emotion, violence and failure together, and we survived it all. You and I have shared more than most married couples. Let me know if you change your mind."

"Well, what can a girl say, when you put it in such romantic terms. To be honest, I do have a stiff neck from being ejected from the plane."

She reached back and rubbed her neck just below the hairline.

Jeff walked across. Her eyes followed him until he moved behind her. She waited, stiff-backed, rigid. Jeff placed his hands on her shoulders and with his two thumbs began to gently massage around her spine. Kennedy did not protest, and after a minute relaxed.

"Hmmmm, it feels good, Jeff," Kennedy said, her voice husky, almost a whisper.

"Let me know when you want me to stop."

As Jeff increased the pressure, her head fell back against his abdomen. He looked down on her hair. So close. He leaned down, the smell of her increasing his desire.

Arina appeared in the doorway.

Jeff pulled his hands back, as if he'd been caught shoplifting. Kennedy sensing the change, opened her eyes. She sat fully upright.

"I want a drink of water," Arina said.

Jeff followed her into the kitchen. He waited until she had filled a glass, then followed along the hallway until she found her room. He rejoined Kennedy in the sitting room but the moment developing between them was over. Disappointed, Jeff sat on the sofa and swallowed a mouthful of beer.

.

He didn't know what time it was when he heard his door open, then close. Kennedy stood beside his bed.

"Say nothing," she whispered.

In the moonlight filtering through the slats, he watched as she let her bathrobe fall away. He moved across the bed to make room and she climbed under the sheet. He found her lips and pulled her body close. They grasped at each other, hungry, devouring, clinging, and when he rolled her onto her back and entered her, a soft moan escaped her lips. She clung to him, her nails digging into his flesh, urging him on. They climaxed together and then lay still.

When he woke hours later, Kennedy had gone.

###

Jeff sat at the table, a coffee in his hand. Kennedy stared into a glass of iced water.

"About last night, do you want to discuss it?" Jeff asked.

She lifted her head.

"I don't do relationships, Jeff. Last night happened. It might happen again. From a male's perspective, I'm the perfect woman; a bout of sex and you don't have to call me again."

"Okay," Jeff said. "No problem. How about I make us breakfast?"

"I enjoyed last night. But it can never go further."

"You don't need to explain. I'm fine with it. Really."

Kennedy turned away from him. Her head bowed.

"As I've already told you, I was a Navy pilot. I had wanted this more than life itself. Not just for me, but to prove to my family I could be the soldier my dad and brothers thought they could become and never did. And as it turned out I was good at it. On a mission over Iraq I was shot down. I managed to eject and land safely but I was captured by ISIS soldiers. For a month I was held prisoner. For a month I was raped daily; sometimes more often. I was a plaything, a delicacy for all to share, passed around like a plate of hors d'oeuvres."

Jeff refrained from comment. He sensed Kennedy needed to unload and his job was to listen.

"Finally, they grew tired of me and the American Embassy was contacted. A prisoner exchange was made. Me, for thirty of their members held in an Iraqi prison. I should have been pleased to be free but I wasn't. All I wanted to do was kill myself. I felt so violated, so ashamed. The doctors told me it was normal I should feel that way. It wasn't my fault and they would help me recover."

She paused to gather her thoughts. Jeff waited.

"My career as a Marine pilot was over. They wouldn't let me fly again. I was offered a desk job but declined it and resigned. I spent a number of months bar hopping, drinking too much and feeling sorry for myself. Each night came the flashbacks that became nightmares and I was too afraid to sleep. I was clinically depressed, I knew that, and the therapy sessions helped to a degree, but no matter how hard I tried, I could not shake my sense of self-loathing. And, I was gripped with an overwhelming sadness. I was never going to lead a normal life, get married, or have children. Those men took away my self-esteem. And if I couldn't respect myself, how could I expect anyone else to. Emotionally, I died in Iraq.

"Then one night in a bar, as I gazed down into my fifth shot of bourbon, I experienced a moment of clarity. If I wanted to take my life back, I needed to avenge myself. I joined the CIA. I take all the dangerous missions. I might not get the men who raped me but I get their followers and others like them. I'm turning myself into their worst nightmare."

Jeff shifted uneasily in his seat. Kennedy half-turned towards him and caught his eye.

"But every now and then I need to be held, to be comforted. Last night was one of those times."

She went silent and turned away again. Jeff wanted to reach out and place a hand on her arm. A voice in his head warned him against it. Right now she was in a secure place and she didn't need him intruding.

He set about cooking breakfast.

CHAPTER FORTY FIVE

Felipe drove the silver Toyota Avensis sedan along the Davao City to General Santos City highway for twenty minutes, and then turned left. Jeff again sat in the back seat and watched Kennedy as she chatted with Felipe. Her earlier dark mood had lifted and her emotions were back under control. She had needed to unload, and he was nobody; the proverbial stranger on a train. Now that she had unloaded, the shield was back in place. Making love to her had strengthened his feelings for her, but he needed to be careful. Just beneath the surface she was fragile. And her state of mind did concern him. Would she take unnecessary risks?

A 'Welcome to Digos City' sign sat atop a pyramid-shaped stand. The road through the city fringe was four lanes. On either side of the road was the usual array of stalls, shops and pedestrians. Under the shade of umbrellas, patrons sat on white plastic chairs outside cafés.

"Up ahead is Digos City," Felipe said. "But we go straight through towards Diwas village. It is on the coast. Somewhere along this road, we turn off. Look out for a black flag on a pole. My friend has placed it there for me."

After another ten minutes, Kennedy pointed out the black flag, and Felipe turned onto a narrow dirt track. The scenery changed to palm trees, banana trees and jungle. Another kilometre and they came upon men, women and children walking in the same direction. Local farmers and their families was Jeff's initial assessment. They wore a variety of singlets, T-shirts, shorts, baseball caps, flip-flops and scarves. A few women wore jeans.

"We have reached our destination," Felipe said, as he pulled over.

The procession made its way through a gap in a fence. Set back from the fence, stood a long house on stilts built from bamboo poles, and with straw walls and a thatched roof. It looked sturdy enough. People milled about outside; others climbed the small log steps and entered. But most passed on by and disappeared behind it.

Felipe said, "Jeff, you and Kennedy need to stay here. I will check if it is safe for you to join the crowd. What is happening here is illegal. They are on the lookout for strangers and cops. I need to find someone I know who will vouch for us."

Jeff gave Kennedy a glance. She shrugged. Neither of them said anything. Felipe was calling the shots.

"Just what is going on here?" Jeff asked Felipe.

"I'll let you know when I come back."

After ten minutes, Felipe returned to the car with a hurried stride; he looked worried.

He climbed into the driver's seat.

"I can't find anyone who will vouch for me. Whatever we do, we'll have to go it alone. I could blend in with the locals, but with you two trailing along that's not possible."

"Are any of these NPA guys here?" Jeff asked.

"My contact informed me they are the organisers. This does not surprise me. This is rebel territory. In the jungle there will be more of them."

"Are they from Diego's village?" Jeff asked.

"I don't know. The NPA are all over Mindanao. All we can do is get one of them alone and force some answers."

Jeff gave Felipe a pat on the back. "Good man. Let's go take a look. How do we recognise them?"

"I told you, we can't go in together."

"Of course we can. Kennedy and I are tourists on our honeymoon. You're giving us a guided tour. Whatever is taking place can't be bad if the parents are bringing their children."

"Have you got money?"

"I've always got money, Felipe, but this trip to the Philippines is draining my bank account. Will these NPA soldiers be easy to identify?"

"They don't look like the scruffy rabble of Omar the pirate's men or the Moro Muslim rebels. The NPA are communists, more disciplined, more organised, but they are dangerous and they look it. Everyone is afraid of them. I will point them out for you."

"Right then."

Jeff turned to Kennedy. He was about to make a smart-ass comment like, 'Are you ready Mrs Bradley? Don't forget to be affectionate. After all, we're on our honeymoon', but he managed to stop himself.

"Let's go."

To his surprise Kennedy looped her arm through his.

"We're a honeymoon couple aren't we, so we'd better play the part."

Jeff smiled. "Yes, we should."

As they rounded the corner of the long hut, Jeff could hear the sound of cheering. He followed Felipe as he nudged his way through the crowd. Kennedy had unlocked arms and now held the back of Jeff's shirt. When they were close enough to view the centre of attention, Felipe stopped, and the threesome stood shoulder to shoulder.

The crowd had gathered around a bamboo and wooden enclosure, and more spectators stood on the embankments. Small children had climbed trees for a better view. Close to the arena, canvas awnings spread between bamboo poles provided shade for spectators. Men wearing red scarves around their necks circled the crowd shouting odds and taking money.

Tethered to a pole in the middle of the enclosure stood a mare; its frightened eyes flashed back and forth, and its nostrils flared, made nervous by the cheering crowd and unaware it was the centre of attention. At opposite ends of the amphitheatre, men held ropes tight, as two stallions, one black, one grey, beat the dirt with their hooves and snorted at each other. Once released, they would cross the distance between them in an instant.

Jeff had grown up on a farm and had been around horses. He knew what happened when a mare was in season in a paddock next to a stallion. The male horse would smash down the fence and trample over anyone or anything in its way. Two stallions chasing the same mare ended one way. The horses would fight to the death.

Jeff had heard of horse fighting, but had never seen it. The expression on Kennedy's face was one of passive indifference, but in her eyes Jeff saw the same anger and disgust that was churning the acids in his own gut. They were both country folk and grew up around animals. Cruelty for fun had no place in modern society. But right now, he could do nothing to stop it.

He turned his attention to the men with the red scarves around their necks taking the bets. Felipe had said the NPA organised the horse fights. They had to be in it for the money and the only money to be made on these fights was gambling. The men wearing the scarves had to be NPA rebels.

From where he stood, he saw no obvious ambush spot. As long as these guys concentrated on taking bets, the crowd protected them. He had to assume the majority of onlookers were NPA supporters. He and Kennedy were already receiving sideways glances. Walking up and grabbing one of these guys was out of the question. The crowd would rip him apart.

A roar from the spectators brought Jeff's attention back to the arena.

The handlers had released the two stallions. The black horse stomped the ground like a bull about to drop its head and gore a matador. They charged each other, reared onto their hindquarters and lashed out with front hooves. When both crashed to the ground, the grey stallion dug its teeth into the black's front leg. The black responded by gripping the grey's mane, which brought hooting and applause. After more writhing and biting, the horses rolled apart and bucked themselves back onto their hooves. Both horses were caked in dust and blood.

Jeff had seen all he needed to see.

"Felipe, I count six men taking money. They're all wearing red scarves. Will they all be NPA?"

"Yes, that's a reasonable assumption."

"I need to get one isolated. How long do these fights last?"

"Depends on how many horses they have. The fights last about twenty minutes. There could be nine fights."

"Bloody hell, we could be here three or four hours. It's time for you to step up and make something happen, Felipe."

"What can I do that you can't do?"

"Use your imagination. You're a cop. Call a raid. Horse fighting is illegal, isn't it? Arrest someone."

Felipe shook his head. "The organisers have strong ties with politicians and wealthy businessmen. They pay the police to look the other way. This is not my district. I can't call a raid, even if I wanted to. But I know the local commander. I'll offer him a payment to come in and do it."

"Good man," Jeff said, and patted him on the shoulder.

Felipe took his phone from his jacket pocket and stepped away.

Hoots and hollers and the crowd were on their feet. The black horse had fallen. The grey snorted and reared then dropped, stomping at the black's head; but the black rolled clear before the grey's hooves struck.

Felipe closed his phone. He caught Jeff's eye and shook his head.

"Dammit," Jeff muttered.

"I'm sorry but the district commander will not help. He has too much to lose and a family to support."

"Then I guess it has to be Plan B," Jeff responded.

"Which is…?" Kennedy asked.

"Something you will appreciate, Kennedy. A stampede, like they used to have in the Wild West."

Kennedy looked to Felipe. He shrugged. She turned back to Jeff. "Are you for real?"

Jeff said, "Beyond the palms on the far side are the horses waiting to fight. There'll be another seven to eight fights, which means at least fourteen to sixteen horses. We release them and frighten them into running at the crowd. Once they get the mare's scent they will go crazy. At least, I hope they will. Even if they don't, stampeding horses will send everyone running. It will be enough of a distraction."

"That's your plan?" Kennedy gave Jeff an incredulous look. "It will never work."

"Of course it will. I can see the horses from here, tied to a fence. Only one man is tending them. We take care of him, untie the horses, and then we 'shoo' them on their way."

"Jeff, you don't 'shoo' a bunch of stallions. They'll most likely find the nearest patch of grass and start munching. I don't see a lot of grass but I'm sure it's there, somewhere."

"Okay, maybe I didn't mean 'shoo', but we get them moving in this direction. Remember, they train these horses to fight and respond to a mare in season. They'll be skittish. Horses have tiny brains. They have tunnel vision. If they think a predator is after them, they'll run until they feel safe, and hopefully, in this instance, straight through the crowd. All we have to do is act like predators. If I'm wrong and they wander off and start eating grass, we call it quits and try something else."

Felipe said, "There won't be a something else, Jeff. You will have played your hand. They will come after you. My advice is, make it work."

Kennedy shrugged. "Okay, crazy man, let's give it a shot."

Jeff said, "Felipe, you stay with the car. Turn it around and stand beside it. When I bring the NPA man, I'll throw him in the boot, and then we'll need to get the hell out of here."

"Jeff, I agree with Kennedy, you are a crazy man."

"It'll work, trust me. Let's do it. Come on, Kennedy."

Jeff watched Kennedy exchange glances with a sceptical Felipe as they walked away. Felipe would go to the car and play his part; what choice did he have? And if Kennedy thought he was crazy, it didn't matter, as long as she helped.

The lone horse minder watched as Jeff and Kennedy approached. Kennedy had her arm through Jeff's and they were playing the happy couple. The minder, a young Filipino not older than eighteen, hesitated, unsure of the couple approaching. Fifteen metres away he spat out an order in Filipino and pointed to the arena. Jeff shook his head.

"Do you speak English?" he asked.

The young man calmed, and then smiled. "A little. What do you want? You're not allowed here."

Jeff took out the map and opened it, then put his finger on Davao City.

"We want to go here. How do we get away from this place and onto this road?"

They now stood alongside the horse minder, who looked to where Jeff was pointing on the map. Jeff's swinging fist smashed into the side of the minder's head. The young man collapsed.

"Okay, he'll be out cold for a few minutes. Let's untie the reins."

As each horse was freed, it scratched the ground and looked about, unsure. Jeff had an idea.

He said to Kennedy, "You untie the rest."

He took hold of the reins of a skittish chestnut and led him toward the arena. For a moment the other horses hesitated then they followed. Fifty metres from the arena he counted fourteen horses following. It was enough. But, the horses thought they were out for a morning stroll. None of them looked ready to run into the crowd. Jeff scratched his head. He looked to Kennedy for an answer.

She shrugged. "Sorry, Jeff, I guess you weren't born to be a cowboy. Any minute the man looking after the horses will wake up. We better get out of here. You can't win them all."

Dirt exploded inches from his feet and a trail of exploding tufts ran along behind the horses. Jeff spun. Felipe had a Kalashnikov at his shoulder and gave another burst. The chestnut, frightened by the automatic fire, reared then fell back on his hooves. He stood frozen to the spot, head high, eyes wide, jittery. Then he began to slowly move forward. The other panic-stricken horses followed. Another blast from the Kalashnikov and the horses broke into a gallop.

On the embankments, alarmed spectators turned toward the sound of gunshots. The thundering hooves of the fourteen horses could be heard but the horses were not yet visible. Then the stampeding herd emerged from the tree line, their necks now extended, ears flat back, nostrils snorting. Muscles rippled as powerful legs thrust the animals forward. Clods of soft dirt were flung in the air. Spectators screamed warnings. Uncertainty turned to panic as the horses raced up the embankment. Men and women were pushed to the ground as the masses behind them surged to escape the deadly hooves.

Jeff ran to the top of the embankment. He looked down across the carnage scanning the groaning bodies and disorientated spectators for a red scarf.

He spotted his man ten metres away and running straight at him.

Jeff readied himself, his hand flattened, as used in martial arts. When the red scarf was beside him, Jeff chopped him in the throat. The man stopped and dropped to his knees, gasping for breath. Jeff took his arm and led the staggering man away. After a few strides Kennedy joined him and held the captive's other arm. The red scarf did not resist, but continued to gag as he struggled to catch his breath.

Felipe was standing beside the car. He lifted the rear lid and Jeff and Kennedy bundled the semi-unconscious man into the trunk.

Felipe slammed down the lid.

CHAPTER FORTY SIX

Near the outskirts of Davao City, Felipe drove the Avensis off the highway and into a banana plantation. Kennedy and Felipe stood back. Jeff ran his fingers along the underside of a ridge protruding above the number plate. He felt for the lever and pushed it. The trunk lid released. As it opened, an arm, a knife gripped in the hand, swung through the gap. Jeff leapt back as the blade slashed through the loose cotton threads where his T-shirt covered his abdomen. He slammed the trunk lid down across the man's elbow. A cry of pain and the knife dropped at Jeff's feet. He kicked it under the car then pulled the lid up again and yanked the NPA man out. The communist freedom fighter slid across the dirt and rolled onto his back. Jeff placed his boot on the man's chest.

"Who are you?" the man stammered.

Jeff knelt beside him. "I have questions for you. I want to know where I can find one of your soldiers. His name is Diego."

"Diego is dead," the man gasped. Puzzlement replaced incredulity.

"I know he is dead. I want to know where his village is. Where does he, and other members of his cell, hang out?"

"How am I supposed to know this? Diego is no longer in our organisation."

"Don't bullshit me," Jeff said. "My friend here is a Davao City police officer." Jeff gestured at Felipe, who waved. "And he is upset because men associated with Diego have kidnapped his sister and her family and they are threatening to kill them." Jeff saw the man's eyes flick sideways toward Felipe. "Now, the choice is yours. Tell us how to find the village and Diego's men, or you will be found dead with a pocketful of drugs."

The NPA soldier stayed silent, but Jeff noted a slight quiver of the bottom lip. A bead of sweat dribbled down his forehead. Jeff took a packet the size of a tea bag from his pocket and dropped it on the man's shirt. "Cocaine."

Felipe drew his gun and stepped forward. He took careful aim at the man's forehead.

"The problem you have," Jeff said to the man, "is you are not the only one who can give us this information. I have so many of you pricks to choose from and I now know where to find your gang members. One of you will talk. And we can just keep on killing you and your comrades, legally. And the best part is you'll be dead. You won't even be able to warn your friends."

The face staring back at Jeff was still vacant.

"Are you going to help us? We have no time to argue."

The man's head fell back, defeated. "I told you, Diego is no longer a member of the NPA. He is with Abu Sayyaf. This is why we threw him out. He had done jobs for them. Kidnapping to earn money. Abu Sayyaf are bad men. Islamist, extremists."

The look on Felipe's face told Jeff that Felipe thought the NPA man was telling the truth.

"Who is this Abu Sayyaf group?" Jeff asked Felipe.

Felipe said, "They call themselves Islamic jihadists, whatever that means. They mostly operate on the other side of Mindanao, down by Zamboanga and Jolo Island. Now and then they venture across Davao City way. Diego was still living in the Davao area, so maybe he had a cell working out of his village."

"I know this group," Kennedy added. "They have sworn allegiance to the terror group ISIS, also called Islamic state or ISIL. Take your pick."

Felipe said, "This is not good news."

Jeff nodded.

"Then nothing has changed. We still need to find Diego's village." He turned to the NPA man. "You walk if you tell us where to find Diego's men. Do you know?"

The NPA man nodded then spoke in Filipino to Felipe.

Felipe said, "I know the region."

###

Felipe drove Kennedy and Jeff to the edge of town. He pulled off the road and parked next to a beaten-up blue Toyota hatchback. Felipe passed Jeff a car key.

"That car is for you."

"Another stolen car?"

"Of course. I cannot afford to buy cars. I still think I should be coming with you."

"We've discussed this, Felipe. If you are with us and they find out you're a cop, we'll never get out alive. This way, if we are seen, Kennedy and I just carry on being two lost tourists. We're growing used to the cover. You just wait for us where we agreed."

"Okay, now get out. I have someone for you to meet."

A man who Jeff estimated to be in his mid-thirties stood next to a twenty-year-old four-wheel drive military Jeep. It was still painted in camouflage patterns. It had a canvas roof, no sides. The man waved when he saw Felipe and walked across. He gave Jeff a glance and Kennedy, a closer scrutiny. That extra attention irked Jeff. The emotion took him by surprise.

"This is Ramos," Felipe said. "Ramos is a nurse and he makes visits to the rebel-held regions. Maybe rebel-held is too strong a word. Where they hide from the military is closer to the truth. He will lead you to Diego's village. Be warned, Jeff; this is a dangerous group. You now know they have links to Abu Sayyaf and to ISIL. Any high ideals they may have once fought for are long gone. Today it's about money; kidnapping, robbing banks, assassinations and piracy. You will follow Ramos to the village. When he gets there, he will signal with a wave of his hand, and then drive on. He cannot afford to be seen with you. He must treat the sick people and he cannot do that if he is compromised or dead."

"Fair enough," Jeff said.

Felipe said, "Now remember, as this is Diego's village, any man you find there will have worked for him. Someone will know who sent him to New Zealand. Find the information you need and get out. Understand?"

"I've got it. Don't worry, we won't be hanging about."

Felipe took Jeff's arm and led him away a few metres. He took a pistol from inside his shirt and passed it to Jeff.

"You might need this."

Jeff slipped it under his T-shirt.

"What is your plan, Jeff?"

"I don't have one. This time I'm playing it by ear. But I will be careful. I will use the jungle. When we get there, I'll hide out and reconnoitre. Someone will come my way and I'll grab them. I can keep hidden and undetected until they do."

"Good luck."

Jeff got into the driver's seat. When Kennedy was seated he turned to her.

"When we get to the village I am going to leave you on your own," he said, preparing for the verbal onslaught he was sure would come. "I want you to drive one kilometre back down the road and find a place to hide. And stay hidden. There's a white rag in the back. I want you to tie it to a tree on the road so it can be easily seen coming from the village." He turned to her, ready to explain his reasoning. Instead, she shrugged.

"Okay. Got it."

"No arguments?"

"Not this time. We're in the middle of nowhere and there's only two of us. You don't need me to grab one of Diego's men and you don't need me to help you hide out in the jungle. If it turns to crap and you come running, I'll have the car pointed in the right direction and I'll be ready to go."

He tapped the gun Felipe had given him. "This time I'm armed."

Kennedy nodded an approval.

Jeff turned the key and the engine vibrated into life. He steered the vehicle onto the road and set about trailing Ramos the nurse through the afternoon traffic.

###

After twenty minutes, Ramos turned off the main road on to what Jeff could only describe as a dried-out mud track. In the rainy season the nurse would need a robust vehicle like the military Jeep. Felipe had said the region had been one of the hardest hit by the typhoon, but apart from a few bent trees there was no noticeable sign of damage. The shacks they passed, which served as homes, appeared to have been nailed back together in the same ramshackle manner in which they had previously been constructed. A few villagers ambled along the side of the road, the women with bundles of branches balanced on their heads. The men gave cursory glances as the cars passed by and then carried on walking. Ten minutes later and Ramos slowed. As Felipe had instructed, Ramos hung an arm out the window and waved. Jeff pulled over and stopped.

"Looks like we have arrived," Jeff said.

Ramos U-turned and drove his Jeep back past them. He gave a mock salute. Jeff didn't bother to respond. With the motor still running, he and Kennedy sat in silence. Jeff scanned ahead, searching for any sign of a trap. He saw nothing. An old man and an old woman pulled on a rope tugging an uncooperative goat behind them. They walked by without giving Jeff and Kennedy a glance.

"I'll go along the tree line," Jeff said.

"Don't get yourself killed."

Jeff pulled on the door handle and was about to climb out. Kennedy grabbed his arm.

"We have company."

He half turned. Men with Kalashnikovs and older rifles, some holding machetes, emerged from the trees and surrounded the Toyota. Jeff had his foot hovering above the accelerator. The ground beneath them was unstable and soft. Any attempt to accelerate would leave his wheels spinning, and the Kalashnikovs would fill them with holes. There was no escape. He switched the motor off. Kennedy gave him an 'are you kidding me?' look. Jeff was relieved to see that her gung-ho attitude had returned. It would come in handy later when he had formulated an escape plan. Right now, he had some fast talking to do if they were to drive away. He pushed open the door. Gun barrels lifted and pointed in his direction.

He raised his hands and gestured for them to be calm. "Does anyone speak English?"

"I do." The voice came from behind the closest rebels. A man appeared from the rear. Jeff's gut churned.

It was Ramos.

CHAPTER FORTY SEVEN

Ramos smiled as he stepped forward.

"Your policeman friend is a foolish man. And you are a foolish man to follow me into the middle of nowhere and expect to walk away. My boss will be happy you are here. He wants to have a chat."

"That's good news, Ramos. I want to speak with him."

Jeff's eyes flicked from side to side, looking for an escape option. He saw none. At least they were not going to kill him straight away. Kennedy walked around the car and stood beside him. None of the armed men tried to stop her. Ramos didn't seem concerned.

One of his men stepped up to Jeff and relieved him of Felipe's pistol.

"Please follow me," Ramos said. "You are my guest until my boss arrives. Don't do anything silly. As you can see, you are outnumbered."

Ramos ordered his men to handcuff Jeff's left wrist to the arm of a wooden chair. His left ankle was cuffed to the chair leg. Jeff was confident that, given an opportunity, he could smash it to pieces and free himself. Kennedy sat on the floor with her back against the wall.

She was unrestrained. Maybe it was because she was a woman. Who knew? It wasn't a totally reckless move; she would never make it to her feet before the Kalashnikov that lay across Ramos's lap ripped her apart. But if he was careless, the rebel leader might learn to his cost that it was a mistake to underestimate a woman like Kennedy Patton.

Ramos pulled out his mobile phone for the second time. Again no answer.

"Your boss must be a busy man."

Ramos shut his phone and slipped it into his shirt pocket. "I am not in a hurry and you are not going anywhere. It will not be long before I speak with him. He will be pleased. Then he will come for you."

"I'm curious," Jeff said. "You don't look like the typical rebel, freedom fighter or whatever you call yourself. You're clean cut; working as a nurse, treating the sick. You people always have a reason to justify killing. So, what's your story?"

Ramos crossed his arms and leaned back until his rump sat on the window sill. "My family were farmers. Like many on Mindanao, the government gave them a plot of land. Three hectares to be exact, but what can you do with three hectares?"

Jeff shrugged.

"There was a stipulation. The land had to be kept agricultural. My family, like the other holders, had little choice but to lease the land to a corporation. They paid my father ten dollars a month. He was given the opportunity to work the land he had leased, so he grew bananas and made a grand total of six hundred US dollars for the year. Deduct the rent from this, and the family income was sixty dollars per month. Not enough to feed a family, and not enough to build a future."

Jeff had seen similar projects implemented in Eastern Europe. The new governments had tried to be fair to the peasant farmers and had given them each a piece of the pie. Most had sold to other farmers who had enough cash to create viable farms.

"I borrowed money from a friend, went to Manila, and trained as a nurse. I had a plan; after gaining my qualification I would go to another country and earn big money. Then my father died, and I had to return to Mindanao to look after my family. I found work in the villages around Davao; the pay was better than others earned, but only enough to survive, nothing more. Then along came Diego, who led a rebel unit for the communists. We knew each other from childhood. He gave me the opportunity to earn real money."

Ramos grinned.

"What can I say? I learnt a valuable lesson. It is better to have money than not have it. Then Diego and the NPA parted company. Funds and opportunities dried up. One of the leaders of Abu Sayyaf approached Diego. He had a special project, if we wanted it. It was of a different type than we'd been used to, but the money was better. We had nothing else, so we accepted."

Jeff offered a wry smile. "And here you are the head of your own clan, a killer and a kidnapper. Well done, Ramos."

"I know about you, Bradley. You're ex-Special Forces. You'll have done bad things just like me. Just because your government said it's okay doesn't make it any less of a crime."

Jeff heard the high-pitched noise of vehicle engines revving.

Ramos walked to the door and looked out. He turned to Jeff.

"Bad luck for you. It seems the boss man had decided to pay me a visit." He tapped his shirt pocket. "This is why he did not phone, he was on his way. He is a hard man, and he is not happy with you. I am not happy with you. You killed my friend Diego, who was like a brother to me. The boss will make you pay and I will enjoy watching you suffer." He slid his gaze to Kennedy and licked his lips. "And the woman will be dessert. My men will look forward to entertaining her when I am finished."

Jeff watched Kennedy's face. It remained impassive but her eyes had gone blank. He had no idea how he might achieve it but he was not going to let her be assaulted by Ramos and his men.

"Let me offer you this advice," Ramos said as he sat at the table. "Tell the boss what he wants to know. You will talk anyway. So why suffer? It makes little sense for you to do so."

The distinctive chattering drone of a heavy machine gun jolted Ramos from his seat. Whatever was going on outside appeared to have caught him by surprise. He looked in Jeff's direction. A frown furrowed his forehead.

Jeff had already worked out what might be happening and at any moment Ramos would realise he was under attack. Would he panic and shoot his two hostages? Jeff had counted thirty rebels in the camp. There might be others he hadn't seen, but for now he'd settle for thirty. They were all armed. They would put up enough of a fight to delay the invading force, but not for too long. The stutter of Kalashnikovs and single shots from rifles and pistols was getting closer.

"You know who that is, Ramos? It's your boss and his soldiers. The same boss who had Diego killed on the flight back to the Philippines. I did not kill Diego. Your boss lied to you. And do you know why Diego was killed? Because he knew too much; now it's your turn. You're no longer needed." Jeff tilted his head toward Kennedy. "She is a CIA agent. The Americans are after him. Your boss is making sure the hunt stops here, in this village. Your boss doesn't need your help anymore. In the next few minutes, his men will charge through that door and shoot all of us."

Ramos looked at Jeff. "What do you take me for? I am not an idiot."

"Near to here, your boss slaughtered a whole village. A young girl escaped, and he sent Diego to bring her back to the Philippines. You know this because Diego must have told you his mission. Now he has sent his soldiers to bury you and your gang, along with the rest of his secrets. It is why he has not answered your phone calls, and that means he does not know I am here. Bad luck for you. Soon you will be lying dead beside me and Kennedy."

Slugs smashed into the wooden door. Ramos jerked his head toward it.

Jeff needed to keep pushing. "Get it through your thick skull. These men are here to kill you. To kill all of you. Your comrades are dying as we speak."

"He wouldn't. Why would they? I have captured you and the woman."

"He doesn't know that."

Ramos bounced up and down on the balls of his feet. Jittery. Uncertain.

"If you want to survive, unlock these cuffs and I will help you escape," Jeff said.

"If I let you go, I am a dead man. He will kill me for sure."

"Your boss sent a shipment abroad and I need to find it. You know I am a Special Forces soldier. Kennedy here is CIA. We can get you out of here and to safety. Without us you will die. Do you understand?"

Ramos took another look out the window, and then back at Jeff. He took the key from his pocket and unlocked the handcuffs. Jeff stood and rubbed his wrists.

"Weapons. What do you have?"

Ramos pulled a cupboard aside and kicked at the wall, revealing an opening behind it. Ramos reached in and pulled out a crate. Jeff picked out a Kalashnikov and removed the banana-shaped magazine. He cocked the weapon, ejecting the round in the chamber then pulled the trigger. The firing mechanism moved freely. It would do. He reloaded the magazine and re-cocked the weapon, loading a fresh round into the chamber.

Kennedy helped herself to a Glock.

With the Kalashnikov in hand, Jeff ran to the window and saw an opportunity.

"Ramos, come here."

Ramos joined him at the window.

"The armoured vehicle. That's our ticket out of here. It has enough room inside for more than six soldiers. I'm going to take it out. Your job is to kill the man standing behind that machine gun. For the moment he has a shield of steel to protect him. When I run through the door, he will swing the gun to target me. When he does, shoot him. I'll climb on board, drop down through the hatch and take care of the driver. Once we're inside, the armour plating will protect us. Then we get the hell out of here."

Jeff saw Kennedy frown. "I could take out the machine gunner. I'm a crack shot."

"Yes, you could. But the job is already assigned. Your job is to shoot Ramos if he forgets to play his part."

She raised an eyebrow. "Got it. Can you drive one of those monsters?"

"Yes, it's an old Commando. They've been around for decades."

Jeff wasn't about to tell Kennedy he hadn't actually driven a Commando, but he had driven an armoured car. They were all the same from his viewpoint. He'd work it out.

Jeff stood by the door. He looked toward Ramos. "Ready?"

Ramos gave a thumbs-up.

Jeff crashed through the door.

He raced sideways, firing at the armoured vehicle as he ran. Two soldiers appeared on his right, swinging weapons in his direction. A burst from Jeff slammed slugs into the first soldier's chest. Jeff, with his finger still pressed on the trigger, continued the arc and the second soldier's head exploded. He turned back to the armoured car. The machine gun barrel was lining him up. Jeff kept moving, making himself as difficult a target as possible. He was putting a lot of faith in a rebel killer who, only a few minutes ago, had wanted to execute him. He heard shots from Ramos's hut. He did not see the machine gunner fall, but when he looked at the space above the armour-plated shield, there was no head. Kennedy was now behind him, firing her Glock. Jeff looked for her target. A soldier fell to the ground and grabbed at his leg. Two more shots and he lay still.

Jeff sprang onto the hood of Ramos's vehicle and from it leapt onto the roof of the armoured car, landing behind the gunner. The top half of the gunner's body was slumped over the turret. Jeff hauled him out of the way and flung him over the side. He looked down the hatch. The driver, coming to his comrade's aid, was looking up. His eyes widened in terror when he saw the Kalashnikov barrel pointed at him. Jeff fired. The driver collapsed to the floor. Jeff climbed inside and yanked on a lever that opened the side door. He pulled the driver's body to the opening and tumbled him outside. He waved for Kennedy and Ramos to climb in. Jeff sat behind the steering wheel.

"Shut the door," Jeff yelled.

Ramos pulled it shut.

"Okay, take a seat and let's get the hell out of here."

The two small glass strips in front of him, for the driver to see through, were splattered with blood. He spat on his fingertips and rubbed the windows until he had visibility. Pushing the gear lever forward, he touched the accelerator and the big vehicle moved. Jeff pulled on the oversized steering wheel that lay almost flat in front of him and the armoured personnel carrier swung away from Ramos's house. It picked up speed. The huge wheels and larger tyres meant the amphibious vehicle could travel at up to one hundred kilometres per hour.

Bullets ricocheted off the armoured plating.

A group of three soldiers twenty metres ahead, knelt and took careful aim. Jeff turned the vehicle, aimed at them and buried his boot.

The soldiers dived in different directions as he sped at them. The vehicle was too heavy for him to feel any tell-tale bump from a body squashed under the wheels. But Jeff was certain he had hit one of them. He swung left, crashing through the trees until he came onto the mud road.

After a half-mile they came across Felipe's stolen car, still parked where he and Kennedy had left it. Jeff drove the armoured vehicle into the jungle until he considered it hidden.

"Okay, everyone out," Jeff ordered.

They trekked back to the car.

"Ramos, I'm going to blindfold you."

Ramos nodded. Jeff emptied the contents of his backpack onto the car floor, then pulled the pack over Ramos's head.

"Now lie down."

Ramos obeyed, spreading himself across the back seat. Jeff climbed into the driver's seat.

Kennedy said, "Even though he's blindfolded, I don't think Felipe will be happy when we turn up at the house with Ramos."

"We aren't going to the house."

CHAPTER FORTY EIGHT

Felipe was waiting for them outside the factory. He lifted the roller door and when Jeff had driven in, he let go of it and the door rattled back to ground level. Jeff studied his surroundings; a workshop of some sort. Old batteries were stacked against one wall. Used and re-tread tyres against another. Two hoists in the middle, the sort used when fitting new tyres to a car. In the corner was a small office, with a glass window that allowed the manager to monitor his workshop.

Jeff and Kennedy climbed out and then Jeff helped Ramos. He removed the backpack from the rebel's head. Felipe glared at him.

"Ramos is the enemy, Felipe. He led us into a trap."

Felipe scowled, pulled out his sidearm and stepped forward. Jeff shook his head and stepped in front of him. He took Felipe to one side. He dropped his voice.

"Not now," he said. His tone was firm. "We're about to find out the truth and the identity of the men who have your family. And at any rate, it's not as if we're about to let him walk out of here, is it?"

Jeff pushed Ramos into one of four chairs around a lunch table. Three dirty cups sat next to an unemptied ashtray.

"All right, Ramos, let's get started. Just who is it you work for?"

Ramos looked from Jeff to Felipe.

"Many people will die if you don't tell me what is going on." Jeff picked up the Glock Kennedy had placed on the table. "We can do this painfully, but why make it tough for yourself?"

Ramos gave a bitter smile as his words were thrown back at him.

"The man I deal with is a Chinese-Malay named Wang, or Colonel Wang. I don't know if he is ex-military. When I have seen him in action, he acts like a soldier and he has almost a hundred men reporting to him. He heads up 'The Heavy Waters' security company."

"I know this organisation," Felipe said. "They have contracts providing security to many internationals operating here in Mindanao. A good reputation from what I hear. The companies they protect have little trouble from criminal gangs."

"The reason is," Ramos said, "Wang controls many of the rebel groups. Cross him and he sends in his 'Whisper Troops'. This is the name given to his men. They are feared by everyone. They wear black uniforms."

Jeff and Kennedy exchanged glances. The soldiers in the compound were in black uniforms.

"I have never heard of this group," Felipe said.

"They are secretive. Nobody speaks Wang's name, he has ears everywhere. Better to stay silent."

"And he is the top dog?"

"No, Colonel Wang reports to General Hono. Hono owns The Heavy Waters, and Wang and his Whispers troops are the General's own private army."

Felipe moved forward. "You are lying. You are making this up." Felipe pulled his gun from its holster and aimed it at Ramos's forehead. "Tell the truth, jackal, or die where you sit."

Ramos's eyes bulged and his chin and lips quivered. He lifted his hands as if he were about to pray. "Please, I am telling you the truth."

Jeff said, "Felipe, keep calm. We need him alive, not dead. Who is this General Hono?"

Felipe turned to Jeff. "This is bad, Jeff, very bad."

CHAPTER FORTY NINE

Felipe explained that General Hono had once commanded the Philippines military in Southern Mindanao. When he resigned, he went into business. "Property development is where he started," Felipe said. "Now he has factories that manufacture shoes, clothing and furniture. All these goods he exports. He also imports commodities; sugar, wheat, rice, chickens, oil and a variety of other goods I can't name. He is a big businessman."

"You seem to know a lot about his business, Felipe."

"When you are successful, others take advantage. His trucks have been hijacked and factories robbed. I've been an investigating officer. These were questions asked during my enquiries. This is how I know he has contributed so much to our community."

"It doesn't sound like he needs money," Kennedy said.

"I agree. It doesn't make sense. He employs many people," Felipe continued. "And he gives money to the poor and to the church. He is a popular man in the Davao region. I have a photo on my wall of me and my family sitting with Hono to have our picture taken. He was an honoured guest in our home. And now this vermin is pointing a finger at General Hono to save his own skin."

"But he does have a private army," Jeff said.

"There are many private armies on Mindanao, but I think this is the wrong label; security companies is a better term," Felipe said. "Mindanao is difficult for businesses. Most companies have security problems. Around election time the local villages and cities use the private armies to safeguard the candidates. We have communists, Islamists and local warlords interfering in the democratic process. But all the private armies, security companies, are legal."

Kennedy said, "The organisation I work for has investigated them. I read the file. Way back when Arroyo was President of the Philippines, she tried to have them disbanded, but failed."

"Felipe, you still have not answered my question. Does General Hono have a private army?" Jeff asked.

"Yes, he does," Felipe acknowledged.

"Tell me what you know about Wang's troops," Jeff asked Ramos.

"The Philippine President ordered the military to wipe out the rebel groups down here in Mindanao. But, as you can see, we still exist. And this is because Wang and his men protect us."

"And money? Do you pay him money to protect you?"

"No. He could have made a lot of money from us and the pirates operating out of General Santos City. But he leaves us alone as long as we leave the businesses he protects alone. But sometimes, he has paid us for special jobs. Like when he sent Diego and some of the men to New Zealand."

An image of Moana holding the hand of Judith Collins, and the two anti-terror squad members who died in the burning car, sprang into Jeff's head. For an instant he wanted to throttle the little shit in front of him. It could wait. Jeff eyed Kennedy. She remained impassive. He read her lack of response as, "keep going, you're doing just fine."

"Okay. What other jobs?"

Ramos hesitated. "I don't remember details."

Felipe pushed the barrel of his handgun against Ramos's head.

"Okay, okay. We assassinated politicians, and some local businessmen. Hono controls the commodities business on Mindanao, especially sugar, rice and steel. Wang's role was to protect General Hono's business interests. Anyone looking to import in competition to him does not stay in business long."

"He kills off his competition?"

Ramos nodded. "A warning is issued first."

"What about the camp in the jungle?"

"Diego talked of it but I know nothing about it. Though it might have something to do with the big job we did over a year ago."

Kennedy straightened in her seat.

"For this, Wang paid us a lot of money." Ramos paused. "There were thirty of my men and fifty men from Wang's unit. We went by ship to a small island east of here and a long way south, in the Pacific Ocean. I don't know where. We went ashore on small motor boats. There were maybe a hundred men, women and children on the island. Those we didn't kill fled into the jungle. Without weapons they had no chance."

"Then what?"

"There was a jetty. The ship had been waiting offshore and now it came in and docked. Some of Wang's men, dressed in strange rubber suits and helmets, came ashore. They looked like spacemen and they went into the underground bunkers. After a while they came out, and we all went in and brought up drums and boxes and loaded them onto the ship. The freighter brought us back to Mindanao."

Jeff looked at Kennedy. "One question answered for you."

She gave Ramos a steely look. "Many people have died at your hands, Ramos. Everyone wants you dead. From this point on your future does not look bright. Just to keep you safe I should take you to the American Special Forces at Zamboanga City. I'm sure they'd love to have a chat."

The whites of Ramos's eyes flashed. He turned to Jeff for support. Jeff shrugged. "I don't disagree with Kennedy's sentiments. I'm in the mood to shoot you myself." Jeff leaned back in his seat. "What happened to the goods?"

"At General Santos port we offloaded the cargo onto trucks. I do not know what happened to the cargo after that. We returned to our homes. I didn't hear from Wang again until he asked Diego for men to send to New Zealand."

Jeff stood. "Where do we find him and his men? Where are they holding Felipe's family?"

Ramos raised his head. "What's in it for me?"

Felipe pointed the barrel of his pistol at Ramos again. His forefinger whitened as it tightened on the trigger.

"How about I don't pull this trigger if you tell us, you piece of shit."

Ramos did not flinch. "We both know you won't do this, so let's not play silly games."

Kennedy stood. She indicated with a jerk of her head she wanted Jeff to follow her. She led him to the far end of the workshop where they could speak privately.

"What's on your mind?" said Jeff.

"We need the bombs and we need to find the compound ASAP. Agreed?"

"No arguments from me."

Kennedy continued, "Ramos has been co-operative until now, but I'd say the little shit is more than confident we won't shoot him without getting the intel we need. He has the connections that will allow him to walk out of any jail Felipe throws him into. You saw how easy it was to break Omar's men out. If he doesn't talk, we don't find the bombs."

"What are you suggesting?" Jeff asked.

Kennedy straightened her shoulders, as if steeling herself for something unpleasant. "We let him walk if he gives us the information we need."

Jeff almost laughed. "You're kidding."

"Look, you know his background, poor family, corruption, lost lands, lost future. It's always the same story with these guys," Kennedy said. "Someone will whack him one of these days. But right now, what we need is locations. We need Wang and we need the bombs, and we need to move now before the damn bombs disappear altogether. Wang and Hono are the brains behind everything, and they and the bombs are our priority."

Jeff stared at her, unbelieving. Ramos was the man who'd hinted he might rape her a few hours earlier. "You're the CIA, Kennedy. You manipulated an eleven-year-old girl to come to the Philippines, knowing they would kill her. Now you want me to believe you feel sorry for him because he says he had a shit childhood. It's crap. You'll need to do better than that."

"Jeff, do you want to wake up one morning and read about dirty bombs exploding in the USA or Europe, knowing we could have stopped it? And the only reason we didn't was because we decided to play hardball with a two-bit thug?"

Jeff tightened his lips. "You better know what you are doing, Kennedy. It could come back and bite you on the ass, big time."

"I'm willing to take the risk if it means finding out Wang's location."

"If we do this, then this discussion never took place. We turned our backs, and he ran off."

"Fine."

Jeff led Kennedy back to the lunch table.

"And now, Ramos," Jeff said, "here comes your chance to win a ticket home."

As Jeff spoke, Ramos's eyes lit with surprise. Felipe's mood turned black.

CHAPTER FIFTY

General Lorenz Hono paced his upstairs living room then limped out onto the balcony of his two-storied home. Though the big house was set back in the jungle, the second floor was high enough to give him a view of Davao City, the coastline and the island of Samal. Jungle shielded the estate from the main road. Whispers soldiers provided by his security officer, Colonel Wang, guarded the dirt driveway and entrance to his grounds. At one end of his property was a barracks, at the other end a small cottage. More soldiers were about than usual. Wang had beefed up security. He insisted that with the New Zealander about, and the mayoral election campaign under way, he needed to defend against unwelcome intrusions.

Hono had not disagreed with the extra security measures. Until the girl had been found and the goods dispatched to their final destination, there was a need to be vigilant. When Hono retired from the military, he had continued to use his rank, as ex-military officers often do, and his private security army was formed along military lines, with military rankings and military discipline. Wang, his security advisor and second-in-command, was given the rank of Colonel. His company's reputation had grown, as had his bank account. Now, his military experience and business success had placed him at the forefront of local politics. The Davao City mayoral elections would take place later in the month and he was leading in the polls. He had heard rumours he was under investigation. Well, let them come.

As Mayor he would be untouchable.

But he needed to be cautious. If the camp and his dealings with the rebel groups were ever found out, all would be lost. He had begun to rely more and more on Wang to eliminate any threats. It occurred to him lately that he was ceding control of his life to the Chinese Malay. When he thought it through, it pleased him. He trusted his security officer. He would never be betrayed by him. They were bound together by the blood of others. And with Wang taking care of business, it gave him time to relax.

Wang was cagey about his past. It was evident in the way he carried himself: he had had military training and he had been an officer. When questioned, Wang declined to comment and Hono didn't push. Wang looked out for him and that was all that mattered. The men he recruited were ex-military, but not from Mindanao. Wang had insisted on recruiting outside the region. When a hard decision needed to be made, which might involve violence against local villages, a recruit from the region might hesitate.

When it came to matters of security and intelligence gathering, Wang was the best he had seen. His head of security had saved his life on more than one occasion. He rubbed the thigh of his right leg. The stab wound had healed and he walked with a slight limp, but if Wang had not been there when he was attacked, he would have died.

Hono heard the engine noise and looked to the sky. After a few minutes the helicopter came into view. Wang had news. Too important, he had said, to relate over the telephone. Hono hoped that whatever it was, Wang would not take long. He had an evening planned. One he was looking forward to. In his lounge, two young Russian women huddled together on the sofa. He smiled at the thought of them waiting for him. When he'd walked into the room earlier, their tired nervous eyes watched him, shoulders slumped, resigned to the evening ahead. Hono offered a comforting smile, but they had not relaxed. He was uncomfortable knowing they feared him. He was kind to them and treated them with respect. They had all the comforts. He wasn't a monster, but he had needs.

The girls had overstayed their visas. Wang paid immigration officials to keep him supplied with overstayers, drug smugglers and any women detained for misdemeanours. The druggies were always the easiest to break down. It wasn't hard to convince the women that sex with him was better than a Philippine prison. At the end of the week he would release his current guests to return home to their countries. A few days to rest up and the next lot would arrive.

The helicopter looked like a bright yellow bubble, a fat bee. It circled once and then descended onto the lawn. Planted in circular metre-high grey-brick planters, palm trees towered over his house, their crowns tossing in the wind from the chopper's blades like wild creatures. The helicopter door pulled back and Wang jumped out. He stooped until clear of the rotor blades. Hono watched him until he disappeared beneath the balcony, then walked back inside.

A tap on the door and Wang entered. The man never waited for an invitation or showed discretion of any kind. The security chief ran his eyes over the girls and made a slight, almost imperceptible, grimace of disapproval. Hono ignored it and pointed to his office. He followed Wang in and shut the door. Wang dropped into the chair in front of Hono's desk and waited. He didn't like small talk and didn't like talking to a moving figure. Hono pulled open a drawer and drew out a bottle of scotch. He poured two glasses and pushed a glass toward Wang. Wang made no move to touch it. Hono sat.

"All right, Colonel, tell me what is so urgent. As you can see, I have a big night planned. I hope you are not about to ruin it for me."

"The goods have been loaded and the ship is at sea," Wang said. "The final stage has begun."

"Where is the ship now?"

"Waiting offshore for my signal. It will not be found."

Hono's tight expression relaxed into a smile. "This is good news," he said. He felt the tension ease from his shoulders and he slumped back in his chair. The bombs sitting in his warehouses had worried him. If they had been found, international investigators would have come, demanding answers. Even the local military commander would not support him, no matter how much he had already been paid. But the bombs had gone.

"And the girl? Have you found her?"

"Not yet."

Hono frowned. "The bombs are useless without the girl. Our buyers will not be happy, Wang. The men we are dealing with will not accept excuses. Not when they have already paid so much money. You must find her."

"I will find the girl. Do not worry."

Hono poured himself another whiskey. Wang's glass remained untouched.

"And what about the meddling foreigners?"

"There's nothing for them to find. The bombs have gone. We have destroyed the camp. There is nothing to lead them to us. We are in the clear."

"I wish I shared your confidence, Colonel Wang."

"But we do have a problem," Wang said.

The tone of his voice halted Hono with the whiskey glass halfway to his lips."

"Oh?"

"The attack on Diego's village did not go according to plan."

"Which part?"

"Ramos escaped. And I have since learned, with Bradley and the woman."

Hono gasped in astonishment. He lowered his glass to the table. "Bradley and the woman are back here on Mindanao?'

Wang nodded.

"Why were they with Ramos?"

Wang shrugged. "This I do not know."

"If they are together, how much could Ramos tell them?"

"Everything," Wang said.

Hono gulped down the contents in his glass and immediately refilled it.

Wang said, "The police and army are hunting for them. My men are hunting for them. This should be enough to keep them out of the way. Don't let it worry you. It is a slight hiccup, but nothing I can't handle."

Hono looked up at his security chief, searching for any sign of hesitancy or doubt. As always, Wang remained emotionless. It might be that Wang was right not to worry over Ramos, or the New Zealander and the American woman, but the girl was cause for concern.

Hono often mulled over the night the girl escaped from the compound. Colonel Wang had stood next to him as their soldiers advanced, hut by hut. Trembling, weeping, hands in the air, the captives knelt next to their neighbours and pleaded for mercy. Wang stood resolute. The decision had been made. The prisoners would not see the dawn's sun. No exceptions.

During the roundup there had been no resistance, no fighting back. The workers had no weapons. Wang had had their belongings searched when they entered the camp. Bulldozers had stood silent outside the compound. When the time came, the huge machines would demolish the buildings and bury the rubble. The bare earth would be replanted, and after a few weeks it would look as if the camp had never existed. The efficient manner in which the first phase of the operation had taken place had pleased Hono.

As they had waited for the head count of the captives to be completed, he had asked Wang again if the killing was necessary.

"You know it is, General," Wang had answered. "We have discussed this many times. If we let the sick walk free, the doctors will identify the cause of their illness. The authorities will be informed and an investigation will take place. Sooner or later it will come back to us. This cannot happen."

"There will be repercussions. The families of these people will go to the police. They will ask questions. There will be investigations."

"And they will find nothing, General."

Hono turned to Wang. "When it is over, I want a marker placed in the vicinity. A tree planted, sanctified by the local priest. It will stay a secret for all time, but these people have died for their country."

Wang stared at Hono in disbelief. "How so, General?"

"My businesses and wealth benefit our nation. Making me richer and stronger makes the country stronger. Patriotism, Wang, it comes in all forms. It's a matter of perspective. I want you to give these people a marker."

"Yes, General. It will be done. This final phase has gone smoothly. Tonight it will be over."

Hono knew from experience that military operations never ran to plan.

Then Wang had brought the news. The girl had escaped.

CHAPTER FIFTY ONE

Ramos chose the crowded activity centre in the NCCC shopping mall to meet Wang. An education exhibition was taking place and display booths and people covered the entire floor area. Parents had brought their teenage children to discuss career prospects. Swelling the ranks of the higher-education seeker's crowd were spectators lured away from the retail stores to watch the inter-school dance competition. The emcee announced the next school group and twenty young teens walked on stage. Music boomed out across the auditorium and the students launched into their routine.

Meeting with the Colonel was a dangerous move, but he'd had little choice. If anything went wrong, he could easily get lost among all these people. He stretched tall and scanned the crowd. There was no sign of Wang. He stepped back a few paces to a less-crowded spot. A sharp object prodded him in the back. He stiffened and slowly turned. Wang was behind him. Ramos looked down expecting to see a gun barrel but instead, saw the nudge had come from the corner of a leather briefcase. The crowd cheered the dancers on stage. Ramos pointed to a quieter spot far enough away from the noise, but not leaving the security that the masses of people gave him. He looked at the briefcase.

"All the money is there?" he asked Wang.

"Five hundred thousand US dollars, as you requested."

"Good. I'm not a greedy man." He knew Wang kept a lot more in his safe. The Chinese-Malay had killed Diego and then tried to kill him. He should have asked for more. Still, all the money in the world was of little use to a dead man. If he had asked for too much, Wang would hunt him down. Half a million was petty cash to the Colonel.

"Where is the girl?"

"Not so fast, I want to count the money."

Ramos held out his hand. Wang passed him the briefcase. He balanced the case on his left arm and with his right hand, flicked open the catches and lifted the lid. Ramos's greedy eyes widened as he surveyed the bundles of one hundred US dollar bills. He checked a few random bundles. They were in order. He closed the lid. Holding the case in his left hand, he pulled out a piece of note paper from his trouser pocket and passed it across. Wang read the text then looked up, sceptical.

"The address is correct," Ramos assured him." You will find her there. I have nothing to gain by tricking you. I have the money and I will start a new life."

"I am curious, how did you find the girl, when my men could not?"

Ramos smiled. "Plain dumb luck. Bradley and the woman rescued me when you, Wang, tried to kill me. They made me lie down in the back of their car when we made our escape. My mobile phone must have slipped from my shirt pocket somewhere inside the car. I asked my friend in the phone company to triangulate for it. His directions led me to Bradley's car. It was parked outside the house he is hiding in. I saw the girl on the veranda."

Wang looked down at the paper again. This time when he looked up, Ramos had a small handgun aimed at his chest. The briefcase hid the gun from the public. Wang's eyes widened.

"A precaution," Ramos said. "You may leave now, Colonel. I have men watching you and watching the men you brought with you. We both have what we want."

Wang smiled, then turned and walked away.

Felipe dropped Jeff and Kennedy at the top of the drive. As they approached the house, no policeman appeared. Jeff stopped and motioned Kennedy towards the jungle fringe. They had no weapons. It angered him that Felipe would still not supply him with a gun to defend himself. Jeff skirted the house using the jungle as cover. There was still no sign of the police. He found himself back in front of the entrance. From where he stood he could see the door was ajar.

He turned to Kennedy. "Wait here. If it's an ambush, no point both of us getting shot up."

"I agree."

Jeff made his way onto the veranda and with his right hand slowly pushed open the door. His shoulders slumped. Mama Soo was lying spread-eagled on the floor, her eyes open but sightless. Blood covered the front of her pale blue T-shirt.

He waved to Kennedy.

Jeff sat on the sofa and stared down at the woman who had become Arina's guardian. Kennedy leaned against the door jamb. Both were silent. Jeff glanced toward Kennedy. Her stony face told him everything. She was thinking what he was thinking. The two of them had brought death to an innocent. They had both liked Mama Soo. She was a school teacher, not a soldier. He knew a quick search outside and he would find the bodies of the two police guards in the jungle.

"They have Arina," Kennedy said. "What now?"

Jeff looked up, eyes icy cold. Kennedy shuddered.

CHAPTER FIFTY TWO

An agitated Felipe turned on Jeff. "You should never have let Ramos go."

Jeff looked at Kennedy but stayed silent. There was no point lashing out at her now. He was equally to blame.

"We don't know for certain it was Ramos, Felipe."

Felipe glared at Jeff. "Of course it was him. In all this time no one has found us. We let Ramos go and suddenly Wang's soldiers have come, and they have taken Arina and killed Mama Soo." Felipe kicked at a chair and sent it sailing across the room.

Jeff said, "Save your venom for Hono and Wang. The Heavy Waters security company, in your investigations did you ever stop to consider why they were more successful at protection than other security companies? Did a red flag never pop up in the space in your head?"

"Why would a successful company raise a red flag, as you put it? Do you investigate all the successful companies in your country?"

"And Hono never came to your attention?" Jeff asked.

"Even if he had, you do not investigate men like Hono. He is one of the richest men on Mindanao and a member of the Chamber of Commerce. He is running for mayor of Davao City, and the word is, he'll win. The people believe the General has the toughness required to deal with criminals and protect the people. And if he does become mayor, no prosecutor will go near him, even if he has done what Ramos says he has."

"Felipe, you are a shit cop."

Jeff knew his lashing out at Felipe was unfair. Right now he needed someone else to blame. Mama Soo was dead and Arina kidnapped. Pretty soon the whole damn family might be dead. He should never have let it happen. He should have broken Ramos's neck when he had the chance.

"I do my best," Felipe said with an edge to his voice. He was clearly angered by Jeff's criticism. "I'm paid a few dollars to protect old ladies and keep the streets safe for ordinary citizens, not investigate organised crime and get my head shot off." He glared at Jeff. "You are pissing me off, my friend. You know nothing of life in the Philippines. You have no right to sit in judgement."

Jeff placed two hands on the table.

"I have every right to sit in judgement. Because of your crap investigative skills, friends of mine in New Zealand are dead. And now these assholes have your family and they have Arina, and they fucking killed Mama Soo."

Jeff gave Felipe his own version of a pissed-off glare.

Kennedy interrupted. "We're losing focus. We don't know where Wang is for the moment, but it sounds like Hono is easy to find. Where does he live?"

Felipe pulled back from Jeff. Their eyes stayed locked on each other.

Without looking at Kennedy, Felipe said, "On a hill overlooking the city. It is a big house inside a fenced-off area. If he has soldiers guarding him, then it will be impossible to get to him. It is like a fortress."

"All the more reason to believe Hono's house is where your family is, Felipe. I'll bet my life on it."

"We are only three."

"What about the police? Can you arrange a raid? Drugs or something?" Kennedy asked.

"No judge is going to sign off on a warrant to raid General Hono. I have no proof he has my family, and no proof he has done anything wrong. Even If I could find Ramos, and dragged him in as my star witness, it would not be enough."

Jeff turned to Kennedy. "How about the American Special Forces in Zamboanga, can you bring them in now?"

Kennedy shook her head. "Same answer as last time." She spoke directly to Felipe. "I'm sorry, but they would not get authorisation to attack a leading Philippines citizen's house to rescue a cop's family. They would say it's a local matter and I should leave it for the local cops to deal with, and they would be right."

Jeff scratched his chin. "We know they have the bombs."

Kennedy raised an eyebrow. "I'm not going to lie to my boss, Jeff. We both know the bombs are most likely on the *Claire Dances*."

Jeff turned to Felipe.

"Come on, Felipe," Jeff said, his voice calmer. "Think of something, and quick. Wang has Arina, and it means Sofia, Carlo and Sarah are out of time if it isn't already too late."

Felipe paced, frustrated. He kicked at a cupboard door under the bench. It split down the centre and fell open. Then he stopped and turned to Jeff and Kennedy.

"I have an idea," Felipe said. "Totally crazy, like one of yours, Jeff, but I have something to do first. Give me three hours and be ready to move."

Felipe left. Jeff turned to Kennedy, a hint of a grin. "Now he decides to be assertive."

Kennedy looked at Jeff. "I just learned something about you, that you can be an asshole when you want."

CHAPTER FIFTY THREE

Jeff drove the armoured car he had escaped in when Wang's men attacked Ramos's village. It was why Felipe had needed time. He had taken a military friend to help him retrieve the Commando and drive it back. It hadn't been hard to find, Felipe said. The villagers knew where it was and for a few pesos he was taken to it.

Jeff edged the oversized vehicle into the jungle a hundred metres from the entrance to Hono's house. It needed to be kept out of sight until Hono's gates were opened. He, Felipe and Kennedy crept up to the outside walls. He scanned Hono's estate with Felipe's police issue binoculars. "Nice property. A large white two-storied home I guess is befitting a man of General Hono's importance," Jeff said, his tone tinged with sarcasm. "The long building will be a barracks, but that small cottage to the right of Hono's house looks interesting. Those three soldiers with rifles slung over their shoulders huddled outside the door look like guards." Jeff passed Felipe the binoculars. "If I was a betting man I'd say Sofia is in that building."

Felipe gave the binoculars back to Jeff, who passed them on to Kennedy.

"Tell me what you think?"

Kennedy said, "Same as you do. The three soldiers are definitely guards and whatever they're guarding is inside the cottage."

Jeff said, "There are two men on the gate and who knows how many more in the barracks. If we assume the guards need relieving every few hours, then there's a minimum of another five men, but there could be as many as ten."

"That's a lot of potential firepower, Jeff," Felipe said.

"It sure is."

Kennedy said, "Too many men for us to attack, even with an armoured car. We'd have to leave the vehicle to rescue your sister and her family, Felipe. When we did that we'd be cut to pieces. You are insane to think this will work."

"What about it, Felipe, are you insane?" Jeff asked.

"We will see."

"What is your plan?"

"In an hour, a fundraising dinner for Hono's mayoral election campaign will be held in the city. At the last minute his campaign manager asked for a police escort. He wanted his own men, but his advisor suggested an escort by local police would give his image more authenticity. They don't want potential voters thinking the new mayor has surrounded himself with a bunch of heavies. The police are from my station. I have appointed trusted colleagues and friends to drive the vehicles. The cars will get the gates open for us. We will follow them in with the armoured vehicle."

Jeff was thoughtful. He picked up the binoculars and scanned the enclosure again. He smiled. "It isn't a bad idea, Felipe. It might just work."

"In the boot of my car are pistols with silencers and Kalashnikovs. These I borrowed from the evidence room."

Jeff smiled. "Is there anything left in that evidence room of yours?" He patted Felipe on the shoulder. "Not a bad effort. Well done."

Kennedy said, "What about it, Jeff, any bright ideas on how to pull this off? The General is expecting his escort. We wait too much longer. He might call a taxi."

Jeff replied, "For the moment we forget about the soldiers in the barracks. We need to take out the two guards on the gate and the three men in front of the bungalow, pretty much at the same time, and silently. Any men in the barracks will have been informed cars are coming for the General so they won't be too concerned when they hear vehicles. We load Sofia, Carlo, Sarah and Arina into the armoured car and drive them somewhere. We can't go back to your friend's house, Felipe. Wang knows where it is. We can hide in the jungle if we need to. Let's just make the rescue. All agreed?"

Two heads nodded.

"Good. Now, ideally, if everything goes to plan as I have just outlined, it will be a breeze. Of course nothing ever goes to plan. So be ready for a fire fight. Kennedy, you're the crack shot. When the time comes can you take out the five guards? They won't be shooting back. You'll be an assassin, not a soldier?"

The expression on Kennedy's face was grim. Her eyes narrowed to slits.

"I can do it. The men at the gates will be close shots. Less than ten to fifteen paces. The soldiers at the cottage not further than thirty yards. I can make that work. What weapons do I have?"

"Take your pick from Felipe's trunk."

"What have you got in your trunk, Felipe?" Kennedy asked.

"I have a Smith and Wesson, a Springfield and a Glock."

"Really," Jeff said, surprised. "Who was walking around Davao City with an arsenal of weapons with suppressors attached?"

"We have hit men in the Philippines just like they have in other countries."

"I'll use the Glock."

"Where would you rather be, in the turret or on foot behind the armoured car?" Jeff asked.

"On foot."

"The three at the bungalow will go to ground if they see the guards at the gate fall."

"Two of them will. I'll take out one before they can react. If they're slow, I'll take the other two out as well."

Jeff tilted his head toward her. He could see Kennedy wasn't boasting. Her tone was matter-of-fact. She had his respect. He'd tell her that later, if they survived the day.

"Anything you want to add, Kennedy?"

"No."

"Felipe, how will you explain it if we end up with a pile of dead bodies. A raid on Hono's house will be big news. Your life and career might turn to shit when this is all over."

"In the boot of one of the police cars are bags of cocaine and methamphetamine, also courtesy of the evidence room. By the time I have finished with Hono, he will be known as Mindanao's biggest drug lord. I will also dump the drug bust in Florida on him. No one will support him. And the cop who brought him down, that's me, will get a promotion."

Jeff nodded. He was beginning to like the new Felipe. "Right then. Let's do it."

When the three police cars arrived, Felipe climbed into the lead vehicle. Jeff, driving the Commando, followed the cars up the winding drive. Kennedy followed on foot, close enough to have one hand on the Commando's armour plating. The guards would never see her until it was too late.

Jeff worried about the unknown factors. What if Sofia and Carlo were not in the bungalow? How many men were in the barracks, and what weapons did they have? Did they have rockets? If they did, his vehicle would be a ball of flame before he got halfway across the mown lawn. Without the armoured vehicle, the assault would be a disaster. It was down to Kennedy; five shots and five dead Whispers soldiers.

The gates opened.

From his limited vision through the driver's window of the armoured car, Jeff could see a man standing on the balcony of Hono's house. Jeff guessed the man was the General himself. Hono watched the cavalcade for a few moments then disappeared inside.

The two guards either side of the gate stood with their rifles dangling loosely in one hand. They were relaxed, not expecting trouble. Jeff didn't doubt Kennedy's ability to shoot a man in battle. For all soldiers, shooting at the enemy in the heat of battle came easily. In fire fights a soldier was in self-defence mode, as well as attack mode, and a soldier was sure as hell going to shoot the enemy before the enemy shot him. At close range it was reactive shooting; in ambushes it was from a distance, and in jungle it was shooting at the unseen.

Kennedy was about to shoot a man, not in the heat of battle, but face to face; upfront. These men might just as well be security guards standing outside a bank. Killing men in cold blood required a special kind of emotional disconnect.

Because of the engine sound, Jeff did not hear the *pfwip* sounds from Kennedy's silenced Glock. He saw one of the three men outside the bungalow fall. The other two looked down at their companion, confused. Jeff assumed the armoured car had blocked their view of the gate. A second guard fell. The remaining man dived onto the ground and unslung his rifle. It would take less than three seconds for him to orientate, seek out a target, and take aim.

Jeff swung the armoured car toward the bungalow, booted the accelerator, and sped toward the last soldier. He knew Kennedy was behind him and he hoped his speed did not leave her exposed. Twenty metres from the bungalow the remaining soldier was set. He was looking through the rifle sight. As soon as Kennedy stepped away from her four-wheeled cover, he would have his shot. No matter how skilled a sharp shooter Kennedy was, she would never hit a target the size of half a head before a slug slammed into her chest.

Jeff had only one option.

He drove the armoured vehicle onto the veranda and over the remaining soldier. His last sight of the man was him trying to climb to his feet. Then he disappeared. Jeff then steered the vehicle back toward the gate and stopped halfway. Leaving the engine running, he climbed out of the driver's seat and pushed open the side door. When he was outside, he saw two bodies lying still beside the gates.

"Climb into the turret and swing the machine gun towards the barracks," Jeff said to Kennedy.

She gave a mock salute. "You got it, boss."

Felipe joined him on the veranda.

"What about Hono?" Jeff asked.

"He can wait, he isn't going anywhere."

"And the men in the barracks?"

"One of my men is speaking to them now. They have a choice. Either be shot to pieces by Kennedy and her machine gun, or, leave their weapons and get lost. They have no boss, so there will be no wages, nothing worth dying for."

As Felipe finished speaking, ten unarmed men emerged from the barracks building and made their way towards the gate. Jeff nodded approval and relaxed. It was over.

"Well done, Felipe."

They made their way into the bungalow.

Sofia stood in the centre of the room holding Sarah. Jeff looked down at Carlo, his friend and Felipe's brother-in-law. He lay on a stretcher, his skin yellow and his eyes sunken into their sockets. He was unmoving. Jeff didn't need to ask; he could see Carlo Marcos was dead. Felipe walked up to his sister and niece and took them in his arms. Jeff stood back, watching the reunited family finding solace in each other. When Sofia saw Jeff, she wriggled out of Felipe's arms and came across to him. They embraced. She stepped back.

"Arina told me how you have helped her and organised a rescue for us, Jeff. Thank you."

"Not just me, Sofia."

She half smiled. Her eyes sad. Jeff knew she must be experiencing mixed emotions. Her family was safe but her husband was dead.

"I can never repay you."

"Nothing to repay."

He scanned the room.

"Where is Arina?"

Sofia's face clouded over.

"Colonel Wang flew her out by helicopter hours ago," Sofia said. "They have not returned."

"Do you know why he wants Arina?"

Sofia shook her head. "Carlo was an engineer. A superb one. Wang hired him to build weapons, but he never told me what weapons. All the men were chosen for their special skills, and between them, my husband said, they had the ability to assemble any bomb. As an engineer he was adept at not only building bomb casings but the variables associated with trigger mechanisms. That's it. Arina is a child. I cannot begin to imagine where she fits in to all this."

"So he was in charge. Where did he learn bomb making?"

"I don't know. I didn't know he had that skill."

"And do you know what caused his illness?" Jeff asked, already knowing the answer.

Sofia shook her head.

Jeff turned to Felipe. "I think it's time to have a chat with General Hono. We need to find out where those bombs are and where Wang is taking them."

"I think you stay here, Jeff," Felipe said, a firmness in his voice. "My men have secured the General inside his house. This is now a police matter." He reached down and touched his brother-in-law's arm. "Hono and I have matters to discuss." Felipe pulled his pistol from its holster and checked the load.

"Now hold on, Felipe, we need the location of the bombs. Kennedy and I will come with you."

"Not this time, Jeff." He turned to his men just inside the door, "Make sure no one leaves."

Kennedy and Jeff exchanged glances. They were outnumbered. They would have to wait it out.

Felipe found Hono alone in his office. He was sitting behind his desk nursing a glass of whiskey. The bottle that was within arm's reach was almost empty. But as arrogant as Hono tried to convey himself to be, Felipe saw fear in the iconic figure he had once idolised. He now knew Hono to be nothing more than a ruthless murderer and a criminal. The people's hero had the same frightened look in his eyes that Felipe had seen in many of the thugs he was about to arrest.

"General Hono," Felipe said. "You have caused me many anxious moments, but those times have ended."

Hono raised his glass. "You are too late. Wang is gone, and so is your niece. We have an impasse, I think.

But I am a businessman. We can discuss terms for her release."

Felipe said nothing.

Hono smiled.

"Ah, so you want to arrest me. For what? And we both know whatever charge you come up with, nothing will come of it. You work for me, remember? You have accepted two hundred thousand US Dollars in payments. Now you will do what I tell you."

"Wrong, General. I do not work for you. And I don't need you to deal with Wang. I can negotiate direct."

Felipe removed his pistol from the holster. Hono's eyes widened.

"You don't know where Wang is. I can help you find him."

Felipe smiled. "I was hoping you would co-operate, General. But I want more."

Hono's eyebrows raised, and he looked surprised. "Money?"

Felipe nodded. "One million dollars." He reached into his pocket and pulled out a piece of paper. "The bank account number. Open your computer screen. I want to watch the funds transferred."

"It's a lot of money. What is in it for me?"

"You walk, General. As you said, you are an important man. No one will bring charges against you. But you will pay for your crimes with money."

Hono smiled. "Very well."

He booted up his computer while Felipe stood behind him. When the transfer had been completed, Felipe ordered Hono to shut the computer down. He then pulled up his account on his mobile phone. The money showed.

His bank manager was a friend. He would spread the money across a series of accounts, making it untraceable. Felipe moved back to the front of the desk.

"Now, General, tell me where I can find Wang."

"He is on the *Claire Dances*."

"I already know he is on the ship, what I want to know is, where is the *Claire Dances* right now?

"On its way to Hong Kong. You are too late."

"And one last question, General, why did you do it? Kill all the people in the camp. Why was it necessary?"

Hono shrugged. "They were more useful dead than alive. And besides that, it was too risky to leave them alive. I needed to make sure when the men the bombs will be delivered to set them off, they cannot be traced back to me. That would make me an accessory to mass murder. Not true when you think about it. I am just an arms manufacturer. Do any of the major powers end up in the world court if someone they supply uses those weapons to slaughter innocent people?"

"But you have committed mass murder."

"Only here in the Philippines. It doesn't count. You police shoot people every day and no one cares, but if internationals are killed, that is a different matter."

"What did you mean, the people in the camp were more useful to you dead than alive?"

"It's a figure of speech; nothing more. Besides, what does it matter now? Money has been transferred to your bank account and now you are a rich man. How do we fake my escape?"

"I'm sorry, General. You should never have killed my brother-in-law and threatened me and my family."

Felipe aimed his pistol. A mix of disbelief and fear spread across Hono's face. A trio of slugs slammed into Hono's chest. The impact from the bullets flung him back into his chair and then he slid to the floor. Felipe heard a low groan. He walked around the desk and looked down into the pleading eyes of the dying General.

He fired again.

CHAPTER FIFTY FOUR

At Hong Kong airport, Jeff and Kennedy were met by Dean Jaggers.

"No talking until we get into the car," Jaggers said. "Everyone has a listening device nowadays."

The three climbed into the back of the Embassy car. "Okay. Now you can talk," Jaggers said, as the car pulled away.

"Jeff, Dean is my boss in Manila."

"Really? I wasn't aware heads of station moved about."

"Normally they don't. But I'm worried that maybe events are about to take a nasty turn. And it is happening on my watch. I don't want black marks on my record. Not when I could have put a stop to it in the Philippines."

"You mean, by going out on a limb and supporting Kennedy?" Jeff said.

"Something like that. But, hey, it's never too late to join the party, is it."

Jeff decided not to offer a sarcastic response.

"What did you find out in Manila?" Kennedy asked,

"That General Hono was under investigation. The investigators had built a file of wrongdoing dating back to his military days. Corruption, racketeering, murder, extortion, what the hell, you name it and our General Hono was up to his neck in it. The investigators even believe that he had rival military officers killed to clear the path for him to become General."

"And Wang," Jeff asked. "Know anything about him? He's our priority now."

"Wang is an interesting character. He was boss of a Chinese criminal gang in Kuala Lumpur and ruled over a territory that stretched south to Malacca. They did the usual organised crime stuff, drugs, robberies, extortion and murders. The murders were mostly rival gang members. It did surprise me to learn there are a lot of organised crime groups in Malaysia, especially in the Chinese community. And Wang was top dog."

Jeff shrugged. "There is organised crime everywhere."

"That is true. But these guys operated large-scale. Wang's gang had over seven hundred members. The Malaysian police believed he had been killed in a bomb blast in Penang. It surprised them to find out Wang was still alive. His real name is Danny Lee and they would like to talk with him."

Jeff said, "Any idea how he came to be working for General Hono?"

Jaggers shook his head. "No, nothing in any of the reports I read. Now that Hono is dead, it doesn't really matter anymore, does it?"

"No, it doesn't. Have you located the *Claire Dances?*"

"Yes, it is still fifty kilometres away but closing. In a few hours it will enter the harbour. You say the bombs are on board?"

"I'm sure of it."

"But you don't know for certain."

"No, I don't know for certain," Jeff said. "I haven't been on board and actually seen them. But we do know they loaded the first shipment at General Santos City and they were not offloaded in Florida before it sailed again. Then they returned to General Santos for the second shipment. Arina was then helicoptered aboard. Her mother said that Carlos, her father, was an expert in trigger mechanisms. Arina said she was taken into the lab once and played with iPads. I'm thinking that what she thought were iPads were in fact a bio-trigger. The father used Arina's hand to activate and then lock them. The bombs are useless unless she unlocks them, which is why the crates were not offloaded in Florida. It's all I can think of that makes sense of them trying to kidnap her and not kill her."

"Well, at any rate, we know where the ship is. The big question, why Hong Kong."

"That is a puzzle," Jeff said.

"If the *Claire Dances'* original drop point was the USA, then why make the change?"

"Maybe because the USA wasn't the final destination at all," Kennedy said. "It might have been because Hono and Wang wanted them away from the Philippines, and loading them on the ship as they were produced was part of the process. Once they were all aboard, as they are now, they could be delivered."

"Sounds reasonable," Jaggers said. "Maybe China is just a transit point and the final destination could be anywhere."

"How did you find the freighter?" Jeff asked.

Jaggers gave Kennedy a fleeting glance. Jeff caught it. He turned his head to Kennedy.

Kennedy shrugged. "Pretty simple, Jeff. We put a tracker in Arina's locket. We've always known where she was."

Jeff shook his head.

"So, right from the beginning the decision was made to send her home and use her as bait, even before I was dragged into the discussion?"

Kennedy said nothing.

"Okay, what's done is done. We have to worry about right now. We need a plan. Somehow we have to stop the ship from docking," Jaggers said. "I think it's a certainty that Wang will have port officials in his pocket and they'll be all over it once it's tied to a wharf. We'll never get near it and the bombs will be gone."

"Can we get help from the Pacific fleet?" Jeff asked.

"Not this close to China. They don't even like it when our ships are a thousand miles away," Kennedy said.

Jeff said to Jaggers, "What do you know about the *Claire Dances*?"

"It's an old bulk carrier, with cabins and bridge at the stern. From the bridge to the bow it's all flat, deck and hold covers and nothing on the bow except the anchor. It's about 277' feet long and weighs 4,000 plus tonnes. Eleven to twelve knots cruising speed. We aren't talking modern shipping here."

"We need to get on board. Do you have helicopters available?"

Kennedy said, "If we used a chopper, we would have to hire a civilian one. Wang's men will see and hear us coming from a long way off. If they have rockets, we will be shot out of the sky before we land."

"Okay, I get the picture. I've been shot out of the sky once on this trip. I don't want a repeat experience. I have an idea. In my days in the SAS we trained for this scenario. I've never done it on active duty. I guess now I get to find out if our instructor was talking out his ass or smarter than I ever gave him credit for."

"What's your idea?" Kennedy asked.

"You're not going to like it."

CHAPTER FIFTY FIVE

Jaggers pointed.

"That's Victoria Harbour and that's the Star Ferry Pier. That seven-storey brick-and-block construction is the Tsim Sha Tsui Clock Tower. It's all that's left of the old Kowloon to Canton railway station. Our man should be waiting for us on the water somewhere."

The Embassy car pulled over near a line of palm trees.

"We have to walk from here," Jaggers said.

They climbed out and gathered at the trunk.

"Grab a bag each."

Jaggers led them under the overhead walkway. It was twilight and the city skyline across the harbour was lighting up and starting to sparkle. Hong Kong at night always reminded Jeff of Christmas.

The speedboat was white. Along the upper edge of the boat's side, written in big blue letters was the word, PARASAILING. The craft looked twelve metres long, and speedy. In the bow was drop-down seating, but there was no cabin and no glass visor. It was going to be a wet ride. Halfway back was the steering, and the stern was flat and clear. This was where parasailers stood prior to launch.

Once they were aboard, Jeff asked, "How far out is the *Claire Dances* right now?"

"Right now, about twenty miles, and closing," Jaggers answered.

"Do we have weapons?"

Jaggers patted one of the canvas bags. "When we are close they get issued."

"Why not now?"

"Are you kidding? Hong Kong might be an autonomous province, but we're still in China. You can't walk around with a weapon in your pocket unless licensed to do so."

"We're in a boat on the water, Jaggers, no Chinese cops anywhere."

Jaggers ignored the remark.

Annoyed, Jeff looked to the stern. The speedboat was leaving frothy white waves in its wake. This was a dumb idea. It would need a dose of dumb luck to succeed.

For an hour, the speedboat Captain, who had said, "Call me Jonny," held his wheel steady as his vessel bounced across the small wavelets. Jeff's stomach threatened to heave up an avalanche of his lunch menu. He grasped onto the handrail to keep his balance. Kennedy stood beside him.

"You'd better move away from me," he mumbled.

He hung his head further out, clinging to the railing as if his life depended on it.

"Jeff, you've gone the colour of chalk," Kennedy said.

"I get seasick," he growled. "It's why I joined the Army and not the bloody Navy."

She grinned. "We only have a few more kilometres to go."

After another ten minutes the speedboat slowed. Anticipating a wet and bumpy ride, the three of them had worn wet-weather tops supplied by the skipper. Jaggers took the wheel, and the captain moved to the stern to prepare his equipment. He connected the chute to the nylon ropes attached to a pole. When the time came, the chute would be released for the backdraft air to fill and it would lift until the harness ropes were at full length.

"You said you had trained for this, but never tried it in action. When was the last time you parasailed?" Kennedy asked.

Jeff smiled. "Training camp. I didn't like it. I don't like heights."

"What sort of Special Forces soldier are you? You don't like heights and you get seasick."

"I'm sensitive."

"What is the plan?" she smirked.

"My plan is the boatman gets me high enough. Once I'm in position, I'll slip the harness and drop onto the deck. The boatman can then reel the chute in. I'll lower the rope ladder over the side, and you and Jaggers can climb aboard."

"I think we should both be on the chute, Jeff."

"And you *have* parasailed?" Jeff asked.

"No, but I've made plenty of parachute jumps. I'll work it out."

"This task needs a soldier. I've done it before. I didn't like it, but I did it."

Jeff had lied. He had never parasailed onto a ship. He had hung from a chute in the air over a vessel. But the day had been windy, and every time he was about to release, the wind swept him sideways, and he landed in the water. If there had been shooters on board, he would have been shot dead. The SAS trainers decided it wasn't a good idea, and the squadron scrapped the project.

"I might have to land while shooting."

Kennedy glared, "Don't patronise me, Jeff. I have been in combat.

"And if this was about aerial combat, the plane would be yours."

Kennedy ignored the comment. "And if you have to land while shooting and they pin you down, how will you drop the rope ladder down to us?"

"Okay, point taken." Jeff pointed at the harnessing. "That is a tandem harness. We go up together and we land together. And if we get seen and one of them has a machine gun then…"

"We die together."

A flash of a smile crossed his face.

"How many men will they have on board, do you think?" Kennedy asked.

Jeff shrugged. "I don't know, you're the Navy girl."

"An old ship like this would need a crew of at least six to eight, I'd say. A Captain, mate, maybe a second mate, two engineers and a cook-cum-crewman. That's the modern-day merchant navy; it's all about electronics even if the vessel is old. But my worry is, how many soldiers will Wang have brought aboard?"

Jeff turned to Jaggers. "Weapons?"

Jaggers pointed to the canvas bag. "Help yourself."

Jeff pulled back the zipper and opened it. "Glock 17s? Is that it? You expect us to go into battle with fucking

Glocks." He held up a gun in each hand. "What the hell am I meant to do with these?'

"They're good weapons. The SEALs use them."

"I know they're good weapons, Jaggers, but when Kennedy and I are floating down onto the deck and a dozen men burst out of nowhere firing machine guns, a Glock 17 won't cut it, will it?"

"Sorry, Jeff, it was the best I could do."

Jeff took a deep breath. "This op is beginning to take on the guise of a suicide mission."

Kennedy touched his arm. "Don't worry, soldier boy, if we pull the trigger fast enough, we can make up for it not being automatic."

"Let's see you laugh when you're dangling over the ship on the end of the chute, and your cute ass is getting shot at."

Jeff checked his weapon. Satisfied the mechanisms worked fine, he loaded it then pushed extra magazines into the pockets of his wet-weather jacket. He pushed the Glock into his belt. He strapped a second Glock to his ankle.

He was ready.

CHAPTER FIFTY SIX

Jaggers steered the jetboat along the side of a large Norwegian container ship. When he rounded the stern, the lights of a dozen freighters of varying shapes and sizes came into view.

Jeff said, "How do we find our ship amongst that lot?"

"There it is," Jaggers said, pointing to a shape a few hundred metres to their left. "The one that looks like it belongs to a Second World War merchant shipping convoy."

"Are you ready?" Jeff asked Kennedy.

Kennedy nodded.

Jonny instructed Jaggers to bring the boat to the stern of the *Claire Dances*. "Mr Jaggers, you need to steer the boat down the port side, that is to the left. This is where the prevailing wind is, and once Mr Jeff and Ms Kennedy are in the air, it will carry the chute over the cabins and bridge, and then when we slow, it will allow them to float down onto the deck."

Jaggers gave Jonny a thumbs-up and steered the boat onto the correct path.

Jeff and Kennedy stepped into their harnesses and pulled the straps tight around their midriffs. Jonny stepped up to the centre pole. He pulled on a yellow cord and the chutes released. The backdraft created by the boat's forward momentum quickly filled the silk. It billowed then pumped out into a fully formed parachute. At the bottom of the chute was a bar. Jeff gripped one side, Kennedy the other. Jonny connected the chute links to the harnesses. He unwound the rope, and the chute climbed into the sky, pulling Kennedy and Jeff up with it.

In an instant they were looking down onto the deck.

"I don't see anyone," Jeff said. "Do you?"

"No, I don't."

"It won't last long. There will be men on the bridge. They will see us come down."

"I'll be ready."

"I see deck cargo. Pallets of freight and one strapped-down helicopter; good luck for us. When we drop, we will have cover," Jeff shouted. "It must be the chopper Wang used to bring Arina aboard."

Was Arina still alive?

The wind drifted them over the railing. "When we get to the right height, we need to release at the same time," Jeff said to Kennedy. "If one of us drops first, the chute will rise without the extra weight."

"Okay, got it."

"Here we go. Three, two, one, release."

They dropped together onto the cover of the ship's hold. Jeff rolled to the left and dropped three feet onto the deck. Kennedy followed, landing behind him.

"That was easy enough," Jeff said. "They must be asleep on the bridge. How the hell did they not see us?"

"It's getting dark," Kennedy said.

"This chute is big and brightly coloured. There are plenty of lights. Someone must have seen it."

"Maybe they did see us," Kennedy said. "And they are raising the alarm."

"Well, no one is shooting right now. We got lucky."

Jeff prepared to lower the rope ladder down to Jaggers.

"Kennedy, go to the ladder under the bridge. Do you see the one I mean?" Kennedy gave him a thumbs-up. "Train your Glock on those upper doors. If anyone comes out, they'll have the high ground. We'll be sitting ducks."

Kennedy moved off. Jeff waited for her to get into position then he looked over the side. The backwash from the moving ship was too rough for the smaller boat to get close. In Jeff's opinion, Jaggers would never be able to grab hold of the rope ladder and climb aboard. Jeff dropped the ladder onto the deck. It occurred to him if he dropped it over the side, Jaggers might risk attempting the climb. No point having him die trying. He and Kennedy needed to stop the ship first. Jeff pulled out his pen torch and flashed the speed boat three times. The abort signal. Danger. Jaggers' torch flashed back.

Jeff, Glock in hand, prepared to move forward. Kennedy stood under the bridge overhang, out of sight from above.

His head spun at the sound of shots.

Bullets hammered into the hold cover and ricochets ripped past his ear. He ducked, and then dived forward. He crawled along the deck, using the cover as protection until he was level with one of the pallets. As he peered over the ledge of the hold, the bridge windows shattered. Kennedy had stepped out from the overhang and was shooting back. She looked over her shoulder and signalled to him that she was going to climb the stair. Jeff shook his head; it was too dangerous. She ignored him and climbed.

"Silly move, Kennedy," he muttered.

He had little choice. He rose above the hold cover and swung the Glock toward the heads looking down from the bridge. He stooped as he shot and freed the second Glock strapped to his ankle. He fired both as fast as he could pull the triggers, and kept firing until the magazines had emptied.

Kennedy was now outside the bridge door.

Jeff ducked behind a pallet and reloaded. He could see what she was about to do. When he was ready, he leapt to his feet and ran across the hold cover, shooting at the bridge as he went. He let out a well-practised battle cry learnt in military training. Two heads popped up. Jeff fired and they dropped out of sight. Kennedy pushed the door open and disappeared inside.

Jeff heard shots. Not at him.

He scrambled up the ladder. When he made it onto the bridge, Kennedy spun at the sound of his footsteps. Her Glock steady in her hand, aimed at his chest. When she saw it was Jeff, she relaxed. He looked down at two unmoving bodies.

He nodded an approval. "Well done."

"Hello on the bridge," the voice came from down the stairs. "We are the crew. We are not here to fight."

"Come up," Jeff yelled back.

Four men entered. Jeff gestured for them to sit on the floor. Backs against the wall.

"Which one of you is the Captain?" An arm went up. "I want the ship stopped. Can you do that?"

"Yes, of course I can stop my ship."

"Make it happen."

The Captain climbed to his feet and pulled on a lever. Then radioed below.

"How many crew?" Jeff asked.

"Six. Four of us here and two below in the engine room."

"And these two men? " Jeff asked, pointing at the bodies with his gun barrel.

"They came aboard with the other passengers."

"How many passengers do you have?"

"Seven to start, but now only five," he said, looking down at the bodies. "The others are, Colonel Wang and a girl, and three men."

"Is the girl still alive?" Jeff demanded.

"Yes, she is alive."

Jeff took a deep breath and then slowly exhaled. An exercise he used to calm himself, to ensure he did not make rash decisions. Arina was alive. He needed to make sure she stayed that way.

"It appears Wang wasn't expecting trouble. He probably thought he was on a holiday cruise," he said to Kennedy. "And then along we come, and ruin it for him."

"That's the way it looks to me."

Jeff could feel the ship begin to slow.

"We have Wang and his men trapped downstairs," Jeff said. "I'll keep watch over this lot. You go drop the rope ladder over the side. We need Jaggers up here. When we go below, I want our backs covered."

Kennedy returned in less than five minutes with Jaggers. The ship had now stopped.

"It concerns me there has been no sign of Wang and his two men," Kennedy said.

"I've been having the same thought," Jeff said. "The answer I came up with worries the hell out of me."

"Reinforcements," Kennedy said.

Jeff nodded. He pulled out his mobile phone and held it toward Kennedy and Jaggers. He had cell reception. "He'll stay holed up below until more men arrive."

Jaggers said, "Then we need to high-tail it out of here."

"This man is the captain. He tells me he is not one of Wang's men," Jeff started. "He and his crew work on contracts. They know nothing of what is taking place."

"You believe him?" Jaggers asked.

"Of course not, but he's all we have."

Jaggers turned to the sailor.

"Right, Captain. I want this boat turned around and headed out to sea. Will you do that, or do I throw you over the side?" The pale-faced Captain, nodded agreement. "Good. Get started.

Jaggers said to Jeff and Kennedy, "I will contact the carrier, Independence II, and arrange to rendezvous with them. It might take a day or two. There is no need to go chasing after Wang and risking your life. He's not going anywhere."

Jeff shook his head. "No can do, Jaggers. Arina is down there. Once Wang realises we've turned the ship around and his reinforcements won't arrive, who knows what he might do. We are still sitting on a stack of bombs, and we don't know where they are. I'm going after him."

"And I'm coming with you," Kennedy said.

CHAPTER FIFTY SEVEN

Jeff climbed down the ladder to the lower deck. Kennedy waited until he signalled and then followed. The passageway was clear, but there were six closed doors to open; three on either side. Wang and his men could be behind any one of them.

Jeff said, "Cover me from here. I'll move forward and check each room before we drop to the next deck."

Kennedy nodded.

Jeff pulled back the first door. A storage room. Mops, buckets, shelves with bottles and cans. The next door was ajar. He peered in. The galley. Jeff stepped inside. To his left, a stainless steel bench top and against the wall a gas cooker. Above the cooker, hooks holding knives, ladles, pots and pans. He could not see behind the bench. To his right were three tables covered with unwashed plates waiting to be cleared. On the other side of the tables was an old three-seater couch. Jeff decided to check behind the bench first. As he turned away he heard a scraping sound. He swung his arm in a half-circle as he dived to the floor. Ricocheting bullets bounced ladles and pots off their hooks. Jeff ignored the clatter as the utensils hit the floor. The man standing behind the couch made an easy target. Jeff fired two shots into his chest. The man staggered sideways. He crashed onto a table, sending plates, cups and utensils clattering across the floor. The gunman looked at Jeff as the table tilted. He slid to the floor. Dead.

Shots rang out in the passageway. Jeff rushed to the door and stopped.

"Kennedy," he shouted.

"I'm fine, one down out here."

"I'm coming out," Jeff said.

"Come forward."

Jeff stepped into the passageway. He could see part of a body lying across the next doorway; Kennedy standing next to it. Then he heard more movement from the galley. He leapt to his right and flattened against the wall. Bullets smashed into the bulkhead opposite. He pushed his gun around the doorframe and fired off two blind shots. When he pulled the trigger again, it did not fire.

He stared at the weapon, then dropped the mag out.

Empty.

He felt for the spare mag. There was nothing in his trouser pockets. Then he remembered. The spare mags were in his wet-weather jacket, now on the floor of the bridge. Going into battle without ample ammunition was an amateur mistake. He looked to Kennedy, who was on the other side of the door opening, and held up the mag.

She shook her head, but signalled she still had rounds in the magazine loaded in the Glock.

He should have cleared the room; another amateur mistake. Soft footfalls advanced across the galley floor. He was unarmed and trapped in a narrow corridor. Even the most incompetent of shooters would not miss him. To get back to the ladder and up to the bridge for his spare mags he had to cross the door opening. Too risky.

He gestured to Kennedy to keep her weapon trained on the galley door. Next to him, on the wall, hung a fire extinguisher; a long red metal cylinder with a pressure hose attached to the top. He yanked it off its bracket. Holding it firm in two hands, he waited. The footsteps drew closer. Kennedy had moved to her left. She knelt, an elbow resting on her knee, the Glock at arm's length; a classic sharp-shooter's pose. If Wang or whoever was inside stepped into view, she would take them out.

The gunman's steps were almost at the door. Jeff flung the fire extinguisher through the gap and raced after it. A grunt as the fire extinguisher caught the gunman in the face. It was Wang. Instantly recognisable from the photo Jaggers had shown him. He stumbled backward, grabbing at his face, his gun hand momentarily off target. Jeff reached out and grabbed a handful of hair. He swung Wang sideways and then smashed Hono's security chief's head onto the stainless steel bench top. Wang collapsed to the deck and lay still.

Kennedy appeared in the doorway.

Jeff picked up Wang's pistol, a Beretta. "If he breathes funny, shoot him. Keep alert. We have one man unaccounted for. I'm going to clear the rest of the cabins on this deck then I'm going to look for Arina."

Kennedy stood aside to let him pass.

He tried each door along the passageway, then went down the ladder to the next deck. He found her inside the second cabin. Arina sat hunched over. Her left cheek was darkening. Blood from a cut on her lip had congealed on her chin. Her bowed head lifted. Tired eyes caught Jeff's.

She smiled at him, the weariness lifting from her face. Jeff walked across and crouched in front of her. He rubbed her arm. Then he pulled her to him and hugged her: she was shaking with fear and fatigue. When he pulled back, he wiped a tear from her eye.

"You're safe now, Arina," he said. "I will take you to Kennedy." She nodded. Jeff squeezed her arm. He guided her back up the ladder. Wang was sitting upright with his back against the bulkhead. Kennedy's arm was steady, her pistol still aimed at his chest. Arina stiffened when she saw him. Jeff's arm tightened around her. "It's okay, Arina. He won't harm you."

Kennedy gave Arina a warm smile.

"I'll take over here," Jeff said to Kennedy. "Arina has been beaten. Can you give her a quick physical examination? Make sure there are no broken bones?"

Kennedy hesitated. "Aren't you the medic on this mission?"

"Only for grown-ups."

"I need him to be alive when I get back, Jeff," she said. "We need to know where the bombs were going. Getting the bombs is not enough. The end user can find more bombs."

"I get it, Kennedy. Now look after Arina. Stay with her."

Kennedy placed a hand on Arina's shoulder. Jeff kept his attention on Wang, but he could feel her watching him, hesitating. She didn't trust him not to kill Wang. Finally, he heard her climbing the ladder. Now, he and his prisoner were alone. Emotions swirled in Jeff's head. The man on the floor had ordered the attack in New Zealand. His order had seen friends and colleagues killed.

He was responsible for countless other deaths, and if he had gotten away with the bombs, many more would have died. And now Wang had beaten Arina. Dear, sweet Arina.

Jeff waved the barrel of the Beretta at him. The Chinese-Malay pushed himself up the bulkhead until he was on his feet. Jeff hesitated. He was not an assassin. Shooting an unarmed man did not come easy to him. But for Wang, he would overcome any misgivings he had. He hoped Wang would make a dumb move and make the whole process easy for him. Wishful thinking gave way to common sense. Wang had information they needed. He could wait until they had it, and then he would kill him.

"Colonel Wang, you've killed friends of mine. I can't tell you how much that pissed me off and how much I've looked forward to finding you."

Wang said, "You have won today's battle, but the war is not lost."

"What the hell does that mean?"

Wang smiled. "The people I work for are determined. And they have plenty of money to pay people like me to get them whatever they need."

Jeff shrugged, "In a way you are right, Colonel. The war against people like you is never won. You people always pop up somewhere, but here is an interesting fact: none of you ever live to witness the results of your carnage. And as you can see, the rest of us are still here. You've lived a meaningless life, Wang, and now it has come to an end."

Wang smiled. "I think you might be mistaken. The woman has said she wants me alive. I will do a deal with her. Give her the details of the man who wants the bombs, for my freedom. She is CIA. She will deal."

Jeff was thoughtful for a moment, and then said, "I think you are right."

Holding the Beretta steadily aimed at the centre of Wang's back, Jeff pushed him along the passageway to the storeroom. The room was the size of a large cupboard. A few brooms and buckets and mops. They still swabbed decks? There were no windows. It would hold Wang until they had finished with him.

As Jeff turned to exit, out of the corner of his eye he caught a flash of movement and spun. Wang lunged at him, a knife in his hand.

Jeff fired two shots.

CHAPTER FIFTY EIGHT

The knife clattered to the floor. Jeff picked it up and threw it into the passageway. Wang held his arm, groaning in pain.

"There are rags in the bucket over there; use them to stop the bleeding. If you're lucky you'll die from blood loss before you die from an infection."

"I need a doctor."

Jeff slammed the door and locked it. When he turned back, Kennedy was standing in the passageway with a questioning stare.

"I heard shots."

"He's still alive. How is Arina?"

"I need somewhere to clean her up. There's fresh water in the galley. But there's also a body."

Jeff said, "Give me a second and I'll get rid of the body."

When Kennedy returned with Arina, Jeff had dragged the dead man into one of the empty cabins. "I'll leave you to it. I'll go up and check on Jaggers."

He made his way out onto the deck, and scanned the horizon. The ship had turned and was heading out to sea.

"All clear below?" Jaggers yelled down.

"All clear."

Jeff climbed the ladder and entered the bridge. His boots crunched on the slivers of broken glass. Jaggers stood with his back against the wall, his Glock loose in his hand, an eye on the Captain

"I've been in touch with the Independence II. I have a bearing. It's a long way off but we have enough fuel to make it."

"Any trouble from this lot?" Jeff asked, inclining his head toward the crew.

"None. They know the cause is lost. They know if they want to live they have little choice but to co-operate."

"Leave them to it then and come downstairs. See what we can find out from Arina."

Arina had cleaned up with Kennedy's help. Her hair was tied back. The bruising around her eye had darkened. The blood from her cut lip had been washed off. She looked shaken but Jeff could see a spark of defiance in her eye.

Kennedy was filling a glass of water in the kitchen. Jeff joined her.

"How is Arina?" he whispered.

"She will be okay. A few bruises and scratches, but no more. She had refused to co-operate with Wang until he persuaded her."

"Thank God she co-operated. It could have been much worse."

Kennedy, Jaggers and Jeff sat at one of the three tables. Arina sat with her back to the porthole, away from the door.

Jeff asked, "Are you up to answering a few questions, Arina?"

She scratched at a spot on the back of her hand. She lifted her head and nodded, "Yes."

"Arina, the bombs. Do you know what happened to them? And where they are?"

"Yes, they are in the bottom of the boat."

"How did you and Wang get onto the boat?"

Jeff already knew the answer, but he wanted to get Arina talking with easy questions.

"A helicopter landed on the lawn in front of the big house, and we flew out to sea and the boat was there."

"Why did he take you aboard? What is it they wanted from you?"

"He told me he needed me to make the bombs work. I told him I didn't understand. I knew nothing about bombs."

"What happened then?"

"He took me down to the bottom of the boat."

"The hold," Jeff added.

"I don't know, maybe. There were big wooden boxes all over the floor. The lids were off. Inside was another box, but it was metal. They had taken the lid off those too. The Chinese man made me stand beside it."

Jeff gave Kennedy a quick glance. They both knew what was coming.

"Then what?" Jeff prompted. "What was inside the box?"

Jeff decided not to use the term coffin. She'd had enough association with death in recent times, without him adding to it.

"It was this long."

Arina stretched her arms. Jeff guessed close to a metre.

"Seven long red tubes. Lying down. Joined together. There were some smaller round things along the side. They looked like clocks. There were lots of wires running in and out of the clocks and tubes. And on top was the iPad I had seen before when my father had taken me underground at the compound."

"An iPad?"

"That's what it looked like."

Jeff nodded. "Okay."

"And then what happened?"

"The Chinese man made me put my hand on the iPad. When I did, a small red light started blinking. Then he reached in and pushed a button but the blinking wouldn't stop. He was very worried, and he asked the man from Egypt what to do."

"The man from Egypt?" Jeff asked.

"Yes, he was an Arab."

Jeff gave a sideways glance to Kennedy. He was thinking more likely an Iraqi or Syrian, maybe Iranian.

"Arina, what happened to the man from Egypt?" Jeff asked.

"I don't know. He was here on the boat."

Jeff said to Kennedy, "The fourth man. We need to go hunting for him after we finish this discussion."

She nodded.

"What happened next, Arina?" Jeff asked.

Arina said, "He pulled on a wire. I could see the clock. It was counting backwards. A digital one, like Papa had. I think from fifteen minutes. The man from Egypt started yelling. He was frightened. The Chinese man yelled out to his men. It was too heavy to carry to the deck. They dropped ropes and pulled it up. Then they threw it into the water."

Jeff looked up at Kennedy and Jaggers. They had guessed right. Arina was the trigger.

"And did you do the same with the other boxes?"

"Yes, one more. And that one didn't stop either. They threw it in the water as well. Did I do wrong?"

Kennedy smiled, "No, honey, you did nothing wrong. The bad men did, not you." Kennedy said to Jeff and Jaggers, "Okay, so now we know. The triggers had built-in scanners that needed a palm print and a pulse. Arina needed to be alive. Without Arina, the bombs were useless." She smiled. "And her clever father sabotaged the trigger mechanism to make certain no one had control over them."

"Sounds logical," Jeff said. "But eventually, once they reached the final destination, someone with the right equipment would find a way to disarm them. Arina, did you count how many boxes there were?"

"Yes, thirty all together."

"Holy shit," Jeff, blurted out. He signalled sorry for his language to Arina. "Thirty to start but still twenty-eight left."

"How do we get into the hold?" Jaggers asked.

"From up on deck," Arina answered.

"Let's go and look," Jaggers said.

The sounds of a revving motor drifted down the stairwells. Jeff and Kennedy caught each other's eyes, then reached for their weapons and raced each other from the mess. The sounds were growing louder as they scrambled up the ladders. Jeff was first on deck. The helicopter was rising from the cargo cover. The downdraft flung a spray of water from the rain puddles into his eyes, blinding him. He wasted valuable time to wipe them clear. Kennedy, behind him, was firing her Glock. It was too late. Kennedy and Jeff could only watch as the helicopter rose higher, then banked away and disappeared into the darkness.

Jeff slapped his hand across his thigh. "Dammit! Well, that at least answers another question that's been bugging me. How did Arina's father know what he was doing? He didn't, he had help."

Jaggers and Arina appeared on deck. Jaggers did not hide his look of disappointment. Arina pointed to a small hatch in the corner of the hold cover.

"That is where the Chinese man got into the inside of the boat," she said

Jeff turned the small lever and pulled it open. Jaggers made to climb down first. Jeff grabbed his shoulder, "Sorry, Jaggers, you need to wait. Someone has to stay up here. If we all go down and the door is shut, we'd never get out. Kennedy has earned her spot."

"That's okay Jeff, I'll stay up," Kennedy said. "I've seen enough cargo holds and missiles and bombs to last a lifetime."

"Okay, Jaggers, after you."

CHAPTER FIFTY NINE

At the bottom, Jeff shone his torch in search of a light switch. "It's very dark in here."

"The light switch is on your right," Arina said.

Jeff flashed his torch until he located the switch and then flicked it on. The hold flooded with light.

"And there they are," Jeff said. "Twenty-eight bombs." He counted them, to be sure. "All here."

Jaggers grinned. The lid on the closest crate was askew. He stepped forward and pulled it away. "Let's have a look at one of these babies." He lifted the coffin lid. "Nasty looking, isn't it?"

"It sure is," Jeff responded.

Jaggers said, "We need to find out where the bombs were going. Wang has the answer. We need to kick the shit out of him until he coughs it up."

"What's the urgency? We have the bombs. Getting them out of Chinese waters should be our priority."

"Well, okay, in an ideal world you're right, Jeff. But in reality, it wouldn't matter if the Chinese grab this ship and confiscate the bombs; they aren't likely to hand them over to a terrorist group and they're already a nuclear power. So whether the Chinese have them or we do is neither here nor there. I want to know who ordered them made. We've stopped this lot but it only means whoever placed the order will look elsewhere. They're not going away. The buyers might be in Hong Kong. If they are, we can find them.

"With the chopper gone, I can't fly back to Hong Kong but the jetboat is there. Now we know for certain what they were up to, the agency will commit resources to tracking them down. We need names, Jeff."

Jeff shook his head. "Sorry, Jaggers, no deal. You can't leave. I can't sail this ship on my own."

"Jeff, you're overruled. The terrorists are more important than the ship and the bombs."

"And if the Chinese grab us, your people will negotiate with the Chinese and have you and Kennedy released, but Arina and I will disappear forever."

"Don't worry on that score, we wouldn't leave you hanging."

Jeff was about to utter a 'yeah right', but said nothing.

"Let's go talk to Wang," Jaggers said. "See how co-operative he's prepared to be."

Kennedy and Jaggers stood back, weapons at the ready.

"Now remember, we need Wang alive," Jaggers reminded Jeff.

Jeff pulled down the handle and pushed the door open. A flaming ball of rags flew toward him. He lifted his arms to shield his face. Wang charged. He held a small axe in his right hand. His arm showed no sign of weakness from the bullet wounds. Clear of the doorway, he lifted the tomahawk above his head and swung. Jeff leapt back, and the axe head scythed past his chest. Wang had full movement. Jeff hadn't checked the wound and now concluded they must have been flesh wounds; lucky Wang. Wang dropped his shoulder and charged, knocking Jeff off balance.

Out of the corner of his eye, Jeff saw Kennedy and Jaggers had their pistols trained on Wang. Jeff could see in Wang's eyes that he believed he held an advantage, and that neither CIA agent was going to shoot. He swung the axe upwards, towards Jeff's chin. Jeff slipped sideways and avoided the blow. He regained his balance and jabbed his fist into Wang's face. He struck again with a right cross, flattening the Chinese-Malay's nose. Blood poured from a nostril.

Wang screeched in pain. This brought a smile from Jeff.

He seized the opportunity and gripped Wang's wrist. He smashed it against the bulkhead and the axe flew from the Chinese man's grasp. Jeff kicked at it, sending it sliding along the corridor. Wang wriggled free of Jeff's hold and made to chase after it.

Jeff took hold of Wang's collar and yanked him back, placing himself between Wang and the axe.

He lifted his eyebrows. "No axe now, Wang, just you and me." Wang looked toward Jaggers and Kennedy and the barrels aimed at his chest. Jeff lowered his voice to a whisper so the two CIA agents couldn't hear. "They won't shoot, they want you alive. Me, I want you dead. So, all you have to do is stop me, and then you can make your deal with the CIA, just as you planned."

Wang snarled, then leapt in the air; he spun and shot out his right foot with the speed of a boxer's jab. The move took Jeff by surprise. Wang's foot struck him in the chest. Gasping for air, Jeff stumbled back a pace. Wang stepped forward and leapt again. His foot drove at Jeff's head, but this time Jeff was ready. A stiff forearm blocked the strike, then Jeff moved in close and brought his fist up between Wang's legs. Wang folded. A right cross smashed his head into the bulkhead. Wang staggered away. Jeff took a moment to catch his breath.

A mistake.

Wang stooped and picked up the axe.

Jeff slipped on Wang's blood, which was spattered across the floor. He fell. Wang rushed at him. Jeff looked up. Wang was on him, the axe raised to deliver a fatal blow to his forehead.

Kennedy fired twice. The bullets slammed into Wang's chest. He staggered backwards. The axe fell, clattering along the floor. Kennedy fired twice more. The impact on Wang's already-reeling body flung it back through the doorway.

Jeff climbed to his feet and stepped into the room. He looked down at the lifeless form amongst the brooms, rags and rubbish. A fitting final resting place was Jeff's first thought. There was no need to bend down and feel for a pulse.

"Wang is dead," Jeff said as he stepped back into the corridor.

"Damn it, Jeff. Didn't you think to tie him up?" Jaggers asked.

"I considered it, yes."

Jaggers glared and turned on Kennedy. "You killed our only link to the terrorists. Bad decision, you shot the wrong man. It will go on your report."

Jaggers turned and walked toward the ladder. Jeff waited until he had climbed out of sight. He waved to Kennedy. "Thanks for saving my life."

"You fucked up, Jeff. Keep the thank you. You've just wrecked my career."

CHAPTER SIXTY

Wang's Davao city apartment was on the third floor. Access was via a stairwell and an elevator. At street level, Felipe's men, dressed in plain clothes, easily blended with the pedestrians and patrons sitting in the sidewalk cafés. One detective was stationed on the roof of a café, with a pair of binoculars trained on Wang's apartment. Cotton curtains prevented a clear view of the interior. But from the moving shadows, he could confirm there were at least three men inside.

Felipe waited below as his men made their way up the stairs. Each stair creaked with each step as they climbed. Perhaps they should have used the elevator. People in the building might hear the elevator doors opening and closing and pay it no attention, but slow, stealthy footsteps were another matter. The men who worked for Wang spent their entire lives on edge and any noise out of the ordinary would have them on instant alert.

Men shouted.

The sound of splintered wood reverberated down the stairwell, as a battering ram breached the door. Gunshots followed. Felipe fought the urge to race up the stairs. He couldn't tell if a gun fight was underway or whether the shooting was his men applying force to gain control.

More shouting. This time Felipe recognised the commands, 'down on the floor' and 'hands in the air'.

Someone yelled, "All clear."

When Felipe entered the room, three men, handcuffed, sat on the floor, backs against the wall. Frightened eyes watched him. They were young, mid-twenties.

One of Felipe's men said, "They say they know nothing. Wang had told them to wait for orders."

"Do they know where Wang is now?"

"They said they don't."

"We'll question them with more enthusiasm at the station," Felipe said.

The apartment was small, just one bedroom. From where he stood in the tiny open-plan lounge and kitchen, Felipe could see along a narrow corridor. The bedroom door was open. The closed door opposite the bedroom door he assumed to be the bathroom. The apartment was not a big area to search. Felipe chose the kitchen lounge to search first. After fifteen minutes of rummaging through cupboards and tipping the contents of drawers onto the kitchen table, he'd found nothing. He made his way down the corridor to the bedroom; two single beds, a three-drawer bedside table and chair between them and a stand-alone wardrobe.

The wardrobe held two jackets and a pair of trousers. There were two pairs of running shoes on the bottom and, sitting on a top shelf, spare pillows and a blanket. He pulled them out, dumping them on the floor next to the drawers. Then he pulled the chair up to the wardrobe and climbed up to look across the top. Nothing. Felipe got down from the chair and pulled the wardrobe away from the wall. Nothing fell to the floor and no envelopes were taped to the back.

The beds were next.

He stripped back the sheets to expose the mattresses. Then he flipped each mattress, checking for slits in the material and any tell-tale bulges that might reveal a hiding place. Again, he found nothing. Each drawer was pulled from the bedside table and the contents emptied onto the bed. The undersides were checked for any taped documents before dumping them on the floor. He rifled through pens, notepads, nail clippers, deodorants, a Phillips-head screwdriver and even an unopened packet of condoms.

He stood in the centre of the room and scanned the walls and ceiling, looking for any sign of a hiding place. Nothing. Disappointed, he was about to walk from the room, when he remembered that prisoners used to hide their smuggled mobile phones in the fluorescent light fittings in their cells. The room did not have a fluorescent light, but it did have a domed ceiling light. He climbed on a chair to have a closer look. Three small Phillips-head screws held the fitment in place. It was too much of a coincidence there was a screwdriver in the drawer. Barely able to control his excitement, he retrieved the tool and climbed back onto the chair. After he removed the screws, he gave the glass bowl a half-turn, and it came away from the chrome-plated frame. And there it was, squeezed between the holder and the ceiling surface, a black computer memory stick. He pulled it out then jumped down onto the floor. He dropped the bowl on the bed and made his way out to the kitchen.

"Carry on," he said to his men. "I'm off to find a computer."

CHAPTER SIXTY ONE

It had taken two days for the *Claire Dances* to rendezvous with the carrier, Independence II. Kennedy had carried on polite conversation for Arina's benefit, but between her and Jeff, their friendship had cooled. Jaggers made it clear that Jeff was responsible for what happened to Wang. If he had secured him correctly there would have been no fight. With Wang dead, they had lost their only connection to the bombers. But Jaggers blamed Wang's death on Kennedy. If she had shot Jeff instead of Wang, she would have been the CIA agent of the month.

Kennedy and Jaggers flew directly to Manila.

A Seahawk helicopter ferried Jeff and Arina to the Davao International airport. Jeff had already booked his return flight to New Zealand via Manila. He would overnight in the city and fly out in the afternoon. He told Kennedy he would make contact when he landed. She hadn't seemed overly interested.

Felipe was waiting at the airport arrivals gate. He looked taller, more confident. At his side were Sofia and Arina's sister, Sarah. Arina's face lit up when she saw her mother and ran to her. Sofia hugged her daughter, and Sarah joined the huddle. Sofia caught Jeff's eye over the top of her daughter's head. With both daughters still clinging to her and each other, she came across to Jeff and kissed him on the cheek.

"I don't know what to say, Jeff. There are no words."

"Say nothing. Live a happy life," Jeff said, uncomfortable with the attention.

Jeff bent over to Arina. "Look after your mum, won't you?"

She hugged Jeff, holding on too long, then she let go. The trio walked away, continuing to hold on to each other. Jeff had little doubt they would need that mutual support regularly for some time as they adjusted to life without Carlo.

Felipe held out his hand to Jeff.

"Thank you for saving my niece, Jeff. Our family is in your debt. If you ever need anything, just ask."

"I see you have a promotion," Jeff said, noticing a new epaulette on the shoulder of Felipe's uniform jacket.

"Documents in Hono's office named a few high-ranking officers working for him and taking bribes. They quit; no fuss. The force doesn't need any more scandals. It's okay to be corrupt, just don't get caught. Gaps in the hierarchy opened and I was in the right place at the right time. Now with the General gone, no one is controlling the rebel groups. Crime will increase, and the new Chief of Police wants to keep Davao City crime-free. His orders come directly from the President. The new chief said he needs men like me. I even got a salary increase."

Jeff smiled. "Good for you, Felipe. Now you're wealthy you can buy me a beer. I have an hour to kill before my flight to Manila."

Felipe led Jeff into the bar and ordered two beers. They small talked until the waitress brought the drinks.

Felipe lifted his glass. "Cheers, my friend. Good health and good luck."

Jeff placed his elbows on his knees and leaned forward. His expression was serious; his jaw set. "How much money did you make, Felipe?"

Felipe smiled. "Aha. I see I did not fool you. Well, you would have disappointed me if you had not worked it out. To answer your question, I made a lot of money. More than I can ever spend in my lifetime."

Jeff looked surprised. "You're not denying it?"

"Why should I? I took advantage of an opportunity and rid my country of some bad people, protected my family and made a profit doing it. And with this new rank," he tapped his lapels, "I have the power to protect myself from any investigation. And, I might add, now Carlo is dead I have new responsibilities; Sofia and the girls. I have two families to support. This costs money. It is right that General Hono and Colonel Wang provide the finance, don't you think?"

Jeff didn't bother to answer.

Felipe reached into his jacket pocket and pulled out an envelope. He placed it on the table in front of Jeff.

"What is this?" Jeff asked.

"A bonus. Call it covering your expenses."

Jeff flicked it back towards Felipe. "Keep it."

"Fine." Felipe put it back in his pocket.

"You almost got everyone killed," Jeff said.

"But I didn't. I admit there were times I worried it was getting out of control, but it worked out in the end. You are a resourceful man, Jeff, and very dangerous. Thank God you were on my side, but I had taken your abilities into my calculations. My judgement proved correct."

Jeff shook his head. He had a desire to reach across and wipe the smug smile off Felipe's face.

"Wang took Arina to the ship. He beat her up, Felipe."

"I admit I did not expect him to do that. But, I warned you at the time that it would be dangerous to let Ramos go free."

"So, it's my fault."

Felipe shrugged. "You have to accept some responsibility."

Jeff had a sudden image of Mama Soo. Another dead face he would carry with him always.

Felipe said, "Arina is home with her mother and sister. Hono and Wang are dead and Ramos is gone. It worked out well, I think."

Jeff needed to board his plane.

"I have a gift for you." Felipe passed across the computer memory stick. "I found this in Wang's apartment. I've looked through it. It has all the information that CIA agent Kennedy Patton needs."

Jeff stared at it before putting it into his pocket. He stood.

"I'll walk you to the gate," said Felipe.

They walked the thirty metres in silence. At the entrance Jeff turned: "Enjoy your life, Felipe. It's unlikely we will see each other again."

Felipe held out his hand. Jeff hesitated, then shook it. Felipe said, "Goodbye, my friend. Keep safe. And again, thank you for saving my family."

###

As Jeff entered the departure lounge, his mobile vibrated.

He recognised the name on caller ID.

"Caldwell," Jeff said. "Why would you be calling me?"

They had worked together in Eastern Europe. Together they had uncovered the identity of the terrorist, Avni Leka. And they had joined forces again in New Zealand, when terrorists tried to blow up an American submarine. Jeff had always suspected Caldwell worked for the CIA, but in the end ruled it out. Whoever he worked for gave him the power to give orders to American Ambassadors and Admirals, and a CIA agent can't do that.

"I heard you've become an American citizen," Caldwell said.

"Not quite, they gave me a passport to get to the Philippines. I'm sure they'll want it back."

"No, they won't. It's yours to keep. When you become a citizen, we expect you to heed the call of duty when the bugle sounds."

"Are you serious?"

"Yes, I am. I have a job coming up suited to your particular set of skills."

"I'm a New Zealander and a wine maker and I have a business to run."

"Someone will be in touch, Jeff."

Caldwell hung up. Jeff stared at his mobile. He had the urge to toss it against the wall. Two airport security guards looked his way. He dropped the phone into his pocket. A second boarding call came over the loudspeaker. But Caldwell's phone call was timely, a gentle nudge to remind him the trip to the Philippines had interrupted his hunt for the terrorist, Avni Leka. Once back in New Zealand and after his house repairs were completed and the vineyard under control; he'd then get back to hunting Leka.

Jeff met Kennedy in his Manila hotel restaurant for breakfast. As she sipped her coffee, Jeff cut into his bacon. Her manner was friendlier than when they had parted.

"What now?" he asked Kennedy.

"I'm on my way back to Auckland. To use a sport analogy, it's the agency's way of putting me on the reserves bench; a smack on the hand for my screw-up. They didn't like that I killed Wang and then let the Iranian, Iraqi or wherever the expert came from, escape to build more bombs. As Jaggers explained to me in the bluntest of terms, in the future, anyone this guy kills is on my head."

The smile she offered was more of a grimace.

"So I'll put my feet up and read intelligence reports for a few weeks. Think about my lack of a future."

"And what happens when you finish up in New Zealand? They won't leave you there forever."

"I have a black spot on my record so it might be time to leave the agency. But I don't know what I would do. I'd thought about going home and helping my father with his business. I don't know if that would work. He would start hassling me about having a family and you know I can't go there."

"Yes, I know." Jeff placed his knife and fork carefully on the plate. "I was looking forward to spending time with you back home. Change your mind about life in general, but as much as I want that to happen, I am in a position to help you with your career."

"You have friends in high places?"

Jeff placed the memory stick on the table.

"This is from Wang's apartment. Felipe found it. It has everything you need on it. The men behind it were ISIL. They had captured a man in Mosul, Iraq, and were about to execute him when he told them about Saddam's stash. Seems he was a crewman on the ship that carried the radioactive waste to Salvation Island. ISIL then contracted the Islamic group Abu Sayyaf, and they approached Wang and Hono to build the bombs. It seems the Abu Sayyaf had quite a dossier on Hono going back to his military days and threatened to expose him if he didn't comply. They were going to use the bombs in Europe. Explode them in a couple of cities to show they were serious, then ask for ransom money from the rest. Their thinking was that while Americans say they don't pay ransoms, the Europeans might. The coffins were to be sent by rail from Hong Kong. They had trans-shipment papers in place. And, it also clears up an issue bothering me; the bodies in the chiller. They had planned to put them in the coffins just in case a nosy customs officer took a peek. We screwed it up for them when we found the camp. They only had time to get the crates out, not the bodies. The bombs were still in the coffins, in the crates, no time to make a change. I'm guessing that once they made it to Hong Kong, they might have changed shipment plans. Or, I wouldn't have put it past these guys to buy some Chinese corpses."

Kennedy screwed her face in distaste at the thought of it.

"If they hadn't embalmed the bodies, wouldn't they smell?" she asked.

"That's my thought. Maybe they had intended them to. A lot changed when we came along and stuck our noses where they weren't welcome. It doesn't really matter now, does it?"

"No, it doesn't. And Wang, he wrote down their plans, recorded everything. Why would he do that?"

"Felipe and I discussed that. Our theory is that he was concerned Hono might get rid of him. Wang was all that linked the killings and crime back to him. He was about to become Mayor and he had lots of money. Politicians don't like secrets."

Kennedy nodded. "That seems logical."

Jeff paused. He pushed the memory stick across to her.

"Anyway, you'll find the addresses of the receiving depots in Europe. Good leads, I'd say. I guess this means you might not come to New Zealand."

Kennedy held up the memory stick, looked at it, and then at Jeff.

She smiled. "It could still happen."

ACKNOWLEDGEMENTS

My apologies to anyone I may have forgotten. A special thank you to Rosina and Trevor McGarry, Valerie and Graham Ellis and Nick and Maria Abbott for continued support. My military advisers Ken McKee-Wright Rtd and Chris Kumeroa of Global Risk Consulting. As always a special thanks to my assessor and mentor Cate Hogan and to Adrian Blackburn technical advisor and editor, and to editors Susan Battye, and Gaydrie Browne. To Vivian Quan who inspired a key twist and Phil Mawdsley who took time out to talk boats. To my agent Nadine Rubin Nathan of High Spot Literary. And finally a special thank you for the continued support from the team at Thomas & Mercer.

ABOUT THE AUTHOR

Thomas Ryan, author of the bestselling Jeff Bradley series, has been a soldier in a theatre of war, traded in Eastern Europe and trampled the jungles of Asia. Ryan considers himself foremost a storyteller, a creator who has plunged his psyche into the world of imagination and fantasy. Taking readers on a thrilling journey is what motivates Ryan as a writer.

website www.thomasryanwriter.com